Digging Up New Business - The SwiftPad Takeover

DIGGING UP NEW BUSINESS

THE SWIFTPAD TAKEOVER

BY

S. LEE BARCKMANN

BW
BARCKWORDS
PUBLISHING

Publisher: Barckwords Publishing

Paperback: ISBN 978-1-7352514-2-4
eBook: ISBN 978-1-7352514-3-1

1 3 5 7 9 10 8 6 4 2

Contents

An Apologetic Warning

To the City of Portland: I certainly can't and don't speak for the city. But I do love it, probably not for the usual reasons.

We have some yucky nastiness to deal with right off the bat, but we won't dwell on that too much. It really isn't that kind of story.

Other than that, any relationship to anything you might think you recognize in this story is a coincidence. It is just a fable.

The Management

Cast of Characters

Starring...

The Killer

His First Victims – Kathy Morton, Regina McKenzie

Kip Rehain (Chubby) – mid-forties, son of a rich Oregon logger

GG (Cynthia Oglethorpe) – late twenties, Computer programmer extraordinaire

Raleigh Highlooper – late fifties, Venture Capitalist

Jim Hunt – mid-forties, IT Professional

Mark Ruskin – GIP Consultant – Outsourcing Specialist

Tyler (Trek, Sebastian, OSWL, VAPOR) – of the CIA/NSA community, former colleague of Snowden

Stan – early twenties, Skateboarder, recent Anthropology Major

Elizabeth Kerns (Easy Girl) – late 30s, proprietor of the Easy Girl Bakery

Macy Ming Cosino – the Woman on the Bridge

Lance Petrovich – late 50s, detective, Richland, WA

Georgia Symaara – late 30s, detective, Richland, WA

Detective Ted Henderson – Portland PD Cop

Walt Rehain – Kip's dad

Alice Hunt – Jim's mom

The KEG Staff (Northwest Consolidated Electric and Gas)

Frank DeFonzaro – CFO

George Robbins – CEO
Dick Swensson – Chairman of the Board, former CEO
Delores – General Secretary for the Board
Tom Freeberg – Proxy voter for the Habitat Group on the Board
Anaka Maheemi – CIO
Art Van Landingham – Chief of Operations
Angelica (Angie) – Jim's boss and former lover

Jim's Crew at the KEG
> Lester – Network – smart but sloppy
> Sonny – Server room tech – backups, general duty
> Arlen – quiet as a brick
> Knute – almost 70, fit and energetic
> Rodney – Always with his briefcase, pants too tight and too short
> Christine – Probably fucking Rodney
> Steve Slater – Calls everybody sir or ma'am.
> Brigitte – big eyes, straight hair. Has filed a sexual discrimination suit
> "Larry" Yang – Best worker on the team. From China

Lesbian DBAs (who are not a couple and are really in charge)
> Janice – Pretty and Black
> Rainey – Southern & Butch

SwiftPad Board members
Hariet Miller, Seb Madison, Michael Kendrick, Mitsuro Mansanato, Pete Hollingsworth, Cook Callahan

Also Featuring
Ken Oren – GIP VP – Big Data; Suzanne – GIP analyst; Persephone Jackson – Mark's GIP boss; John – GIP Sales; Mary O'Hara – Crockett Group; Renate – East German (double?) spy, Spritzer; Heidi – (spy?), Quark

With...
Archimedes, Emma, Hadley and Rina – SwiftPad programmers; Judge Van Ritter – Lance's friend; Sharon Rodriguez – VP

of Bonneville Power; Heber Young – Walt Rehain's accountant; Enrique – Walt's foreman; Rosa – Walt's housekeeper, Enrique's wife; Portland DA; KOIN News Girl; FOX News Guy; Rich Dunner – Oregonian reporter,

Prologue

The first woman had worked with me at Bonneville Power. It was dumb luck I got away with it. It just happened, although I admit I had thought about it, and of course I planned it. I was just sort of daydreaming really, but got more and more specific in my mind about what I was going to do, as the days passed. I am not a deviant predator, and I am not sick or bent. I didn't want to go to jail, which anyone would say was a normal and sane reaction. I am not suicidal or looking for martyrdom. I was not, and am not a monster. A monster is unthinking and unfeeling, and I am certainly not that!

Kathy thought I was funny and probably handsome. She told me she had received critical letters about "environmental issues" with the utility sub-station and she didn't know how to answer them. When we talked, there was that undercurrent of flirting that both of us were too professional (or too shy) to openly acknowledge. I told her I helped design the station, which was not true. I was an IT guy, but I can read plans. Then she said she would get back to me for the structural details and might have other questions too.

But she didn't contact me that day, so I waited for her as we were leaving work and I timidly asked her out for a drink. She said no, but in a nice way. I acted embarrassed (because I was) and apologized (to hide my anger at her for refusing my invitation). She touched my arm and smiled and said she would like to see the electrical transformer that I told her about. She said she had to answer the letters from the "bird watchers." I said when the transformer is completed, they will hardly notice it, "low impact," very unobtrusive. She handed me her keys and I drove her car to the site. This turn of events upset my plans because I expected we would take mine. However, it was a stroke of luck, because getting rid of her car later was what saved me from getting caught.

It was a beautiful isolated spot that overlooked the Columbia on the edge of the Yakima Delta Nature preserve. The hole was dug and the survey points showed precisely where the electrical box would be set. The wooden forms for the concrete were in place. As I stopped the car there was a nervous silence between us. She began to fidget with her purse and suggested we go get that drink, but it was too late, for me or her. I pulled her out of the car by her hair. Halfway out of the car she stopped struggling, although she continued to cry and beg me not to. But as I said, it was too late.

After we made love, I had to strangle her. At that point I had no other options. I buried her where the transformer was to be placed. The hole was dug, but I knew there was enough space for the concrete and the dirt that covered her. The rake and shovel were in the unlocked portable shed (as I knew they would be). I left the top rough and dirt clods strewn around the surrounding area. I knew that the next step was to tamp it down and compact it with a hand roller and then pour the concrete base. It was just an electrical box.

I drove her car away and left it on the street several blocks from my apartment. The next evening, Friday, I drove it to Seattle, wiped it down very thoroughly, parked it and took a bus back to Richland, through Spokane. I got back just before ten A.M., showered and crawled into bed, totally exhausted. But I knew I had left too many clues, and I really didn't sleep.

I went over everything in my mind, trying to figure out what I had forgotten. I had been very scrupulous in not talking to her or showing any interest in her before that day so she would not tell her friends about me. But I worried she might have mentioned me to someone in the office. I was almost sure no one had seen us leave and was pretty sure no one had noticed us in the break room previously, but as each hour passed, I lay awake worrying more and more – about what, I wasn't sure.

There was evidence all over: footprints, tire tracks, who knows what else. The tire tracks scared me most of all. By Friday afternoon the police were looking for her. This was of course years before I had built my access into the police communications system (that wouldn't come for another ten years, after I moved to Portland) so I only knew about what they were doing from the local newspaper and TV. They found the car in Seattle Sunday afternoon, and that brought heat on the staff at Bonneville Power. They questioned everyone, and the detective in charge questioned all of the men, and it seemed he took special interest in me, because his questions were very brusque and aggressive. And, I really didn't have an alibi, other than reading in bed.

But, as you must have guessed by now, I was never charged, although I suspected then and know now that they kept a file opened on me. I never made it into the FBI NCIC (National Crime Information Center) as a "person of interest." (I had access for a little while, before they changed the lock.)

They never connected the transformer site with her disappearance. It was never a crime scene.

I didn't begin to think about doing it again until I got to Portland. You think I am lying and that I could not wait four years without doing it again? Well, then you don't know me. I am very disciplined. For me the memory of an event becomes bolder and clearer as time passes. It, for the most part, suffices. Anything can be overdone. The Epicurean principle of "moderation in all things" applies to everything of course, but after a while...

Anyway, I wasn't the only one who couldn't take my eyes off of Regina. I walked by her cubicle carefully, head down, not too fast or too slow, staying out of sight, never looking directly at her or anyone else. I walked by the construction site early in the morning, watching, noticing who arrived first and when. Sometimes I would leave work early and notice who left first, noting the progress they made each night, watching who locked up and when. As the work on the station progressed it inflamed my imagination; it was just like before, I thought. I walked down to the construction office on the sixth floor and figured out the pecking order of the staff. I watched as they pulled the project plans from the rack. Sometimes I would see the crew chief talking to the engineers or the inspectors. I noticed where he sat. The crew chief had a set of keys and I noted where he kept them.

Getting her to go out to the lake was easy. It was the same drill, shy flirting, meek, never letting her know that I knew everything about her. Led her to the subject slowly. "Have you ever seen a liquid natural gas pump station? That technology is going to be the company's bread and butter...Let's take a look at the utility vault..." No hesitation, her eyes lit up. I could tell it wasn't the technology that interested her...

It was dark and deserted and I didn't even need to rape her. I was always surprised how attracted women were to me. She wore a skirt, and as I started taking her panties off, she lifted her derriere to make it easier. I have to admit, that got me angry. Her animal desire shocked and disgusted me, to be honest. It affected my...I suddenly was not "ready," as they say on TV. So I started to beat her. But then it was good. Very good.

When I finished I strangled her slowly. I let her recover her breath and beg. Then I fucked...I really fucked her! It was the greatest experience of my life; the release was total. I came like a fire hose and then finished the job.

I unlocked the gate and carried her in. They had even left shovels and rakes out for me again. It took me ten minutes and she disappeared under the ground and concrete, above the utility vault.

Chapter 1

Kip, an Alternative Energy business failure, goes to JAVAPALOOSA, and takes a Picture

Kipling ("Chubby") Rehain didn't know much about what made computers work or how, after he typed a URL in the top of a web browser, it would almost instantly find the website. He liked to search Google for whatever he was thinking about and would chase the links around the web, and get lost finding other things, whether they were related or not. He didn't understand the IT business either, and had only recently learned that IT meant "Information Technology" but thought that it was something he could learn easily, with a little bit of study, because his whole life was about information.

After all, he had learned enough to get into the "alternative energy" business in the early nineties, before it took off. Back then, Kip had still been in his early twenties, and his father still believed in him and helped convince some of his rich friends to invest in Kip's pilot project for tidal energy. A Croatian (or possibly Serbian, Kip was never clear on that point) engineering student designed the key piece of the technology, an anchored ocean buoy with a little turbine in the middle that was chained by a power cable to other buoys. The drunken Yugoslav thought it up at a late night poker party in Corvallis, after he ended up in the hole for a couple of thousand, and agreed to complete the proposal and design and give it to Kip in lieu of payment.

About three months after that, Kip met an Australian sailplane pilot in a sauna at a private folk music luau on a goat farm near the mouth of the Columbia River. After deep discussions that went on all night by the fire, where they consumed more than just the pig, they established a company to sell the floating buoy idea, along with a plan for a modular and flexible geodesic solar panel. They even got a loan from a local public utility district for prototypes. But the solar panel prototype set fire to the attached goat barn (even though the sun wasn't out at the time), and the buoy's turbine made it so top heavy that it didn't float upright. The money plug was pulled soon after that and the Australian went back to Perth.

After that Kip did not see his father very often, but inexplicably, he allowed Kip to tap into his trust fund occasionally, and that was what he lived on.

This is all by way of explanation, because in October of 2013, Kip found himself in a coffee shop in the Portland's Pearl District at about 11:30 in the morning, tired and a bit hung over. He had taken over a table as far from the service counter as he could, against the wall, with his usual accouterments spread out, his stained and weathered leather book bag, with his soft, dark pencils and big erasers at the ready, his rag paper sketch pad, and notebook, and the book –*The Idiot's Guide to IT Start-Ups* – which he had found not to be as simple as the title promised. Information Technology was definitely the business he wanted to be in, but he still used the computers in the public kiosk at the library because he didn't have a laptop and his phone was not particularly smart; all he ever did with it was talk and text.

Kip had the passion and the brains to be successful at almost anything he put his mind to, but he could never finish anything he started, which was a problem. He read constantly and knew something about almost everything. But that aside, almost everyone who knew him agreed he was a wonderful person to have as a friend, that he was fun and generous, insightful into people, kind, and usually very polite and solicitous, especially to people who he could see were hurting in some way. He seemed to know "everybody" in Portland and maybe, because he was older than most of his friends and had a deep resounding voice, everyone he knew respected him and often came to him for advice. At least five or six people thought of him as their "best friend" and would do anything for him.

In any event, he was sitting at the table in the coffee shop, doodling on his sketch pad, when he gazed up at a bulletin board right next to him, and as he reached for some change in his pocket to buy another cup of coffee (and a Danish if there was enough change) he noticed a poster tacked up on the board. He recognized it as computer gibberish.

```
public class WelcomeCoders//COME TO THE JAVAPALOOZA!{

public static void main(String[ ]args)//@MISSION THEATER{

System.out.print("Oct-23 9 PM - LET's GET IT STARTED!"); } }
```

It was titled "The Emerald Empire Java Collective," and it was some kind of "happening" at the Mission Theater in northwest Portland. The Mission Theater, a former union hall, built with solid red brick, was owned by an Oregon brew-pub chain, McMenamins. Various organizations often rented it for alternative type affairs, writers or activists would occasionally speak there, sometimes there would be music or dance performances, and they served great beer and bar food. Kip looked at the poster for a long time, and was not completely sure "JAVAPALOOZA" wasn't some come-on for starting your own coffee shop.

Two nights later when he arrived at the Mission Theater, he quickly discovered his first instinct had been correct, it was some kind of Nerd Fest, and that Java was a computer language. The "vibe" in the room was good, and the people seemed pretty hip and there was free coffee too, so he stayed around and just let things happen, to see what was going on.

Kip sat in the corner in the darkened former union hall. A young man in dark-rimmed, slightly tinted glasses, wearing a heavily starched, plaid shirt, buttoned only at the top (like a Mexican gangbanger) and new jeans rolled up above black boots, was talking about Java programming, which made absolutely no sense to Kip. He noticed a girl who looked slightly bored, and who seemed just about ready to pack up and go. She had sly, hidden beauty and long dark hair, too dark to be her real color, he thought, braided into thick pigtails, with frayed, uneven ends. She had eyes like moons. She couldn't have been over 25. Kip pulled out his Leica and without a thought in his head, shot her. The slight flash startled a few people, and by the time he put his camera back in its holster, she was up and over him, right in his face.

"You can't do that. You have to erase that right now," she said. She was taller than he had first thought and was wearing an oversized, ugly black sweater, a tight black skirt, black tights and Chuck Taylor high-top sneakers. Her eye makeup was probably intended to make her look ghoulish, but her raccoon eyes couldn't completely hide the coquettish, slightly vulnerable, All-American girl behind it all.

"I can't delete it. This is a real camera, not some digital piece of...," he paused, looked at her, and broke out into a Hollywood smile. "Are you going to make me rip out my film?"

"You can't take a picture of me. End of discussion. I will make you sorry if you don't get rid of it, and prove to me that it's gone."

"I can't destroy the roll; I have too many shots I want to keep."

"I don't care," she said. They were both pretty calm and she continued to stare at him. Part of the calm was Kip's smile and charisma. His eyes sparkled and did not contain a hint of threat or malice and she saw that. But she was insistent.

"What do I call you? Little Orphan Elvira?"

She smiled. "Elvira. Good guess, I used to be Goth Girl. So call me GeeGee."

"Gigi?" asked Kip.

"That is what I said, GG," she said. In fact that was what everyone called her. No one in Portland, as far as she knew, knew her real name. They continued to stare at one another.

A guy with thick, flaxy, bleached-out hair, complementing a too-perfect dark tan, approached them. He was wearing polished leather boots, narrow faded jeans with no belt, and a hand-stitched off-white linen shirt. He had the craggy face of an aging soap opera star. "It's the Code Queen!" he exclaimed, drawing curious looks from those around her. He was Raleigh Highlooper, tech entrepreneur and the MC of the Javapalooza. He had just come down from introducing the Java gangbanger, who was now talking about "multiple inheritance techniques," which Kip thought must have something to do with genetics. As Raleigh approached GG, he held out both of his hands as though pleading, as if to say, "What, no hug?" GG reluctantly nodded to him.

"I saw you do that, man," he said, frowning, turning to Kip. "That is very uncool. Very uncool. Come on, man, you know you can't take pictures of people here without permission. This is a private affair and a safe place...for everyone! We have an unspoken code." He looked at GG for affirmation, but she remained impassive. "You can't be here if you don't respect people's privacy, especially women. Everyone knows what I am talking about! It's creepy and invasive. You are not a programmer are you? Why are you here? GG, is he bothering you?"

"Hello Raleigh," GG said, glancing at him, then back to Kip. "No, it's OK."

Kip, who had worked as a choker setter on his father's logging operation and could be a tough guy, if the occasion required it, smiled hard at Raleigh. Not threatening, just confident. "I am putting together an IT company," he said. "But you are right, I don't program. I am looking for programmers."

Raleigh half rolled his eyes, looked at GG, and put his hands out again, but when she still didn't respond, he shrugged as if to say it's OK. He pulled an embossed business card out of the air with a nonchalant magician's flair, and offered it to GG. "I don't remember if I ever gave you my card." It read, "Raleigh Highlooper, AdVenture Capitalist."

She looked at it but didn't take it. "I think I have one from last time," she said.

"I've seen you here at least twice, but we have never talked," he said to GG. Which was no accident because GG had avoided him. She had watched him try to recruit programmers with big promises of money and wild, hedonistic work environments, but no one she knew ever vouched for him.

"We were just leaving," she said, looking at Kip, "right?" Raleigh made a pained, squinty face and turned away and then waved at a young man who called his name from across the room.

"Hold on, Gee," said Kip, quickly assuming an air of comfortable familiarity. She realized, to her complete surprise, that she trusted Kip, even though he had taken her picture and she knew nothing about him. "I've seen you around, what's your story?" Kip asked Raleigh in his deep authoritative radio voice.

"Well…," Raleigh smiled as he looked knowingly at GG. "What is that thing?" he asked looking at Kip's camera. "Some kind of stone-aged Etch-a-Sketch?"

"Surprised you don't remember it. It became popular just after the daguerreotype."

"I remember a lot of things." Raleigh smiled, and looked at GG, "I know you have asked around, looking for talent. If you're serious, you should be thinking big." Raleigh shifted an eye toward Kip, who was unconsciously rubbing his knuckles.

GG grabbed Kip by the arm and started pulling gently.

"I can help you," Raleigh persisted, relaxing his shoulders and taking a deep breath. He looked as if he were communing with an unseen muse, then turned back to GG. "I don't know what you have heard, but I am very plugged into venture cap money. I know Hariet Miller – personally. You know who she is right? Cascade Sportswear? She wants to invest locally. I am connected to several other wealthy investors, in addition to my own resources, which are substantial. So, I can pull together money. If you have an idea, and I think you do, so…let's talk. Really, think about it. Ask around about me. I have made things happen." He looked dismissively at Kip. "Here take my card, in case you lost it." He held it out again and this time she took it and nodded, noncommittally.

In fact, she had asked around about him, and she heard about two semi-solid gigs he promoted. One was a high-paying, long-term contract with unspecified overseas employers. The other, a web development project for what sounded like porno sites. But Raleigh did get around, and had been in the business a long time. His web bio said he used to do technical network consulting, and he had a long list of A-list companies he claimed to have worked at. GG knew she had to stop slamming doors in people's faces if any of this was going to go anywhere.

"Bring your friend," Raleigh said. "Maybe we can use some old-time photos. Ciao."

Kip let GG lead him out of the hall.

Chapter 2

Jim wants to grab Wet snow from Mount Hood while explaining what a Union General has to say about Portland

The 737 flew across the eastern Oregon desert, from southeast to northwest, hitting the great Cascade mountain wall just above Bend, where it veered due north. The bright sun lit up the dry eastern side of the mountains, but dark clouds were piling up on the other side, in the rain forest of the Willamette Valley.

Jim could see it all from his window seat on the port side, first class. He hadn't spoken to his neighbor, a young white boy with dreadlocks, who had been pounding down the complimentary vodka Collins the whole flight.

"Going home?" Jim asked, after ordering a Courvoisier cognac, which was his long-time pre-landing ritual.

"No – first time in Portland. I can't wait. You live there?"

"Well – I will. I used to and now I am going back."

"Cool! My girlfriend goes to school there."

"Where?"

"Lewis and Clark."

"Nice school," said Jim. He had looked at the campus once in when he was in high school – but there would have been no way he could ever have afforded it back then.

"Yeah – this trip is my birthday present to myself. Never been to Portland and never flown first class. I am going to surprise her – I am moving out here to be with her."

"Oh – you haven't told her?"

"No, man. We lived together in Boston. She graduated ahead of me and got into law school out here."

Jim smiled. "So what are you going to do?"

"I'm going to hang out, man – do the Portland thing! Get some kind of gig, and take care of her, know what I am saying?"

Jim smiled again. "Check that out." They were coming up on Mount Hood. "We'll be heading into the Gorge."

"Columbia Gorge, right?"

"Yep." They began the slow turn to the left, right next to the top of the mountain. It seemed close enough to reach out and grab some of the snow.

"I can't wait to get up there and do some boarding!"

"Snowpack is down again this year. Five years ago the whole upper half of the mountain in the winter would be covered with snow. Now – mostly just the top."

"That's messed up."

"Yeah it is." One more time, he thought. One more trip and he would be done with traveling. Next week will be easy. Timed it just right, he thought. He resigned from GIP yesterday, effective in two weeks. He was quitting just as he finished his last project, so no one could be unhappy with him about leaving. He was going back to the power company, to a tame, low-stress job, home every night, and intended to enjoy the coming summer. Reconnect with family, friends…

In other words, Mom and Chubby. His mother was a shoo-in to be mayor of Corvallis later this year. She was the star of the city council, wife of a hot-shot professor, and was running a volunteer agency. She's come a long way. They both had. And Chubby. We'll have to see about that.

Why was he moving back, going back, coming back, back to a comfortable job where he had once been the hero? At 44 he was old enough to know…you can never go back. Period. No expectations.

Anyway, he didn't know what else to do; he just had to stop doing what he had been doing. He had been away long enough.

The drinks came just in time before they started to descend. "So what do you do, man?" His neighbor toasted him.

"I'm an IT guy. Networks, servers, software. I've been a generalist, but that is starting to be difficult. It's like everything else, all specialized now. I am getting tired of it, so I just took a job in IT management, and I am starting next week. In Portland. I'm getting my apartment set up this weekend."

"Wow, management. Can you get me a job?"

"Do you work in..."

"No, I'm just kidding. I studied Anthro at BU. Primitive cultures is my thing."

"You going to continue with school?"

"No. I just want to hang out for a while."

"Well, you won't lack for company."

"Huh?"

"They say Portland is where young people go to retire."

"Oh – yeah – that's pretty funny."

Keep Portland Weird. But really it's Don't Be Awkward, thought Jim. Anyway, weird covers a lot of ground. First thing tomorrow he was going to get a bicycle. That would be his contribution. He sold his VW Passat in San Jose. He wasn't going to buy a car; he was going to live in the city, so he could bike to work.

They gulped their drinks as the "Fasten Seat Belt" sign came on, and the attendant came through collecting the last of the cups. "So – what's it really like?" asked his neighbor.

"What – Portland? I grew up here – not in Portland, but in Western Oregon...And I always thought it was a backwater and couldn't wait to get out...In other cities...they still have stains of the tribes that had passed from memory, and the streets are still alive with the dead who used to live there. You could feel them. I am not sure that is true in Portland, because it's still discovering itself, the way London must have been after the Romans left, but before the Saxons moved in. It used to be something and now it's something else. It has a very recent past, which is not really connected to the future. Do you know what I mean?"

His aisle neighbor looked real serious and nodded sagely.

"Who will be here in a hundred years? There is turnover, every twenty years it seems like. The rain chases away a lot of people who think they will like it. So it seems like a group of newcomers are always discovering the place. There is so little continuity. Which is good for guys like you, looking for a new start. I mean you are free to be what you want."

"And now you are a newcomer again. So you are free too. I'm Stan," Stan said, reaching over to shake Jim's hand.

"Hey Stan, Jim...you're right, that is kind of what I want to do."

"Reboot – isn't that what you guys say?"

They came around to land from the west. The east wind coming out of the Gorge always brought a chill. Looking down, there weren't enough words that meant the color green to properly describe the view. They came over Sauvie Island where the Willamette comes into the Columbia and as they descended Jim could see the open parade grounds at Fort Vancouver.

"One hundred and sixty years ago Portland was just a mud flat, a river raft stopover between Fort Vancouver and Oregon City," he said pointing down. "Ulysses S. Grant, the future Union General and President, spent more than a year down there at Fort Vancouver in the 1850s, just on the other side of the Columbia, and he only once mentioned Portland in his famous memoirs. I remember this phrase. He said there were 'a number of remnants of tribes' near Portland. Even the Indians were newcomers to Portland, at least in the 1850s. That's what I mean when I called Portland a backwater with no continuous history, still waiting to be defined."

"What did he mean, 'a number of remnants of tribes'?"

"You're the cultural anthropologist. But then he said that those 'remnants' eventually all died from smallpox and measles."

"Yeah – it sounds very sad. That things fell apart for people and – and they had no home anymore...why did they come to Portland?"

"Well – it's the meeting point for two big rivers. But maybe it was something else too – something about Portland that attracts people from different tribes trying to find a home."

"I dig where you're coming from. This is the reason I wanted to move here. To meet people like you that – you know – can talk about things."

"Thanks." Jim gave him a look of real appreciation.

The 737 landed and they got off. It was raining.

"Good luck. I am sure she will be happy to see you," Jim said as they headed up the terminal.

"Maybe. I guess I'll get a cab over there and see if I can surprise her. Maybe I'll get lucky."

Maybe I will too, thought Jim.

~~

Trapdoors and Easy Money - A Word from Our Killer

I wish sometimes that I had a friend I could share my story with, someone I could talk to directly, personally, without holding back. Of course there is no one I could trust enough to really do that with, but still, I think about it and like to pretend that you are out there, listening to me.

But who would listen? Who could listen? I know when I explain it all, in the proper context, it will make sense and – while most of you wouldn't want to emulate me or follow my road, but at least, maybe if you knew it all, you would understand it. So I am going to pretend you are here now, not as a friend, or an admirer – but certainly more than just a witness or cold observer. You are not a colleague, and not a Sancho Panza either. I can't control what you think of me, but let's pretend I can insist that you listen to the whole thing and that you will "reserve judgment." I love that phrase for some reason – saving the judgment, putting it aside, not including it in the story as it unfolds. I do that. I don't judge anyone.

You probably have to be a man to really get me – even though it is women who are the primary object of my attention. So whoever you are – maybe it's better if I don't know who you are – then I'll just be frank and not assume I know what you want to hear – I'll just talk and address you as – you.

Who can know what anybody thinks, or can guess what is in anybody's head? I suspect you will think me Beyond the Pale – unworthy of the normal respect we give anyone who is honestly telling their story. Perhaps you will think I am impertinent and cheeky. But believe me, I am very serious. You'll have to wait to see what I mean by that.

As to my business, I actually have several businesses, as you will subsequently learn. In a sense I am a pirate – to that, for now, I'll admit. A pirate, in it for the easy money and protection from discovery. I sell my information and make a lot of money. It is information I sell – like I said – easy money. I am an information technologist, and it makes sense that my product is information, right? I think you will find that there is nothing that crosses my mind that hasn't crossed yours – perhaps you decided a long time ago that what I do isn't for you, the risks aren't worth the reward, or that you simply don't have the talent and nerve to pull it off. That is OK.

But my business – it really is not so bad. I use my skill as a computer guy, hacker if you will, to invade and steal data. I have a view that stealing information is not so bad – it's not like stealing a little kid's bike after all. I am definitely not a hacker in the way that you think, not in the way you probably understand the word. I'm not some tattooed snarly long-hair who sleeps until noon and lives on energy drinks.

When cops used to stop people with pot in Oregon, they had to let them go if they have a medical marijuana card, which anyone could obtain with a note from their doctor. The cops said that the card was easy to counterfeit, so about ten years ago, they hired me to build a little program that could look up the names in the Med-MJ database with a special text message and confirm it – and then respond to the messages. That way they could arrest people who were not in the system. That gave me access to the entire cop communication system, in Oregon anyway. I built a little back door and with it I can spoof any cops account and send or receive orders or other info. I don't use it much, because I don't want to tip them off. But in a tight spot it's handy.

The other project, which in some ways is much cooler, I did for the Oregon Arms Collectors Association, which is like a local auxiliary for the NRA. When Oregon passed a law requiring that vendors at gun shows could not sell Uzis or AK-47s to convicted felons, the OACA got their representatives in the legislature to attach a rider saying that the police had to provide way for gun show vendors to be able to check on the record of their customers in real time, so that the law wouldn't seriously affect business. They hired me to build the application, which required that I get access to all of the criminal data, including the FBI records. I have sold it to a couple of other states too, but have stopped marketing it, because I didn't want to show up on any anti-gun political radar. Don't need that.

The data from the criminal databases is my product. I sell it to my other customers, former East bloc guys, mostly Russians, Central American narco guys, and others whom I am careful not to inquire too closely about. B-movie bad guys, if you catch the drift. It is all done from a distance – I don't know them and – hopefully – they don't know me. My business is too big to handle all by myself of course and I have partners who handle a lot of the technical details, keep the lines of communication open if you will, and I have the same deal with them – anonymous transfers, no names or places. I don't even know where some of them are from and have met none of them. If they fail to live up to their agreements, they are cut off and left out in the ether. They are not nice guys, so I protect myself, we just wire money to numbered accounts and I give them what they need. So – I got that going for me. Like Caddyshack Carl's deal with the Dalai Lama.

So those are some of my businesses. We'll continue this discussion. Now – you go away. I'm busy.

Chapter 3

Kip Takes GG back to his Room and they Found an Internet Social Media Company

Kip and GG left the JAVAPALOOZA together. They walked fast at first – it was about half a mile from the Mission Theater to Kip's walk-up on 11th and Stark. It was chilly, and a bit windy too. They didn't say much, and after crossing over 405 they began to feel comfortable strolling together closely, without overt romantic affection. From the outside, Kip's place appeared to be a half a step up from a junkie hovel. "Let's go up to my photo lab; I'll cut that picture out for you."

GG had amazed herself that she went with Kip up into the rundown apartment building and felt like she was in a daze as she followed Kip. Something drew her forward and it wasn't completely about erasing the photo. It was a dark, small space, but she didn't hesitate. In the far corner by the sink were four trays and she stood in the darkened room, just outside the open curtain, while he washed the film and hung it up. Kip quickly demonstrated he was an expert in the developing room. He mixed the solutions, getting them to 68°, processing at each stage, hanging up the negatives with a sure practiced hand, never wasting a motion.

"We are done. I'll cut out the negative and you can have it, or burn it, or whatever you want," said Kip.

"Aren't you going to make the picture?" she asked, with a voice she didn't recognize, one she hadn't used since...long ago. She stopped thinking.

"We can make a print. Sure," said Kip. He pulled out and opened his serrated, single-blade folding knife and cut the negative out of the roll and set the rest of it in a can and put it in a well-organized drawer. He ran it through the mixture and set up the glass, "We won't bother with a print proof, or with the others for now." He pinned it to the enlarger. GG saw his profile as he exposed the negative, and saw a different man than the one she saw at the Mission Theater a few hours ago. The smell of the chemicals made her a little dizzy.

"Why don't you wait in my room, while I clean up?" said Kip, handing her his keys. "This solution is a bit toxic if you aren't careful. Its 309, two floors down." She took the keys and went to wait for him.

Afterward, they couldn't sleep and walked across the street to have breakfast at the Roxy. GG hadn't had sex in six months and she felt amazingly happy. It was 3 A.M., but the joint was full of the usual crowd for that time of the morning, young musicians and their crews talking excitedly about their most recent session, three or four homeless people savoring a cup of coffee or soup, waiting for the sun, a couple of women who looked to be in their late thirties (but were probably much younger) with big purses and wearing very short skirts. A cop, who had his hat on the counter, was talking intently to a very distraught young man. Kip and GG split a four-egg omelet with lots of toast, coffee and bacon.

GG held the 6" by 8" print and stared at it. It was black and white, and it captured an expression on her own face that she had never seen in another picture, in any mirror, in her imagination, not anywhere. Her smeared eye shadow was haunting, not comic or pathetic like she assumed. The shot placed her just off to the side, and her eyes were smiling, even though her mouth was turned down. She had a little crinkle just above the right side of her upper lip. It went with her eyes. Kip had cropped everything below her shoulders. He had made her a way she had never imagined herself to look.

"OK, listen we need to talk, I don't usually..." Kip began, but she cut him off.

"We are fine, Kip. Just fine. I am very happy and am looking forward to getting to know you, but as a friend. I have too much to do to become..."

"Yeah, yeah, great, we can work together. I mean I want to, but, that guy, that old guy...Raleigh..."

"Raleigh?" she said. "I don't know. I don't think he's..."

Kip was wolfing down his food, listening.

"I know who he is..." she continued, picking at her eggs. She shook her head and waved her hand, as if she were erasing something, "...and it bothers me that he knows who I am. But people vouch for him. Some people. He says he is a 'Venture Capitalist' and is looking for a software project to put his money into but, I think he is just trolling, looking for ideas, or...Most of the projects he talks about don't seem that great. It's all real basic, commercial IT stuff. At least that is what I have heard. But I don't really know. But...I am not crossing him off any lists. I have to stop being so... judgmental about people, especially if they can help me."

"I see. Was I trolling?"

"If you were, you were not very good at it." GG smiled.

"Well, as the man said, by their fruits ye shall know them." She looked at him and rolled her eyes. "So what is it that you want?" Kip asked.

"You really want to know?"

"Yes," Kip said, and then he put down his fork and looked at her. "Yes."

"I want to build a new kind of social media application. The concept is so cool, but they are all missing the point by a mile!

I want to architect it right so it actually means something. Not endless pictures of cute pets and birthday greetings."

"Huh? I guess I don't follow you."

"Do you use Facebook?" she asked. "Can we have some more coffee?"

"No, but I know what it is…coffee? Here…" He leaned over and got the pot off the recently evacuated adjacent table.

GG shook her head. "You know how it works…you mix and relate to other people's input. You write or post a picture or video or something and other people, 'friends,' respond to it. If something interests you, you add to it. It is an electronic town square or something like that."

"I thought it was for Mind Control," said Kip. "Advertisers see what your weaknesses are and exploit them, right?"

"No. Well, yeah, that is part of it too…" She looked at him at first wondering if he didn't get it and then, if maybe she was missing something. "But, I want to get away from that angle. I mean it has been done, and can be replicated, and improved. But I want to do something that matches people based on their 'anti-interests.' Suppose everyone had friends who were the opposite of themselves? Wouldn't that begin to…?"

"…You mean the people you pick as Facebook friends should be 'assholes' instead of your friends?" Kip smiled as he wiped his chin with a napkin.

GG looked at Kip and flashed an impatient smile. "Maybe people need help picking their friends. People who agree tend to band together, so if you make that easier like Facebook does, then I think it is actually contributes to the fragmenting of society, so people only communicate with other people like them…So I was wondering if the opposite could work?"

"It sounds like it might have potential as a dating site. I mean, in my experience people who are alike make lousy partners. What are you going to call it?"

"*SwiftPad*. SWimming In Freezing Temperatures & Practicing Angry Dancing."

"Huh? What does that mean?"

"I don't know. Satire maybe, Jonathan Swift...and a pad is... something to write on, a place to live, a soft place to land. Also, you know what SWIFT numbers are? Those hieroglyphic numerals on the bottom of your check that banks use to track who is paying who...the big checkbook. There is big money in successful applications and sites."

"Sounds like a reach. OK, so the software would match unlike people..."

"...and push people into uncomfortable situations," she interrupted. "Push them away from their comfort zone, instead of reinforcing it."

"OK, OK. But you have to have a larger strategy don't you? Dig this – do you know who Daniel Ellsberg is?" asked Kip.

"Vaguely, something about Vietnam..."

"Yeah, he released the Pentagon Papers to the public, which was a history of the US involvement in the Vietnam War," said Kip. "He helped write it and then it was marked as Top Secret, and he lost his clearance to even read it." Kip took a sip of coffee and looked around the room. "Anyway he was also an economist, studied game theory, and his PhD thesis is now called the 'Ellsberg Paradox.' Ellsberg applied it to the choices that Presidents, from Truman to Nixon, made regarding the war. That was his most famous example of the Paradox."

"I don't follow."

"In Vietnam, Ellsberg said there were two rules for American presidents," Kip said. "Rule 1: Don't lose South Vietnam before the next election. Rule 2: Don't get into a ground war in Vietnam."

"If you follow Rule 2 you will almost surely break Rule 1. But if you don't follow Rule 2, you will lose thousands of men, waste billions of dollars, cause horrible chaos in the country and still, most likely, eventually break Rule 1. Following Rule 2 was a better long-term bet than not following it. History had demonstrated that many times, with the Chinese in ancient times and with the French in the fifties. So it stands to reason we should have just followed Rule 2 and taken the consequences eventually, right?"

GG nodded, and looked intently at Kip.

"But we didn't know when or how we would lose if we got into a ground war. We just knew, people who studied the culture and understood the practical military options knew, we could not win. The sequence of how we would lose was of course 'unknown.' The problem was that if you can delay the inevitable, there is always hope, always a chance for a miracle of some kind. So they would not make the key decision, to end it. Even though rational analysis said we couldn't win, we still broke Rule 2 because at the time it seemed like the safer choice."

"So," said GG, "minimizing the risk by adding a few troops at a time to keep from breaking Rule 1 but eventually we broke both Rule 2 and Rule 1."

"Couldn't your social media software help people understand when they were falling into the 'Ellsberg paradox'? Make them aware they are victims of the Ellsberg Paradox almost every time they make what they think is a 'safe' choice about their lives, and end up marrying the wrong person, or never traveling, or staying in a shitty job, always making the 'safe' choice rather than testing the odds to try something 'unknown,' something that if they think about it, would be better for them?"

GG looked up Ellsberg Paradox on her Android phone. "This is interesting, he has math associated with it. Ambiguity aversion. Hmm. People could set their...decisions...which are always ambiguous because the future...This might be interesting."

"You know," said Kip, "I might know some venture capitalists. Or at least one."

Chapter 4

Jim meets the Easy Girl, and Learns of A Disturbing Discovery

Jim Hunt walked quickly down the hill, crossing the Vista Bridge, looking out over fog-covered Portland, out toward the unseen, cloud-enshrouded Mount Hood. He considered this gray monochrome outlook a personal failing, an inability to see the shades and hues. He knew the world was different in different places, but to him it didn't seem to matter, it was all the same, a whitish haze surrounded by shadow.

His work had taken him to many places, but wherever he was, it never seemed exotic to him. Jim was easy to please and generally hard to disappoint, but he was getting older and knew he had better figure out what he really wanted pretty soon. It was beginning to bother him that he could be happy anywhere, with anyone. "I could survive prison very easily," he thought. "There is something wrong with me."

It was fifty and drizzling, a typical winter day, and the streets were shiny and slick. The Westside, the hillside, upscale Portland neighborhood, had the same lush, overgrown flora that he had known all his life. Jim had grown up in the Oregon woods, living in a trailer with his hippie mother, up a dirt road by a creek about ten miles west of Philomath in the northern shadow of Mary's Peak.

His mother, Alice, a former logger's wife, had broken away from the world of axe men and almost all of its values and social mores and had decided to follow an alternative West Coast lifestyle. For Jim this meant he had eaten healthy food his whole life, in fact, he didn't know any other kind until he joined the Army. But beyond this, her hippie-ness barely affected him. His mother had tended a wild, productive and luscious vegetable garden, and they ate fish, quail (that Jim and his friend Kip would trap), brown rice, sweet potatoes, and fresh fruit such as berries, pears and crab apples. She had raised him in a converted trailer with an enclosed addition on the back, which she had had several of her succeeding men friends build out of discarded lumber. Away from his mom and the trailer, Jim just seemed like a crew-cut country kid from poor circumstances. He had learned to mimic the rudiments and gestures of civilization, but had never learned how to be part of it. Maybe that was why nothing seemed distinct to him, and that the high-tech world of airports, mid-town hotels, and Fortune 500 companies that he inhabited all colorlessly blurred together, along with everything else in his life, or so it seemed to him.

He was going downtown to meet his oldest friend, a grammar–to–high school buddy from Philomath. Kip Rehain was in some ways the smartest person he had ever known, although he had also been perhaps the stupidest, and most self-destructive. And to top it off Kip was a force of nature, a whirlwind of energy that sparked out in unpredictable and random directions, sucking anyone around him into the gravity of his charisma. Most of their time together as kids, when they weren't in trouble with school principals or the local authorities, had been spent tramping through the woods along the upper reaches of the Mary's River, building dams and tree houses, trapping fish and frogs.

But they both had a bookish side too. They had been a two-boy science fiction club, and when they were eleven they hitched a ride to Portland to see Harlan Ellison read at Powell's Bookstore and came back with a treasure trove of "speculative SciFi" books by writers who saw man's interior life as separate universes or dimensions. When Philip K. Dick died in 1982, Kip wore black for two months and didn't speak to anyone.

Jim went into the Army after high school and lost track of Kip. In 1994 Kip was living on a farm outside Canby, as an "Energy Consultant," with plans for tidal power plants and mass-produced solar panels. They met up briefly once back then, but they were on different wavelengths. Kip had told him he had tried to catch the wave too soon, but Jim suspected that other factors were to blame, such as Kip's chronic pot habit.

So as Jim walked down Vista Avenue, he was thinking about Kip and what a mistake it probably was meeting him today, or for that matter, quitting his six-figure job at GIP and moving back to Portland, when he saw a pony-tailed, ruby-cheeked woman standing across the street from him, on the corner of SW Vista and Madison, a block down from the "Suicide Bridge," twisting from her waist back and forth, her eyes closed. She had light brown hair and something good from within her coming out, maybe it was the rhythm of the music pumping through her ear-buds, radiating out, but it was something else too and Jim felt it. She was different, not the same. He felt that clearly as he watched her, he felt her…goodness…was it possible to feel goodness from someone? A slight shiver and a mild shock briefly colorized the white fog in his head.

As Jim walked past her, he looked at her and smiled. At that moment she opened her sparkling eyes, completely composed and unstartled and smiled back at Jim with red lips and pearly teeth. Her tight, gray cotton sweatpants outlined a wholesome kind of perfection. She leaned forward to stretch and put her palms on the ground without bending her knees.

As Jim walked by, he realized he was unhappy, and he was tired of it. He finally turned around when he was a block away from the stretching woman in the tight cotton sweats. But she was gone. Must have run up Vista, from where he had just walked down.

He crossed Burnside and continued walking down 23rd. Most of the beautiful old houses of the Westside of Portland, which used to be the center of the city's society, were now divided into apartments and filled with Millennials looking for a kinship with others who came of age when the two towers fell. Young seekers of something hard to define had been moving to Portland, attracted by a high-tech, laid-back, liberal frontier ethic that offered the possibilities to do things differently, maybe even better. They were too earnest and un-cynical to be "hipsters," and something about them had broken permanently with the past in a way that was very different from other recent generational groups. Jim was only approaching his mid-forties, but he felt old here and slightly out of place. Nevertheless Oregon was home, where he had been brought up. It was the Emerald Empire. The drizzle was verging on rain.

Jim stopped to get coffee at the Easy Girl Bakery on 23rd and Truman. He was the only one there and he struck up a conversation with the owner, Elizabeth, who appeared to be almost his age. She told him she wrote a blog about her cakes and cookies and he promised to read it. They chatted about the weather, and then two customers came in and he pulled over a copy of the *Oregonian* and glanced at the front page. Sewer rates were going up, the City Council was arguing about what to do about homeless people sleeping on the street, and then he saw a story that he looked closely at and read.

Body Found in NW Electric and Gas Pumping Station

A NWEG repair crew discovered a human skeleton buried just above an underground liquefied gas pumping station in outside of Gresham near Blue Lake Park Friday afternoon, a company spokesperson announced Saturday night. The crew was performing some "scheduled maintenance" and came across the body in the course of digging.

The pump station was installed in the late nineties, but was never brought on line due to political and regulatory considerations.

A NWEG crew member, who did not wish to be identified, said that the body appeared to have been buried when the pump station was originally installed because there was no indication that there had been any new digging in the area.

Arthur Van Landingham, Operations Chief for the power company, discounted that, saying, "No conclusion can be drawn regarding the date or even the year of the burial." Van Landingham also said they were cooperating with Portland Police, and that NWEG staff was manually sifting through the files of past operations.

Van Landingham refused to comment when asked why maintenance was being done on an inactive pump station.

Van Landingham indicated that all further comments would be handled by the police and declined to elaborate further.

"It's weird...that body they found, I mean," Elizabeth said.

"I am going to work for them," Jim said.

"Who?" asked Elizabeth.

"Northwest Electric and Gas," Jim said.

"You mean the KEG?" she asked.

"Yeah. This is the second time actually. I worked for them... damn, fourteen years ago! In the main building down in Chinatown. And now I am going back. My first day is a week from next Monday."

The headquarters of the KEG, Northwest "Konsolidated" Electric and Gas, looked like a beer keg. Even the *Oregonian* occasionally used that tag in its more informal references. He thought about Art's statement, "No conclusion can be drawn regarding the date... of the burial." It seemed like they don't even know when they built the vault or else they are lying about not knowing. Jim wondered if the CAD drawings and files had been misplaced, or maybe they lost the backups. He knew how things were done there. Probably can't find the vellum-finished maps either. Even in Jim's day, when mechanically drawn plots were absolutely required, the hard copy maps and drawings were sometimes not maintained properly, people would forget to put them back or someone would borrow them and not return them. Apparently they can't find the construction notes on the project either.

Jim thought back to the missing girl. He forgot her name. But he had not forgotten her – after all these years. She had flirted with him the day before she disappeared. Back in the nineties...back in the nineties, Jim had stabilized the KEG's faltering computer network and more importantly, banished a whole team of expensive GIP consultants. What fucking irony, he thought. The GIP guys (Global Industrial Processors, the oldest and still one of the largest IT companies in the world) had planned, installed and operated the whole system, and they had screwed it up royally. Jim first official act had been to fire the chief malefactor and ringleader of those consultants, who never bothered to come to meetings or even acknowledge emails from Jim. Even Van Landingham, who had hired Jim and gave him carte blanche, had been shocked when Jim fired the guy. The other IT people at KEG were scared of the consultant and what he knew. But Jim got rid of him first. Fired him, because he was the most expensive of the group and because he pissed Jim off the most. That meant Jim had to do his job.

Jim remembered that it was the scariest thing he had ever done, but it worked out. The guy had threatened him on the way out the door, said he would never work in Portland again. What the fuck was his name...? Was it that long ago?

He remembered it took about five months, but step by step Jim took the infrastructure back, moving down the network stack, step by step, patiently, staying late every night, spending hours on the phone with vendors. He stabilized the whole system and soon there were no more GIP consultants working at the KEG.

Returning to the present, Jim showed the Easy Girl the text on his phone:

Hi Jim,

I am not supposed to contact you but I thought I'd give you a little encouragement to apply for the job below. I'd be your boss, and I would strongly consider you, based what I know of you and your recent experience.

Hope to see you,

Angie Warkel

"Who's Angie?" the Easy Girl asked. She handed Jim back his phone.

"A woman I used to work with at the KEG. She is a boss there now and I guess she, or somebody there, wanted to hire me to manage the infrastructure team."

"Why would you want to be a manager?" asked the Easy Girl.

Jim liked Elizabeth, the Easy Girl. "I am actually taking a pay cut. But I am tired of travel. Mostly though, I am tired of lying to whoever I have to work with. I feel like I am always hated by the local staff where I get assigned, because I work for GIP....Companies hire GIP when they want to get rid of people. I still have some self-respect – not much, but some."

The Easy Girl made her lopsided grin straighten out, which was how she told her customers she liked them.

Jim didn't mention that sixteen years ago, when Jim first started at the KEG, Angie and he had had a brief but passionate affair and kept it secret from everyone, including her live-in boyfriend. It was "meaningless" and purely physical, an "Oh shit, somebody's coming!"–Coitus Quickus Zipus Interruptus kind of deal. Their love nest had been the meeting room adjoining the balcony on the twelfth floor. Doing it during working hours in the middle of the day was crazy, but they had avoided detection. Angie seemed to dig it too.

Two weeks ago, he had come in for the interview, on a Saturday. It lasted ten minutes. Six people were there including Angie. It was so perfunctory that he was sure that his return had been squashed by the chain-of-command.

"I guess it was probably some homeless guy who fell in and got buried when they originally built it, don't you think?" she asked as she wiped the counters.

"Buried what? Oh..." He looked back at the article. It said, "human skeleton," the sex not indicated.

"I don't know. You would think maybe they would be a little careful about projects like that. Do they just leave the hole open?"

"I really don't know, to be honest. Like I said, I haven't worked there in fourteen years. I like your shop. Great pastry." Jim used the napkin to wipe crumbs off his closely shaven chin and waved goodbye.

"Come back and see me..." she said.

The rain had let up, and there was a hint of sun peeking out, as it almost always did on wet, winter days, for a little while at least. Jim was trying to savor the aftertaste of his apple strudel. He wished he wouldn't gobble his desserts. He had to start pacing himself in all things. Elizabeth's shop didn't have the usual Portland pretentiousness that he noticed some shops had, especially on 23rd Street. It was a place he could eat slowly and savor his pastry. He would have to come back and try again.

Jim was trying to start over, to build a little community, just trying to find people he could be comfortable saying hi to, just people he could stop and talk to without consequences. He was coming back to Oregon, back home, and now he had to face Chubby...Kip.

Two months earlier, Jim had received a letter written in Kip's large, almost medieval scrawl, sent with a Portland postmark to his apartment in San Jose. It was a strange letter, even accounting for the strangeness of Kip himself.

JIMMY!

I was visiting the Rehain Hacienda last month driving past our old haunts, thinking about our plans and schemes and realized we had a great childhood, those were the best days of my life and the only reason I can think of why is our special simpatico, you my friend. It was strange that we were thrown together when we were young, because that is still something that hasn't been equaled for me – the intensity and synchronicity of our friendship might have been a once in a life-time deal, but at the time it seemed like it would never end. But fuck that nostalgia shit! We are still here aren't we? I thought that it ended when you went into the Army and I started college – (Four times)! It seemed like the end back then but it wasn't even the beginning.

I made a couple of interesting films – anyway I'll tell you about that when we meet – which will happen soon when you come back to Oregon – to Portland, where we can resume our Tom and Huck rain forest adventures.

(Here Kip scrawled a pencil drawing of a somewhat sinister portrait of a neo Huck Finn – straw hat pushed back, shirtless under overalls, straw in his...NO FACE! Huck's face had a video screen instead of nose and eyes, from which a grainy image of himself projected.)

You have to move back to Portland! I know you worked here in the early '90s – was it the power company? Now you are working for GIP? Jesus Jimmy, come work here! We can get it going again – and I know how! I saw your mother at the Beanery coffee shop in Corvallis on my way out of bleak Benton County and she told me all about you – she wants you to move back to the Empire and get a girl pregnant – And I want you back here to help me with my new company – I am a co-founder and CHO – (Chief Hallucinatory Owlphsir) for SwiftPad (SWim in Freezing Temperatures Practice Angry Dancing) – which is going to be the next Facebook once we launch our master product – we are already out there among the initiated and more important than any of that it is the most subversive stone righteous thing since the Trystero! We are talking about an IPO – We have backers – big evil money looking for absolution. We have a staff – sometimes we have 10 sometimes 20 people here working on the project! We are going to conquer everybody.

Anyway – no email – no internet email! Not without special handling – We are being watched – all of us – so trust the US Mail – Postal Carriers understand the muted horn – and can be trusted.

Chubby

Chapter 5

Petrovich and Cop Partner Georgia are roused by the Disturbing Discovery

About 200 miles up the Columbia from Portland is the town of Richland, Washington. In World War II it was a strange kind of boom town, with hundreds of government-built and owned Levittown-style, cookie-cutter houses set in the middle of square, unlandscaped lots. The purpose of the town was to produce nuclear material for the Manhattan Project and its population went from 250 to 21,000 during the War. It was a top secret place until the mid-fifties and there were no private houses; nearly everyone who lived there worked directly on Manhattan Project or in service to project workers, even the grocery clerks. The streets were all named after famous engineers. George Washington made the cut because he was a surveyor. By the late fifties Richland gradually began to change to become more like other towns, but its strange history still radiated in the town's collective subconsciousness.

And so on a Tuesday afternoon, a Richland native son, Detective Lance Petrovich, and his cop partner of the last two years, Georgia Symaara, who grew up in Spokane, were sitting in the Uptown Tavern on George Washington Way, pretty much by themselves.

They were both pretty quiet. Petrovich, approaching sixty, was retiring the next month. Georgia was normally perky and talkative, but not that afternoon. She had grown to like her older mentor over the last couple of years, even though he became more and more withdrawn and morose as his last day approached.

She had been on the force for fifteen years, and still drew somewhat formulaic and predictable sexually tinged comments from her cop peers, but she liked the way Lance treated her, with just a hint of swagger that never went over the line. She learned more working with Lance than she had in all her previous thirteen years on the force. But for the last six months she had been his cheerleader/therapist, trying to keep him focused on the job, for her own preservation as much as concern for the older detective. Until recently, it had been the perfect cop partnership. They kept their private lives separate and supported one another. But for the last month, Lance had been withdrawn and quiet. She knew he was obsessed over a case he hadn't solved.

Petrovich noticed his partner was quieter than normal. He pinged his half empty beer glass with his pinky fingernail, trying to get a smile out of her. It was his third of the afternoon and it was still two hours until quitting time. That was when Georgia nudged him and showed him the story on her *PoliceOne* iPhone app. They had just dug up a skeleton in a Portland, Oregon, power utility vault.

They returned to the station and as Lance read the report from Portland Police Department, he literally shook with excited anger, anger at himself and at the gall and arrogance of the prick. The skeleton, he was sure, would be of a young woman, the same woman who had disappeared from the Portland power company about sixteen years ago. The *modus operandi* was now clearly and painfully obvious; he was sure that the same guy was responsible for the missing Portland woman as for the vanished woman from Bonneville Power several years before that.

At the time there had been no evidence linking the Richland construction site with the disappearance, but the coincidence of the company employee vanishing at the same time as the construction had occurred to Lance several months after her disappearance. As his other leads dried up and he had begun to think that maybe she had never left the area, the site had bubbled up in his mind as a possibility. He had even gone out to look for clues, but too much time had passed.

But back then, he didn't yet understand how important hunches and intuition were to criminal investigation. His boss and colleagues all thought it was some kind of white slavery situation, that she had been taken to Seattle in her own car after being drugged or that her car had broken down, or she had got lost and ran into the wrong guy or guys. From Seattle she might have been taken to Vancouver BC, where she would have been shipped off to Asia or South America to be a high-end slave-whore. It was a theory that could be made to fit the facts and now Lance was deeply regretting that he had gone along with it. Lance had spent months looking into the connections and where none existed he found himself inventing them. He made a list of suspects from her workplace, but no one popped up. Although there was one guy...

That guy was in Portland now. No alibi either time. For the first few years, Lance had checked him out every six months or so...but the last couple of years he had been less vigilant.

In the end he looked in other directions. He traveled all over the Northwest and British Columbia, and even up to Alaska, focusing on all the leads available for sex trafficking. He never cracked the case, but sex trafficking became his specialty. Five years later he moved to the Seattle Police Department and within a year had broken up the biggest child porn–kidnapping ring in the history of the state. His techniques were copied worldwide and he was known as one of the premier detectives on the West Coast. Five years ago, after a storied career in Seattle, he came back to Richland to be close to home, to help with his mother during her last years. But even in Richland, each case was harder on him than the last one and he was getting tired of being a cop.

Georgia was excited by Lance's sudden renewed interest in his work but she knew, she had finally learned, that sometimes it was better to be quiet. She listened more, anticipating him. She followed him around the station as he checked the reports and got updates from their colleagues in Portland.

"Still haven't ID'ed the Portland body yet," he said. "But I know it's her. Come on." They drove out toward Badger Mountain. "The same thing happened here. We are going to dig up another girl. Something I should have done twenty-two years ago."

Chapter 6

DeFonzaro wants to Bring in GIP, while Swensson can't wait to hit golf balls

---

hief Financial Officer DeFonzaro felt hemmed in. The board meeting fell on the 125th anniversary of the company, so it was a full house and he wanted to get to his place at the table, but it was crowded and he couldn't just push people out of the way. He had important business to go over, and these old emeritus shits couldn't sit still for very long, either getting up to pee or gabbing on and on like they were at a damn reunion. He wondered if he should have brought his embossed leather document folder, but he wanted to be unencumbered. No executive comes into an important meeting with a folder, like some kind of junior assistant. He was done with that. He looked at George Robbins, the CEO, and impatiently gave him a circling-index-finger hurry up sign.

"OK, we have a lot to cover today. Dick, you aren't going to play in this weather, are you?" Everyone laughed and one person even began clapping at the mention of Dick Swensson, the Chairman of the Board, former CEO, who merely smiled and nodded.

"We need to mention the unfortunate discovery of the body at our LNG pump station by Blue Lake," said Robbins, not even realizing he seemed to be emphasizing that finding the body was what was unfortunate. "Unfortunately, some of the notes describing the construction of that pump station are missing as well. We had to go to the utility commission to get their records just to pin down the dates that the station was last excavated."

A murmur ran through the board and senior staff.

"What does that mean?"

"We should never have installed that pump station, without getting full approval," said Tom Freeberg, who served as a proxy voter on the board for the Habitat Group.

Robbins ignored Freeberg.

"We won't know until the body is identified. The police are going through missing persons and trying to match the remains."

"Do we know anything about the...body?" asked Irene Schweitzer, KEG board member, steel magnate widow and noted local arts patron.

"It was a woman, between 20 and 30 years old. That is all we know now." Robbins paused and looked around the room. "OK, let's let Frank get started. Dick, did you have something to say before we started?"

"One more thing, George," Freeberg persisted. "Did the maintenance at the LNG pump station have anything to do with the recent stock offering tendered by 'Bum' Crockett?"

George looked with exasperation at Freeberg. "No, Tom it wasn't. It was a regulatory requirement related to insurance..."

"I am just saying it is quite a coincidence." Tom sat down and the volume of the murmuring rose.

Dick Swensson stood up and waited with a slight smile for quiet. "OK, let's settle down, I have a tee-time in two hours, and I need to get to the range first," he announced. Swensson, still popular, and ruggedly handsome, was now Chairman Emeritus. The room transformed instantly, and everyone found their place and sat. "I don't have too much to say; you all know we have to make some tough decisions this year, and I think Frank has some ideas to bring up. Delores, could you make sure he has some water, in case Frank needs to cool off. We want to minimize the fire breathing, in case we had any gas leaks from George."

There was an eruption of laughter, and DeFonzaro smiled. George Robbins, the CEO, looked confused. "OK, Frank, take it away."

"Thanks, Dick. I'll try and get you out of here so you can get some putting practice in as well." Someone broke the silence with a mirthless chuckle.

DeFonzaro, with a frozen smile, slowly made his way to his place at the ancient polished oak meeting table in the middle of the pentagonal top floor. The table in front of him was sticky from some honey-sweetened spilt coffee, and DeFonzaro was trying to find a place to leave his cue cards that wouldn't rub against the sticky spot. He should have brought the damn folder. Delores should have had the table cleaned before the meeting. There was so much incompetence in the organization, he thought. He had heard that Delores had been Swensson's mistress a hundred years ago, when that sort of thing was common. DeFonzaro was a believer in not shitting where he ate. Swensson shat where ever he felt like it. Why doesn't he just play golf and not gum up the table with his honey-sweetened coffee!

DeFonzaro stood behind his desk and waited with his Nixonian forced smile. He took deep breaths and nodded to those around him, most of whom didn't acknowledge him. He wasn't well liked and he knew it. He was the new broom and had no illusions about his role and what it meant to the old guard.

He looked at Swensson, who was still nodding at whispered quips, accepting accolades from the throng.

Swensson smiled and gave Frank a thumbs-up. Dick Swensson looked over at the senior officers. He cursed himself for allowing such a bunch of dishrags to be promoted. Robbins, the lifer lawyer, now CEO, who never offended anybody. He's there because he spent the last 20 years sitting in State Utility Board committee meetings, arguing over fractions of fractions of percentages for rate structures. Operations, goofy Van Landingham, taking over his daddy's position. HR, who cares? He still didn't know her name. IT...an Indian or something from over there...Anna something...? They say she is smart…Being smart has nothing to do with leadership. Otherwise, Swensson thought, I have been in the wrong business.

Swensson knew it was his fault. The only one with any gumption is Frank, the bloodless accountant, and he wants to gut the company. Dick Swensson was old school, a liberal Oregon Republican of the Hatfield, McCall brand. The company was 80% workers…guys (mostly) in the field, laying pipe and installing relays, etc. Dick had always been loyal to them and they loved him. Dick liked to think his legacy was that people liked working for a successful company.

Swensson continued to half-listen to DeFonzaro deliver the fiscal state of the company. Not a bad quarter, but trouble looms. Global warming will drive down winter heating revenue. The Feds are threatening Bonneville Power and we might be next. Need to upgrade the IT infrastructure, but don't have the revenue…

Dick Swensson was sure he knew who they had found in that hole. The project records vanishing was too close a coincidence. He remembered the girl; she was so pretty, and rumor had it so willing, that men would make up excuses to walk by her desk. She disappeared and they found her car down in the San Francisco Bay area. So Portland stopped looking for her. He had had a bad feeling about it then, and now he was sure, almost sure, it was her.

He really did have a tee-time in a couple of hours and was half thinking about his swing keys as he remembered her. My God, when the press finds out we lost all the notes, who was there, comings and goings, all of the logs…it is not going to be good. And worse, there were blank notebooks and vellum sets used to replace the missing ones so they would not be noticed. Until now. Which meant, it was some kind of inside job. It had to be somebody who worked here. Robbins will undoubtedly bring me into it, Swensson thought; I was on the bridge when it happened…Shit.

Head still, feet still, elbows stiff, not stiff but…the whole company, the people in the company who loved golf anyway, used to play every Wednesday afternoon during the summer. Turn from the waist, eye on the ball. Had to let that one go. The company golf league, damn women managers and their assistants brought it down, said they were denied access, which was bullshit. He always thought it had been a mistake to not fight to keep it. Fuck, he thought, he should never have let it go. He had a bad feeling about it and now, like the old skull in that play, it shows up. Alas, poor... he forgot her name. He could see her face now. He would find out soon enough. He looked at the woman running HR. He couldn't remember her name either.

Did she play golf, he wondered? There were a few cutie pies who came out back then to play. The company golf league was the best part about working at the KEG, he thought; he would play and partner with guys from the field. He learned more about the state of things than he ever did in meetings like this one.

Suddenly he half-heard something that startled him.

"You want to bring GIP in?" Swensson blurted out, instantly regretting it. Back in the nineties, Global Industrial Processing had left a mark of spousal abuse on the KEG. They took a twelve million dollar loss in fiscal 1997 on GIP's failed upgrade of the financial systems that year.

But DeFonzaro wasn't here then; he wouldn't remember it took everything we had to get GIP out...almost 15 or 16 years ago.

"We have to consider the idea," the CFO said, "Our IT systems are unprepared for the new paradigm."

Swensson made a face, then pulled back. I have no power anymore, he reminded himself. A low murmur rose up from the audience.

"Smartphones, social media, the way you organize the employees. Younger people have different ways of socializing than existed in the past."

Who is this old asshole telling us how young people think, Dick thought, but he remained impassive.

"Collaborative engagement, working anywhere, crowd sourcing, we need flexibility with productivity. We have to focus on the product and eliminate everything else. What is our product? Energy, the energy that heats homes and powers industry, everything else is not our core..."

Oh Christ, thought Swensson, here we go with the 'core business' crap. We should get rid of everybody, contract it all out, sell our headquarters and outsource everything but the pipes and transmission line...hell, sell that, and lease it back, he thought with a stifled laugh.

Take a deep breath, he thought. Why did I let him be hired? But then MBAs keep rolling off the loading dock and they are all alike. Anyway, this was not the time or place. He had never wanted this prick but then he got old and Frank slipped past the door...

"But why GIP?" asked Van Landingham, "They are a dinosaur. We had them in here in the '90s and it was a disaster."

"They are a totally different company now," said Anaka, the CIO. "Dedicated to the Cloud, sold on collaboration. It's not your father's GIP."

DeFonzaro said, "We need to bring in a consultant to see what our options are. We need an outside opinion, someone with the experience to see where we are and where we need to go..."

Swensson didn't like it, but he had been hitting the ball so well on the range lately that he couldn't wait to get out on the course. It was his course and it was wet and windy, just like he liked it. Dick loved this kind of weather, playing golf in his spiked cork boots during the winter. This California fuck with his five handicap... Swensson smiled to himself as he thought about it.

Thank God we have our own hired gun though. It was a stroke of luck to hire that kid, Jim...Jim Hunt. Army veteran, former GIP too, great kid. I guess he's not a kid anymore, he thought, more about himself than Hunt. He helped us get rid of GIP once before. He doesn't know that's why I had Angie recruit him. Neither does DeFonzaro or Angie.

Angie...he should have helped her more, made her senior staff, but they had not been careful. It was his fault, he knew. Delores had caught them in his office. He never heard a word about it, but he knew he couldn't have promoted her after that. He looked at Delores and frowned. Angie had been his swan song, his last throw of the dice, but Delores...He smiled at the memory of Angie. She knew Jim pretty well, he remembered. As he hurried to his car, he knew he would regret not fighting against all this shit harder, but in reality, there was nothing he could do.

Chapter 7

GG and Kip get Dressed and Petrovich plans to flush out the killer

CyberTimes

*"Silicon Valley's source for
the New Millennium"*

SwiftPad Seeks to Reinvent Social Media

A ghost-like social media site with the obscure
title *"SwiftPad"* has been popping up and down on
the web for the last two months, and those who
have seen it are gushing with praise. More than
five thousand web-stalkers "liked" the comment
by the frequently prescient *snarkopath*, who
goes by "SoftStool": "...the most amazing time
wasting tool to come along in a decade..."

SwiftPad sends up a link every week or so,
but it is never valid for more than a few
hours. But it has the Valley buzzing. The link
spreads like wildfire. It appears to be sourced
from Seattle or possibly Portland. "There is
some serious cyber-talent working to mask its
origin," one source told this reporter.

"Posted items get automatically catego-rized and pushed into strange and unfriendly spaces," says Mitch Granoli. "You never know where you will end up. It seems to take the 'interest recognizing' concepts that Amazon and Google have perfected to another, almost bizarre level, to perfectly position anyone into a cyber war of ideas and never allows you to stay put. It might be the final realization of Herman Hesse's 'Glass Bead Game.'"

"If you see it, click on the link and sign up right away, because you will be notified later when it is available," added Granoli.

"The trolls seem to be weeded out by a machine-generated benign sarcasm, which some-how doesn't get bogged down in the usual obscene hate that takes over any discussion. It is not being 'monitored' by the politically correct police, in fact it is the opposite," said one commenter. "It's totally incorrect, with a 'suave awkwardness.'"

"It might be the new 21st century battle-field, the future of intellectual knife fight-ing, because the machine is a player too and is pretty good at it."

Joe Thomas, a Wall Street social media analyst, says it appears they are positioning for a major capitalization through Crowd Source funding.

"G...you see this?" asked Kip, who sat in bed with his orange iPad.

GG leaned over and read the article.

"Wow. Good press for drumming up the investors. Speaking of which, we better get going. Phew! Kip, you stink!"

"No worse than you," Kip said.

"I know. Now! That is the problem!" GG got up and found a towel on the floor and wrapped it around her compact, white butt. "Next time, you have to take a shower before…" GG said. "…In fact, I don't want to do this anymore. We are in business together. We are going to get all cloudy in our thinking." She went into the bathroom, and Kip heard the shower start.

"It doesn't affect my thinking," said Chubby, who sat on the edge of the bed. "My mind is clear." He went into the bathroom and got into the shower with GG.

～～

She pushed him away as she dried off. He went hunting on the floor for a towel. "I'm serious. We need to stop doing this. You should get your own place."

"What does that have to do with anything," Chubby asked, opening her closet.

"Why don't you get an apartment? It was stupid to move out of your old one. We are talking about raising a million dollars today. What is your problem? Why are you afraid of the slightest amount of stability?"

"I had to move out. Most of my photo lab gear got stolen, and then they raised the rent! Said they would need more for security. It was a dive anyway." Kip held up a shirt he pulled out of his duffel bag and sniffed it, and held it up for GG to smell, which she declined. "Anyway, I am pumping everything into our company. If I sleep on the floor, the rest of the crew can't complain as much about not getting paid. Besides, I don't want him to think I am just like every other trust fund loser. I can't get soft."

"Him?"

"You know who. Once we start generating some income…"

"Well, you can stay on the floor at the office from now on. I am not bringing you home anymore."

"Even if I take a shower?"

"Get your own place and your own shower," said GG. "Are you wearing that?"

"Why do you care? Are you my girlfriend?"

"We are asking for five million dollars from these people and you look like you have been Standing by a freeway entrance for the last three days. Your pants are too short, the cuffs are ripped, your socks sag and don't match, there's a gravy stain on your shirt, or smock, or whatever that thing is.. It all stinks...why even take a shower if your clothes are dirty?"

"I thought I just washed it. Are you sure this is a good idea? We'll lose control of the company once we start bringing in investors."

"You have a pee stain there...and if we don't get more money the company will die. People need to eat and pay rent. We are going to start losing our best programmers quickly."

"Pee stain? Where? Show me?"

"This won't be good. Let's go."

GG and Chubby drove her Honda Civic down I-5 to Lake Oswego. Kip wanted to drive his truck, but GG said they already looked like refugees. They wove through the leafy neighborhood, then down along the north side of the lake. The house they came to wasn't particularly big and certainly wasn't new. But it was a fabulous combination of muted colors and hyper geometry. "It looks like Frank Lloyd Wright designed this on acid," said Chubby.

"Everything strange or unusual is on acid with you. You don't have to take drugs to think outside the box," said GG. "You think Michelangelo was 'on acid' when he painted the Sistine Chapel?"

"Well, I bet he was half drunk at least," said Chubby.

GG shook her head and decided the conversation was going nowhere. They both got out of the car and Kip gently bumped her with his shoulder.

"Why didn't we just crowdsource this through the Web? Are you sure you want to meet these people? Crowdsource Funding is perfect – you read the article. We are getting buzz. I don't know why we have to meet with these people."

"We wanted to keep the funding local, right? I want to know the people who are financing us. I am old-fashioned that way , I guess."

"OK. Here we go. Don't embarrass me, dweeb," Kip said, walking ahead of her and ringing the doorbell.

Another Word from our Killer

If you know how to start rumors, be at the right place at the right time, and drop the right hint to the right person, you can do anything. For the last five months I have been setting the stage to get in on the ground floor and to have total control of the idea, the big idea. That is my talent! And all big ideas need money, so it is about ideas and money. That is all. There is really nothing else involved.

So you see, the socially proscribed diversions I have described previously, my forays into the ultimate erotica, they don't define me. They don't drive me or control me like they do some, who are almost always caught. Just because you enjoy a glass of wine now and then doesn't make you an alcoholic. I enjoy it when the opportunity presents itself. Victorian gentlemen had their naughty proclivities and I suppose I do too. More in good time – business before pleasure ensures pleasure isn't just business.

In any event, this will take me into the midst of Fortune 500 affairs. Even so, I only consider it a diversification strategy, which goes along with my business of selling crime data to various concerns both national and international. (My handle with them is "Raskol.") And – since my new business is about to take off too – for that business I'll use my real name, which you will know soon enough. That is my main focus. I have had to work behind the scenes to get on board with that one. In any event, I'll be on the inside and the outside. Then...

"Yeah. Henderson here." The Portland cop gave the universal "jack-off" sign to a woman walking by his desk, who responded with her middle finger.

"You any relation to Ricky?"

"Petrovich, you fuck. Yeah, Ricky's my long lost cousin. Who'd he play for? The Knicks? Hold on," Lance heard a muffled *"Hey!"* and listened to distant voices, barely recognizing Henderson's.

"*Busy?*…No, it's just some asshole calling about my cousin…*Captain wants to see you*…Yeah. Yeah. OK. Right. I'll be there in a minute.*" Henderson resumed his call. "Yeah…So, Petrovich, you still there?"

"You got to go?"

"Fuck no. I'd rather talk to you if you can believe it…"

"He led the league in steals I think."

"Who? Oh. My cousin. What do you want? Still live in that hick-water town, what is it, Kitschland?"

"Yeah. We call it the 'Tri-Cities,' sounds more cosmopolitan."

"Isn't that a drink for fruits?"

"What, Tri-Cities?"

"So what's up, Lance?"

"How's it going with that body you found under the electric vault?"

"It wasn't an electric vault. I assume you're talking about the girl we found under the LNG pump station."

"What's an LNG?"

"LNG is a Lesbian Nookie Grotto. We find a lot of girls there."

"Didn't you meet your ex-wife there? OK, so it's some kind of gas or power thing. A big box in the ground with a fence around it. Right?"

"Liquefied Natural Gas. What do you want to know, Petro?"

"Who is she?"

"We are working on the theory that she is a young woman that went missing from the utility company about sixteen years ago. Things seem to match up on it. Still waiting for a positive. Dentist went out of business five years ago. So we are doing DNA with the parents."

"That is tough…I think I might have a connection over here in Eastern Washington. I don't have anything solid yet, but I am working on it. While I'm getting that done, I thought we could do a little fan dancing…"

"What's that, Lance?"

"You know, show a little skin, see if we can get the perp to stick his head up?"

"But you got nothing, right? And you want me to potentially hose my investigation for your…I don't know…your hunch?"

"You mean my itch. When I scratch, it shows up somewhere else, like a Lesbian Nookie Grotto. But yeah, I want your help. Just a little hint that you might have a witness. I'll provide the witness too."

"But it won't really be a witness. Just one of your fan dancers, right?"

"You catch on so fast, Ricky. That is why I love working with you."

"Send me your plan. I'll run it by the DA."

Chapter 8

Jim finally meets Kip again after Years of Separation

After he left the Easy Girl Bakery, Jim rode the downtown streetcar toward Powell's Bookstore, and realized that the principal reason he moved back to Oregon was because he had no real friends in California, just acquaintances. Life was passing him by and he felt as though he had no connection to it. He didn't know what else to do, so he went home – or the closest thing he had to it. Portland was as close as he wanted to get to Benton County. Looking around Northwest Portland made him realize it was going to take a long time, but at least there were enough potential friends in the neighborhood – and of course there was Chubby.

He had driven up the 101 to SFO at 4 A.M. almost every Monday for the last two years, when he could just as easily have flown out of San Jose, but they had bigger planes at SFO and he was more likely to get a first class seat (based on his airline mileage) by spending an extra 30, 40 minutes driving. Besides, there was no traffic that early in the morning, and doing 70 on that stretch of 101 was almost like flying on a magic carpet, because in daylight you could skateboard as fast as drive, and the morning after he got the letter from Chubby, Jim needed a reason to do something and he realized that even though everything he had ever done with

Chubby had always backfired in the most bizarre manner, he had never had more fun, before or since.

Jim Hunt had been the first to call Kip "Chubby Welles." As teenage stoners they had watched Rodney Dangerfield allow Bill Murray (his "talent agent" in the *SNL* skit) to change Rodney's name to "Chubby Welles," and Jim started calling Kip "Chubby" after that and they extended the persona at school with Jim acting the Impresario introducing the great "Chubby" Welles, who would straighten a nonexistent tie and deliver no-respect jokes.

"I told my Dad to take me to the zoo, he said if they want you, they'll come and get you." Baboom.

In any event, it seemed that everything Jim and Chubby did turned out wrong at first, but then ended up OK, often because Kip's dad owned half the land in rural Benton County and was able to pull them out of their messes. The old man's Christmas tree farm made millions, and he had other businesses, solid waste collection and a landfill, long-term leases for logging rights on some of the best timber still standing in Western Oregon, and he had between five and fifteen loyal Mexican workers who lived and worked on his property during the winter months, ready to take advantage of any quick and profitable project that came up. Kip's father was one of the richest men in Oregon. He wasn't too popular with his neighbors though.

Kip's mother left when Kip was 10, and remarried. She called Kip on his birthday and at Christmas but otherwise was gone for good, with minimal remorse or regret. Kip's dad brooded alone on his compound with only his housekeeper and her husband Enrique as company. He didn't speak Spanish and their English was *muy mal*.

Kip's father liked Jim, especially when he heard he enlisted back in 1987 right out of high school. He often said it was what Kip needed, but that line of reasoning never went very far. Kip used to tease Jim that he was the son his father had never had. And of course, there was that week when ol' man Rehain and Jim's mom took off together and returned separately.

So Jim decided it was time to get out of the permanent gridlock in the Bay Area and get back to the Emerald Empire. He had never had so much fun in his life as when he and Chubby roamed the rural outback of Benton County, Oregon, in spite of their bizarre parents. He realized that moving back to Portland and finding Chubby would probably be career suicide, but he didn't care, at least it would be different, and different was what he knew he needed, not the slow death he was experiencing now.

So he flew to Portland, found an apartment that overlooked the city and had a view of the mountains. It didn't matter where he lived, as long as an airport was handy. And now that he was going back to work for the KEG, that settled the matter.

He was thinking all of this and about the letter he received from "Chubby Welles," sitting on the streetcar at 23rd and Lovejoy, across the aisle from a pretty girl carrying a violin case. He thought about the body they found near Blue Lake outside Gresham buried near a pumping station vault. He had just got hired at the KEG fifteen years ago, when the young intern disappeared. The cops had interviewed him and were not nice about it either. A single guy, new at the company, and suddenly a pretty girl disappeared? Made sense to talk to him. But it all got dropped when they found her car in Palo Alto. He knew who was buried out there. Elizabeth, the Easy Girl, said it was probably a homeless guy…no, she was wrong about that.

He looked at the girl with the violin case. Who was she, he thought, was she a student, a privileged daughter, or a vagabond with most of her belongings in the old faded black violin case? It wasn't easy to tell because the line between a vagabond youth on a voyage of self-discovery and a destitute homeless waif was not always well defined. Jim had read somewhere that there were more homeless in Portland than almost any other city in the country.

They turned south on 11th, passed Jamison Square, and the upscale Pearl District condos. It appeared to be a community of café sitters, reading *Willamette Week,* or for the edgy ones, *The Mercury.* Around the square's fountain on this unseasonably warm winter day were urban dog walkers, shirtless and sunbathing body builders, women with severely trimmed hair, wearing cut-off black Lycra jogging tights, some managing kids with toddler tethers while others, childless yuppie poseurs or young immigrants from places that no longer seemed like home, sipped coffee and looked on with anxiety disguised as stylized contempt.

As the streetcar passed some high-end condos, Jim eyes landed on Stan, the young guy from the plane, shaking out his dreadlocks, arm around a young woman who's perfectly spheroidal glutes and rock hard tits were painted over with torn and faded $500 jeans and a size-too-small gray "Lewis and Clark" hoodie. She was looking at a newspaper and then up, in front of some very high end property. There goes law school, thought Jim. Good for Stan. Love conquers all.

Jim had been born in Oregon and he knew he didn't fit in, but then he didn't need to, he didn't need to belong to anything other than the silent society of all those other unconnected, untethered loners. A lot of us out there, he thought. It sucks sometimes too. He should have listened more closely to Stan on the plane. He seemed to have figured it out better.

Jim got off the streetcar at Powell's and walked up to the Burnside door and immediately noticed it was different from what he remembered. The Burnside entrance he remembered used to be seedier and grittier and was almost always staked out by several sad people, who had written out stories on cardboard, sometimes with a punch line, a story with pathos, perhaps a lost wallet, a dying sibling, needed medical procedures, sick children, a thrown rod in an old car. But they fixed up the door and windows around the entrance since Jim's last visit, put in more glass and now it feels a tiny bit more corporate, and streamlined, with more cashier stations. And maybe it is a little less inviting to all of the out-of-luck people who used to camp out there. Jim felt a little strange about it, like he did all gentrification.

Jim came through the Burnside entrance to Powell's and turned left into the door toward the literature stacks passed the novels and the poetry, row after row of Classical Greek and Latin literature, Aeschylus, Euripides, Sophocles, Virgil, the two Plinys, etc., up the short steps into the detective and science fiction section. Jim stopped and found a copy of the sequel to *Tinker Tailor Soldier Spy*, *The Honorable Schoolboy*, then put it back, he wanted something with more grit and maybe more...American, something easier to read too, he thought...Chandler! There must be something Chandler wrote that he hadn't read...oh yeah, Chubby, he was here to meet Chubby. He pulled himself away from the Noir fiction and went into the coffee shop.

Kip was sitting at a table by himself even though it was pretty crowded. He was wearing a water-stained fringed Buffalo Bill leather jacket and had a couple books about old films scattered in front of him. His serrated single blade pocket knife was opened and laid on a sketch book that displayed Chubby's almost finished dark pencil drawing of Vlad the Impaler, whose burning, recessed sinister eyes seemed more medieval and dark than any Hollywood vision ever made. Jim could sense Chubby was making some of the other patrons nervous.

"Why did we meet here?" Jim asked, as he walked over to Kip and looked down at Vlad.

"Remember the library back in school, detentions for talking during study hall? Come here, man..." Kip got up and hugged Jim. "It has been...I was just thinking about this. It has been 18 years since we last saw each other."

"I know, I was just trying to remember, it was here in Portland, I met you at that Chinese dive..." said Jim.

"Hung Far Low, just down the street," Chubby said. "And that's not even there anymore. I think it moved out to Hillsboro or maybe 82nd – some place out past the buoys."

Kip stood up and stretched. He began shoving the books into his grease-stained leather bag.

"They used to kidnap sailors to Shanghai there," said Jim.

"Maybe."

They continued to look at each other. "Chubby, it is good to see ya." Kip got a little twinkle in his eye. No one had called him Chubby in years. And now, well, it began to fit, even if it didn't when he got the nickname. "Remember when we came up here as kids? This place was like heaven. Did you look at the SciFi sections?"

"*Clans of the Alphane Moon*," said Kip, holding up the PK Dick novella, laughing, "The paranoids and the depressives ran the place, just like Philomath High. Principal Smith, he should have been institutionalized. The English teachers were the schizos, the coaches, and gym teachers were manics, and then there were the Heebs, the hebephrenics."

"We were the Heebs, weren't we?" Jim looked at Kip with awe.

"Yeah, I guess we were. The disorganized schizophrenics, major issues in the house! It is amazing we ever escaped. Powell's saved us," said Kip. "I am here all the time now. It is my office away from my office."

"We met some characters hitching up to Portland."

"Nothing we couldn't handle though." Chubby made a fist and a knowing look.

"When I worked at the KEG, I walked up here half the time on my lunch hour, just wandering through the stacks looking at titles and covers, and dreaming about reading it all, but you can't live long enough, so you have to choose."

"It the same with women," said Kip.

"Yeah, more so. So what are you doing now?"

Kip had always looked a bit like Orson Welles, the other reason that "Chubby" Welles had stuck as a nickname. He had the same eyes, the swept back brown hair, the cleft chin and wide cherub cheeks that still seemed boyish even at 44. Chubby did what he could to accent the resemblance. He copied his mannerisms, at least those of the young, buoyant Charles Foster from the first reel of *Citizen Kane*. He was big, about 6'1" at least 220 lb. But the voice, the melodious voice that once you heard would stick with you, it was one of a kind; you could never get it out of your head. It was made for radio, bold, unapologetically rich and deep, like Orson Welles.

"It's a long story," said Kip. "For both of us I am sure. Let's go somewhere that we can talk without whispering. I want a beer or something..."

"OK. Lead the way."

"Fresh start, huh? I have been staying down across Nicolai, crashing in my office, it's cool, I got it fixed up. You got my letter? I stay with this woman sometimes, I got to tell you about her, she is...too much for me by a mile. But, *SwiftPad,* baby! It's in an old warehouse, I have a little corner of it, not too private, but every-body in that building is, well we have too many people. I had a great place downtown, but it got robbed, and...Anyway, last week we hired eight or nine. There will be more soon, many more, we got money flowing! Maybe I should move out, how big is your place? Come on, my truck is outside..."

Chubby had a canvas duffel bag where he kept his stuff, books, an orange iPad, his first computer, with a black Skull & Crossbones stenciled on the back, dirty clothes. When they got to the counter he opened the duffel bag, releasing the aroma of mildew and some-thing else...he quickly pulled out the books and closed the duffel bag for the duration of the transaction. It flat-out stank when he opened it.

"I have to buy these," he said. He had copies of *R. Crumb: The Complete Record Cover Collection,* the first book of *The Illuminatus! Trilogy,* and *The Complete Idiot's Guide to Tantric Sex.*

They got into Chubby's truck, a 1951 Chevy pickup, and he threw his stinky duffel bag in the back.

"In your letter, you said no email. You mean, internet email?? What is that about?"

Kip looked sternly at Jim, who was smiling.

"It's not a joke, Jimmy," Kip said.

"I guess if you have reason to be paranoid..."

"You work for GIP for Christ's sake!" Chubby looked ahead, working the gears on the hilly stop, and headed up toward North-west Portland, where Jim had just come from.

They ended up on 23rd, across the street from the Easy Girl Bakery, found a parking spot and Kip led Jim into the Nob Hill Bar. Jim paid for a couple of beers and they sat in the back away from the other customers.

"You ever eat over there?" asked Jim.

"Easy Girl? You kidding? Lizzy and I go way back. I met her at the Sturgis Rally ten years ago. I'm in there more than I should be; the pie is too good, gotta watch my figure."

"She seems nice. I stopped in this morning..." They ordered beer at the bar, found a table and sat down. "So how about you? Tell me about your girlfriend."

"It's not just her. But yeah, we're business partners, which is probably not a good idea."

"What's not a good idea, fucking or business?"

Chubby thought about that for a few seconds. "Which brings me to what I want to talk to you about."

Jim shook his head and rolled his eyes.

"I have finally hit the mother lode! I am helping to run a software start-up, like I told you."

"Well, I have a job. I am not looking for another one right now."

"I am not talking about a job! First, I need to vet you. GIP? How can you work for them? Jesus, I have to say that concerns me. You are like some demon coming up to Heaven and saying, "Yeah, I've been working for Satan, but I think it would be cool to hang out with you guys now." Kip lowered his head to sip his beer and looked at Jim through half closed eye slits, suddenly morphing into Sheriff Hank Quinlan from *Touch of Evil*.

"Fuck you, you fat fuck."

"That doesn't matter. You would be working with me," said Kip.

"When you say working...you mean you pay people..."

"Soon, yeah, but now we have some subsidies, we are always having open dinners for everyone and we have some contingency funds...but that is changing fast. We just signed up with some investors and..."

"Kip, I need to make money. Anyway, I am going back to the power company. I start next week."

"But you can still quit that. Or do both! This is going to be big. We will be rich! Richer than my Dad, within a year. What are your expenses? Are you supporting anyone? Any kids you know about?"

"No, but still..."

"OK. Can you keep an open mind? If I take you over there, can I say you are thinking about it?"

Jim smiled and for about 30 seconds stared at Kip, who never cracked a smile or broke eye contact.

"Yeah, I'll think about it. What is your position in all this?"

"I told you, I am one of the founders and I squeezed some seed money from out of my trust, anyway, it is all on the up and up. Investment, depreciation, tax stuff. You know what I mean? Now we have real investors. I am designing the overall...ya see, it is GG and I who kind of came up with the concept. There are about three of us, four...no five of us running it...But if you came on board...we just formed a board of directors and like I said, money is about to flow ,my friend! And with your experience and my recommendation..."

"OK, OK, don't get ahead of yourself. Alright. This is software, right? I mean your product?"

"Well in part. Yes. It is a...it started as a Facebook rip-off. But it is taking off...!" said Kip.

"You mean you are going to sell advertising like..."

"No. Well, yes, but..." Kip shook his head like he was tired of talking to idiots. "You still don't get it," said Kip. "But that's OK. We don't have all the answers yet either, so you can help us answer those questions."

Jim made a face and looked away, then back at Kip.

"It's good to see you, buddy." said Kip. "We'll figure something out."

Chapter 9

Mark Ruskin, of Santa Monica and GIP, plots Outsourcing of the KEG's IT Team

M ark Ruskin (MBA), a "Business Consultant" for GIP, stretched and twisted in his striped silk pajamas in front of the opened sliding glass door, and looked out into the morning darkness of his Pacific Ocean–facing Santa Monica condo. He had just taken a piss, but still had his morning woody, and he tried to remember the last time he had sex in the morning, and why it had been such a long time since it happened.

He knew there were two kinds of women in Santa Monica, or at least in his condo building. He was clear about which ones he wanted to sleep with. There were the needy ones that said hi to you and the other kind, usually thinner, more elegant and stylish, the ones that smiled slightly or only lifted their eyebrows. Those were the ones. That is what he wanted, that is what he was waiting for! He had seen them on the elevator, in the park, at Whole Foods, in the gym, they were everywhere. He dreamed about having a girl-friend who always looked gorgeous, whose hair was always perfect, yet natural, a woman with that perfect uplift on her breasts, but not too big. Cheekbones, he really wanted cheekbones. That is what he was waiting for.

He knew if he kept a clear head, didn't compromise, didn't fall for a needy girl, one that was too quick to say hi or who continued talking too much, those were the ones to avoid…if he could stick to his plan, eventually, when he mastered his professional life, the rest would fall into place. He knew that. It takes money to get a perfect woman and he knew he was on the right track.

5:55 A.M. Mark was getting ready for the call. It was starting to get light out and he saw a strange flash out over the water. A plane taking off from LAX, catching the sun? He reminded himself to take out the trash.

He dialed in. "Hello, who's on?" It was his boss, a woman who he had never met in person. Her name was Persephone Jackson. The name Persephone was a clue, could she be Greek? Mark didn't think she liked him. She might be black, he thought. But he couldn't picture her as black. Persephone…in some Greek myth, didn't she fuck the devil?

"Mark here," he said.

"Hi Persi, it is John. Ken just texted me that he can't make it. Suzanne will join later if she can."

"OK, let's get started," Persephone directed.

Mark's heart sank a little. Ken Oren was the VP in charge of BD Outsourcing. Big Data. He wanted to get connected with him. "John, why don't you lay out the project?"

They heard a "BIP" on the line.

"Well, it is a small energy company up in Or-ee-gone…" John began.

"Hi, this is Suzanne, I just joined. I think we can say it is a mid-sized company, John…looking at the balance sheet, it doesn't sound like much as these things go, but it is a chance to refine our approach, get requirements aligned with the model, analyze strategy. We want to go through the process on a small scale and figure out where we need to focus resources going forward. This could be a big play we use again and again. That being said, here are the main points.

"The company is Northwest Consolidated Electric and Gas. It is an old company, and they have a protected market, a franchise from Oregon to sell natural gas...and electric power. Electric co-ops compete in outlying areas. It is all one big valley up there, isn't it? Great football team lately. Ducks, right? They are about to break into some new markets. Potential regulatory nightmare, but we have people working that and the state legislature is..."

"But," John jumped in, "the price for expansion is that they might be losing the lock on their franchise. If they want to grow, they don't have a choice. They have to take the risk. Furnaces and appliances have IP addresses now and power is getting managed down to the milliwatt. They want to start exporting gas across the Pacific. So they will be international soon and need to get ready for that. They have an LNG plant but no LNG. Can't convince the regulators and politicians to let them turn it on. They have facilities for storage with a terminal being built on the Columbia, and a pipeline from Canada. They could really take off," he paused. "Suzanne, what do you think?"

"If any of that is going to happen," she paused, almost certainly, thought Mark, for effect, "they need to upgrade their whole way of doing business, and their IT department is a Mom and Pop operation." She stopped. "Hang on, I have to take this..." There was some dead air.

"So what do you think, Mark?" Persephone asked. "Who joined?"

"It's Ken." The Big Data VP! Mark's heart skipped.

"Hi, Ken. This is Mark Ruskin..."

"Oh, you're the Scout on this project, right?" There was a collective nervous laugh.

"Yeah," Mark laughed again, this time by himself. "I am going up there on Monday, Ken," he paused then continued, Scouting...so John..." *Take charge!* he thought. "...You were the primary for sales on the Northwest Energy Project?"

"I was not primary, but I am working on it..."

BIP! "Hi, it's Suzanne again. Did Ken join?"

"I'm here."

"OK, do we have a statement of work?" Mark asked.

"No...we have an understanding..." John sounded unsure.

"Do we have a contract?" Mark felt the power coming to him. Don't let up!

"Oh yeah, yeah, we have you there for three months. But extending it should be doable, if we need to..."

Suzanne was good, Mark thought. She handled all the real work for clowns like John. He remained quiet. Clearly they didn't know what he was supposed to do, which was fine with him. Mark thought the key was to give them as little as he could so they couldn't micromanage him. Let Ken know that he is in charge, not the Project Manglers or the Sales Monkeys. No milestones. The best plan was no plan.

"Our big goal is to provide them a path to migrate their IT services to our facilities offshore. When they grow, we grow with them. There are some other business angles to this but we don't need to worry about that. There will be staff resistance. It could even get political because of the franchise, etc. They have a Utility Commission..." He wondered who Suzanne was, a business analyst obviously, but she didn't seem like she was shilling for John like he first thought. "...that controls rates. So we need you on the ground to track all of it and help us come up with strategies to mitigate that resistance."

"Got it," said Mark emphatically.

"Excuse me a minute, Suzanne, hold the fort, I have to take this..." John's phone BIPPed off again.

"In addition to your services, the contract includes the Social Cloud. We threw it in for a three-month trial. Don't worry about licensing. Six months, even a year free, OK, as long as we make progress. The plan requires, absolutely requires, that they utilize our business tools. The collaborative tools will allow all activity by the entire company, both on and off the job if it really takes, to be tracked and directed to unified goals. All of it, the whole package, has to be implemented. That is your charge, Mark. The first thing is to get some beta testers happy."

"I've heard that we don't have a product yet," said Mark, "Social Cloud is really that start-up...*Jammit*, right? I understand we are still in the process of re-badging it, but it hasn't been through any integration testing...for smartphone data sharing..."

Shut up, he thought, realizing he was just digging a hole he would have to climb out of. He knew the "Social Cloud suite" or whatever it ended up getting called would get sucked into that massive Ooze that was GIP Software. It had to integrate with this, that, and all the other GIP products, most of which were acquired, none of which talked with each other, even though each of those other products had the same requirements when they were brought in, but none of them had really been brought up to snuff yet. What did work was slow and buggy.

More dead air, about 30 seconds. "I'm back." It was John. "So where are we?"

"Well, Mark, we can take that offline, but the key thing to remember, 'Don't let perfect be the enemy of the good.' I think we are done, John," said Persephone. "Do you have any questions, Mark?"

"No." Are you kidding, he thought? Don't let perfect be the enemy of good? Mark looked up the quote on his iPhone. Voltaire? What did he know about software integration? Mark knew that none of the people on the call had any answers for his questions, so he kept silent. Questions would only make more work for him.

He got pinged on *GIPtalk*. IT WAS KEN!

KEN: Mark, great job! Call me when this ends.

MARK: k

"Mark, get us a plan as soon as you can. We told them we'd start Monday. Can you get up there by then?" Persephone asked.

"No problem." It was Wednesday. "I'm going to drive my own car up. Any problem with reimbursement?" Mark had a Bimmer; he didn't want to be driving a piece of shit rental for three months.

"Probably not. Copy me on your first expense report. One more thing," it was John. "They recently hired a new Operations Manager. He was working for us until last month."

"Really?" Persephone exclaimed.

"Came out of the blue. He didn't tell us where he was going when he gave notice. We found out about it from their CFO."

"What's his name?" asked Mark.

"Jim Hunt," said Suzanne. "He was in delivery, a Systems Management guy. Our internal people didn't have a particularly high opinion of him." Suzanne hesitated, "And, he used to work there, at the client's, years ago. So he probably has friends."

"Have we talked to him?"

"Mark, that would be wrong," said Persephone, "As well as risky..."

"We have to be careful about tampering, it's true," said John. "But as things develop, in the right setting. This is your thing, Mark. Everyone says you know how to handle these situations."

"So our angel there is the CFO, what's his name?"

"DeFonzaro, Frank DeFonzaro. He is new to the company so he has to be careful. I understand he has some plans to push. 'Bum' Crockett is planning to set up a hostile takeover. Try to remember that we have a solid, long-term relationship with the Crockett Group. DeFonzaro thinks they would be a beneficial partner but he will need to bring his people along on that."

"Like you say, John," said Persephone, "we can't..."

"I know, I know, but it is better to know what is going on across the field, right, Mark?"

"Sure."

"Just," John hesitated..."Just...let this guy Hunt, Jim Hunt... you got to make sure he is still our guy. Feel him out and let him know if things go well, he will land on his feet. See that he understands the welcome mat is still out."

"No problem." Mark sensed an awkward silence. He heard a cough. It was probably Persephone. "I'll see how it goes." He knew that the other side of the coin held true too, that a company like GIP could remove a lot of welcome mats, not just at GIP.

"OK, any questions? No? I have another meeting, if anybody wants to stay on–" Persephone said. "No, thanks everyone!"

"Bye." "Bye" "Thanks." BIP – BIP – BIP – BIP – BIP – BIP.

Mark got up and walked to his balcony to breathe. Holy Wow! He was reeling and now he had to call the VP. This was becoming exactly what he wanted, MORE! Alright. Mark dialed.

"Ken, it's Mark Ruskin."

"Mark. Great job! You ready for this?"

"Absolutely! I think this is going to be a big play for us." Mark was excited and he didn't mind letting it show in his voice.

"I have something to add, which I didn't want to say in front of the rest of the team. We might have another deal in Portland. It is more long term but maybe not. It is not related to the Energy Company play. It is a start-up, a Social Media Company. They are staying completely off radar. They are putting simulations out on the Web which are getting amazing amounts of traffic. It is becoming a bit of a cult phenomenon. You still can't google them. I have a guy looking into some things and will send you the update as soon as I have it."

"Great!" Mark was confused. Is this legit? Can't google them?

"We want you to do some recon work while you are there. Just sniff around. Once you get something, we can darken the skies with people flying into Portland. But we want to know what we are dealing with. It is called *SwiftPad*. We don't know what it means, but it looks like they might be doing a business collaborative deal, or even going after Facebook. I'll send you the details, but it is really only one address and one name, which I do know, and we are looking into one other...Like I said, I'll keep you posted...We've dealt with him before; he is kind of slippery so be on your toes. You will know him as 'Lonnie Wolfe.'"

"OK, I'll check it out."

"For business, you can trust him, don't be afraid to utilize him. Just..."

"Just what, Ken?" asked Mark.

"Keep on your toes around him, keep it low key. And keep us out of it for now."

Us? Mark didn't ask him who us was.

"Understood. Thanks, Ken."

Chapter 10

Petrovich seeks Info from Tyler @NSA who notices GIP Seeking Same

"Trek," Tyler Ambrose (his undercover working alias was Sebastian), his feet up on a conference table, deep in the Black Monolith at Fort Meade, shook his head and laughed as he listened to the daily summary they were preparing for "Waterfall," the White House Group advising POTUS on measures taken to close the barn door that Ed Snowden open-sourced. Tyler multitasked as he listened to a mid-level "Assurance Officer," who must be a legacy (oh yes, the Agency has legacy hires, called trans-generationals, one of the last residues of OSS–Ivy League nepotism). He was listing through all the reasons why it happened and why we don't know what was missing, while sliding away from any inferences that he or his sponsors might have prevented it all. Tyler of course knew, because he had helped Snowden, not out of ideological reasons, but because...the system was a bigger threat than all the Al-Qaeda bad guys put together. And rat-fucking the Black Monolith was fun. He had a blast watching America's Security Establishment run for cover when Snowden pulled back the curtain. And strategically, it was better for the United States to be outed this way than to be bled for decades and not even know a needle was in your vein. He and Ed had done their country a favor.

He had left the NSA six months ago to work for the CIA, and was taking advantage of the new openness insisted on by the President between the two spy citadels. Actually he had never even cleared out his desk, and all his badges still opened all the doors in the NSA citadel.

While listening to the internal propaganda podcast, he was reverse traversing some net traffic back to a GIP consultant, whose cubicle happened to be just on other side of the wall. Tyler had snuck by and peeked in; the guy was all wired up, listening to Springsteen or possibly instructions from his Mothership, while sloppily scanning the 'Lode.' The GIP consultant's back was scrunched up, his laptop up close to his chest, his elbows out. Tyler knew he had been running searches for one person in particular, Jim Hunt, also a GIP employee. Why were they spying on one of their own? Was this laptop jockey a rogue, or was he under orders? Was Hunt fucking his girlfriend? Tyler let it run, see where he goes.

The GIP consultant seemed to have figured out some of the holes still out there, and was exploiting them. Of course being inside the Agency's primary firewall helped. Tyler had been watching him for the last week, and told his boss in the most general terms what was going on, but he was told the GIP guy was OK. So Tyler just sat back and watched.

He looked up Jim himself, only yesterday, as a favor to a cop he had worked with once, over the phone and online, helping find a kidnapped victim in Thailand. Jim Hunt's Army career was quite fascinating. Almost a year and a half as an agent of military intelligence without portfolio, at 19 years of age. And for all that, nothing, no reports, no memos, all direct reports to then-Captain, now-General Michael Graham, who had shimmied up the JCS chair short list. We watched Graham too, it appears he had a long affair with an East German woman who is now one of the most powerful women in the world. No, her name is not Angela, but that doesn't matter.

Tyler wove a complex tale that he embellished with an international angle for his boss to pass up the chain. "This was how the Germans helped Snowden; if we want to get him, we shut down GIP's spying, then take over where they leave off, catch the

Germans in the act and shut them up about American eSnooping."
He peddled this, knowing it was stupid, but exactly what his bosses
wanted to believe.

His phone rattled, and the alert he had set for the GIP Consultant's Lode searches went off again. Tyler almost fell out of his chair.
Cynthia Oglethorpe! Now he was searching for Cynthia too! He
wanted to walk around the wall and put electrodes on this GIP
creep's balls. He breathed deep and watched. Hunt and Cynthia.
Both in Portland. What is GIP after? Was Hunt connected to
Cynthia...and a serial killer investigation?

He pulled Petrovich's number off his phone and rang him.

"Hey, Lance. Getting back to you about that guy you were
asking about."

A few years ago, some rich girl from Seattle whose daddy was
connected to the Bush family got kidnapped while on vacation in
Thailand, so it got flagged as NatSec. Tyler and Lance had worked
the case together, successfully, and in the course of it, he learned
that Petrovich had broken many big cases with old school style,
no massive "technical means," only an untrainable combination of
logic, intuition and persistence. He was one of the few cops Tyler
really admired. He had no trouble ethically or otherwise breaking
the rules for Lance.

Petrovich had asked for "a peek" at the military records of a
suspect he was investigating, the same Jim Hunt that GIP was looking at. Hello! Somebody was farting in Denmark. And now Cynthia,
his Cynthia...

"Yeah, Sebastian. Thanks, did you find out anything?"

"Nothing bad, he wasn't discharged because of anything criminal, he had some semi-espionage stuff hanging about him, but it
was honorable. It was a strange career for a guy that young. I'll do
some more digging for you. Why? Do you think he might be..."

"No. That adds up for me. But my partner still thinks he's fishy.
Anyway, I am still nowhere. The utility company doesn't want to
dig up the vault."

"Why not?"

"They are afraid it will cause power disruptions, and incur a huge expense on the utility as well. But the reason they are using is that the site is in the middle of one of the biggest great blue heron nesting areas on the West Coast. It's not even 'endangered,' just on the Fish and Wildlife Watch list. So for next three months, no construction activity allowed in that part of the delta."

Tyler knew Lance would be retired in three months. In fact, he was scheduled to retire in three weeks.

"Why not petition the court?" he asked.

"This isn't a FISA deal, it is just a hunch, a wild ass hunch. More important, if we petitioned it would be public, and we could never keep it secret. The whole point is not to tip him off. Anyway, we don't have shit. We can't get a court order to disturb the birds without some evidence, something."

"I seem to remember you mentioning having a good friend who is a judge?"

"Yeah, but he is a past president of the local Audubon society."

"Oh, maybe not a good idea."

Tyler heard Georgia on the speaker.

"Hey, boss, who we talking to?"

"Fed spook. He's OK."

"Hi, Spook," she said into the speaker. "Lance, I have been looking through your old notes."

Lance looked at her. "No wonder you don't have a boyfriend."

"Your detective skills are seriously slipping, boss." She smiled and shrugged. "Hey, Spook, tell him he's too young to quit."

"Somebody is always killing somebody. He should get out when he can," said Tyler.

"Anyway, Georgia my dear, if I am so young, then I need to get laid once in a while too. I have to stop booking so many sex perverts…"

"What?"

"Hey, Lance," Tyler sensed he was intruding on a partner-to-partner moment, "I'll get back to you with more on Jim Hunt's Army resume, but I think that is a dry well. But please keep me informed."

Georgia shook her head. She wasn't so sure.

"OK, Seb, thanks. I'll be in touch."

She looked at Lance with just a hint of concern. She had never associated what sex criminals did with her own love life. "I looked at the transcripts of some of the interrogations in Portland on the '97 disappearance of the McKenzie woman."

"Yeah?"

"Jim Hunt. I don't think it's a dry hole, as your spook friend suggests. After he got out of the Army, he enrolled at Eastern Oregon in La Grande. In March of 1992. Two months before the Morton woman disappeared."

"Well that is why I am having my buddy in the NSA informally look into it. Just remember though, it wouldn't have been a crime of opportunity for him. La Grande is 120 miles away."

"Less than two hours, big deal. Look at Bundy, he worked from Corvallis, Oregon, to the north of Seattle."

"I know, I know."

"So we don't know what he did in college. Did he have an internship anywhere? He was never a focus of the Morton case. After he gets out of college, he does Info Tech work, down in Eugene, then moves up to Salem, and finally gets work in '96 at the Electric and Gas company in Portland, two months before…"

"I checked him out for the Portland case. He is a milquetoast. No way. I am sure of it. But keep checking, OK?"

"Did you read the transcripts? Here, listen…" Georgia pulled a notebook out of her purse. "…Uh, yeah sure I noticed her. But I didn't know her. I mean, she was really pretty…' That is from Portland, Detective Henderson, see?" She showed him the transcript but Lance just nodded. "It goes on, the guy couldn't shut up talking about how much he liked her. Like he might feel guilty? They bring up her name and it sounds like he is going to ejaculate all over the tape machine. He gets out of the Army two years before his tour is up. What's that about? No record, no decorations, nothing. If he was smart enough to get into intel, why did they let him go?"

"Like I said, it is worth a second look, but I am sure it's just coincidence." Lance gave Georgia a tired look. "But, you might be right. So we'll take a second look. Or you can after I am gone."

"Lance! In three months the birds hatch and we get a court order to dig up the Morton woman."

"What if she's not there?"

"Then you say sorry to Bonneville for causing a fuss and retire."

"It's not Hunt. I am sure of it."

Georgia rolled her eyes and drew a laugh out of Lance. "You might be right, Lance, but on this case, you haven't exactly hit it out of the park on your suspicions."

"No way in my book. I remember him. No way."

"So you'll stay?"

"I'll think about it."

Chapter 11

Jim at SwiftPad HQ Admires Programmers (Sans Panties)

Gentrification had not yet arrived to the Nicolai Street area. Seedy warehouses, mostly wooden and many still used for industry, spread out on the flats that extended from the northern edge of the West Hills down to the river. Unlike the brick and mortar structures being turned into lofts and shops in the Pearl District of Portland, there was still a blue-collar, industrial feel to the area.

"Nice, huh?" Kip said. Jim shrugged.

"Typical really," said Jim. "Just like the Dallas Yahoo data center in '99."

Chubby parked his truck, grabbed his stinky duffel bag and led Jim into the *SwiftPad* headquarters. The lobby was small, with walls of mismatched graffiti-covered plywood. A white half-filled Styrofoam coffee cup sat alone on a rough unfinished wooden bench just inside the door. The vestibule's sole light hung from a single precarious electrical cord. The door matched the exterior wrought iron handle and an oversized reinforced steel lock.

Kip unlocked the door and they walked in and were greeted by GG. "Hey Kip, did you get the checks?" she asked.

"Not yet, later today," Kip said.

"Really?" She looked as if she didn't believe Kip, and then quizzically at Jim. She was wearing a tee-shirt embossed with a leering Founding Father embedded on some futuristic currency.

"Yes – I just need to get the transfer notarized...it's good, I talked to the guy..."

She didn't look happy and looked back at Jim without changing her expression. Without taking her eyes off of Jim, she asked loudly, "And, did you start the New VM on the Pittock server?"

"I tried but it said, 'Not enough memory to load...' or something like that..."

"There's enough, did you stop the TEST VM first like I told you?"

"Ah, I tried, but it kept asking for a password and the one you gave me didn't work."

"We change them every day. You need..."

"Oh yeah. Sorry. I forgot."

"I'll drive over and do it..." she said.

"No. Arky, you do it," interrupted Kip, looking at a smooth-faced young man with spiky blond streaks working on his laptop on the floor. "Do you know how?"

"Of course."

"Good – please get it done. We have to stop fucking up like this!" They all abruptly chuckled, because it had been Kip himself who had fucked up.

"Hold on," said GG. "Arky is working on something far more important..."

"GG, it's OK. I think I have it worked out. I just emailed you the equations and a first cut at the code to use them. And I need a break, to be honest."

"Really? Before you go – show me the highlights. Come on, let's go over to the conference room." The four of them went into an adjoining room, which had three stained, broken down, ratty couches pushed around a big white board.

Arky took a picture of the board and then erased it. He looked doubtfully at Jim, but Kip said go ahead. "He works for GIP, so maybe they'll hire you." The three men laughed but GG didn't. "OK – Rina is working on the linguistic model – which will take language, written, audio, or both, and break out the meanings into parameters. It is pretty sophisticated, and like we talked about, is not yet ready to encode all meaning that language conveys. But that is OK. We all understand that we will miss some things and sometimes it will be funny, but rarely serious – people can be outraged or not – it doesn't matter."

"I don't understand?" said Jim.

"Say you post some long diatribe stating that Conservatives are afraid of sex. You put in history, and sociology studies and personal experience. Every point you make is broken into a 'variable' by Rina's model. It is not meant to be perfect, but just approach say 65–70% accurate."

"Most people get bored after a few paragraphs anyway," said Kip.

"So each 'point' of meaning is made into a variable and this gives you a long string of variables the meaning of which is stored, so that it can be reused the next time," GG said, with a worried look as Jim appeared to follow the conversation. "But your example is not true."

"What isn't true?" asked Chubby.

"That Conservatives are afraid of sex. I lived with a guy for two almost two years that worked for the NSA – or maybe DIA, I was never sure. I think he still does anyway. I told you that didn't I?"

Kip looked at GG, started to speak, then stopped.

Arky staring at the white board pretended not to have heard the exchange. "Of course we have each person's profile who associates with this rant – some people try to split hairs and say yes – but sometimes no – you know? We can store all that," Arky continued to write pseudo-code on the white board. "All this can be used by the equations we use next."

"So – the goal is to push the conversation," Kip said. "Anyone who says anything must be dealt with – either by others or by the 'SwiftPad user.' Right?"

"Right. The App will create fake users – or reuse existing fake users. If someone else pops up – a real person – fine. Better in fact. Otherwise we maintain the same variables with the same meanings throughout the whole exchange. It doesn't matter if we are wrong…" GG added.

"That is step one. Take the input from users and break it into variables," said Arky.

"OK – Kip – before we go on." GG stood up and smiled tightly at Jim. "You've have told me about your friend here, but…"

"GG, this is Jim, we have known each other since we were, when was it?"

"Mrs. Allen's class, I think," said Jim. "We must have been six or seven."

"OK," she gave Jim a look that wasn't unfriendly, but otherwise he couldn't read. "OK. It's Kip's show too. Nice to meet you." They shook hands. "Please turn off your smartphone while you are in the building. OK?"

"Sure." Jim pulled out his iPhone and powered it off while letting her watch.

Meanwhile, a letter arrived in an anonymous Portland post office box.

Confidential Memo
From: Mark Ruskin, Business Consultant, GIP
To: Lonnie Wolfe, Portland Oregon
Subject: Cynthia Oglethorpe

LW,

As per the protocol, will continue to drop communication at the agreed location until otherwise instructed. Read with great interest memo re: capital venture "SwiftPad." Discussed with VP of Big Data at GIP. Will be arriving in Portland next week.

Regarding inquiry, SwiftPad "Architect," name, Cynthia Oglethorpe – father in Procurement @DoD & lives in Bethesda, Maryland, mother – primary school teacher. Two younger sisters, both accomplished. Discreet inquires find Cynthia had a series of depression-based episodes and discipline problems ensued. School assistant VP – "...sociopath, self-destructive, twice suspended, associates with Goths and Gamers." And finally she was expelled. Briefly reported missing, but after two weeks turned up in New Jersey and soon after completed GED. Then perfect SAT scores.

'Goth-Girl' – exploits legendary in the gaming community. GG – "public" online **nom de plume**.

Conflicting reports – lived with "Trek," identity not determined, analysts posit in intel community.

Profile changed – Gamer to Hacker. Relationship with Trek correlates with assumed "relationship" with the tech side of the intel world. Hacked corporate/government systems around the world, according to anonymous dark web blog, "for sport, playing cat and mouse, learning distinctions between the 'real' and the 'bait'..." Sped through Rensselaer, double major, Comp-Sci, Math. Voted "Most Likely to Virtualize" at the 2006 Def Com convention.

Trek disappeared off-grid and Cynthia soon followed, until she turned up in Portland, spring of 2009, writing code for CoLab, an open source business app. Six months later CoLab bought by JAMMIT, Portland open source firm that built secure teleconferencing applications and document sharing for far-flung businesses and organizations. @ 24, head developer for security of the apps at JAMMIT. Designed advanced PEN testing, influence at the company immense. Full disclosure, GIP purchased JAMMIT in 2010.

Your information seems to correlate with what we have. I will forward more as I learn it. On behalf of GIP, I am looking forward to working with you

Mark Ruskin, Business Consultant, GIP.

"So Arky – before you drive back into town and fix that VM, please explain your solution for converting the 'Input Variables' into data that SwiftPad can work with," GG directed.

"Right – well, we have two goals – one to push user input into a logical choice framework. Which we do with the latest work in game theory."

"Kip introduced the ideas of Daniel Ellsberg..." said GG.

"And two – to take those choices and subtly change them and rewrite them through the 'SwiftPad user,' and create and sustain discussions about anything. Create believable controversy."

"Ya see, Jim," said Kip, "People are lonely and nobody thinks anybody else understands them. The goal isn't for SwiftPad to be everybody's friend – it is really a 'Miss Lonelyhearts' project – the ultimate dating site – not for marriage – but for worldwide conversation."

"Right," said Arky, looking at GG with a roll of the eyes and mock confusion. "But many refinements in Ellsberg's model have occurred since he developed it. Many economists and researchers have expanded and modified his original theory and built solid mathematical models around it. Ambiguity aversion/uncertainty avoidance vs. risk aversion. We have several tested equations with which to create models. Studies have shown that societies that are risk averse don't accept change. So our theory is that some people, like some societies, are risk averse for the same reason. So we are looking to the 'input variables' to mathematically determine how far we can 'push' people without causing...aversion."

"How do you do that?"

"Well people who agree tend to reinforce each other. So SwiftPad enters the fray as a wildcard – an independent variable. A machine-created 'user.' We create 'friends' for people – friends, colleagues, strangers with candy, whatever – they all have IDs and bios, which I suppose an overeager investigator could see through – but everyone will know that this is how it works so there is no fraud. Anyway, these computer-generated 'friends' push them away from what they think they believe."

"No politics. Liberals and libertines get the same treatment as Rightwingers and prudes," said Kip. "We are constantly creating more 'containers' – Sports fans, History buffs, Romance Novel lovers, pot enthusiasts..." said Kip.

"That is Kip's favorite. If we can get a simulated user to change him on that then we know we are on the right track...anyway, then we push these variables that Rina and Arky have modeled and run them through a Mandelbrot set – a closed set of course – it wouldn't make sense if it was opened and ran out to infinity."

"No – of course not." Jim looked at Kip with a look of bewilderment. "Do you understand any of this?"

"I was pretty good at math – I can follow it but…Arky and Rina are out there, they are not normal…" said Kip.

"Thanks, boss. I thought everybody jerked off on the Euclid theorems. No – Jim – Mr. GIP – I thought all you GIP guys were smart? Anyway we feed the results of the Mandelbrot sets back into Rina's linguistic model and it is pretty cool what the results look like. By keeping the Mandelbrot set closed – less than 2 – it creates 'natural patterns of behavior.' You know like those trippy computer-generated patterns that can draw trees, or Tibetan Sand Mandala. Anyway, this is GG's model. She drew the big picture, so if anybody is not normal, it is she. It is easy to fill in the blanks once you have the architecture," said Arky. "I got to get over to the Pittock Building and reload that VM. Anything else, G?"

"No – I'll masturbate to your equations tonight."

"Great." Arky grabbed his bicycle helmet and headed out the big doors.

"So, G, what's the status?" Kip asked. They walked through the main section, which Chubby referred to as the *SwiftPad* Great Room.

"We are hitting it. It is starting to live."

"What do you mean?"

"After a certain point of complexity, there is unpredictability to software, which even the most well designed systems can't avoid. Actually, it is what I find most interesting about making computers do things. You discover things about it…there is quirkiness, because Java and Ruby and the rest of languages you work in are abstracted at such a high level. You tell it to do something, and then something else, and there are so many micro choices being made for each of those commands that soon it gets out of control. Anyway, we should be ready to put out another revision for maybe three or four hours next week. Every time we come up, we double the number of hits."

"Sounds like a corollary to Moore's Law," said Jim.

GG nodded and looked at Jim.

A Cisco 6500 switch, about 4 foot high, sat like a Mayan Idol in the middle of the room, a tangle of "cat 5" cables tapped down and snaking across the room, tentacles connecting other switches in other parts of the warehouse, and particularly into the laptops of three young, seemingly interchangeable spiky nerd boys, and two barely post-nubile women who were as different as sweet and sour. The redhead, a Java programmer, who wore a Peruvian poncho, and a bright red star tat on her cheek, was bent over, intently typing, her glistening dreadlocks jiggling.

"...Emma's a 'meta-coder', linking parent types and categories with their child specifics..." introduced GG as they walked by. The other woman wore what looked like a real silver fox fur coat, boots and Russian policeman's fur hat. "And this is Rina, nobody gives her any shit about endangered species..." ("because the fur is synthetic," said Rina with just a hint of a Russian accent) "...and I have never met anyone who understands variable linguistics, or writes tighter code to represent it..." ("...except maybe you, GG.") It was chilly, in spite of all the humming hardware.

Pillows carpeted the floor except for a rough pathway to the wooden stairs across the room.

"OK – listen up!" Everyone stopped and looked at Kip. "The paychecks are cut, but try to make them last – We should have them tomorrow by the end of the day. We are almost there...make sure you fill out your time so we can get your pay converted to shares. Hopefully, we will be hitting a regular pay period...consider this one as what loan sharks call 'the vig.'"

Squeals and cheers reverbed and echoed from the ceiling, not just from the programmers that Jim could see. Apparently the acoustics carried around the whole building from here.

"The chili is ready now and Chinese food arrives at five, and the wine and beer kegs at seven."

"Gonna get fucked up! WOOOH!" yelled Hadley, sitting until then unobserved by Jim. She was the head SQL query writer, and could pass for a voluptuous Tracy Flick, in her monogrammed sweater, plaid skirt and knee socks. She had an especially long cable, with lots of slack, because she liked to relocate around the room as she worked. As she plopped down on a big floor pillow, Jim caught just a flash of her white legs akimbo, sans panties, and then he tripped over her cat 5 cable.

"Hey, be careful!" Hadley yelled and that got a titter from the other developers.

"Yeah, be careful, man," said Chubby with a wink.

"Careful? I see nothing but trouble, of course I'll be careful," whispered Jim.

It was not much over 60 degrees. They were spread out around the Great Room, wrapped up in sweaters and blankets, working on what looked like disk-less laptops, like Chromebooks with Ethernet ports, but more generic. But they were all wired into the switch.

"I wish we could get a dedicated link…how come other companies don't get hacked?"

GG smiled. "They all do, believe me. Once we get it right, we can get a link permanently, then we'll need a large team just to fend off dumbshit denial of service attacks. You'll see. If we did it now, we would be dead in two hours, believe me."

Kip looked at Jim with a raised eyebrow. She looked at Kip, then at Jim with a quizzical expression he could not read. "I got some more systems to bring up before noon. You still have the keys to the cage?"

"Yes," said Kip, as he pulled out change, paper with notes, a rabbit's foot, a USB key and two rings of keys – "Yes, I have it here…"

"Let me see 'em – OK. Jim, nice meeting you. Maybe see you around. Kip, I have to take care of some stuff with the coders, then in about twenty minutes I'll drive downtown to the Pittock exchange. I need to make sure Arky got it right. He is smart, but is sometimes in a hurry. It's too important…Jim, we'll talk later, I am sure," she said.

"Love ya, Gee," Kip said.

She walked away with an expression on her face that Jim found impossible to read. It amused Kip.

"Come up to the orifice, Jimmy." Everything was unpainted and raw, mostly wood, but some steel and a little wrought iron, mostly in the doors and banisters on the stairs. Like downstairs, there were lots of big puffy pillows on the floor and St. Vinnie de Paul couches.

"A pillow wholesaler went Chapter 11 and we picked up a truck-load for a hundred bucks."

Chubby had a big, polished oak desk. Unlike anyplace else Jim had seen in the building it was covered with paper. He did have a computer, but it wasn't on. He had open space in front of him looking down on the Great Room below.

"So, I pay the bills, keep track of the kids and what they are working on. I am learning still...and trying to keep us from getting too corporate. My dad's accountant, Heber, remember him telling us how he was one of Brigham Young's descendants?"

"Yeah, I remember we gave him a slow barge of shit over Joseph Smith's story."

"Anyway he is coming up every couple of weeks to help me keep it straight. This is not what I thought I was signing up for, but..." Kip looked at the pile of paperwork that overflowed on his desk. "...I also have to do some of the shit technical work for GG that I always seem to fuck up. I was supposed to start that server the kid is doing."

"What did you yell at him for then?"

"He knows I was pissed off at myself. Sometimes it pays to be an irrational boss anyway. I read that somewhere. I am not handling this very well. And it is getting worse." Chubby looked at the ceiling.

"So you met her at a Java programming recruiting event that you thought was about the coffee business?"

"Yeah. Well, I thought it might be coffee, but I knew..."

"...I can see she is good. Am I wrong or is your company not connected to the Internet at all?"

Chubby smiled, proud of Jim's compliment. "No, we are not directly connected. We are very careful. No wireless in the building, none. We model against real traffic though and have probably 50 K users, who lurk and wait for us to show up. We know a good portion of them are other companies spying on us, and governments too. We run our model, then replay it with a massive set of VMs on a real connection. Well...actually it is nothing compared to the big boys. We rent a space down at the local IXP to get close to realistically seeing how it works on a big pipe. Then we bring it back and GG scrubs it before we put in on our system. Or we don't scrub it just to see what happens. Then flush it and reload the base VM. She does something to mask the real IPs."

"Seems like a lot of trouble. If you are going to put it on the Web and isolate it...maybe it makes sense."

"A lot of back channel buzz about just what we are and how come we aren't online all the time. But they haven't jammed us yet. Your company, fucking GIP, is especially interested. We see your hack attempts all the time. Pitiful."

"Like you would know the difference. Between good and bad hacks I mean."

"I know what you meant. We are expecting a legal assault soon. G says she is being tracked but isn't worried about it for some reason. She smiles when I bring it up...But we are lining up our shysters getting them ready to do battle. Heber is running that angle."

"Are you attacking any systems?"

"Absolutely not. We are just a parasite. We suck off the life force of the internet, and then hide under a rock so it can't suck on us. We don't probe or even look if we are not invited. If it is open though, we use it."

"This is too much like work for me. I have laundry to do, got to get on a plane in about 18 hours or so, and then go fuck with GIP software. It's my last week."

"Don't you want to have lunch? Mondo Extremo Chili – hearty and hot!"

"Mmm! Another time."

Kip got up and yelled down the fireman's pole hole next to his desk. "GG! Have you left? Are you going downtown soon? Give Jim a ride?"

"Leaving in five!"

"OK, buddy, careful with her, she might be a little too..."

"Too what – too hot for Conservatives? Definitely too hot and too young for you! I better not tell her I was in the Army then. I mean, she used to live with a CIA spook, right?"

Kip laughed, but then looked at his childhood friend blankly. "Be careful," he repeated.

"I am sure we will be fine," said Jim enjoying his friends discomfort. "I'll see you next weekend when I get back from Texas."

Jim and GG left in her 2002 Honda Civic and went downtown. She made a point of telling Jim that she had not slept with Kip, but Jim was pretty sure that was not true. Jim suspected that they had had some kind of tryst, although it had probably ended awkwardly. Chubby had a history of making friends with ex-lovers. Jim told her that he hadn't slept with him either and she let him out on Burnside and 23rd. He walked the rest of the way up Vista.

Chapter 12

Jim, back "Tapping" the KEG, Reacquaints with former Lover, Angie, now his Boss

Jim, wearing all black for his first day of work at the KEG, looked out from behind the glass partition of his new office at the cubicles where, theoretically, his team labored. There went Knute Jepparsen, his short-sleeved white shirt displaying his bulging old man Popeye forearms, hurrying to the bathroom for the fifth time today. He waved. He'd pick up a cup of coffee on his way back. Knute was the company's last mainframe programmer. Old history coming back to haunt Jim. It was the same mainframe application that the GIP team tried and failed to replace 16 years previously. Still the bread and butter of the company. Knute wasn't going to last forever in spite of his seeming indestructibility, and Jim knew that he would have to solve that one sooner or later. He looked at his phone – 9 A.M. – Showtime.

As Jim walked into the eleventh-floor meeting room, it all came back. The spectacular view from the southeast corner – he had forgotten the view. The river and the bridges – the Steel, Burnside, and Hawthorne bridges all looked like an elaborate hobby board for a Lionel train set crossing the dun-colored river, which seemed to stay still while the land around it moved south. It was a gray day, like most were, and the sliding doors were closed. They kept the rooms warm in the KEG; they were an energy company after all.

His boss's boss, the CIO, was Anaka Maheemi. Large-eyed and coffee-complected, she spoke with an emphatic flat Midwestern accent, but with a syncopation that de-emphasized the final syllable of her sentences. It was almost a Chicago singsong. She was attractive, and smiled, but ended her smile with a slight nod that seemed to transform into, not a frown, but almost a questioning look when it was acknowledged.

"I have several things to cover today, but first let's welcome the newest member of the team to his first staff meeting." She walked over to Jim and introduced him with her hand like a game show host. Jim stood up and bowed, to restrained laughs and sarcastic applause. "I understand that it is a welcome back rather than a welcome. It shouldn't take too long for you to get acclimated then?" Jim wondered if she kept that little subcontinent head nod-tilt as an affectation. Maybe she didn't like the way he was dressed. Oh well, she wasn't his problem, she was Angelica's boss.

Beth Rockford was still the manager of the developer team. Her team averaged over 15 years at the company. What kind of developer worked for less than $100 K in this economy? Beth brought cookies and Jim noticed he was the only one eating them.

Anaka took the floor again. For the next fifteen minutes she went on as if reading from a well-memorized script: the company was in trouble long term, global warming was cutting into the receipts, warm winters meant low gas usage, earnings per share were flat and projected to decline unless they could get their costs under control. Corporate blah blah, thought Jim.

"We have no web presence," she said, with a nod and almost a frown on the word "presence." "Customers don't feel they can communicate with us." Jim started to speak, but a glance at Angelica told him to stifle it.

"We need to get Linux on the desktop," said Anaka. She stopped when Joan, the "desktop support" manager, whose team consisted only of two help desk jockeys, suddenly looked up from her laptop, which she had been staring at through the whole meeting, with concern, almost alarm.

"Sorry. We've got an issue with the utility exchange. Lester says there is no problem with the connection, but, excuse me, I have to attend to this..." she got up with her laptop and left. Nice timing. Angie had told him Joan had applied for his job and was pretty pissed not to get it.

"I think we should reconsider the plans to modify our Desktop platform. I have done a study of the applications..." It was a big guy, with hipster horn-rimmed glasses and white socks.

"I am sure we will have a chance to discuss that, but..." Anaka looked over at Angelica and then at Jim. "...Rodney, we need to eat our own dog food," Anaka said. Rodney looked confused, but said nothing. Jim smiled.

Anaka looked at Jim with a quizzical head nod as he smiled. He nodded emphatically, thinking, she doesn't like me already.

Meeting over, Angelica walked out with him. Jim looked around the room and then at her. She smiled. This was the place. This had been their boudoir, where they almost got caught. Why did she hire me, he wondered. And why did I take the job? To get off the road? To come back to the scene of his greatest professional triumph and see if he could repeat it?

He got on the elevator by himself and pushed five.

"JIMMY!" Arthur Van Landingham caught Jim as he was coming out of the elevator. "Like a bad penny!"

"Yeah, I'm back," said Jim. "How are you, Artie?"

"Great!" They shook hands and Arthur could not contain his smile. "I am glad you are back. We need you now!"

"Well, I don't know about..."

"No, no, no, remember what it was like last time you were here? Those bastards at GIP were running us into the ground."

"I was one of those GIP bastards until last week."

"I know. Last month Old Swensson said he was gonna get you back."

"Swensson, huh?"

Arthur Van Landingham laughed. He was a second generation KEGGER, and if nothing else, he understood how the company really worked. His dad had been its chief engineer in the glory years, during the big expansion after the Second World War. Artie had been a fighter pilot in Vietnam, getting into the action just as it was over. Said he flew one of the last sorties over Saigon as the NVA tanks rolled in, but couldn't shoot at them. The war was finally over, just when he was getting ready to join it. After Vietnam, Art tried his hand at various schemes. Today they would be probably be called industrial design start-ups; all had failed.

"You must be thinking about retiring soon, huh?"

"Me? Naw! What am I going to do? Listen, I am only telling you this because I really don't know what is being planned up on the top floor. But I heard they hired a GIP consultant that will be reporting directly to the dot."

"The...oh..." Anaka. Jim smiled weakly and shook his head. "You mean the bindi?"

"Huh?"

"Nothing – it's what they call the dot on an Indian woman's forehead."

Artie laughed and slapped him on the back. "Watch your back, Jimmy. Come talk to me any time. OK?"

"Thanks, Art," Jim said. He had to be careful. Art might be unfireable, but Jim had no such protection.

Chapter 13

Mark drives Beloved Bimmer up to Portland and begins to Understand his Task

Coming up to Portland from California, making the trek north, getting off the LA Grid, getting in touch with the City of Roses, feeling the vibes and getting into the Pacific Northwest flow of it.

Mark had paved the way for three successful outsourcing gigs in tough environments and he understood the importance of blending in, of learning to laugh with the client and not be laughed at. Mark's pulse quickened; his senses began to vibrate. He was excited and scared, like he usually was when he started a new project.

He didn't fly into PDX, or even rent a car; he brought his own. He was going to be in town for a while. He would have to fly back in a week or two to finish putting plastic over his furniture, and flush his goldfish, and then focus on Portland. He had a complicated set of marching orders that he broke down to: (1) Complete the outsourcing of the gas and power company and (2) Figure out how to take over (or shutdown) this pirate social media company.

One, then two, and finally three. Who knows what three would be! There were no limits on what three would be. Three gave him a boner just thinking about it.

He told himself he needed to settle into sleepy Portland ways. He would have to accept a new way of dealing with people. He had heard that younger woman in Portland didn't even shave their armpits, much less wax. That might be a problem, but he was sure it wasn't universal. Mark prided himself on his skill in satisfying women. He would adjust. That is what he did, adjusted.

The gushingly lush blooming, the flora swallowing all and spreading out and overwhelming the stumps and boulders, fences and trees, the bushing out with blackberry brambles cascading over brooks and the margins of the roads, it made him nervous. There were no boundaries and he didn't understand why they just didn't spray it and clean it up! He liked plants and shit, but he hated the jungle wildness of Oregon's roadside greenery. The desert was clean, this was...like bush. He noticed his nose had been running but he was sure he didn't have a cold.

Coming on up I-5, he got out of the farmland when he crossed the Willamette River at Wilsonville; he then stopped for gas in Tualatin and put down the top on his convertible Bimmer. Back on I-5, up and down, then up again, then flying out of the Terwilliger curves, blasting down the hill, only to have to break quickly as he hit the two P.M. traffic. He missed his exit and had to cross the Marquam Bridge. The traffic stopped moving completely, and he had a spectacular view over the city from the top of the bridge. Nestled tightly into some hills along a river, it was like a miniature settlement of displaced earthlings built by some hobbyist in his basement, all packed up together in one spot. He wondered if he had made a mistake.

He could see a mirror-covered octagonal office building from the Marquam Bridge, where I-5 crosses the Willamette River. He swerved as he looked down, recognizing it right away from its Wikipedia photo, in three lanes of speeding traffic, as it glimmered at the end of the Portland Waterfront. Driving north it came into full view, a shining silver can, "The KEG," thirteen stories, tapered at the top, shimmering in the sun, next to the iconic Reindeer "Made in Oregon" Sleigh along the waterfront. Pretty cool, but is that all? So hokey, he thought.

Mark got off I-5 at Weidler, and crossed over into town on the Broadway Bridge. He expected to be embedded in the company for the next six months, advising and helping to guide them into a new model for their IT plant. That was the plan, agreed to by the KEG CFO. This was to be his final on-the-ground, hands-on outsourcing project, and while not the biggest company he had ever "transitioned," it was the first time he had ever got to start at the beginning and make it happen from the inside. And it was in Portland, green but fun, or so he had heard. He had to make it happen; this was his chance. He knew it would depend on them accepting and trusting him. Then next year in Santa Monica he would have a real woman, a tight, perfect woman.

The CFO, Frank DeFonzaro, was completely on board, but he didn't have the total support of the company. He maxed out his signing authority with a $500,000 surety bond with GIP as a sign of good faith. He said the major players were "on board." It would happen, if it came together. For now, it was a three-month contract to study process and efficiency. He just had to figure out how and put the plan together. Don't rush, he thought. No hurry.

In the back of his mind though he was dreading meeting this guy "Lonnie Wolfe." He knew it was a pseudonym. It made him nervous. Keep "us" out of it, Ken Oren had said. Who is us? GIP? Ken Oren and Persephone? Whoever it was, it didn't include him. He couldn't keep himself out of it. If he was not part of "us," then who was he?

Chapter 14

Petrovich and Henderson Set Up a Sting and mark Georgia as the Bait

The Multnomah County District Attorney knew he could move up the food chain, State of Oregon Secretary of Something or Other, maybe Attorney General if he played his cards right. The next election was in two years, so he had to seem dynamic without doing anything too risky. The sting Henderson was planning to run screamed out "potential career-ending Shit Storm!" But if it blew up, most of it would get on the Blue Uniforms and not him. The DA intuitively knew that what he didn't know couldn't hurt him, so the key was to stay way up above it all, yet be ready to swoop down and claim credit if it panned out.

He stood outside his office, giving his usual weekly update to the regulars. The local FOX News guy, the KOIN News Girl, as well as the investigative guy from *Willamette Weekly*, all sat in the cheap uncomfortable press-room chairs, looking at their phones. KGW, which was currently number one in the local TV News ratings, didn't even show.

"Is Rich coming?" he asked his aide. Rich Dunner was the old metro columnist for the *Oregonian*, who had assumed the Police Desk after the last round of layoffs at the paper. His column, once popular, had been cut to weekly, but now, sometimes they cut his column altogether out of the print version and relegated it to the "web," like some common blogger.

His aide shrugged so he continued.

"Thanks for coming everyone." FOX guy made a mock serious face at News Girl, whose eyes flicked back and forth from her steno notebook to the DA. "As you know we have agreed to a 'guilty-with-intent-to-sell' a controlled substance plea from…," he looked down at his notes, "…Malique Witherspoon." The WW Investigative Guy started to make a 'Reese' allusion/joke, but held his tongue.

"How do you spell that?" asked News Girl. "m-a-l-i-k?"

"l-i-q-u-e. Sentencing is next week. There is an ongoing investigation of higher-ups in the Cartel Organization, which we believe will bear serious fruit." News Girl nodded seriously at the WW Investigative Guy, who ran his tongue over his lips, which caused her to widen her eyes. She wrote in her notebook, with an amethyst-colored pen, in her ornate print style, "Serious Fruit!!"

"Sorry I'm late," said Rich Dunner, disheveled as usual, with his frayed khakis and checkered sport coat, pulling out a complicated, slightly obsolete digital recording box out of his REI carryall, which was strapped to his waist.

"As you know, we have identified the body discovered under the Blue Lake LNG pump station and have been using that knowledge to review information gathered at the time of her disappearance 16 years ago. The sad final chapter of Regina McKenzie's life is, however, providing new clues. We will solve this murder. Her employment at NW Consolidated Electric and Gas has led us in new directions." The DA stopped and looked around. Nothing. No questions. Journalism certainly has taken a turn for the worse. Do I have to do their fucking job as well as mine, he thought, as he continued. "Other information has come to light recently that is independent of the relationship with the power company."

"What information is that?" asked NEWS Girl. Finally, he thought.

"I am sorry, I can't comment on that," he said.

"Hold it," said FOX Guy, as he signaled his camera man. "Could you repeat that?"

The DA smiled slightly, before putting on a stern face and looking up at the camera. He repeated his "other information" quote. Fortunately there was so little local news of consequence in Portland that it was sure to make the news tonight. Now if only the suspect was watching…

Portland Police – Internal Morning briefing – January 14, 2014…We have one more thing for everyone to be cognizant of, a high-value witness is in town regarding the investigation of the murder of Regina McKenzie. As you all know, McKenzie is the woman found under the pump station near Blue Lake last month. It is sensitive and important that this witness's anonymity be protected.

Her situation is as follows: She is staying, at County expense, at a hotel in the Lloyd district. She doesn't want any police presence, so we have agreed to allow her to come in to talk, but we will be monitoring her movements by Text and GPS.

She is scheduled to give a statement at the 2nd Street station tomorrow.

She will disembark from the MAX train in the late morning on 2nd and Yamhill. The MMT will be positioned to observe persons of interest, who might have their own interest in the witness.

Her situation is delicate for several reasons: Because of her "past" (i.e., some B&E in BC, an illegal entry into the U.S. from Canada, and her relationship with a man now housed in the Sheridan Fed pen), she does not want to be IDed publicly until legally required. She is not happy about the situation.

Her former boyfriend/inmate alerted authorities as to the possible connection between McKenzie and his girlfriend/witness, undoubtedly to score points with the parole board.

Witness claims to have gotten a good look at the man with Regina on night in question and can ID him. She was a high school classmate of McKenzie in British Columbia, but didn't come forward 14 years ago because of her sketchy status at the time. Now she has a new life and is afraid that too much publicity will upset her new situation.

Also, if any officers have mechanical issues with their bicycles, a gear tuning class will be held at the Eastside station…

The morning report was broadcast to all the cops in the metro area and if the spook friend of Petrovich's was right, somebody, possibly the perp, was monitoring cop communications. If the perp was tapping Cop-Comm, he might see the report, and maybe react to it. And maybe even try and stop this "witness" from testifying. Or at least come out of hiding and show himself.

In any event, the story of the witness to the McKenzie murder could never be made public, because it was a total fabrication. It was probably a stupid exercise, Lance thought (Henderson had told him as much), except making the detectives in Portland aware of the "high profile" nature of the case. Maybe it would blow some dust, and they would pick up the trail. Maybe the perp would react. The spook was watching internet entry points, trying to see if somebody poked his head up in response to the DA's vague announcement of "new information."

There were hundreds of accounts to hide behind, as well as various software holes that allowed the right sequences of buffer banging that would give an outsider ownership. Like most organizations, Portland PD didn't keep their servers patched, too labor intensive, too expensive.

"We are watching everyone within a three block radius of the station, photographing, looking for a face that might register," said Henderson. "We'll see if he is interested in the witness."

It was 10 A.M. and Georgia was lingering over her complimentary continental breakfast at the Crowne Plaza. The lobby overlooked the Steel Bridge, the river and the Moda Center, where the Portland Trail Blazers play their home games. Georgia had been a basketball fan her whole life. She was brought up in Spokane and her father always had tickets to Gonzaga home games. She never saw Stockton play there, but had watched him year after year come oh, so close, with Malone. She had always wanted to see a game in

Portland. Maybe she would hang around until Friday when they would be back in town.

Her iPhone was on the table, having recently been loaded with the Portland PD VPN and the secure messaging software. She was waiting for the signal to start. She was the bait, taking a leisurely trip across the river to the downtown police station on SW 2nd between Main and Madison, trying to draw out a murder suspect, who just might be curious.

She wore a print India dress, black athletic tights, a black pull-over she bought online from Talbot, a blue silk scarf, and Dansko walking shoes. With her medium big sunglasses, she looked like a slightly athletic, suburban divorcee, whose kids were with Dad for the week. Her shoulder length brown hair was coiffed up and puffed just a tad, a way she never wore it. She thought she looked slightly Canadian and was determined not to look like a cop on her day off.

Her iPhone rattled on the table.

Georgia picked up her phone and looked at her message.

7:30 PM: FROM HENDERSON TO MCKENZIE MURDER TEAM – Witness will proceed from Crowne Plaza to the 2nd street station via MAX. Departure scheduled for the first train after 10 AM from the Moda Center MAX stop.

Everything was in place. Georgia thought about visiting the lounge downstairs, but opened a couple of vodkas out of the mini-bar and fell asleep.

The Next Morning

9:20 AM: FROM SYMARRA TO HENDERSON – proceeding on foot to train.

9:27 AM: FROM HENDERSON TO MCKENZIE MURDER TEAM – Maintain stations – subject proceeding on MAX train in 5 minutes

The Portland PD had let Sebastian VPN (connect with strong encryption) into their command systems, but the Communications team was clearly uncomfortable. He had a brief meeting with the two techs, saying only that he worked for a "Federal Agency."

Tyler got the feeling he was not a welcome guest, especially when he discussed the possibility that the Portland cop shop had been hacked. The techs didn't want to hear it. Tyler suggested that they watch the VPN logs. What are we looking for? they asked. Inserts out of sequences, "unusual activity," multiple "acks" for the same response, he said. He could feel their eyes rolling.

"We have 510 accounts who have been authorized – they can be connecting from anywhere."

"Do you purge accounts when they no longer have a reason to log in?"

"When guys retire or move, their accounts are deleted."

"What about others...contractors for example?"

"We don't have too many..."

"During this operation, please watch the log."

Tyler knew Petrovich was not in charge here, but was humored because of his reputation, and that limited his options. So, he watched the traffic as it moved, and let the techs watch the logs.

9:30 AM: FROM HENDERSON TO SYMARRA – Stop! Do not take the train! Change of plans. Proceed on foot to station. – stay alert.

9:31 AM: FROM SYMARRA TO HENDERSON – Copy. Will maintain access to weapon.

Georgia walked down 2nd from the Crowne Plaza, then past the Legacy Hospital building and along Multnomah, and finally to 1st and over to the MAX stop, across from the Moda Center. She looked around, from behind her big sunglasses, trying to figure out what or who had caused the change in plans. She almost messaged back for clarification, but decided to focus on her task, and let Lance and Henderson do the thinking.

Georgia was surprised at the number of young, apparently homeless people who were circulating around the Moda Center and the nearby train stop. Some carried ratty backpacks or pushed shopping carts. Oh wow, she thought, a Hornacek jersey! There is a statement. The Blazers were on the road, she remembered from looking at the paper at breakfast.

〜〜

Back at the cop IT shop, they never saw the last transmissions. The techs watching the logs missed it. The IP addresses on both Symaara's phone and Henderson's terminal suddenly changed. They saw something, but didn't think to compare the new IPs with the ones that the devices were using previously.

Then a new message from one of the field officers popped up.

> 9:45 AM: FROM MMT#5 TO MMT – Witness did not board! Repeat – Witness did not board!

Now they saw it! The IPs flipped back. And the lines just above it disappeared! Someone hacked in and changed the logs. And they weren't backed up! One of the techs scrolled back, but they were missing the most recent ten minutes of the VPN logs.

> 9:45 AM: FROM IT TECH TO HENDERSON – We have been hacked. Your conversation is not secure! Repeat – Conversation not secured!

> 9:46 AM: FROM HENDERSON TO SYMAARA – What is your 10-10?

> 9:46 AM: FROM SYMAARA TO HENDERSON – Proceeding on train – As instructed.

"Something is afoot," Tyler, who had logged back in to watch the VPN log, said. "Or at least an inch. That wasn't her replying," he told the tech on the phone.

"Yeah…that is what we thought."

Petrovich had insisted that Tyler not be sneaky, but that he share his exploits or problems with the local cops, that he not alienate them. He listened as the Tech told him there had been another blip and someone deleted the lines with the hacking IP address.

Ten minutes later, Tyler returned to his call with Petrovich. "He didn't see it. In fact he wouldn't have known what happened if he had. We lost it. He covered his tracks. It won't happen again. We put in a trigger to save as a copy of any changes. But that's for next time. Which unfortunately won't happen."

"But, why wasn't that..."

"Look, this is labor intensive and when you got one guy watching 30–40 logs he is going to miss shit. It is automated now. We shut the door, if he comes back we got him. But I think he's too smart for that..."

"OK, OK," said Lance. Christ, he didn't remember Sebastian being that touchy. He got off the phone and told Henderson, "Georgia's on her own, get some people to the vicinity quickly. Don't use the messaging!"

Having been a plainclothes cop for more than a decade, Georgia was of course was a trained observer, but she took it to another level. It was her superpower. Her secret was she always associated what she saw with something else. She would build a little castle (or office, or piazza) in her mind and populate what she saw around her imaginary castle. Memory was what she put in the castle.

Her memory populated a piazza, the open square west of the Moda Center, and she placed each face in a spot and marked its place with a hydrant or bike rack, or scrawny curbside tree, or even on a radial line connecting on a point on the arena, flaring out from where she now stood. It was out in the open, overcast as usual, but not raining. She had to wait to cross Interstate Avenue, and as the MAX train went by, she noticed a young, thin, possibly Hispanic man standing, seeming to talk to himself, watching her closely from the train. Bad planning. She met some of the team, but not all apparently. She wanted to get to the lower pedestrian walkway, and she crossed against the traffic to get the stairs on the south side of the bridge. She walked down on the pedway, right next to the

Amtrak tracks. The pedway over the river was filled with people and bicycles. She scanned faces, trying to categorize them, file them, put them on her own imaginary Steel Bridge. Most of them were young, twenty-something kids, jogging, groups of three and four women gabbing and walking fast, an endless stream of all kinds of people taking their exercise seriously. She had the pictures of the faces of all the suspects in her head and she tried to overlay them against those she saw, but got no matches.

She expected to see minders, cops looking after her, going in one direction or the other, but she was sure they weren't there. The bridge was like an island floating above the Willamette. She looked up at the buildings, particularly the KEG, which towered over the Steel Bridge. She imagined some of Henderson's task force team were up there with telescopes checking everyone. She knew better than to try and guess who might be following her.

She strode down the walkway off the Steel Bridge and stopped at the crosswalk at Everett. Why not continue down the Waterfront until getting to Salmon? But then a patrol car pulled up across Naito and stopped with flashers spinning. They opened the doors, drew weapons, and looked into the green area to the right, under the off-ramp to the bridge. Then she heard two sirens wailing a syncopated duet, one coming down Naito, another coming over from Chinatown. The two cops started toward the semi-hidden area under the overpass, and Georgia immediately crossed, flashed her badge and followed them into the foliage. She pulled her gun from her handbag, and covered her colleague's rear and moved in slowly, until she was under the off-ramp and stopped. Ten feet away, she saw a leg. A nude female leg behind a pile of transient refuse.

Petrovich walked under an overhanging branch, through the bushes and ducked under the yellow Do Not Cross tape. Henderson and Georgia were standing together, but not talking.

A couple of techs were down on the ground, with their lab kits out, going over the body, which Georgia had had the presence of mind to insist they cover immediately.

"Petrovich, looks like your perp struck again," said Henderson.

Lance reached down and lifted the blanket. The "body" was a full sized, inflatable "Judy" doll, naked, with dark pubes that appeared to have been drawn with a magic marker, blond hair, with a policeman's hat angled jauntily off the side of its head.

"We got called in a few minutes ago," said Henderson. "Digitally disguised voice. Looks like you were right, Lance. About what I am not sure. But this guy is pretty fucking good. A blow-up fuck doll. There can't be too many places that sell these things. We're checking…"

He's been saving this doll for years; they won't find any recent purchases, thought Petrovich, as he looked up at the KEG building. He covered the dummy. No sense having people wondering why we're investigating a manikin murder. They were about thirty meters away from the building and it towered over them. The east-facing windows had a clear view of the interstice between the off-ramps. The mirrored windows blocked his view in, but Lance imagined that hundreds of KEG employees were staring down at them.

"The power company office, kind of convenient it is so close, isn't it?" said Henderson.

Georgia looked knowingly at Lance.

"We've been covering for the last hour," Henderson said. "Hunt left the building an hour ago…" She looked around at the platoon of cops investigating and chasing away gawkers. Although the foliage was thick, you could get in or out from the back.

"We should look for footprints over there," she said pointing.

Henderson gave her a sarcastic thumbs-up. She still hadn't figured out why Lance thought this guy was his friend. "I got a guy over there waiting for Hunt. He apparently told his buddies that he was going for a run. I think I'll go over there and wait with him."

"Can I come?"

"No, this is Portland, Lance. I'll let you know what I find. You should bird-dog the autopsy."

Jim walked into the lobby of the KEG building in his running shorts and waved to the security guard at the front desk. He pulled his sweatshirt hood back and made a face of feinted exhaustion.

"Have a good run?" the desk cop asked.

"Yeah, it really felt good. Finally starting to get in shape. What's going on out there?"

"That's what we'd like to know," said a man dressed like a bicycle messenger who was waiting by the elevators. He pulled out a police badge and showed it to Jim. When he went to put it back in his back pocket, Jim held up his hand for him to wait as he read the badge carefully. When he finished reading, the cop–bike messenger said, "Would you come with me? We have a few questions."

As they started out the west side door they heard a shout from behind them. Another unfamiliar face came in from the east side of the building and joined the bike messenger–cop. The three of them turned around, and walked out on the plaza in front of the MAX stop, and the bike messenger took off and left Jim with the plain-clothes cop on the MAX platform.

"I'm Detective Henderson. You Jim Hunt?"

"I don't have my ID; it is in the locker room..."

"That's OK. I know who you are. Where you been?"

"What do you mean? I went for a run."

"Where?"

"Down the waterfront bike path toward where the gondola takes people up to Pill Hill by those new high rises."

"And turned around and came back?"

"Yeah."

"You carry a phone?"

"No. Why?"

"You know, keep in touch with work, use one of those apps to measure how fast you run..."

"I run to get away from the digital choke-chain." Henderson looked closely at Jim in his plain, sweat-stained pullover and shorts. Jim lifted his hands and then patted himself down on his shirt and shorts.

"OK. Go back in and get dressed. Come down to the 2nd Street station, meet me about two this afternoon. Give you a couple of hours to take care of things. OK?"

"What's this about? Do I need a lawyer? What are all the cops doing over there?"

"Oh that...we found a transient beat up under the off-ramp. He'll be OK. No, we have some questions to ask you. Don't want to cause you any grief. If you think you need a lawyer, you can bring one of course, that's up to you. You go get cleaned up and tell your Mommy you will be out this afternoon. It shouldn't take more than an hour. See you at two?"

"Can you make it 2:30?"

"Sure. Like I said, just need to clear a few things up. Here's my card."

"Yeah. I'll be there."

6 PM: FROM HENDERSON TO PETROVICH – Talked to Hunt. We need more to shake him if he needs to be shook. He has a solid story and we can't prove otherwise. We cannot eliminate him as a suspect. No CCTV footage from the scene during crime. We'll try and find some witnesses down the waterfront who might have remembered him. I asked for his phone and he asked for a warrant. I told him to forget it. If it is him, he tossed his phone or tablet in the river. You can get Tri-Cities PD to pay for divers if you want. We have nothing.

Chapter 15

Lester, Jim's old colleague, seems to have Little Hope For the KEG's IT Crew

Jim got out of the elevator on the second floor and tested his new badge on the Server room door. Bingo. It worked and he walked into his old haunt.

What a dump! The server cabling was a rat's nest, some unplugged, meandering across the floor, connecting the firewalls with stacked computer systems packed against the wall like discarded fast food containers. They seemed a little too familiar... the power lights in the front of the old boxes still flickered. One rack was labeled with his own shaky scrawl on masking tape, "DMZ," and each machine stacked on that rack was similarly labeled: DNS, Intrusion, Honeypot, Content filter. Jesus – they were his internet connecting boxes that hadn't been upgraded since he left – 14 years ago? He looked – they were connected – to something. What had Lester done all these years? He remembered how proud he had been when he left – it all was new, patched, maintained perfectly. Now they were working ghost ships, apparently.

Jim saw Sonny over by the consoles. Sonny was an operator, responsible for backing up, restarting and physically racking systems. He had done the same job during Jim's first tour. Jim waved at Sonny and he walked over.

"Welcome back Jim," Sonny had a big smile. "Changed a little, huh?"

Not really, thought Jim. "Yeah, looks good ..." Sonny was lost if his routine varied. "What's new, Sonny?"

"It's weird how they found Regina, huh?" said Sonny.

Jim felt a sharp thud in his solar plexus. "I didn't really know her..." Jim remembered back when he first started at the KEG, so many years ago, being grilled by Portland PD about her disappearance and he had basically told the cops the same thing. And now – it was coming back again. It was never going to end.

"I had lunch with her once. She was a Canuck too."

"I didn't know you were from Canada?"

"Calgary. I'd do anything to kill the son of a bitch."

"Maybe they will find some clues..."

"Maybe..." Sonny turned his attention to a console and watched the progress of a backup he was running. "Something about that transient who got beat up, huh? Christine said you could see it from the east side of the building, but that it looked like a naked woman before they covered her. Fishy, huh? They blocked off Naito and Everett for three hours, had cops all over and an ambulance. For a beat-up hobo? Nothing but a tiny mention in the paper about it?" Sonny never looked over at Jim as he talked.

That cop, Henderson, Jim thought, hadn't even just asked him, "Did you beat up the transient?" Just asked where he was...only explanation why was that his description and a witness's matched. Some guy in jogging shorts? Beating up a transient? Who looked like a naked woman?

There was something in the wind, something happening – finding Regina's body after all these years, him coming back, Chubby acting like a responsible adult...kind of anyway...the world seemed off its axis. He looked at Sonny again, who had his eyes firmly attached to the console. Line after line of file names zipped by and it held Sonny's attention like a cat watching a bird flit around tree branches. Sonny seemed uncomfortable. Think, Jim, you are his new boss, in his server room. Nothing is odd here. He wondered what else was being said around the building about Regina and the transient, but realized he couldn't really ask Sonny about it.

He shook his head and tried to focus on business. He was getting a sense that he was expected to make something happen, that he had to choose sides, and he decided that now, right now, he had chosen. He looked at the tangled up and knotted, yes actually knotted, cables that were clearly in Lester's domain. It was a fucking pigsty, nothing labeled. It would take weeks figuring it all out, if stupid Lester got hit by a truck. But he was the boss. Lester was going to clean this up, even if it would be easier for him to do it.

As he walked out of the server room, he thought, who else worked for him besides Sonny and Lester? Jim looked at the list Angie had given him along with her caustic comments.

Arlen – Internal switches, desktop network - quiet as a brick, avoids being noticed by anyone.

Knute – Mainframe - almost 70 if not older and could easily beat up anybody on the team (including me, thought Jim).

Rodney – Supports Windows - going to be a battle, him fighting "Linux on the Desktop." Always with his briefcase, pants too tight and too short.

Christine – Exchange servers, help desk for 10 years – she is probably fucking Rodney.

Steve Slater – Technical security, former Marine - calls everybody sir or ma'am. No apparent other skills.

"Larry" Yang – Scripter, developer, social media interfaces – Best worker on the team. From China, of course he is good.

Brigitte – Intern turned support specialist – works mainly with Christine, big eyes, straight hair, she has already filed a sexual harassment case against somebody.

Janice and Rainy, both lesbians – Rainy southern and butch, Janice pretty and black –DBAs and Sys Admin – not a couple and are offended if you ask them if they are. Everyone is scared of them.

That was his team. He walked into the conference room. Sonny came zipping in behind him. The rest of them, except the lesbian database admins, who, according to Angie, didn't come to meetings very often, were looking at their phones or tablets. Jim smiled and waved everyone on, to continue talking as he set up his laptop and got settled.

"Hello! I don't know all of you but that will change over the next few weeks. Rather than go around the room and introduce yourselves, for my benefit only, because you all know each other, I presume," he paused for laughter, which never came, "let's assume that I will get to know you all personally very soon so we can skip all that high school introduction crap and let me tell you what I think we are about, I mean who I am and why I think I was hired and then, you tell me why I am wrong."

"Let me stop you right there, Jim," said Lester. "I can tell you why you are wrong now."

"OK. Fair enough, tell me..." Jim was smiling but Lester was not.

"First, welcome back to the company, not sure why you left in the first place, but..." Lester let that thought drift, "...this company has a habit of ignoring technical people and then pulling ideas out of their butts at the last minute. Project Managers rule the world now." There was pathos in his voice.

"Well, Les, I intend to try..."

Christine started laughing.

Jim looked at Christine and she put her head down and pretended she hadn't laughed.

"Les, you must have more to say..." said Larry, also with a laugh.

"You know I prefer Lester, Larry," said Lester.

"OK. But now we know you used to be called Les, didn't you?" Larry laughed and looked at Jim.

He is right, Jim thought, I had always called him Les.

"Les! Les! Les! It is demeaning if you hear it over and over again...I am not Les. Less than what?"

"Ah, Larry," Jim liked him already. A good man to have as an ally. "I hear you speak, your accent, and I think you are from China originally?"

"Beijing. Yes. I escaped fifteen years ago. Now people in IT business make more money in China than here." Larry knotted his eyebrows and suddenly stopped talking.

"Alright, you all must know that this is my first management job," Jim stopped and looked out. Mostly concerned faces. "When I was here fifteen years ago I essentially did Lester's job, and in my career after, and I have been consulting since. Mostly doing technical stuff, Installing and configuring GIP software..."

"Trash! GIP is overpriced, clusterfucked-up software...I hope you aren't thinking of bringing that shit into the company..." said Lester.

Jim interrupted Lester. "Well, there is some truth to that. But we have to keep our options open..." he let that one lay there. "I have a different perspective than when I was here, back..." Lester was looking at his phone, so was Rodney, in fact only Steve Slater, and Brigitte, the intern who filed the sexual harassment suit, were still looking at him intently. He should have planned this meeting better. "So...I'll be coming around to each of you in the next couple of weeks and we can talk about your concerns and I can tell you more about what I have in mind." When I figure it out, thought Jim. First victory. I didn't say what I meant or thought. Have to keep that up. "So thanks for coming and we'll talk more later. Any questions?" Lester was already out the door.

That didn't go well, thought Jim. He had to figure out how to get a lot more out this crew. They had to finish some big stuff and make it help the business and get more people to stop saying our IT department sucks. Otherwise it was curtains for all of them. But he didn't want to scare them the first day.

Chapter 16

Jim's Hippie Mother dreams of a Bohemian, high-brow community in the Oregon woods

Jim vaguely remembered his childhood home, perched on a hillside overlooking the Siletz River. And his father...he remembered the fights, the drinking...his father moved to Alaska after his logging business failed, and soon after, he and his mother left that old house. Jim was about three or four at the time. His father died a few years later, found in a Juneau motel room with about fifteen empty vodka bottles for company. Jim didn't learn that until years later though.

His mother's name was Alice and even as a young boy he always called her Alice, which she seemed to encourage. Jim's family, on his father's side, had been in the Oregon logging business since the late 1800s. He knew that he had aunts, uncles, and cousins all up and down the coast, but he also knew that most of them were not well off. Staying close to home had not been a winning strategy for his family.

Alice kept no pictures of the time. She didn't like any of her husband's family, and had never talked about hers either, other than they were supposed to be related to some Scandinavian royal family.

Other than a sister in Corvallis, they were all either dead or had moved away, at least as far as Jim knew.

His father had been a big man physically and was popular up and down the coast, from Coos Bay to Newport. He remembered some of the other men who worked with or for his father, who carried him on their shoulders and let him ride in the giant logging rigs. He remembered them talking and laughing and but then the laughing began to stop and the drinking became angry and nasty.

After Alice left the house on the Siletz, they stayed in an apartment in Corvallis, near Oregon State University, with his Aunt Sally. Then after a couple of weeks his mother kissed him and left. His aunt lived with a man with a strange accent who always smiled and laughed. He had just started kindergarten in Corvallis. The kids were different, prissier, better dressed, likely to complain about things he didn't even notice. He was always surprised that he remembered his preschool and kindergarten classmates so clearly. Jim liked going to school and playing with all the different toys and the teachers were very kind to him, and he liked the man who lived with Aunt Sally. He sometimes missed his mother and his father, but he didn't cry about it, at least not in front of anybody else. Aunt Sally's man friend always asked Jim about school and what he was learning. They would play number games together, which Jim liked.

But after Christmas his mother came back and without much warning, he and his mother moved to a house off the highway in the woods west of Philomath toward the coast. He started going to a new school, which wasn't as nice as the one in Corvallis. But he liked the kids better and slowly discovered he was the second smartest in class.

Later that spring his mother, Aunt Sally and he drove up into the woods past Blodgett up a dirt logging road along a creek to a rundown house with a rusted logging rig and a pickup on blocks out in the front, as well as a gray but recently washed Rambler, with medium sized tail-fins. The house was half covered with shake shingles, the other half was bluish vinyl siding. A couple of Australian Heelers sat silently in the dirt, watching Jim and his mother as they walked up the rickety wooden front porch stairs and knocked on the greenish-yellow door.

A guy came to the door and hugged his mother, and she pushed him away, but with a smile. He wore calf-high cork boots, a plaid shirt and jeans held up with suspenders and had a long woolly black beard. There was no rug in the house and it smelled like grease, dogs and something else which he would later come to know as marijuana.

Alice and Aunt Sally and the guy sat on the stained, torn couch and drank beer while Jim looked at a car transmission that was torn apart on the kitchen table. The guy came over to the table and moved the rotating assembly up and down while talking to his mother. He told Jim he used to work with his father, and Alice told the guy to shut up. They were discussing the price of the Rambler in the front yard. His mother got up and made the "come here" sign to the guy with her index finger, and started toward the back. Jim and his aunt went outside and walked around the yard. Later he and Alice drove home in the car, which was the only car they ever had while he was growing up. She still had it, taking it in for maintenance at least every six months, or anytime she heard the slightest rattle.

Every July, he and his mother made the trek to the Oregon Country Fair outside Eugene and then to the "Rainbow Gathering" down near Roseburg. Jim met other kids like him, raised by hippies, many of them had never attended school or had any idea of the "world." Some smoked pot even though they were not much older than he was.

Jim had one thing in common with other hippie kids, besides having a mother who could dance by herself to Grateful Dead music, and that was they had no TV. He had noticed in Corvallis that almost all of the conversations revolved around TV shows that Jim had never seen. At the Country Fair, nobody talked about TV and Jim liked that.

His mother had many men friends, but she never allowed them to talk to Jim much beyond hello and goodbye. She never got senti- mental about any of them, and that really never bothered Jim. This situation did bother some of the men his mother brought home, and Jim felt sorry for more than one of them, when his mom put on her cold, "it's time for you to leave" face.

Alice would drop him off at school every morning in their Rambler and she would drive into work. Jim would take the bus home, up Highway 20, and would get out and walk up the driveway to the double-wide. Jim would usually go out in the back and play by the Mary's River unless it was raining real hard. Sometimes he caught enough crawdads for dinner. Kip, the smartest kid in class, came over sometimes and spent the night. Kip and Jim slowly, even warily, became best friends.

Alice had big dreams that kept changing, but she always managed to keep her job and actually did very well, moving up and making more money. Her real dream, the dream she stuck with through it all, and that she told Jim about, and that Jim saw as hopeless on every level, was to one day, "get some land," and build a commune, one that mattered, for people who had their "shit together." It would be based on Hobbiton, the village where Bilbo and Frodo grew up in the *Lord of the Rings,* constructed with wood, with a giant communal garden overflowing with delicious food, with some folks living in barrows and some in tree houses, and the horses would be owned by everyone and would be cared for like kings. Jim said they should have modern mountain bikes too, and his mother said that would be cool. And almost every week there would be festivals and music. They would make things, practical things, that they would sell for lots of money in Portland. They would all read books. Film would be OK, but not movies. Jim sort of knew the difference between film and movies by the time he was 10. A huge guest house would be built too, for all of the famous people who would drop by, to stay for a while and entertain people.

"What about police?" Jim would ask, because he thought that might be a good job for him, but Alice would only laugh and shake her head. There were some things Jim didn't understand, in spite of his precociousness.

As he got older, many of Jim's friends slipped off the edge. Poverty slowly destroyed a lot of families as the timber industry failed. Their parents often fell to meth or booze or even too much pot. Alice, on the other hand, got stronger as things began to fall apart for her neighbors. She began to evolve from a hippie momma to government worker and then to a community leader, going to meetings late on week nights, and shaking up the Benton County Commission and the Philomath City Council. She joined a church for a while and spent a lot of time with the minister. Jim didn't like church and after a summer of Sunday school, she stopped making him go.

By the time they were in fourth or fifth grade, Jim and Kip were inseparable and Jim spent a great deal of time at Kip's huge house, which was on the western edge of Philomath. It was in range for him to bike, and he spent a couple of nights a week there. Later, in their junior year of high school, Kip and his father moved to "The Compound," which was even further away, deep in the Coast Range, but by then Kip was driving and continued coming to Philomath.

Jim was a good student. He ran cross country his sophomore year, and he was pretty good, probably from all the biking he did, but it took too much time. Kip's dad bought a Tandy TRS-80 and it ended up at Jim's, where he and Kip spent a lot of time learning how to program it. He took all of the college prep classes offered and even drove into Corvallis every day in the summer between his junior and senior year to take a Physics class at Oregon State. He wanted to get out of Oregon though, and planned to let the Army help pay for his college. He wanted to see the world, and talked to the recruiter in town about the specialties that they needed overseas. He didn't know what he wanted to study anyway. His mother kept working at the county and he graduated from Philomath High School in 1987, signed up, and headed off to Texas to train for the Signal Corps.

His mother told him to be careful, and that women could be more dangerous than enemy soldiers, but he already knew that somehow.

Chapter 17

Jim wakes in a Strange Bed and flashes back to
his Secret Affairs with East German spies

Jim opened his eyes, and knew immediately he was in a strange
bed. He looked at the ceiling. Directly above him was a paper
mobile: A fisherman wearing a conical, Asian peasant's hat was in a
boat, and a fish was below him and a bird was flying above, and the
whole thing was spinning slowly. He blew a stream of air straight up
and saw that it moved the mobile ever so slightly, spinning it and
seesawing the flat paper fisherman's line and pole up and down.

As the mobile floating above his head moved in response to
the air movement, the two-dimensional fisherman dipped forward
and his fishing line moved down and brushed against a mobile fish
and attached to the fish with a weak magnet, and as the fisherman
rebounded back up it lost connection with the fish. Every time Jim
blew up at it, it repeated, almost catching the fish, then losing it. Jim
looked around the powder blue room with white ceiling. Centered
on the walls hung three small reproductions, in plain frames: a Song
Dynasty painting of finches on a bamboo tree, a Monet of a willow
tree overhanging a water garden, and Jackson Pollock's "orangy" dark
and light painting *The Flame*, which he stared at for at least a minute…

"Where am I?" He looked over next to him.

She silently looked at him with feigned suspicion out of the corner of her eye.

"OK, OK, I have to get this out of the way," he continued. "This is probably the wrong time to ask, but your name, it's right on the tip...it's not Mary, or Mandy, Mindy? No. No. it's, Marcie, um, no, that is wrong..."

"Well, JIM...," she said with mock profundity, "...let's see if we can remember..." she frowned and put her hand under her chin and looked up at the ceiling as if deep in thought.

"Anybody can remember my name. Jim is so common for Christ sakes, but your name...is not a regular name...is it?"

"Not regular?" She sat up in the bed and revealed her magnificent and perfect breasts.

"Unusual...uncommon." Jim tried to maintain eye contact, and an air of innocence. "I am admitting what most people would try and fake their way through. You gotta give me points for honesty, right?"

"Oh, OK. Points for honesty. Let's make sure we record that." She licked her finger and swiped it in the air. She couldn't hold it any longer and broke out laughing and climbed on top of him and leaned over and began kissing him, and was grinding him in a way that began to focus his attention...

"I remember! Macy. Macy!"

"Goosed your memory, huh? Let's try it all together now. Macy Cosino Ming."

"I knew that, Macy."

"I never told you."

"Chinese department store...Italian trigonometric function. Got it now."

"You better got it."

Later, they sat in bed drinking coffee. It was still dark outside. "Don't you have some place to be?" she asked. "Friday is a work day isn't it?"

"Kip and I are going down to Newport today, to go fishing. You want to come?"

"Did you plan that last night?"

"Yeah. Yeah we did, then I called my boss right after the meeting. At the gallery. Where we met, remember?"

Macy continued to stare at him.

"Kip and I have to meet my father on Saturday about business."

Macy furrowed her brow.

"It would be overnight – two nights."

"Your father? I thought you told me…"

"Did I say my father? I meant Kip's father." Jim shook his head, puzzled at his mis-speak. "But my…"

"…What about my daughter? I can't find a sitter that quick."

"Bring her. There is plenty of room."

"That makes sense. We just meet, you sleep over, and now I am going on overnight trips with you, and bringing my daughter. That sounds real smart." She pulled the pillow from under her head and put it over her face.

"But you could meet my mother."

She peeked at him from under the pillow. "Are you insane?"

"Haven't you ever done anything crazy?"

"Yes, and I know how it usually turns out too. No! No! You don't even know my name for shit's sake!"

"I just had to remember which department store it was."

"You tell jokes so good! Yes, that's it! Do that thing with your eyes, it makes it twice as funny. Department store. Asshole!"

"Thing, huh? You're the first person I have ever known who noticed that I do 'a thing.' I suppose I should be flattered."

"Don't get cocky," said Macy, looking at him with open and measuring eyes. His contrite look satisfied her. She rolled out of bed just as Jim was beginning to get interested again. "So I have to pick up my daughter from her friends in two hours. I want you out of here."

"Perfect. We can pick her up together. Then get Kip and head to the coast. We can take your SUV, right?"

Macy looked very hard at Jim.

"She can miss a day of school. She'll learn about Ichthyology."

"You don't think I know what that means, do you?"

"Probably not. Even Aristotle talked about how beautiful woman don't like to discuss icky stuff."

"Aristotle, huh? What branch of Icky-ology? Be careful..."

He sniffed and "did that thing with his eyes.""We will do better than your friend up there," said Jim pointing to the mobile of the fisherman above their heads. "Steelhead are running, but I like the bottom feeders myself." He began to slide his head down her torso.

"OK – OK! We'll go fishing...but no bottom fishing now! Come on. We better get going. You can join me in the shower, but no funny business. We can talk about this science lesson then."

"I promise," he said holding up his hand with his two big fingers crossed.

As might be suspected, Chubby was partly responsible for Jim ending up in bed with Macy on Friday morning. He had badgered Jim to come to the First Thursday meeting of the *SwiftPad* board. Now that Jim was working in Portland at the KEG, instead of flying out of PDX every Monday, he could not avoid it anymore. Chubby said that they timed the meetings to coincide with the First Thursday art openings, because one of the board members owned a gallery that had a great meeting room in the back.

On the First Thursday of each month, about thirty downtown art galleries, mostly in the Pearl section, opened up their storefronts to the public to come in and browse. Some of the more "upscale" galleries would serve wine and cheese, and others were workshops where the artists could be seen framing and cleaning paintings, etc.

Jim knew a bit about art, at least as much as you can learn when you spend a year intently studying the wall hangings in the greatest museums of Europe. He had taken formal painting lessons in West Berlin and declared himself (to himself) an "artist." Even though he was still officially a soldier in the US Army, he had openly traveled to Communist Poland, East Germany and Czechoslovakia and never had any trouble, even at border crossings.

After basic training, he spent six months training in electronic signaling methods, and another six months at the Monterrey Language School learning German, after which he was immediately sent to the Teufelsberg Listening Post in Berlin. He was assigned to general duties, which included maintaining and servicing the technical equipment, listening to signal traffic, and sorting and collating the recordings. The East German Foreign Intel group, *Hauptverwaltung Aufklärung (HVA)*, commonly known as the *Abteilung*, a branch of the *Stasi*, was getting desperate by 1988 because they knew they would be exposed when reunification happened (which proved correct), and they were frantically trying to penetrate the security at Listening Post Berlin hoping for a miracle to slow down or fudge up the inevitable. There was no fear of attack though. They had stopped repairing the tanks in the east. Jim had seen intercepts that seemed to prove that.

The best assets of the East Germans were beautiful young women with perfect English. One of them managed to find her way into the bed of Captain Graham, Jim's CO. Through a series of coincidences, Jim overheard her phone call back to one of her friends, right after she delivered a coded report to HVA headquarters. It was his job to listen to such things. The second call was quite detailed and juicy and included part of a tape of one of their amorous encounters. It took him two hours to unravel all of the sexual German idioms she used. There was no web internet back then of course, so he hunted through the heavily laden shelf of dictionaries in the translation section, trying to understand what exactly she had learned and was telling her spymasters on the other side of the wall. When he heard the captain referred to, he had more than an instinct that this one shouldn't be passed on in raw form to the analysts. Jim didn't know exactly what to do with it, so he reported it directly, yet formally, to Captain Graham and pretended he didn't recognize the captain's voice. He knew he was treading in very deep, shark filled waters.

The captain was quiet as he listened to the recording, and Jim provided the translation commentary. Then he just left the recording with the captain, and cleverly altered the duty logs, so it never "happened," and found he was rewarded with two years of Army pay, but no duties, except reporting to base once a month to leave a one-word voicemail for Captain Graham – "No" – which meant no progress yet on his unspecified assignment, and that was all Jim ever had to do for the rest of his tour. Officially, he was doing "general intelligence work" according to his orders.

He had strange and conflicting feelings about passively black-mailing his CO. If he were a patriot, he thought, he would have reported him. But if he had, he was sure he would be thanked for his loyalty by being crushed in some way. Best case, a dishonorable discharge for defaming an officer. He knew that it was dangerous to have something on a powerful person. So he kept digging into "the case," hoping to stay one step ahead of whatever fate had in store for him.

From the intercepts, he knew the woman's name, or at least one of her names, and where she had met the captain. He staked out her West Berlin neighborhood bar, and by subtle clues that he let out as he drank and chatted around with his stilted German, he eventually met and "lured" Renate into a short but intense relationship. She swore she wanted nothing but a romantic experience and to practice her shaky English (which Jim knew was better than she pretended). Jim let Renate think that she was spying on him and he led her on with bogus tales of his access to classified stuff, but she never acted interested. She either caught on to his ruse and thought he might be a clumsy, long-term double, or perhaps decided he was full of BS about his access. She might have even decided to quit spying in order to live freely in the West. But if she wasn't still spying, why stay in Berlin and date American soldiers? He was interested in the answer, but he didn't want to pry. Jim then realized he was not a good spy.

In the end, she seemed to grow bored and disappointed that he wasn't playing the game correctly. She introduced him to a friend just as young and beautiful as she was, and then she disappeared, moved out of her apartment and was gone. The second woman (Heidi) demanded sex more forcefully and gave him orgasms that left him wobbly. But otherwise she wasn't as romantic as Renate and when he asked her about where Renate had gone, she got mad and disappeared too.

He was certain that the West Germans, and probably the Americans as well, were watching him and maybe even had turned Renate and were trying to set him up. He suspected he was being groomed – for something…Since espionage was not that interesting to him, he decided to resume his tour of European culture, even as he also continued to look for Renate.

To Jim, Renate and Heidi were Spritzer and Quark, his Deutscher Mädchen Doppelgängers, white wine and gooey cheese; they went together in his mind when he thought of them. He was not too sentimental about them, though, and as it turned out, he never found either of them.

But Spritzer and Quark were only part of the reason his two years of retreat in Europe had freed him from his past and opened his eyes to the possibilities of life. It was "Art" that changed him. Art showed him "The Meaning of Life." He said this to himself and constantly tried to change it into something less dramatic, like "The Window into the Soul" or "The Now that Never Leaves, but Is Already Gone," but he came back to "The Meaning of Life" as the real impact of his Concert Hall and Museum *wanderung* hiatus from Army duty.

The scratchings and splatterings of charcoal and oils on animal skins and canvas said to him, "I see life too! I see it so well, that you are staring at it 500 years after I died. I am dead, but look! I am still alive." Jim understood then why people believed in Art. It was life after death, it was the meaning of living, even the secret germ of feeling. Michelangelo, Dürer, Caravaggio, Rembrandt, Beethoven, Mozart, and Bach! They were real and art was real in a way that went beyond the temporary existence of life. They were real people, smearing colored paste on stretched canvas, chipping at rock, hammering on wire, sliding horsehair on catgut and blowing through pursed lips into brass tubing, and singing! It was something beyond time and space. His mind came alive like never before and it made him realize the spirits of the dead could see and feel and sing. He wanted life to be like that all the time. He took classes at night, and attended lectures all over the continent at universities from Paris to Bologna, Heidelberg to Smolensk, on every subject he could find, in English and German and by the end even in Russian.

He took painting classes too. "Slow, slow, slow the brush down!" his teacher said as he struggled with a bowl of fruit. As he painted, his teacher, an old German man who never talked about himself, moved to another student, "You seem to have repealed the laws of gravity, Mr. Hunt."

But every week Jim went back. His teacher asked him what he wanted.

Jim said he had been in many museums. "Show me how they do it!" he begged.

"Perhaps if you had started younger..."

"But I didn't...I am looking for the meaning of life..."

His teacher only said, "You have to look closer and keep trying. Don't hold the brush so tight."

So, it was First Thursday in the Pearl District and Jim, not wanting to go to the *SwiftPad* Board meeting, hoping he would miss it in an excusable way, wandered around the Pearl, from gallery to gallery. It was raining. He stopped at a little, barely stable tent out on 13th and Hoyt, and looked at landscapes of an artist who was exhibiting his pictures and trying to keep them dry. The artist stood in the downpour, to leave room for his paintings, and passersby who might be interested. Jim remembered his sketch of a fruit bowl that so disappointed his German art teacher, and realized he was lucky his lack of talent had been so pronounced. He looked at the amazing painting of a spiky cactus plant in a grungy apartment window that looked out at a tiny corner of sky, and at the 40-year-old artist standing in the rain. He thought to himself that at least the old German had taught him how to see, if not paint. A woman friend of the nearly drenched artist came up and hugged him in the rain, and they both laughed. Jim put his hood up on his North Face jacket and moved on.

Still a half hour early, he wandered into the 68 Gallery, very upscale, on 9th and Flanders, crowded with a perfect mix of Bohemians and Glitterati. 68 Gallery's style was "art school modern," with pieces by artists unknown to Jim, mostly knock-offs of set pieces of the NY scene, particularly MOMA. High quality but "derivative" (a word that applied to everything, he thought), negative photography, latex fossil-like paintings, odd familiar non-functional furniture, a post-apocalyptic garbage dump, it all made him sleepy, and when he spied the wine and cheese table he began to slowly wander over to it.

The woman pouring his wine had sparkling eyes, with long, silky brown hair, wrapped up almost haphazardly behind her head, and as he looked closely at her, Jim remembered her stretching next to the Suicide Bridge in old-style tight fitting, cotton sweatpants. He remembered she had been different, not "the same as it ever was." A blue satin dress hung, precariously and seductively from her left shoulder. She looked closely at him as she handed him his Chablis.

"I've seen you. Were you leering at me a couple of months ago… over on Vista?"

Jim hesitated briefly, then smiled and liked her right at that very moment. "Leering? You mean at the train station? Do you remember? In Copenhagen? Or did we meet before that?"

"Yeah, right. I've never been to Copenhagen. Next…" she said, looking behind Jim even though no one was there waiting.

"Oh, you mean…yeah, I remember, of course. You were… preparing to run. I didn't think I was leering, but yes, I did look, as I walked by. Then you were gone." Jim looked at her intently.

"I remember too." She smiled.

"I couldn't stop looking at you."

That apparently was the right thing to say. She drew him in, not letting even a tiny rough edge show, smooth as her dress, and yet there was a blunt directness to her that refused to allow them to fade off into polite chitchat. It was all natural and unforced and she smiled enigmatically, but with soft fire shooting from her eyes.

"Jim!" Kip trudged into the gallery in his stained leather fringe coat and beige wrinkled Dockers, his hair slicked over and back, reeking of some generic version of Old Spice, carrying an etched leather documents folder under his arm. "Have you seen GG?"

"No." Jim froze, not able to decide whether to introduce...

"Hey, Mace, how you be, Babe?" Kip leaned over and kissed her on the cheek as he went by. "Are they back there?"

"I haven't seen them yet," she said, quickly glancing at Jim, enjoying his discombobulation. She reached over and rubbed Kip's face. "I love your beard, Kip. It's so soft and furry."

"I don't think G likes it much. What do you think, Jim?"

"Why would I give a shit?"

"Oh well – I looked too young before – this gives me some – what's the word...gravitas. You need that in business right? I better go get ready, I'm supposed to..." he looked at Jim and then at Macy. "Jim, I'll be in the back, my hands are full, could you bring me a glass of wine when you come? Mace! Love ya, Babe!" Chubby walked back behind the panels to some place in the back of the gallery.

"So you know Kip, huh?"

"Who doesn't?" she said. "Well, I don't know him that well. So you are here for the *SwiftPad* thing?"

"Yeah. But, I like art too."

"Art who?" she asked with a straight face, as she looked at the couple waiting patiently behind him. Jim stood to the side and let the other patrons imbibe.

A few minutes later GG came in followed by Raleigh, his hair now with a little salt and mostly pepper, the surfer look a thing of the past, still dressed as an urban cowboy, sans hat, with tight jeans, etched pointy boots and a Mexican embroidered linen shirt. Just behind him, an old lady in a floppy hat and ski vest over a white long-sleeved blouse with frilly cuffs at the wrists was nimbly shuffling. GG stopped when she saw Jim, who looked spooked. "Is he here yet?" she asked.

"Kip? Yeah, he already went in." He nervously glanced away. Jim knew the man with GG, but Raleigh looked back at Jim and showed no recognition.

"Jim, this is Hariet Miller," GG said. "She is on our board."

Jim suddenly realized where he had seen the old lady before. On TV advertising the ski jackets and boots for her company Cascade Sportswear. In the commercials, she would carry stacks of firewood and giant packs around the campsite while a bunch of handsome young campers would lie around exhausted. "It is nice to meet you," he said, all at once realizing he was wearing a North Face jacket.

She smiled at him and looked askance at his jacket. "Darling, he obviously wants to talk to this young lady, let him be."

GG made a face behind Hariet's back and waved him in. Jim looked back at Macy, trying to think how to ask if she would still be there when he got out.

"Don't forget Kip's wine," she said.

He stood close to her as she poured the second glass and filled Jim's as well. "I start cleaning up at nine," she said tapping her bare wrist. Jim pulled out his phone and peeked at it. It was just 7:30.

Chapter 18

Petrovich, the Judge and the Bonneville VP
Plan to Dig after the Birds Hatch

The discovery of Regina's body under the Portland LNG station, and then the confirmation that the killer was still out there, mocking efforts to catch him, was a double blow to Lance Petrovich. The first blow, finding McKenzie's body, woke him up and forced him to face his biggest professional failure, and set his determination fast on catching the murderer. The second, finding the blow-up doll on the edge of Chinatown in Portland, had nearly knocked him down for good, while at the same time confirming that his instincts about the killer were correct. The fact that the killer mocked him like that was really a good sign, because it showed he was cocky and prone to foolish acts of bravado. It would have been much worse, Lance thought, if the killer had not taken the bait, or if he had actually killed Georgia, which Lance had no doubt he could have done. Lance had learned in almost every case, that serial killers long for attention and that sooner or later that craving rears up. Lance felt comforted in the knowledge that this one was finally fitting the pattern, after 22 years.

The son of a hydroelectric engineer, Petrovich had only just made detective in 1990, when he was almost forty. He seemed headed for an obscure career when Kathy Morton disappeared after leaving work at the Bonneville Power office in downtown Richland. Her disappearance had been his first real big case. But he had nothing, just a vague feeling about one particular suspect. The guy was as cold as ice, and all this time had never showed any cracks. Lance had let his instincts be overruled, because he didn't have the evidence. It was his only unsolved case and now 22 years later, it suddenly reappeared to him like a bolt of lightning, shaking him out of his somnolent march toward retirement.

He was sure of one thing, though, this guy would definitely kill again. Someone else was going to die because of his incompetence 20-some years ago. He knew he was always going to have to live with that.

He was leaning against his unmarked squad car off to the side of a dirt road, halfway up Badger Mountain, looking down on the old transformer and relay station. Another car pulled up behind him. Driving was Judge Van Ritter, the "Dour Dutchman," who made all lawyers who came before him, regardless of the side they argued, squirm and mutter. He and Lance were old friends. The judge brought his binoculars. He waved to Lance and immediately began scanning the marshes. From the passenger side, Sharon Rodriguez, an Operations VP at Bonneville Power, skinny except in the hips, in her early forties, dressed in jeans and collared tee-shirt, walked forthrightly up to the detective, introduced herself and immediately got down to business.

"Why wasn't it dug up back in what, 1992? It would have been easy then. Wouldn't have interrupted anything to speak of... but now..."

"It is my fault, I missed too many clues. I was inexperienced," said Lance. "But I know now she is under there."

"Look at that," said Judge Van Ritter. "A double crested cormorant!"

Lance and Sharon looked out on the Yakima Delta marshes to see what he was talking about, without success.

"You know," continued the judge, "the Chinese use the cormorant to help them fish. They tie a leash around it and it dives and brings the fisherman what it catches."

"I think I saw that on a PBS show. Was it *Nature*?" said Lance.

"Right. I saw that too, fascinating. Look!" A long-winged bird was lifting off the water slowly, seeming to barely get airborne.

"Is that a blue heron?" asked Sharon. Lance looked at her over his glasses.

"It's, yes, it's a female," said Ritter.

Please don't tell me it is going to nest again, thought Lance. The judge and Lance both looked at Sharon.

"Did you grow up in eastern Washington, Sharon?" asked the judge.

"No. I'm from California, the valley near Delano."

"This murder, even though it happened 20 years ago, still haunts Richland. I was here, working in the Public Defender's office. Lance and I have been tangling for a long time."

The detective smiled and looked away.

"They had only caught Bundy a few years before that. He worked his evil near here and it still spooks us."

"So you thought it was murder back then?" said Lance.

"Oh, yeah. I thought it might have been a copycat. I was pretty sure you were off the mark back then. You pursued the kidnapping angle, didn't you? Back then, from what I read, I thought it was somebody who she knew, and...I had a feeling that she never left Richland."

Lance shook his head and shrugged. I had the same feeling, he thought, but I ignored it. The blue heron was circling around and landed only 20 yards away from them.

"An old lady called to complain about a strange car parked in front of her house. She had a way of calling the cops about anything, so it got filed. It was two miles from Morton's apartment and it sort of matched the description. But it didn't dawn on me until a couple of years later when I was going through the case. Anyway, then the car disappeared and showed up later in Seattle and it was matched up then. So even though the trail was cold, I tried to build a timeline around that," said Lance, as he picked up a rock, and flung it sidearm, skipping it across the marsh. "We canvassed the neighborhood near the old lady's house, but I still chased the theory that she was kidnapped. Nothing. Was she in the trunk, dead? Or tied up in a nearby basement? Or maybe it wasn't that car. I am scheduled to retire next month. I want to nail this guy before I go out."

"Who is it?" asked Sharon.

"They just found a woman buried in a utility relay station near Portland. It's a liquid natural gas pump station, not electricity, but still, the station was in the same condition as this one in '92, almost completed, almost ready to be brought on line. My prime suspect was here in '92, and in Portland in 1997. I actually helped them work the case back then, but once again, nothing. They never found the body or suspected it was buried at the LNG station – until now. This guy – he is a lot like Bundy, smart, charismatic, successful. If it really is him, and I am almost sure it is now, he is a pure psychopath. But he is beginning to break down – he has poked his head up to taunt us, and now – I am sure he is going to strike again. It's classic behavior."

Lance didn't mention Georgia's suspicions, that there was another guy who might have been here, and who definitely was in Portland when McKenzie was killed.

"I don't know, it sounds kind of iffy to me," said Sharon. "You know your job, but I have a responsibility to the company…this is going to cost…"

"And, even if you find her, it still does not prove…" said the judge.

"No," said Petrovich, nodding in agreement, "you're right. I agree. On the face of it, it's a long shot. But, if I get this order, it will be my last case, either way. Anyway, remember, she worked for Bonneville. She was your colleague, Sharon. Don't we have a duty to her memory, to say nothing of her next of kin?""

"We will have to divert power and probably shut off some customers for a little while at least. This is not going to be easy."

"Sharon," said the judge, "I asked you if you grew up around here because…we had a Sharon from here, back when I was a kid. Miss Richland, 1959. You're too young to remember, of course, but your name brought her to mind just now. I had just started high school and I still vividly remember her, anyone would. She was the most beautiful girl I ever saw, even to this day I think. You remember *Helter Skelter*, the Charles Manson murders, 1969? Sharon Tate was nine months pregnant when she was murdered. She had been Miss Richland."

Lance continued to look for the double-crested cormorant.

"I have a ten-year-old daughter," said Sharon, nodding in surrender.

"I'm going to approve the order. After the birds hatch. So you will have to stay around for another two or three months. OK, Lance?"

"Yeah. I will."

"Good. Sharon, once nesting season is over, I'll give your engineers a week to plan it and get your customers notified. So start getting ready. But it has to remain secret until the last minute. At least, until we find out if she is under there or not. Put together a plan and schedule with the detective."

"OK, Judge."

"If we find her, then it will be announced. That should give Detective Petrovich time to do what he has to do."

"Yep," said Lance. "Yep, it will." He was going on instinct that he would know what to do. Because at that moment he didn't have a clue.

Chapter 19

At SwiftPad Board Meeting, Kip pulls Jim into a Scheme to get Funds

Jim followed GG through a curtain to the back area of the 68 Gallery, up the raw wooden stairs, into an immaculate artist's work area. They walked up the polished hardwood stairs to the upper floor and into a well-appointed meeting room. People were sitting and standing while awkwardly chatting as they waited to start. There was a clear glass wall that looked out at the narrow courtyard surrounded by old brick walls, within which was a little pissing cherub statue, and a couple of moss-covered benches.

Jim handed Kip his wine and nodded questioningly toward the bar.

"I quit the hard stuff, Jimmy. Too much to do. Weight of the world, my friend!"

"I'm glad you are finally beginning to understand the gravity of the situation. Cheers," said Jim. Out of the corner of his eye Jim saw Raleigh approach them.

"Evening, Kip and…look what the dog dragged in! Hunt! Now I remember," he said. "You worked at Consolidated E & G. Back… back before Y2K. Right?"

Kip heard himself referred to as "the dog," but took a deep breath, and watched out of the corner of his eye. Jim tried to hide the fact that he had immediately recognized him by intently search-ing Raleigh's face.

"Yes, I did, I do, actually, again…I…" said Jim, squinting, looking close, pretending to look for something familiar in his appearance.

The other stared back, giving nothing away. "Jim, I am Raleigh Highlooper, remember?" Jim nodded with feigned fuzziness. Raleigh gave him a glimpse of all his teeth, a gesture that appeared friendly. Jim however saw something else.

"So you guys know each other?" said Chubby. Raleigh made a point to ignore him.

"You worked for GIP…back then," said Jim.

"I was a subcontractor. You had me fired."

Jim of course had remembered him right away. He remembered Raleigh was a local legend and that when he fired him, everyone said he was crazy to get rid of the most famous IT guy in Portland, the most sought-after consultant in town, the most technically bril-liant, allegedly. But Jim never really saw the brilliance, although he admitted to himself at the time that maybe he just didn't under-stand it.

In actual fact, Raleigh didn't invent anything, but he person-ally commercialized and consolidated some basic techniques, such as basic scripts for installing and configuring DNS, SendMail, and basic OSPF and BGP Cisco routing. Those three technologies were edgy stuff back in the early to mid-nineties, almost secret knowledge. It was the key for organizations to get on the Web, and Raleigh was the go-to guy around town. He could pull in $15K to $20K for two or three weeks' work just connecting a company up to the internet and configuring their email.

"Oh, yeah – well – I didn't actually fire you, there were some budgetary issues and they asked me if I could, you know, take over some of the duties…"

"Believe me, I had plenty of work – it was a loser project. I was about to bail anyway. Don't sweat it." Raleigh flashed his toothy, slightly carnivorous smile.

"Yeah – loser – GIP fucked the KEG hard in the bung – you're right about that…" said Jim. Raleigh was one of the main reasons it was a loser project. Jim had spent most of his time during his first tour at the KEG ripping out and redoing Raleigh's work.

In the nineties, the names of the computer systems, the server-names, were often assigned from characters from *Lord of the Rings* or *Star Wars*. Raleigh had sold himself as a wizard or a Jedi. He was the Paladin of the Portland Tech world, with no boss, lots of money and living on his rep. Jim would occasionally see him out at the bars, presiding over young tech-nerd wannabes.

"...I get it now. You are the other partner here at *SwiftPad*...!"

"Yeah – I'm the other partner."

They continued to glance at each other as more people came into the board room. Jim returned a weak smile to Raleigh. Kip looked deep in thought, but kept it to himself.

"Let's get settled," said Hariet.

"I move we bring the meeting to order," said Heber Young, Kip's father's accountant and his representative on the *SwiftPad* board. Heber was there to keep track of what Kip spent of the advance on his "inheritance."

"Second," said Seb Madison, former four-minute miler and Nike shoe company executive.

The rest of the quorum consisted of Michael Kendrick (Intel executive); Mitsuro Mansanato (Subaru); Pete Hollingsworth, twice a runner-up in the PGA Open, now a fixture on the Senior tour; Cook Callahan, a popular Portland left wing radio host and nationally followed blogger; along with Hariet, Raleigh, Kip, and GG.

"New business?" said Hariet. "OK, financial report. Heber?"

"We are broke," he said with finality. "No income, no reserves. We have payments due next week for server space, rent on the headquarters, general bills, line leasing, it is all due before the end of the month. That is not to say anything about salaries, which I understand are also in arrears."

GG kept her head down and Raleigh nodded to himself and began softly whistling. Kip glared at him and he stopped.

"It is not as bad as that," said Kip.

"No, it is actually worse," said GG. "We have to start paying people or it all falls apart. You started the trouble, Kip, by paying them for one week, then having to cancel after that. We have to follow through on our promises."

"But you said the last time it was up on the Internet we got a tremendous response," Seb pointed out, with some anger in his voice. "That we had thousands of hits and updates."

"Hundreds of thousands of updates and almost a million hits," corrected GG. "It's going better than we hoped, better than I thought possible. But we also got hit very hard. The competition is snarking us big time and hijacking conversations on a massive scale about us. In some ways, though, that is good, because it is driving people deeper to find us. Quality counts in the early stages. But we have to prepare for battle now. They know how we come up, where we come up. Next time they will be ready for us. We are not an underground phenomenon any more. I know Facebook has a team dedicated to shooting us down preemptively, to say nothing of all the freelance trolls. We depend on content from out there, and if they inject bogus or negative feedback, they can hurt us. But it is risky for them too...and we can't assume our enemies have perfect knowledge about us."

"Unless they have a spy on the inside," Kip whispered to Jim.

"So..." Heber sensed something in Kip's muffled comment and it threw him off for a couple of seconds. "Where does that leave us? What do we do?"

"We've come too far to back down now," said GG. "We have about two hundred servers in eight different locations. Which is nothing! A feather. We can be shut down with almost a basic denial of service in nothing flat. We need a stronger presence. Which means..."

"More money! With no income..." exclaimed Hariet.

"We need to inject twenty million dollars now," said Kip. "It will keep us afloat for six weeks..."

"...We have it all lined out," said GG. "We just need the money in the bank, and we can fire off the spending. We have vendors lined up, we have the process tested and ready to blast. We have been able to convince three companies to give us big space. Fortunately a gaming company in SoCal went Chapter 11 last week so we can spin up their servers in a week. That will give us the resiliency;

it will make it possible, I think. We just need assurance money to reserve it all."

"We should prorate the staff's shares of the company," said Kip. "They need to be paid two times going rates for shares in the company."

"Twenty million!" said Hariet.

"I've looked at the numbers," said Heber. "Other than the fact that I think it is outrageous and foolish, the requirements match the dollars. Or vice versa."

"How much will the Rehain estate be able to put up?" asked Hariet, looking at Heber. "Also Raleigh, you have not posted what you promised. Is there a problem?"

"My investors have been coming on slowly. As you might suspect, they are careful about doing anything high profile. They don't want to be noticed by the press."

"Or the Feds," GG whispered to Jim.

"I think some of them are having second thoughts," said Raleigh glaring at Jim. "But I will talk to them. No worries, it is in the bank."

"Well," said Heber, "I can speak for Mr. Rehain..."

"Hold on, Heb," said Kip. "I am going to visit my father this weekend and I will have an answer by Monday."

Heber shook his head slightly and looked down, then spoke. "Kip, we have nothing. No collateral, no receipts, no big customers throwing money at us. This isn't business; it's a big crap shoot."

"They will!" said Kip. "They will!"

"But is it timely?" asked Michael Kendrick.

"We are not racing the headlines. This is not some form of journalism. That is not our bag," said Kip.

"Twenty million, though?" asked Mitsuro.

"We need to see it," said Hollingsworth.

"We are having the BUDHI on Saturday. It is on. We can't delay it any longer. If it goes and if it is successful and we get high participation..."

"What do we need? How much participation?" asked Seb.

"Forty, fifty million I think."

"Wow. Is that possible?" asked Hariet.

"I think so," said GG. "It is the big question, for sure."

"We need a yes or no right after BUDHI. We need to start spending the money on Monday or Tuesday if we are going to take advantage of this," said Heber. "By the end of the week, our option on the Death Angel data center lapses. We'll miss the…"

"We'll get the money. We'll get a decision by Saturday," said Kip. "Jim and I will do it."

Jim looked at him.

Chapter 20

Jim's Tiff with Angie - A Staff meeting is interrupted by Art - Angie and Mark have a Personal Discussion

Macy dropped Jim at the KEG early Friday morning so he could explain the situation to his boss, Angie. He came in jeans and sneakers so he wouldn't get stuck at work, which seemed like a good plan, until he realized it was the quarterly Casual Friday. Macy would be expecting him outside the KEG in one hour. She went to pick up Kip and GG, and they would be heading south on I-5 for Newport before 9 A.M.

The cold curtness in Angie's voice message told him that she was pissed off at him for bailing on the meeting with the GIP consultant and DeFonzaro. She asked him to "Please, if possible," come briefly into work and come up to her office, "but only if he had time," before leaving for the coast. Back in the old days, she had been a young project manager, vivacious, ambitious and energetic. She had the right stuff to make a go at the corporate ladder. But she had stayed too long at the KEG. On some level, Jim blamed himself for her situation. Maybe he thought he could make amends by coming back, but it clearly wasn't going to work out that way. It probably never could have been any different.

They had been colleagues, working hand and glove, with Angie explaining and promoting Jim's radical, but often poorly articulated IT technical ideas, many of which led to sweeping changes in the way the company did business. Now she was his boss. When he torpedoed their meeting with DeFonzaro and the GIP guy, she made it clear, in every way, that the party was over.

"Anaka has been pushing me about this meeting for two weeks, and now I have to go to into it without my operations chief," Angie said.

"I'll email her and DeFonzaro about it and tell them it is a family emergency," said Jim.

"No. Don't do that." She said it as an order.

"I admit I am not looking forward to meeting this guy."

"What do you mean?"

"I want to make it work with this team, but we are not ready. We also needed to get the business message clear from Frank. The thirteenth floor has to decide, don't you think? Not just...Frank?"

She stared at him for a minute. "You were hired to carry out the wishes of the corporate structure senior to you. That is what you will do. Frank doesn't want the thirteenth floor involved. And neither do I. Go do your, we'll call it an off-site planning workshop or whatever. I'll handle the rest."

Angie's office was a tiny hole in the middle of the fifth floor, the same one she had when she was a project manager fourteen years ago when Jim had left. It was small and the stairwell was right behind it, and she could hear its conversations two floors away. No outside windows. She was almost never in her office though, always in meetings somewhere else.

"You need a better office."

Angie rolled her eyes. "So what is going on with you, Jim? We haven't talked much since you came back."

He shrugged. "You still seeing Carter?"

She laughed. "Carter? I haven't thought about him in years. He moved to Denver I think."

"I met someone."

"Oh?" Angie looked at him with no visible reaction.

"We just met, earlier this week actually…"

"That's great, Jim. I'm happy for you." She looked blankly at her monitor, and listlessly moved her mouse.

"I'm sorry. It is a family issue. My mom…"

"She's on the City Council in Corvallis, isn't she?"

"Yeah…" Jim had never mentioned that, at least to Angie.

"OK." She looked down at her desk, shook her head in disgust, and pulled another file off the pile on the desk corner. "I'll cover for you, don't worry, do whatever you have to."

"Anyway, I'll be back Monday and we'll move forward. Do you trust Frank?" he asked.

Angie smacked her pen down hard on her desk and looked at Jim. "We work for him, at least my boss, Anaka, does. So it's not part of our job to 'trust' him. We have to earn *his* trust. That's the way it is…"

"Yeah, I know." Jim looked at his former lover and saw clearly that without a doubt, the light had gone out, which was good. But he felt the rumblings of something threatening and unpleasant.

"I'll see you Monday," she said, dismissing him.

"Good luck, have a good weekend," said Jim, immediately regretting it.

Angie didn't look up as he left.

Mark Ruskin was staying downtown, at the Hilton, next to Pioneer Square, and was not returning to LA each weekend as he normally would. He kept his Bimmer parked in the Hilton garage all week. He was trying get the "feel" of Portland. Mark spent a day riding the MAX train, first out to Hillsboro, then took the Westside spur south to Wilsonville through Beaverton, Tigard and Tualatin. It was hard for him to understand Portland after LA. The "sticks" were so close to town! It was so green, it almost hurt his eyes.

There seemed to be a disdain in Portland for things he thought were important: style, cars, fragrance, and the statement you made when you stood up and took off your sunglasses. And they had a thing about body odor, or rather didn't. It was especially evident on the MAX train. And then there was the look, the cool. In LA it was important to show up with a well-practiced nonchalance, the attitude that you had nothing important on your mind. You hide yourself with a smirk and Versace with crossed Crockett and Jones suede loafers under the table. Style matters, dammit! In Portland people seemed to strive to reveal their inner-selves, and didn't care about their exterior – it was an anti-style style, one that doubled down on earnestness.

Mark came to realize as he wandered the Portland streets that it wasn't a simple, one-size-fits-all anti-style. There were tribes with particular missions – runners, grungers, bicyclers, beer crafters, cheese-makers, vegans, purveyors of the salted meats (and various subcultures of that, munchers of pork fat mixed with grains and beans, fish-eaters, free-range bird eaters, who called themselves semi-vegans so as to keep their place at the table). Within the food groups there were hikers, walkers, thinkers, woodworkers and dog lovers – big dogs, little dogs, show dogs, even manicured and well-behaved attack dogs. There were Deadheads and cellists, Claptons and Segovias, folksters, and lone singers in the park, fiddlers sitting on the sidewalk, and squads of drummers, whose beat reverberated whole city blocks. And of course, there were the dour, more normal than normal hipsters, who took a whole different path in their cool ironic commentary. From perusing the various free newsprint weeklies found on the Portland streets, and reading local blogs on the web, Mark found sprawling manifestos, sometimes apologetic sometimes angry, an ironic chorus sung, grading and balancing it, based on some self-justifying "understood" moral and social code that all knew better than to ignore. Everyone seemed to get it, but exactly what it meant seemed elusive. He knew he was missing something.

Mark knew that every city had these tribes, but in Portland, they flew their flags and made their personal statements loudly. The various bicycle tribes were particularly prominent, men riding with waxed Barbershop Quartet mustaches, shaved chrome-domes and lots of embedded metal. Sometimes twenty or thirty bikers rode three or four abreast like a posse out of a Louis L'Amour novel, or a Mongol raiding party, tattooed and pig-tailed swarming through Portland neighborhoods, stopping to eat and sort out the cannibals from the headhunters. It was a rich ecosystem that had evolved from something like standard Americana, but was different all the same.

Mark was pretty smart in odd ways, an astute observer and a bit of an amateur sociologist, even if…but Portland put him off his game, because people responded to the cues (money, status, clothes, cars, etc.) in a way that wrong-footed him every time tried to join a conversation, particularly if it involved trying to flirt with a pretty woman with nice cheekbones.

In the end, Mark thought it all came down to sex, because as he saw it, that was the ultimate goal. What did sex mean in Portland? He knew what it meant in LA – it was ultimately about money. Was it different in Portland? Surely not, it was just buried deeper. What did you have to do to get laid in Portland? He couldn't figure it out. It was some kind of unspoken code that eluded him. He began to think that maybe they didn't know themselves, and were hoping someone would tell them. He missed Santa Monica.

In any event, for the first week in Portland, he came into the Consolidated Electric and Gas offices (the KEG) for about four hours each day. Mark had been successful in the past by becoming a chameleon, blending in, feeling the culture. He had lots of time during that first week, so he would walk the streets, stopping in shops, even (once) having lunch from the food carts. He took the MAX train at Pioneer Square, traveled three stops to just before the Steel Bridge, a short walk really, but he wanted to ride, to see and feel it. He got out and took the elevator up to Frank's office on the ninth floor.

"We have to get you in front of our Info Tech people," Frank said. "It's important that you know what is going on in detail, because if we are going to trim things and make the kind of changes that I know we need to make, and get GIP involved in a big way, you are going to have to be ready for hand-to-hand combat with those people. They will defend their turf to the death. There is practically no daylight between staff and management, so we are going to have to come up with a very strong case to make the changes we need."

Frank was the CFO, but he wasn't a VP yet, and so he didn't have an office on the thirteenth floor like most of the rest of the executives, even though, he was (at least) the second most powerful person in the company. Frank had previously been the assistant CFO at MiddlePoint Energy in Dallas, which was about 50 times bigger than the KEG. When he was hired by Consolidated he was told he would have almost total control of the financials, but no one said anything about an office on the top floor and it pissed him off. But there wasn't anything he could do about it without seeming extremely petty.

"I think we should start by introducing the GIP Social Cloud Suite, get the company using collaborative software, then…"

"We need a win first," Frank said, tapping his pen on the desk, his chin in his other hand. "There are too many people in the company that can shit all over new software." Frank got up and paced around his office with his hands behind his back. Mark silently sat and stared at him.

"It's time. Let's go talk to Anaka and her managers. Apparently your former GIP colleague Jim Hunt isn't going to be there."

"Why not?"

"He is on some 'Planning Retreat' or something."

"Wow, that is strange, don't you think?

"Let's not focus on it. We can get the others out of the way first."

Angie took the elevator up to the executive conference room on the twelfth floor. It was the old love nest, with the balcony that overlooked the river to the east. The place had lost its charm for her. She wondered if Jim remembered it like she did.

DeFonzaro and Mark Ruskin were waiting. They chitchatted for five minutes when frumpy Beth Rockford and high strung Joan Shimaski came in, followed by Anaka, who somehow looked bird-like in her new, low-riding Levi 505s and a simple monochrome white blouse. Angie wore a soft denim skirt and a black sweater. A dark suit, and a tie painted with a modestly dressed hula girl, hung lifelessly on Frank's stocky frame and Mark sported an off-white shirt with beige Dockers and Crockett and Jones suede loafers.

They forced a few laughs and insipid remarks regarding the lack of Hawaiian shirts in the building and Frank repeated a line from the movie *Office Space* that ended with "...that would be great." They all hooted and laughed together.

"It's too bad Mr. Hunt isn't here, but, in any event, my objective is simple – find ways that GIP can partner with Consolidated to improve IT service delivery and look for opportunities to achieve cost savings," Frank continued.

Anaka talked fluff and IT buzz gobbledygook for what seemed like a long time.

"Thanks, Anaka," said Mark, nodding as if he understood exactly what she was saying. Angie smiled, in seeming bewilderment. Frank looked at his phone.

At that point Angie introduced Beth and Joan, who each gave a little introduction to their staffs, and their workload and their amazing productivity.

Angie thanked them as did Mark.

"We respond to the business," said Angie, summing up her team's status. "If the business needs different levels of quality, we can respond to that."

"No one disputes that, Angelica," said Frank, putting his phone in his breast pocket and looking at her. "But the field is shifting, new technologies are in play and..."

"Well, yes, but as Jim says, IT is still fundamentally about securely transporting Tee-See-Pee-Eye-Pee between different computers," said Angie. Jim had said that in one of the staff meetings and she had written it down.

Frank looked at Angie and then at Anaka. Now Anaka was looking at her phone. He was crazy angry that Hunt had skipped the meeting. Nothing was going to be accomplished here today. He bit his tongue.

"My role," said Mark, "is not to upset the chemistry of your teams. Let's forget about staffing, and talk services and then I think we can walk it backwards. I think we should look at the way the company communicates. The email platform Consolidated uses is not up to modern requirements of collaborative..."

"Excuse me," Art Van Landingham stuck his head into the room, "am I interrupting?"

"Art we have the conference room reserved…"

"I know, I just wanted to meet the new consultant. Heard some great things! Are you hiding him, Frank?" Art said with a laugh.

"Mark Ruskin, this is Art Van Landingdam," said Frank with a slight sneer.

"Landingham. Well, the real reason I popped in, now that they have positively identified Regina's body, we are having a memorial service for her in the big conference room, so people can share memories. We will have food…"

"When?"

"We are starting now. I know many of us were touched by her, even though it was so long ago."

Angie started crying. "I remember it like yesterday. We were such good friends." She began to tear.

"I suppose she would have been in her forties now," said Frank.

Angie looked at Frank with barely disguised hatred.

"It's terrible," said Mark. "I think maybe we should put this meeting off until next week perhaps. Apparently we need Mr. Hunt…"

"Fine, we'll do it next week then," said Frank. He picked up his black folder and walked out.

Anaka smiled at Art, and asked him to explain a point regarding the Operations budget that she thought might be associated with her department. Art smiled, said sure and they walked out, leaving Angie and Mark at the table.

"Aren't you going to the…" said Mark.

"I can't do it," said Angie.

"I know it is hard to lose someone close. My fiancée died last year."

The closest Mark had ever been to having a fiancée was a two-week romance with a woman in his building in Santa Monica, but she moved out with no forwarding address.

"That's terrible. I am sorry," said Angie, temporarily forgetting Regina. "Was it illness?"

"Yes – well – no – she – aah – she had an operation that led to her…"

"Oh. I'm sorry. Did her illness..." she wasn't sure what she was asking.

"She had breast problems..."

"Cancer?"

"No – uh – the real cause was...it was an elevator accident." Mark was flying without a net. "She had – it was a botched breast reduction – and – that bothered her – and distracted her, I think. She never could bring herself to look down...And that's when..."

"That's horrible. She fell down the elevator shaft?"

He nodded. "She was everything to me. She had beautiful cheekbones. Would you like to have lunch with me?"

Angie looked out at the river. She looked around the room, and toward the back of the room, where Jim and she...she looked at Mark.

"Sure. Let's get out of the building. You like Chinese?" she asked.

"No," he said.

"OK," she said. "Let's take the MAX uptown and find something else."

Chapter 21

GG and Kip Watch Charlotte while Macy and Jim get away for a Walk on the Beach

"This is weird," said Jim.

"How do you mean?" asked GG.

"I have to sleep on deck, on a cot," said Kip. "On my dad's boat. That's what is weird."

"Would it make you feel better if Jim slept on deck too?" asked Macy.

"It absolutely would," said Kip. "Which deck?" It was a big boat.

"We'll see."

"I'm glad you came, Gimbel," Jim toasted Macy.

"Huh?" asked Kip. "Let's stay here and go fishing again tomorrow. Today was fun."

"And blow off your dad?" said GG. "We might as well keep sailing to China." GG smiled at Macy, who looked back blankly at her. "I have to make sure you don't screw this up, Kip. I'll even pretend I am sleeping with you, if that is what it takes."

"The old pervert will be proud of his son if you do," said Jim.

"But I am not pretending," said Macy. "Does that help?"

Jim smiled at her. "Maybe it will with my mom." He paused, "But then again maybe not."

"Not pretending what, Mommy?" asked Charlotte, standing in the lower cabin door.

They all looked down at her from their deck chairs. "Charlotte, honey, I am not pretending when I say you better get to bed now!"

"That's not what you said," said Charlotte.

"Good night, Charlotte."

"Good night."

They sat back and watched the harbor. Jim and Kip had been taking Walt's boats out together since high school, but this one, a Formula 40, was a bigger, newer one, with all of the modern conveniences of navigation and luxury.

Macy had worried that Charlotte would be bored, then worried she would get too much sun, but neither happened. She made the boat her personal playhouse, and scampered all over. The four adults all took turns minding her, and Chubby had caught two giant sockeyes and GG a sea bass, which Macy and Jim had cooked up with various greens they had brought along with rice. Dinner was over, the galley was clean and squared away and the four adults were on deck, tied up in the harbor enjoying a batch of rum Mai Tais.

They all sat with mellow reflection, enjoying the last glimmer of the sunset, quietly thinking about tomorrow. Tomorrow would be the day they had the final test of the *SwiftPad* application, worldwide. The team had dubbed it the BUDHI. Kip thought the concept of BUDHI was provocative. The word BUDHI was Sanskrit for "Awaken," but of course "bud" and "hi(gh)" had different connotations, to some people anyway. GG didn't particularly like it, but it caught on very fast and the idea spread around the net and created a lot of anticipation. The plan was to demo it live to Kip's father, when they asked him for money. It was a big deal, they were asking for a hefty chunk of his fortune, twenty million dollars. Kip didn't know what his Dad was worth, but it was maybe fifty million, probably less, most of it tied up in land and equipment. It was early spring, but the sun's encore seemed to go on forever, like it was late summer. Seagulls patrolled, loudly looking for their evening meals.

"What's he like?" asked GG.

Jim and Kip looked at each other but said nothing.

"Don't we have to go to Corvallis..." said Macy.

"Yeah, Kip, I meant to tell you, I stupidly told my mom we were coming up and she..." Jim looked down and shook his head. "Macy and I are going to leave after saying hi. My mom is expecting us in Corvallis tomorrow afternoon to have dinner with her and her husband."

"Shit. Jim! You have to stay through the BUDHI. You are the key, Jimmy. You know that you're his boy, his favorite son...he'll never believe me if you don't back me..."

"Remember the line in *Prizzi's Honor*, 'Sicilians would rather eat their children than part with their money, and they are very, very fond of their children.'"

"You telling me?" said Chubby, looking at GG. "To answer your question, G...He's a cold-hardhearted bastard when it comes to money. He is going to make us grovel, and then still will probably dropkick us out of his house. I am not sure I want to deal with that. We are asking for more than half his fortune. We're fucked."

"Well he already dropped a mil on the first round...so maybe we say, in for a penny in for a pound..."

"That won't work with him," said Kip. "You remember all those poker lessons he gave us...don't bet on what happened before, bet on what's going to happen."

"Then I am screwed," said GG. "I'll have to marry a rich Arab, because I am not going back to contract programming. Should I act cute for your dad? Would that help?" GG did a little pose with her finger on her cheek and her head tilted. For some reason at that instant she looked grotesque, like a drunk peasant woman in a Bruegel painting.

They watched another boat come into the harbor and turn toward the pier much too fast. It slammed into the bulkhead, four or five boats over. There was laughter, and some cursing as they tied up.

A woman, mid-forties, wearing gold clamdiggers and hoop earrings, got off the boat, stormed down the dock and the boat's captain, twenty years older, sullenly followed. Chubby got up and made another batch of Mai Tais and they held their comments until the people from the other boat were out of hearing.

"You're in the business, Jim. If you have a hand in helping get us the twenty mil, then you are a full partner. The key will be the demo. You have to help make him see the economic return...explain the business in ways he understands. He only understands big ticket, moving-shit-around kinds of business. He doesn't get this stuff."

Jim looked at Macy, who shrugged. "I think he probably gets it, otherwise he would have told Heber no deal, no way, no how." Jim got up and poured himself another Mai Tai. "OK. I'll call my mom from your dad's and tell her we'll be late. Which will catch me a raft of shit, but…" He shook his head.

"We have to pitch him before he gets drunk," said Kip.

"Right. Get him when he is sober. It will be harder at first, but more likely he won't change his mind later." Jim and Kip had often plotted various schemes as teenagers around the predictable drinking schedule of Walt Rehain.

"Does he really have the money?" asked GG.

"I am sure it is tied up. He will lose a lot making it liquid quickly."

Macy, who was clearly impatient or uncomfortable with the conversation, stood up. "Jim and I are going to take a walk over on the beach now. Keep an eye on Charlotte, OK?" She pulled Jim's hand into hers.

"Love ya, Macy," said Chubby. "You know I saw you first."

"I am sitting right here," said GG, "I thought I was supposed to be your girlfriend this weekend?"

It was a long walk to the beach. They had to walk across the Yaquina Bay Bridge, over the channel that flowed out into the ocean. The bridge, built in the thirties, had successively larger arches going north, and was designed with an Art Deco style that somehow looked like the staging for a black and white musical from the Depression. It made Jim think of those movies where people dressed in tuxes and gowns in the afternoon and talked like they were on stage, without mumbling, in complete, declarative sentences. As they walked, he thought of those fast-talking, suggestive black and white comedies of the period with Fred Astaire or William Powell and Myrna Loy...The Thin Man! That was who Macy reminded him of! Nora Charles!

"What are you laughing at?" she asked.

"I think I just figured you out."

"Oh that's just great – But I bet you don't know where I hid my gun though, do you?"

"I got your gun..."

They took a short cut across the dunes and ran down the hill in the dark.

The half moon seemed hooked onto Orion's belt and the last rays of the sun flickered behind the western horizon. They walked north up the beach, holding hands and listening to the rhythm of the surf.

"Think they are doing it now?" asked Macy.

"Wouldn't surprise me. They are always playing grab-ass when they think no one is watching."

"OK – next question. Are we moving too fast?" asked Macy.

"If we were kids, maybe...we both know life is too short..."

"...Actually, if we were kids it would make more sense, you know, Romeo and Juliet. But I guess we both have some..."

"Battle scars?"

"I was going to say history, or experience," said Macy, "but yeah, we should know better. This is different though, I think..."

"Come here," he said pulling her gently down on the sand. They listened to the surf and stared at the stars.

"I am scared," she said.

"Of what?"

"Meeting your mother tomorrow. This is crazy. I just met you last night!"

"But I saw you months ago and knew then too. You saw me too, remember?"

"Yes, I remember. I might have thought that, but I don't remember. But I liked it when you looked at me."

"See? We've been at this for a while, just slowly working up to it."

"Right." Macy laughed to herself. "I guess it will be cool if you guys get the money." Macy sat up. "Right? Do you think it is going to work? I am not sure your dad is going to like GG. You guys say she is smart and all, but she doesn't seem that smart to me. For starters, she dresses like she is mentally disabled...if Kip's dad thinks it all depends on her, I doubt he will give you the money. She is too flaky."

"I guess we'll find out."

"And the name, *SwiftPad*, sounds like a something to use when your period starts unexpectedly."

"How about *FaceButt*," said Jim.

"That should be the name," Macy had a deep-pitched laugh. "Wouldn't you be happier working with Kip on *FaceButt* than working for the power company?"

Jim gave Macy a stone face. "I feel responsible at the KEG. I...I am comfortable there. At Chubby's company, it's just a bunch of ADHD rehab survivors. They follow an ironic order of behavior that I have no way of ever joining...Kip can roll with it because he has his own, aura, or whatever...He fits in because almost none of the *SwiftPadders* have real problems – at least outside their own head they aren't real. Like Kip...They are all just floaters in the current around them, like amoeba in a pond or something."

Jim then started kissing her.

"What are you doing?" she asked.

Jim looked at her quizzically. "I thought you'd be shy on the boat because the acoustics are so good."

"So you want to make sure you get a screw in tonight?"

"Even a semi-screw would do. I get so turned on when you say screw."

Macy looked at him with a grin. "OK. Point for honesty." She licked her finger. "Now I will be honest. Portland is a hard place to live. I have been volunteering at the Gallery for the last year, for tips, hoping somehow to get a regular job. But it's not going to happen. I am in over my head – living beyond my means. I am on waiting lists, call-back lists. I saw you once last year – remember eating at Hibiscus Bowl last year?"

"Yeah – it was great food. It's out of business now, isn't it?"

"Just as I was getting full shifts waiting. I thought, why is that guy eating alone?"

"I was traveling for business – Wells Fargo...no it was US Bank. Short visit. I was living in San Jose at the time."

"I wanted to be an actress. Or actor, whatever. But I didn't want it enough to live in LA or New York though. Now..."

There was silence.

"See – you are stuck here at the beach with me, looking for the exit. We did move too fast. This was a big mistake."

"No, I was just thinking about tomorrow, if we make that happen and finance *SwiftPad*, some of these problems..." Jim sat up and looked out at into the darkness of the ocean. "The real problem is, money means absolutely nothing to Kip. He has told his dad to go fuck himself more than a few times. It's not GG we have to worry about, it's Kip. So tomorrow is going to be hard – we have to help Kip get along with his dad and then...go visit my mother. You gotta to understand something about her..."

"I doubt I'll understand anything; I am a complete amateur when it comes to..." said Macy.

"Crazy, impulsive women? I don't think so."

"To be one, and to understand one, are two different things."

"Well you've got a kid, that changes a lot of things. It means you've lost your amateur status, my dear."

"You mean I went pro?"

"Something like that. Anyway, tomorrow you will see why I am all fucked up."

"I doubt I'll figure you out. Anyway, I have my own demons."

"I have been meaning to ask..."

"Too much talk. Let's get that screw in."

Chapter 22

At Kip's Homestead, Deep in the Oregon Coast Range, SwiftPad is Introduced to the World

They left the boat early the next morning, with the screeching of feeding seagulls and the blasts of the fog horns serenading them. Jim had not been to the Oregon coast in ten years, and he was not eager to leave, especially to go spend the afternoon with Kip's father, asking for an unimaginable amount of money. He took in a deep breath, smelled the fresh salty air and got in the SUV.

They stopped for breakfast at the Newport Café, and lingered over breakfast. Charlotte wanted to play on the beach, so they walked down to the ocean and dug a sandcastle at the water's edge. They all watched Macy's daughter play in the sand in silence, not really ready to talk or even think about what the day had in store for them. The plan was to run the worldwide public demo on the old man's computer, letting it all hang out and trusting that the product itself would be enough to convince him to jump in with a considerable percentage of his fortune.

When they finally got ready to go it was almost noon. Jim drove Macy's SUV through the western side of the Coast range, climbing up past Toledo, the old county seat, now little more than a sign on the highway. When they got to Eddyville, they turned north on the Nashville Road and wound up the little two-lane road alongside of the Yaquina Creek, heading toward the Rehain Compound.

As they drove, each of them still keeping pretty much to themselves, staying quiet, Jim thought about his run-in with the cop over the "transient." Two or three people from the upper floors of the KEG building saw what looked like a naked woman. He shook his head, and looked out the window. It had been years since they had been down to the Coast Range. Jim had a vague fear that he kept to himself.

Kip's dad had always shown Jim a special respect, even when they were 10-year-old boys. He never felt mistreated because he was poor. Life was primal in the Coast Range, a bedrock equality. Everyone lived like the mushrooms that sprouted out of dead rabbits, close to the bone, sucking out what they could, before it washed away or rusted over. The rain was the overriding reality and everyone was almost equal before it. Green life overwhelmed everything; even when it died, it fed whatever was sprouting on top of it. There was an innate democracy to the Old Oregon, the Oregon of the loggers and knock-abouts who inhabited the perennially wet and fecund Coast Range. It was hard, but that disguised an underlying equality among all those who could handle the wet isolation of Northwest winters.

At least it used to be like that, when it seemed that big, easy-to-cut trees would never be scarce and when the California drought wasn't threatening to move north. Nothing stays the same, which usually meant it was getting worse.

"So, G," asked Kip, "What are you going to say when the old man asks you about yourself? Before you came to Portland, I mean."

"I don't know."

"I am sure he has had you investigated. You have to assume the worst of him," said Jim. He looked at Kip and said, "We better get our story straight. This is kind of important."

They turned left again at Norton Road and kept heading up the hill.

The *SwiftPad* BUDHI was set for Saturday at 4 P.M. Pacific Time. GG had thought it crazy for her not to be at headquarters for the event, but Kip had said if they don't get the money, the BUDHI would not matter, successful or not. Timing was the critical element, as it usually is with important endeavors.

They pulled off the side of the road next to an ugly clear-cut patch, determined to go over their plan one more time. They got out and walked down to Yaquina Creek, and sat by the stream bank. It was springtime and the creek was running high. The running water, in the Oregon rainforest, the scent of hundreds of years of compressed flora, moist, cool and spongy life on top of life, deep, clean and rich all lifted their mood. This was Western Oregon; this was what it meant. Charlotte took off her shoes and stepped into the running water and turned over rocks, and tried to catch a skittering crawdad. They forgot about Portland and lay back in the moss.

"I wish we could just stay here," said Kip.

"We are going to be fine," GG said, mostly to herself. The air was so sweet next to the fast-running creek. Nobody disagreed, but Jim and Kip stayed in their own thoughts and anyway, they didn't believe GG believed her own words.

They went over the plan one more time. GG was eager to plug her laptop in and see what was going on. She had been over and over and over the *SwiftPad* code in her mind, how it would respond to the push and pull of the entire world trying to break it and fool it and bend it to its will. She thought she had programmed in an answer for everything but also, almost within the same thought, knew that that was impossible. If Kip's dad wasn't a fool, he would sell everything he owned to invest in *SwiftPad* before the day was over. Either that or throw them off his property. GG thought her head would explode.

She pulled out her phone, no service, and pulled up the cheat sheet she had written the night before as she lay in the pullout bed on the Rehain cabin cruiser. Kip forgot to bring condoms, and that was enough for her to exile Kip to the deck (until he ran out to a Newport pharmacy when Jim and Macy were walking). She had deliberately left the technical start-up steps to the team back in

Portland. Kip had insisted she assign all that to others, to pull her out of the weeds so she could think strategically. She was worried about connectivity out at the Rehain Compound, but Kip assured her it was solid, fiber to the house (Walt brought it in along with the gas lines, and he even had satellite backup). She sat by the creek and breathed in the cool, wet air and tried to just listen to the creek below her.

The BUDHI was widely anticipated around the Net, chatting was voluminous with speculation extremely detailed, the team had been watching it and feeding back, and they had even recruited some new staff from the user base. The speculation was especially intense in Portland, which was the center of user activity. They had a large fan base in Japan, and northern Europe as well. The international interest was extremely intense, even more than in North America.

A grungy bar on Portland's Eastside, The Bong, was hosting a BUDHI "Phenomenon." The core of the *SwiftPad* staff would end up there tonight. Around the bar, on the walls, ten 85-inch interactive screens hung, surrounded by beanbag couches with interactive controls linked to customized tablets that were scattered about. BUDHI phenomena like that were springing up all over the world, almost fifty that they knew about, in Norway, Germany, Spain, Korea, Vietnam, New Zealand and all through the old East European Bloc. It was scary, because attacks were increasing enormously. If it failed, they would be shackled in laughing-stocks and their business would be dead.

"You have to stay for the BUDHI, Jim," said Kip. "You can't leave for your mom's until it's over."

Jim promised that they (Macy, Charlotte and himself) would stay until after the BUDHI started, and that he would talk to Walt.

They got back in the van, and continued up the hill toward the Rehain Compound, noticing as they gained elevation and as they got closer to the Compound, that it flattened out and a herd of Roosevelt elk waded into shallow Yaquina Creek meandering in a high meadow. They passed over the hill, into the east side of the Coast Range, and they looked down on a huge valley. Then an unmarked dirt road appeared almost unexpectedly and after a half a mile, they drove through the gate and up the gravel driveway into an open lot. Nothing pretentious, barely maintained, pickup trucks were parked haphazardly around the huge hard-pan gravel area in front of the airplane hangar–like barn, which was what you came to first. The house, big as it was, seemed like an afterthought as you approached, off to the side, about 50 yards away, sitting on a rise that overlooked both the Coast Range and the northwest side of Mary's Peak. The entrance to the compound was very commercial and utilitarian, which matched Walt Rehain's personality to a tee.

A front-end loader came out of the barn, Enrique was driving it and when he saw Kip, he put on the brakes, skidding and had jumped off the tractor almost before it came to a halt.

"Aiya!" he shouted and suddenly eyes, then people, began to appear around the Compound looking at them. *"Kip ha vuelto! Y con su amigo Jimmie!"*

Jim parked in the middle of a bare area between the main house and the storage shed. The house was half painted and the scaffolding was in place and unattended.

"Enrique. Que pasa!" said Kip, shaking both hands of the short, thick, middle-aged man in tight-fitting brown work pants and a denim Guayabera shirt. Enrique had worked for his father since Kip and Jim had been in middle school and was the de facto boss of operations.

"Muy bien. Very good here. Jimmie! Mira! You bring beautiful girls!" Enrique looked at Charlotte, waved and smiled, showing his yellowing teeth. Charlotte moved closer to her mother but gave him a smile back.

Kip looked over toward the porch and saw his father. He waved, but his father just looked at him. Heber, the family accountant, stood behind him. "What's that flabby-arsed troll doing here," he said to Jim.

Jim didn't answer because he then saw a polished 1965 Rambler Ambassador with new whitewalls parked in the shade under the huge oak tree just off the side of the house. "That your mom's car?" Kip asked. Jim looked back and put his arm behind Macy, who held Charlotte's hand. GG walked behind and Jim looked hard at Kip.

They walked up to the solid oak, newly painted steps of the wide, ancient porch that wrapped around the three-story house. The Byrds were playing on Walt's formidable custom Blaupunkt stereo system, "Are we gonna fly, down in the easy chair," music that only made sense when Jim saw his mother standing in the screen door. She had never denied the rumor that she had a long-running affair with some famous writer or politician whom she never identified, even to Jim. Jim tried to guess in the beginning who it was, but she never "confirmed or denied." Sometimes she would disappear for a few weeks, bringing home souvenirs from Africa or Asia. She was happy then, and Jim never tried to figure out any of the details. She still looked amazing; no one ever believed she was as old as she was.

"Jim, it's been a long time," Walt Rehain stepped toward Jim with the biggest smile he had ever been seen to wear by either Jim or Kip.

"Walt...it's been what, almost twenty years?" Jim held out his hand. They shook and Walt put his hand on Jim's arm. Jim was a little shocked at how much he had aged. How old was Walt, at least 70, maybe 75. He'd lost weight, but not in a good way.

"Kip, it is good to see you." Walt turned and stiffly punched his son on the shoulder.

"Walt," he corrected himself, "Dad – this is Macy, Jim's friend, and her daughter Charlotte."

"Pleased to meet you both." He bowed so gently and deferentially to little Charlotte that she broke out into a laugh.

"And this is Cynthia," Kip held G by the wrist, and she resisted the impulse to pull away from him. Walt smiled and bowed deferentially again, and held his hand out to lead them into the house. Jim caught Walt's sly look at his mother as he walked past her. Everyone but Jim went in, as he waited on the porch with his mother.

"I left Gregory yesterday," she whispered to him. "Sorry, I know what you think, Jim, but I just couldn't stand it anymore, and anyway I hated living in town..."

"But you are on the city council! And running for mayor in the fall. Right?"

"I don't know, one step at a time," she looked over at Walt, who ignored her. "Just let's make peace today. She is very beautiful, Jim. I have a good feeling. I hope me saying that won't mess it up for you..."

Of course, Alice, it's all about you, Jim thought. "I guess we aren't having dinner in Corvallis tonight..."

"No. no...Walt wants us all to eat here. I sometimes run into Walt and we have kept up with each other for the last few years, you know, old friends are those who end up living longest, I guess."

"Staying out here?" he asked.

She gave him a neutral look that morphed slightly into a wry smile. "Aren't you going to introduce me to her and...the child?"

"Sure. Let's go in..." but he didn't move, "so are you OK?"

"Yeah...I am great, Jim. Really. It is so good to see you." Alice leaned over and awkwardly hugged her son.

"What about...?"

"I don't know...come on," she said, hiding her frustration at her son's coldness, opening the screen door for herself and after passing through the "coat and boot" room, they walked into what he remembered Kip's mother calling, "The Slaughterhouse," where the ceiling was vaulted and a big fireplace stood cold, just across from the entrance. Heads of a black bear and a 12-point elk bull hung on opposite sides of the room. Dead ducks posed alertly on the mantel. It was all worn and faded but, surprisingly to Kip, extremely polished, and dusted. It smelled fresh and clean. In the far corner, a sturdy couch squared off a quarter of the room and faced a couple of huge velvet throne-like chairs with low thick backs.

"Rosa," Kip hugged the woman who had raised him since his mother left. Rosa, five foot, two hundred pounds, hugged him back so hard she nearly lifted him off the floor.

"*Kipito, que bueno, has vuelto, muy muy bueno. –* So good..." she looked over at Jim, and her smile became a little tight and she said, "*Himmie!*" She suddenly seemed nervous. "I get drinks," and she left without asking what anybody might prefer.

"Well," said Walt, "how's business, Kip?"

They all became quiet.

Kip looked at Heber. His father's business agent stood next to the fireplace, pretending to ignore the conversation. To make it even more awkward, he wouldn't be drinking either.

"Hmm...so Jim..." Walt looked over at Macy, then back at Jim. The old coot missed nothing, thought Jim. "Are you part of this venture?"

Jim looked at his mother and quickly at Macy.

"Hold on, Walt," said Alice Hunt. "Are you going to introduce me, Jim?" She forced a tight smile and looked at Macy.

"Macy, Charlotte, Cyn...this is my mother, Alice Hunt."

"Hello, Alice. I have been looking forward to meeting you," said Macy.

Alice, in round granny glasses, wearing a worn, gray sweater, snugly fitting jeans, her gray-streaked light brown hair pulled back in a tight pony tail, suddenly seemed relieved, and silently walked up to Macy and hugged her and then got down on her knees and solemnly took both of Charlotte's hands. Jim realized how formidable Alice was when she wanted to be. She had gone through so many phases in her life, loyal wife of a hard-working logger, free spirit hippie, spiritualist, feminist, bureaucrat, mistress to the rich and powerful, university wife and doyen, politician, and now was on the run again from her most recent husband. Yet no matter how many doors she slammed or bridges she burned, she was never without options, even now. Through it all, she had been more like a big sister rather than a mother to Jim. Jim resented her, especially when she made him feel hardhearted, when she "out-empathized" him with other people. She always saw the pain in others and seemed to take it into herself. No wonder she had never lost an election. Everyone loved her. Jim had learned how to avoid emotional pain as a child and that made him feel mean and hard compared to her, yet he at the same time blamed her for his...Jim shrugged and let it go. This was his life, he thought, and all in all it wasn't bad. He returned to Walt's question.

"I am still just an adviser. It is amazing what Cynthia and Kip have going. It's turning some heads. But my day job is running IT Ops for Portland Consolidated E & G."

"So you left GIP, huh? Well that's good. I never thought you belonged in an outfit like that." Walt casually leaned against a chair and seemed to labor a bit. "Everyone I have ever known who worked for a big outfit like that ended up regretting it. Adviser, huh? Well what would you advise me? I assume you are here with Kipling to try and shake more money out of me, right?"

Jim gave Walt a look of mock surprise, but then relaxed. He hadn't seen Walt in a while and it came back to him that this was the man who, along with Enrique, stood up to a posse of angry loggers at a Grange meeting after buying up most of their repossessed rigs. He gave a better price than the bank, but he had always heard complaints about Walt's cutthroat business dealings. He looked at his mother, who moved closer to Walt.

"Key Pee, you help me bring, OK?" Rosa called from the bar area.

Jim looked next to him and said to Macy, "While we are waiting for the show to start, let me show Charlotte and Macy around. So – hold that thought, Walt. I'll start shaking you down then…" Jim and Walt looked at each other, and he didn't look at his mother.

Macy, Charlotte and Jim walked out onto the porch, and Jim led them down around the far side of the house. The entire valley was covered with newly planted Christmas trees. They walked along a dirt road that led into a wooded area of old growth. Jim pointed out the remnants of an old platform nailed to a huge Douglas fir.

"We used to perch up there for hours. We fastened up a huge rubber inner tube crossbow-slingshot and we'd shoot sealed up cans of sand out into the valley."

"This is what you are proud of? Launching garbage into the forest?"

"Yeah – we actually did the math to see how far they would go."

"Were you right?"

"Not even close." Jim took Macy's hand. "I could do it now though."

"Oh?" Macy looked him over top to bottom. They smiled at each other.

Walt had taken over an old railroad spur that led into Albany, and from there he shipped trees all over the world. Asia was booming. Hong Kong people paid as much as $700 for a fresh, perfectly proportioned six-foot spruce and Walt shipped tens of thousands of them every November. Charlotte walked ahead of them.

"Why don't you talk to your mother?" asked Macy.

"I did," said Jim.

Macy nodded, clearly not convinced.

"I don't know, she and Walt have a history that isn't pretty; something happened between them when Kip and I were in junior high school. It's her life. She is not a bad person," he said, as if he were trying to convince himself. Macy looked at Jim.

"What happened? Did they have an affair?"

"Affair? A drunken fuck fest more likely. But who knows? They took off together and came back apart a week later, then Kip and I were both told we weren't allowed to see each other. Well, we both said fuck that, we were about 13 or 14, and we let them know they were not the bosses of our lives anymore. It was a strange time, but that was when Kip and I became real close friends. Like brothers almost, which is another reason this feels wrong to me."

"And here she is, obviously there is some passion. Or something. You think they are...?"

"I don't know. I don't want to even try and figure it out. Let's face it, they are both old. Mom is in her late sixties....You and I met what, two days ago? Here you are in the middle of...we're not..."

"I am a big girl. I don't know if it's...but I know it is a good feeling, almost wholesome or maybe that isn't the right word."

They watched an eagle float over the valley below.

"I know all the rules. Take it slow, don't crowd, stay in the shadows until it's time to come out. I suppose they look at me as a desperate mother latching onto a lonely guy. But I don't care. Even though, if we are honest, we should admit, I don't know you, Jim, and you don't know me. But for some reason, for the first time in my life, I just don't care. That is what worries me the most. I *have* to care..." she pointed at Charlotte, who had run up on the embankment and was skipping ahead.

Jim looked at Macy and thought about the last two days, and here they were. He hadn't even thought about his job and he couldn't ignore it, because too many people were depending on him. And now, suddenly he felt lucky to have all these burdens. He felt radiated with a kind of power he had never known before. He loved a woman and maybe she loved him. He put his arm around her.

"Tell me again, your ex-husband, Charlotte's father...both you and Charlotte are so beautiful, how can he not be insane with grief being away from you?"

Macy looked at him, hurt as though he had violated a rule they both understood was supposed to be inviolate.

"You can't be coy now."

"I don't know why he left. It has been over almost a year. His phone's disconnected. His sister pretends she doesn't know me. I am desperate, Jim. God that sounds so fucking melodramatic, but I don't know what I am supposed to do. I am so scared and feel so guilty!" Jim took her hand. "I will stay tonight because I know this business with Kip's father is important to you. But we went too fast. It is not fair to you, me throwing myself at you. I can't...I am feeling very overwhelmed..."

Jim shook his head at her. "When did you see him last?"

"About six months ago, for two days. He tried to recruit me to the Falun Gong and was going to take Charlotte. He was irrational and a bit threatening. So I called the INS on him. He lied about some things on his green card application and when they showed up he agreed to just leave, to fly to Hong Kong the next day. It is not something to be proud of, getting your husband deported. He claimed I would be hounded by lawyers forever, but he kept money in the bank, until last month."

"So it's not so bad."

"It's not good. It's bad for Charlotte. She asks about him less and less because she knows it upsets me, but I can see that it bothers her more and more. I haven't told her where he is..."

"You know?"

"He went back into China. At first I thought it was because he was tired of being married, but I think he believes in, you know, the Falun Gong, I think he wants to be a martyr and I know his government will gladly oblige. It seems like such a goofy religion to me, but I don't know."

"Alice dabbled in Falun Gong about 10 years ago, but as usual, she had only been halfhearted about it," said Jim. "It was something to fill the void somewhere between chanting, Sufi dancing with drunk Jesus at the Wedding of Cana and kundalini meditation."

"Anyway, I am pretty sure he is in prison, in China, or maybe not, I don't know. His sister told me he was in a demonstration in Beijing, and we stopped hearing from him – or his family."

"Maybe Kip's dad can help. He does a lot of business with the Chinese."

"Jing's family is well connected and they can't do anything. I don't think a foreign businessman can help. They won't even admit they are holding him."

They looked at each other, and both shrugged and Jim put his arm around her. "I know what you mean about a feeling. I have it too. Maybe I am just a desperate bachelor."

Macy licked her finger and made a checkmark in the air. "But an employed bachelor. That counts!"

Jim smirked. "It's scary to give in to a vague hunch," he said.

"I think vague hunches are all we ever know," Macy said.

They came back in the house and Jim joined Kip and GG standing behind Walt, who sat in front of his 48-inch computer screen. The large window overlooked the Christmas tree valley below.

"OK. How do I make this go…"

Kip leaned over Walt's shoulder and navigated his Chrome browser to the *SwiftPad* site. The home page started on the back of a long-haired woman sitting on the edge of a cliff overlooking the Pacific. Some gulls flew by, and her hair gently fluttered in the wind. "What time is it?" Kip asked.

"Two minutes," said GG.

"This is kind of hokey," said Alice. "Is she the Oregon Goddess of the Internet waiting to bless *SwiftPack*…"

"…and all those who use it," sputtered Macy, as she laughed uncontrollably and fist-bumped Alice.

GG and Kip looked at each other alarm. GG mouthed, "Swift-Pack?"

"So why isn't it live all the time? Isn't that the point of the Internet?" asked Walt.

"Until we get funding to buy more systems we have to limit availability. But the Oregon Goddess...she sits there all day. The sky matches the ambient light normal for the Oregon Coast in real time. It even matches the current weather. She will wear a floppy hat when it is raining. When it's cold she wears a wool jacket. A Cascade Sportswear jacket. Product placement for our major investors. Think about that, Heb."

"Didn't Andy Warhol make a movie that was nothing but some guy sleeping?" asked Alice.

"It sounds Orwellian," said Walt. "Soma for the masses."

"Dad, you're mixing up Huxley's *Brave New World* with Orwell's *1984*. People have these conversations all the time. Take us, you and me..." Kip went on with a little history of his and his father's arguments and disagreements, how each time it came down to Kip's inability to accept responsibility. He admitted that he had rejected whatever his father had thrown at him, even when it made perfect sense in relation to what Kip had said he believed. When he called Walt "Dad," it seemed to bring out feelings that went beyond the pure intellectual arguments they had, which usually fell into a predictable pattern. Your business practices, buy low, sell high, were they worth it to those who lose out? Our neighbors still think you screwed them, that you took advantage of their weakness. It was getting out of hand, because Kip was supposed to be sweet-talking his father, but nothing could change the pattern. (Alice's eyes swelled and her face reddened. Years ago she had railed against Walt's business blood-lust whenever she thought Jim had been spending too much time at Kip's as a boy.)

But Walt didn't back down. "Life is a knife fight boy," he said, not looking at Alice. "Everything you eat was once alive. Eagles that fly with doves starve to death."

Neither Walt nor Kip was raising his voice, but the tension was building with each volley. This was an ancient scene at the Rehain Compound. Doors would be slamming soon, thought Jim.

It didn't look good for the money, GG thought. Kip's father was from another planet compared to her own suburban bureaucrat father.

"It's time to start," said GG, trying to ignore the loud father-son spat. "Kip, log in and show us what you see…"

They pulled in closer to the computer. Walt slid over, and Kip sat almost up against his father and started to navigate in. Walt punched him hard on the shoulder. Kip smiled.

"So tell me what I am seeing," said Walt.

"The main difference between this and other sites is that it generates its own content, which is based on human input," said Kip.

"This upper half of your screen is the user's panel, you can expand it and drill in, but it uses all of your existing profiles – Who you follow, who follows you, Friends, GooglePlus, Facebook, Amazon, Tinder, Pinterest, YouTube, Twitter if you tweet, or are tweeted at, even Yik Yak, and more, we are vetting new apps all the time. It takes everything you 'do,' and guesses at posts and applies them to you even if they are not about you. What things seem like, as much as about what they actually are. Interests and purchases, which is the same thing. The weighing algorithms are pretty cool, I think. Each level of permission is explained with examples. But if you turn everything green, allow all permissions, you are going to get a personalized experience that will take you where you really want to go, even if you don't know it. That is the goal."

"Its goal is to move you off your mean," said GG. "To change you. Or rather to push you to change yourself."

"It begins to create content, to lie, but just a little, scans the recent news and creates composite events, without skewing away from the user."

"It doesn't have a sense of humor. It is just a machine…but the juxtaposition of information is sometimes almost ironic…"

"On every level it synthesizes choices."

"Here, down here, this is a pull-down of all your groups, politics, your Christmas tree sales data worldwide, Christmas tree discussions, Druids complaining that Christianity stole its tree worshiping traditions, old car restoration websites, why Jay Leno sucks, just jump on or off wherever you want."

"Here is what we watch, though," said GG, "the Admin Panel… or as we call it, The Big Bored."

"We have to think of a better name for it," said Kip. "It isn't 'public' yet. We might monetize it. High-end subscription service or something. Use it for some other purpose. But it is completely unpredictable. I don't think we expected it to function like this."

"Theoretically, I thought it might work like this…" said GG.

"The synthesis of syntheses makes it almost Artificially Intelligent. It is almost creative, if only because it 'creates' something new and unpredictable, yet is somehow 'related.' Re-computations against other re-computations, right?" asked Jim.

GG nodded. "It's based on the slightly 'random' choice functions of everybody in the world…there's some Mandelbrot and Fibonacci built into the algorithms."

Macy looked at Alice. "Did she say sauerkraut and fettuccine?"

Jim looked at his girlfriend and mom. "Math talk. Sorry."

Alice made a long, wide-eyed face, "The great geniuses are talking math." Macy was nearly rolling on the floor laughing. GG looked away, impatiently.

"I like the way you parse the video," said Macy, seeing that GG was pissed at her. Everyone was waiting for Alice to get control of her laughing. Jim looked at her with a surprised smile and she smiled. Alice moved next to Walt and put her hand on his shoulder.

"It parses the content of video and allows it to be searched and exchanged," said GG coolly. "Automated real time video photo-shopping, and face recognition, driven by the internal software engine."

Chubby's picture morphed, he got older. Kip clicked on the news.

The lead is another murder. They bring out a body on a stretcher and it switches to bodies, bodies piled high; it is an old Jack Palance movie and Genghis or Attila mounts the pile of bodies and looks out at an unseen vision of desolation and gives a speech; his voice has modulated into a Boston accent about paying any price.

Then it switches to an old clip from *Rawhide,* but instead of Rowdy Yates, its Kip sitting on a horse and he is riding and shooting, then cut to Jack Palance dying in Billy Crystal's arms from the end of *City Slickers.*

"What the hell was that?" asked Walt.

GG shakes her head. "I have no idea." She looked at Kip, who shrugs. "It must be some beta code for 2.0 that we forgot to comment out..."

Jim slips over to the comments sections, and suddenly it is cute dogs, sad dogs, jumping dogs, that morph into cats then mice, then a montage of a man born about 1920, colorized black and white baby pictures, that change to teenage pictures, young man, family, in the office, getting an award, sitting at poolside watching, then in intensive care, but each time his eyes stay the same as he grows up, and then fades away. There is a B&W photo still from some scholarly convergence (Einstein is in the back and Bertram Russell is sitting near the front), and sound track is the singing of Monty Python's "Immanuel Kant was a real piss-ant."

"If you click the 'Chooser,'" said GG, pointing at an icon that recalls Mr. Peabody's 'Way Back' machine, "and click "Enter," you see a series of decision icons that result in more choices, favorite colors, favorite teams, players, politicians, causes, and it predicts, based on age, occupations, background, origins, likely choices of people. The Chooser changes its design for each user, and creates a whole new environment where people can see themselves and when they do, it changes again. It changes any 'history' that is too consistent. When they finally choose, they enter a mirror world of what they thought they chose."

"Phony and real updates change 'reality,'" said Jim.

They continued to watch and saw saved puppies become dead bodies washing up on shore, reports of massacres in the Middle East turn out OK, with happy women villagers ululating, playgrounds are happy places, then jungle gyms turn to gallows. Happy times in villages, in the Himalayas, and in the African jungle, Inuits dance in front of an igloo, interviews with TV personalities go off the rails and cameras are smashed, truthful outbursts are silenced.

A town in Wyoming is not perpendicular to ground, a scientist discovers a slight tilt in houses and people, just a tad, but measurable, slightly off kilter. SCTV's Dave Thomas's Bob Hope character meets the real Bob Hope, only to be joined by Woody Allen and Rick Moranis. It was mostly a juxtaposition of stills now, but in two point oh, the splicing of video on the fly will be almost constant. How is it controlled? It's not.

"Remember Mandelbrot and the predictable randomness of nature?" said GG. "Facebook updates, tweets and political columns stream and are interrupted by questions, then, slow careful words, become found poetry. It is always familiar yet…"

Oil covers a seagull. A Sufi master dances.

Alice looked more closely.

"Slightly random variables are inserted everywhere, between 10% and 30% of all posts (which are randomly decided) are changed," said GG. "Different people say what others say, only it is slightly changed. It is a Bizarro world, but not completely. The software engine constantly scouts for Ellsberg Paradoxes and forces the user to confront the consequences of their choices. Content is constantly being categorized. And re-categorized. In the end it always comes back to you, in the here and now."

"How does it find the ones that are 'changed'?" asked Walt.

"Embedded Google queries. We automate the creation of the queries…"

"What about your posts? Or my posts."

"You don't 'like' things – you 'rate' them, associate them, move them around, see this palette? Slide it over here…"

"…but they disappear as fast as you see them," said Walt.

"They are changed too, but not by much, and usually not until enough time has passed that the user might believe the changed post was theirs rather than what she actually posted. We just can't control it…it's not just from you, it's about you."

"So the machine fucks with you?" said Walt.

"A little bit. Actually, more than I thought. It is different every time. We've given over a certain amount of control of choices to the machine." GG looked at Kip, who had not said anything since they sat down and began the BUDHI.

"And you think I would like that?" Walt asked incredulously. "What is the purpose? It's delusion," said Walt.

"Is it?" Kip said. "Delusion? I know you watch sports on TV with the radio on, so you don't have to listen to fucking Jim Nantz. Watching without some corporate hack narrating is always better. Closer to truth anyway. We think that will get eyeballs, which will pay the bills."

"It reminds me of dialogue in a Robert Altman movie," said Jim. "Or Firesign Theater."

"Welcome to the Future!" said Kip. Walt snorted shook his head.

"Out of the fog, into the smog, he's Nick Danger, Third Eye!"

"There is another technology we are incorporating, which will be out there soon," said GG. "Take video with your phone camera and stream it to your followers – friends, or the world, if they're watching. So the next step will be to incorporate this 'alternate history' with reality and broadcast that."

"We just passed 70 million users," said GG. "We have to start the shutdown or it will freeze and people will see we can't handle it with the existing infrastructure."

"If we are going to make this happen, we have to maintain the illusion that we are in control," said Kip. Until we get the horse-power to keep it going full time…"

"I am starting shutdown," GG said. "We have it under control. Your network out here is very good, Mr. Rehain. It is just like being in Portland."

"Good Christ, I hope it's not like being in Portland!" said Walt. They all laughed.

Suddenly the screen went blank and the clip came on of the girl watching the ocean on the cliff.

She stands and turns, and she says, "It's time to go back now. I'll be right here in the meantime…waiting for you – we will be back very soon..." She put on a pair of sunglasses, and sat down on the cliff again, facing out to the ocean.

"That is so beautiful!" said Alice.

"Eighty-one million real users logged in and actually did something, updated something, in a half hour with no advertising, on a Saturday afternoon," said GG.

"Maybe we won't need your money, Walt," said Kip.

"Bull crap!"

They all turned around. It was Heber – almost cursing! "That was pretty amazing..." Heber looked like he had seen a ghost. "If we are going to hit our horizon, we have to get the money cleared by Monday at noon. Or we lose a month," said Heber, who was shaking. "It...It's pretty amazing..." He looked at Walt, then turned away.

They all sat down in the dining room. GG, dressed like a college girl, sweater, jeans, Chuck Taylor's, was charming Walt and Alice with stories about the software business. Walt kept asking how companies get valued so high with no income, everything was promised. Sign up for free if you like it, subscribe, no receipts, IPOs go for billions? "What is it based on?"

Alice listened intently but was quiet and kept looking over at Jim and Macy, who both talked to Charlotte, who was doubtful about the food, venison and salmon, grilled sweet potatoes, asparagus, etc. Charlotte put on a brave face and nibbled carefully. Rosa was also watching Charlotte, and shaking her head while muttering to herself silently. She clearly didn't like Alice showing up, invading her kitchen.

"It is based on the future, Dad," said Kip. He hadn't called his father Dad or Pop this much since high school.

"Every investment is based on the future, son, that is the definition of investment."

"So does this have a future?" Kip challenged him.

Walt looked at him and shrugged. "It is a lot of money. Best case, we will lose at least $60 K in early withdrawal penalties, having to sell too soon. Right?"

Heber nodded. "Probably a little more, actually."

Walt looked out, thinking and chewing. "The future? I used to think that I knew. Sometimes I think the Bible thumpers might be right, that the world is winding up for a big kapow. But if we prepare too well for that, we are just ensuring its arrival. We have to believe in ourselves. We can keep marching forward. Right?!?" He looked at Charlotte.

"Right!" she said stabbing her fork into the air.

"We'll pull the trigger Monday morning," said Walt. "We're in!"

Chubby and Jim looked at GG. The realization hit them like a ton of bricks and it was as scary as it was exhilarating.

"Rosa - ¿qué hay de postre?" asked Kip.

"A casa hecho helado de la zarzamora," she said.

"I'll go get the good brandy – it will go good with homemade blackberry ice cream," said Kip. "Might as well enjoy being home, right, Dad?"

"You better not fuck this up," said Walt with a whisper.

Chapter 23

SwiftPad is Launched in Portland - At the Bong, lonely Mark finds Solace

Raleigh sat in Chubby's office, looking down over the railing at the enthusiastic, young *SwiftPad* staffers. The BUDHI was shutting down, and they were working on getting ready to disconnect the back-end systems from the Net. He glanced at the company's activity stream on Kip's monitor and saw GG's announcement from the Rehain Compound, that funding was secured, they would all be paid. Since they all had small pieces of the company, everybody was buzzing "IPO," thinking of the small fortunes they might be coming into soon.

They all had another hour or so of shutdown work and then would pull the plug and be off to the bars to celebrate. Raleigh opened a browser window on a live feed of the local Fox affiliate KPW's Ten O'clock News. A reporter outside the Bong was interviewing a trio of vapor-smoking Millennials, including two young women and an intense, wide-eyed guy who probably could almost pass for a young Judge Reinhold, except that he was overweight, had a wispy goatee and puffy, side-of-the-head pompadours crowned with a barber-inspired bald spot. They were a tight crew, though, you could tell by the postures and the faces made by whoever was not speaking at that moment to the camera. The two women were skinny young beauties, perfectly matched, yet visibly opposites, right out of a Gap photo shoot, with heavy eyelids, and who appeared to be alternating the intake of rice cakes and Everclear shots. The Judge look-alike was calling the *SwiftPad* BUDHI "the most important event of my life," while the ladies signaled with derisively animated faces that he was totally full of shit. They alternated mugging for the camera, fingers down throats, each taking a turn to act obsequious toward *SwiftPad*, as the News video turned to them. How fucking pathetic, he thought.

GG was fast becoming a Tech Celebrity. She was the face of the company, so perfectly cast that no one would believe she even worked for *SwiftPad*, much less created it. Raleigh was very pissed off. He had made this whole thing happen, and yet had been pushed aside like so much trash. GG's tweet, "Next time *SwiftPad* comes up it will be a permanent fixture of the Internet," was retweeted more than five million times. Raleigh pulled a bottle of Chubby's Sangria out of the mini-fridge. A couple of the young programmers glanced up at him and seemed to be laughing behind their hands.

Laugh now, he thought. Go ahead and laugh.

He had taken Hadley who he thought was shy, to lunch, but as it happened she wouldn't shut up, so keen on impressing him with her technical chops. They had gone for sandwiches at the Easy Girl Bakery over on 23rd. It was his first visit and the waitress had it going on, mid-to-late 30s, still cute, hint of crow's feet around the eyes, which was nice. She gave him the crow eye, like, "Come on dude, she is your daughter's age," but did it in a way that made it kind of funny. Still – it was an insult he could hang it all on. It enraged and excited him at once.

Hadley told him she could suck anything out of relational tables with sequel queries. No cutesy, innocent double entendre, just a simple fact. She slowly moved her head back and forth. She was just playing him the whole time, he realized, and now he was really mad. He asked her back to his place and she laughed at him. "In Gresham?" She said it like she would get cooties. Who lives out there? He told her he had eight K square feet and she said, So?

Disgusted with her, he thought, It's a fucking mansion – especially compared to the cramped squirrel cages close to town! The backyard bordered the west side of gigantic Blue Lake Park. As for the lake itself, well it sometimes smelled a little ripe. But no matter, he had an indoor pool in the basement. The pool and jacuzzi were next to the panic room, which was his favorite room, soundproofed, reinforced concrete walls, eight inches of steel on the door. He had other toys too.

When Easy Girl brought him his BLT, he knew that soon... soon...things would be rectified.

~~~

That afternoon Mark Ruskin, the GIP Consultant, was lurking around the Bong watching the BUDHI, which was the worst "bar" he had ever had the misfortune to enter. It stunk like mildew and pot – years old, paraquat-tainted pot, the smoky odor permeating everything in the seemingly claustrophobic bar. He had worn his most casual clothes, whole cotton, skin-tight white tee, and stone-washed, super skinny Levi's (that couldn't hide his butt crack). Now it all would need to be dry cleaned.

The whole *SwiftPad* thing was completely stupid to him. There were ten big screens around the "Bar" and (Mark had done a mental inventory) one kind of whiskey, one vodka, one gin, two beers on tap, and Oregon "pinot" poured out of a pitcher. All "crafted" in Portland. Each screen was surrounded by velvet-covered beanbag couches, thick theater curtains around the walls, with lots of cheap Android tablets handy on highly varnished cable-spool tables.

The app could be an asshole. Attacks on the machine were futile. The popular strategy for users was to fool everyone by pretending to be the machine, which made conversations very civil, if nothing else. It was like the beginning of a cocktail party for robots, which slowly evolved into the game Broken Telephone (or Chinese Whispers, although that is now considered derogatory, as the application will clearly point out). Losers fell out and started their own journeys, which enhanced, enriched, degraded or "adjusted" their experience, falling into place as it got closer to what was true for them, but somehow less powerful and distinct as information moved away from its source. By the time the story had moved a certain distance away it was almost unrecognizable. Events from the outside, news, sports, entertainment gossip, etc., also mutated, in most cases not enough to notice, unless you compared it carefully to the original. But by then the world has moved on. The goal was NOT to be isolated in your own little world of course, so everyone would be led back, as they got closer and more comfortable with their true self. While there was no political or cultural bias, no one could agree that it wasn't rigged in some way, because almost all of the choices pleased no one. But as it was clearly seen, it was all randomized and completely unpredictable.

It all made no sense to Mark, who watched as each screen was surrounded by groups who seemed to have their own agendas.

A libertarian grunge team kept trying to push away whatever came their way, and they would seem to be winning, only to be outwitted by the distinct liberal bias of the *SwiftPad* algorithms at the last minute.

The Fine Young Nihilists (a hard-edged band of self-hating, ridiculously bad musicians) had a posse of about fifteen, who had taken over one of the couches.

But the FYN, even if (as they never failed to remind you) they had balls, still, it couldn't hide the fact that their music sucked. Most of their songs used the repetitive, grinding, death rattle that seemed vaguely similar to the chorus of Nirvana's "Smells Like Teen Spirit" (which ironically was playing somewhere in the background), but their songs went nowhere and had no context to anything and always ended with five minutes of nothing or way too much. Their roving gang of bicycle-riding fans, the PNA (Portland Nihilists Auxiliaries) were a tame, smart-aleck bunch who were trying to ratfuck *SwiftPad* by updating their statuses with alcohol-infused, crazed randomizing gibberish, which *SwiftPad* fired back with the steady prose stylings of calm, Victorian Anthony Trollope admonishing a witless footman. On another couch, three Indian geeks, in dhotis and turbans, were a little bouncy, sir, technically correct, elbows high, spin-balling all the way, incomprehensible, even among themselves veering into and out of Hindi, and English. Five snappily attired Chinese men all under the domination of two bespectacled woman in long red slit-skirts, crowded on top of each other like crazed, Macao crapshooters, shouting at each posts, offering addendums and answers (their posts were in English, hence the domination, because the two women appeared to speak no English, yet seemed to be making all the decisions). A machine-generated post told them there were plans to internationalize *SwiftPad* down the road. This news saddened them immensely.

There were eight other groups of highly engaged Portlanders, completely in their own space, half of them unable to not shout and scream, the other half, less animated, but deep into themes that made no sense to Mark. While it seemed like a game, there was no game, and Mark couldn't see the point to anything, a point that everyone else clearly saw.

So Mark walked out of the bar into the parking lot. No way GIP would be interested in this. He wondered if this assignment could possibly benefit him. He understood what he had to do at the KEG, the cost/benefit was clear. But this was just a waste of time. He would be 38 in four days. Jesus, he thought, what happened to my life? He had to start thinking about what kind of assignments he accepted. He still believed in GIP, at least he thought he did. As he got into his Bimmer in the darkened parking lot, his iPhone dinged. He checked his email.

From: suzanne.jenks@us.gip.com
To: mark.ruskin@us.gip.com
Subject: SwiftPad Update and Portland Consolidated E & G

SwiftPad just completed their much ballyhooed demo. Not sure if you had a chance to check any of it out, but according to analysts, it has clearly moved the bar higher. GIP's Senior Team is very impressed. The ramifications are far-reaching, and it is imperative that we put resources toward understanding this company with an eye on a possible acquisition or other move. The technology has serious social implications. GIP senior leadership (and their contacts in other areas) are very concerned that we not miss this opportunity. It is important that you meet LW as soon as it is possible to arrange. He will contact you and identify himself.

I have discussed this with Ken and we both agree that LW should coordinate local tactics regarding Swift-Pad and that you adhere to this protocol.

You are the EYES and EARS of the company. Ken (and I) have implicit trust in your judgment. However, there are extremely important reasons that LW lead operationally.

Continue assignment at Consolidated and report progress. We are hoping you can hold the two forts until we know more. Too many cooks etc. But you must trust and share with LW.

Regards etc.
Suzanne

Mark sat in his Bimmer and cursed, but without using any words, silently or otherwise, that referred to female body parts. He had trained himself not to use the "C" word after calling a woman that in a Sunset Blvd club. She beat up him up pretty badly, and he often wondered if she hadn't actually been a "tranny." But he was angry at Suzanne, and he needed to "direct" that anger and feed off it. He had read about this technique in the self-help business book, *Acquire your Target*, by Will Powers. How do you feed off your anger and re-direct it in an email? With words? Come on, that doesn't work. It doesn't work on a phone conference either, unless you are the boss. He was stuck, and he was still angry. Suzanne had turned Ken against him and was now moving in to be HIS boss. Fuck that, he thought. He needed an idea, a plan to get out from under Suzanne and back reporting directly to Ken. Because in the end that was her message, you are reporting to me and you work with the LW guy, whoever he is.

He thought about Angelica, and God, that was embarrassing. She had come to his hotel room yesterday evening, after work and going to dinner, and she laughed so much, because he was totally on, like he was doing an old *Tonight Show* monologue. They watched TV on the couch, sitting pretty close to each other. Then they had talked about work, big mistake! He had told her that he wanted to introduce the GIP *Social Suite* to the KEG, but she thought it might be too soon. It frustrated him that she didn't understand, so he tried to explain that outsourcing did not mean that the whole staff would get laid off. In fact, he quoted studies showing that two years after most *GIP* outsourcing projects more than 30% of staff remained employed. It was a huge opportunity for someone like Angie. It might even mean a raise for her. But she didn't want to talk about it.

So they watched TV. They made out a little during commercials, but when he went in for it (the big C), she got up suddenly and left, in a hurry. It was mondo awkwardo.

Sitting in his car, outside The Bong, on a Saturday night in a strange town. Very strange. He had never thought it would come to this. He decided to text her.

> MARK: What are u doing Angie?
>
> ANGIE: Getting ready 4 bed.
>
> MARK: I have some news – about what we talked about!
>
> ANGIE: Huh?
>
> MARK: Can I meet u 4 a drnk?
>
> ANGIE: Just come over

He realized he didn't know where she lived. He was pretty sure it was downtown.

> ANGIE: 1125 NW 12th #5

He looked it up – Pearl District – probably $1800–2500/mo. Nice, he thought.

> MARK: Give me 15m

Chapter 24

Angie conspires with Mark to put in New Software at the KEG - Jim and Lester make a Pact

When they got back into Portland late Sunday from the Rehain compound, Jim had no trouble convincing an exhausted Macy that he should go back to his own apartment. They both needed sleep, and Jim was pretty sure they both needed a little space to think. He was beginning to realize what his and Macy's impetuous attraction was beginning to mean. It was all still hazy, and unformed but powerful and he knew it was going to change his life. It felt special, although why, he wasn't sure, but it didn't scare him.

He knew a shit-storm of meetings and posturing by the GIP guy was coming, and he had to come up with a strategy, to think through the next steps. During his six-year GIP career, he had never met or even heard of Mark Ruskin, but that wasn't unusual. It was a big company.

Jim walked down Vista Avenue from Macy's to his apartment, about a quarter mile. It was getting dark. Jim walked up the stairs to his two bedroom plus den and stood at the door looking. He had developed some habits when he was in Germany, during his walkabout from the US Army, when he thought he was being watched.

He always left markers around to track if someone had been inside his apartment or hotel room, a trick he learned watching *Dr. No*, an early 007 movie. Just line up a hair in the door jamb, or a tad of talcum powder on the floor with a slight print, or a document lined up on his desk with a seam in the wallpaper, just slightly off center. Or all three, as he happened to have done when he left his apartment on Friday morning. Back in Germany, he occasionally found what looked like a disturbance, but almost always found a rationale for it. Most of the time it was his fault, failure to follow his own rules. Sometimes it had been Spritzer or Quark looking around while waiting for him. But, he emphatically told himself, they aren't here now.

He entered the apartment and checked his other markers. There was no doubt. He had been hit; someone had come in and looked around. And it was the way he was hit that concerned him. Whoever had been in the apartment had made some very good attempts to put things back, although of course they still missed his markers.

Nothing was missing though, as far as he could tell. He didn't know what it meant or what to do about it, so he filed it away under "other shit to worry about."

Next morning, early, Jim coasted his bike down, ignoring stop signs (there was almost no traffic on the road), and barely had to pedal all the way down to the KEG by the Waterfront. He took his bike up the elevator. Lester was lurking and followed him into his office. It was just 6 A.M.

"Let's get some coffee, Boss."

"Good idea. The Perk was just about to open when I came in."

As they rode the elevator down, Lester said, "We're fucked, Jim."

"Well," Jim thought about his cased apartment and shook his head, "Maybe, but I think we might be a little better than..."

"No. This is different." Les looked at him, and saw he was clueless. "I got an email from Angie this morning, a multiple cluster forward from the GIP asshole to Frank then to Ange, finally flushed down to us."

"I didn't see it," said Jim. He heard his phone jingle. There it was. "Fucking Exchange Server. How long does it take to relay... when did you get it?"

"Late Friday. You weren't copied originally, I don't think, so I relayed it to you just before you came in. I think they are rat-fucking you, which means all of us are getting it up the bung."

"So it would appear...but it's probably just an oversight. Just missed me in the cc: list..."

"Yeah, maybe..." Lester started to say something, then stopped.

Jim looked at Lester and saw he was really disturbed. He continued reading. "Let's see, GIP has generously offered blah blah, Social Cloud Suite – shit! Now it's called GIP-SS; that has a nice ring to it..."

"Sure, if you're setting up a concentration camp," said Lester. "It's that retro-fitted JAMMIT pile of crap they bought two years ago. The best review it got was that GIP's market position makes it a contender, despite technical problems. It is garbage. And it only runs on Windows. They actually retrofitted a Linux package to Windows and then didn't market the software on its original platform!"

"Yeah, I remember hearing about a side deal with Ballmer...and then that VP leaving the company for Redmond."

"Well, not my problem. It is Rodney's baby."

"No Lester, that can't be our attitude – got to work together right?"

"It's bullshit, man!"

"Let's not panic. I'll talk to Angie when she gets in..."

"Didn't you read the whole thread?"

They walked into the Perk coffee shop, ordered and sat down. Jim continued looking at his phone, scrolling down. "They already ordered the servers! No. FUCK! No." He kept reading. "Angie flew to Chicago with the GIP shithead. And she *EXPECTS*??? the systems, as well as the patched OS, to be completely installed and ready by next Monday..." Jim was moving his lips as he read now, "...and GIP is sending one of their 'Top Engineers' to install it." Jim looked over at Lester, who was smiling.

"GIP-SS...I wonder why they dropped the Cloud? I would think that Storm Troopers could fall out of Clouds just as easily."

Jim smiled weakly. He had to pull it together or it could all unravel right here. He had to get himself under control. He was still worried about the break-in at his apartment. Were they bugging him? They? Who? It's not about Germany. is it, after all these years?

"I'll talk to Anaka this morning. This can't…"

"You want some advice?" asked Lester.

Jim looked at Lester and nodded.

"You need do something heroic again, Jim. We are fucked otherwise."

Jim nodded and took a deep breath. "I'll be completely straight with you from here out, at least about our business shit. So, you ready? Gonna take this the right way?"

"OK. Shoot."

"You got to clean up the wiring in the server room. Quickly. Like today."

"You mean data center?"

"Yeah, the 'data center,'" Jim rolled his eyes. "It is a fucking pigsty. Remember what Hunter Thompson said, 'When the going gets weird, the weird turn pro.' We gotta get professional, Lester. If the GIP guy takes a picture of that and our execs see it, they will eat us alive. They will be shocked, shocked that the 'Data Center' looks like a Bangladesh shipbreaking yard. We can't give them a reason to fuck us over. Gotta straighten up and look exceptionally sharp if we are going to ride this out."

"OK. 10-4."

"You want a scone? A chocolate croissant?"

"Yeah, thanks, Boss. I can handle the server room. I'll get it in shape today."

Jim took Lester's advice and went into the only "hero" mode he knew, which was working his ass off. First he prepared the ground for the introduction of the social groupware software GIP-SS into the KEG. He organized a beta-test group/user committee and connected them up with an online version of the product to practice and begin figuring it out. He got Rodney to commit to getting the Windows OS patched and ready even if he had to work all weekend. The boxes arrived on Wednesday right on schedule, thin, vertically racked GIPBlades, fortunately shipped exactly to spec. Jim personally took over the racking, the network installation and configurations, and had them ready for OS by Friday morning.

In between it all, he got Larry Yang started writing up an integration architecture of his customized messaging systems, telling him that there was no way that GIP-SS would replace his stuff. The business would stop if they did. Larry understood that it was just for show, but as usual, he was very discouraged.

Jim took the whole team out for dinner on Thursday and charged it to the KEG (almost $1500). That was when he finally met the lesbian DBAs. Janice pulled him aside, and Rainy stood in front of them, like a bouncer.

"So you used to fuck Angie in the eleventh-floor conference room?"

"What?"

"Don't worry about it. Everybody knows."

"Bullshit."

Rainy turned around and looked at him, and nodded.

"So boss – she doesn't know that we know. So don't tell her we know, or I'll tell her you told us. Cause we know other shit too," she said. "Just so you know – we know."

"I don't think boss Jim here likes having a couple of dykes own his balls," said Rainy over her shoulder.

"No, he doesn't," said Jim. "But the boss doesn't see a problem, at least not so far. I would just suggest that you don't push him too far." He didn't try to sound dangerous and that seemed to concern them both, as if Meyer Lansky had told one of his capos that perhaps someone might have miscounted on the light side. Jim and Rainy kept their eyes locked on each other as he walked back to the table.

"Good work on getting the GIP database schema setup by the way," he said.

"Thanks. Did you ask permission to buy this dinner?"

"No, let them suck on it." Big cheer from the team; everybody ordered more drinks and desserts. Janice looked at him and laughed.

Angie got back from Chicago and came into the office Friday afternoon. Jim saw her as he walked by her office. He smiled, and she reddened a little and waved him into his office.

"I got your email and it is amazing you got the prep work done for GIP-SS. I wasn't expecting..."

"Weren't expecting what?" Jim got a sudden, cruel impulse to singe her a bit. "That we could do it or that we would do it?"

"No – I – I – should have talked to you before I left, but it was so sudden..." Angie looked down, her cheeks suddenly reddened.

Jim looked at her quizzically.

"This conference came up and Mark thought it would be good if we started getting to know some of the..."

"It's good that you went," Jim said. She's fucking him, he thought.

"Anyway, I have some bad news," she said, her voice shaking a little. "We can't install yet. I should have told you from Chicago, but I didn't believe it either...I didn't..."

Jim knew that she was trying to say she overloaded him, thinking he would fail and she would have her foot on his throat.

"Their software has been hacked," she said, "seriously breached and they don't seem to know how. GIP is shutting down their own implementation of the Social Suite, the one that their employees use, worldwide and at their corporate site and some big customers are...they are advising us not to go forward yet."

Jim listened and nodded politely. "I was talking to Lester, and he has some ideas about re-imaging those boxes with Linux and putting in..."

"No, no. We can't do that, accounting issues, you know. So we are going to switch gears and we are going to attack staffing up front. That is the biggie so we might as well face it sooner rather than...up front."

"I guess I'll see you Monday."

Jim had won the first scrimmage, but now he knew the big guns were coming.

Chapter 25

Tyler, in Der Große Tiergarten, Exchanges Information with Renate

A great deal had happened to Trek (Tyler Ambrose, "Sebastian," now codenamed OSWL, pronounced "Oswald," the secret meaning being, "Oh Shit We're Lost!") since he had disappeared from Cynthia's (GG) life five years ago. His left earring hole had healed (and the scar surgically removed) and he had gone into deep cover for the Company. His alter ego in the NSA didn't even acknowledge his CIA connections or his direct link to "Waterfall," who was some person or persons on the staff in the White House. Trek pretended to trust Waterfall and sent him (or her) semi-regular status updates on his search for other Snowdens – potential leakers and Cyber-scofflaws within the National Intel Community. It was an easy list to make, since there are over four million people in the US with "Top Secret" clearance.

Trek had changed his appearance since his days living with Cyn (she was never Goth Girl to him). Even though he patched his earring hole, he was careful not to look too normal or nondescript, because that was a tell-tale sign as well. He drove a Bronco, wore fashionably sheared-off at the ankle Desert Storm boots, with his khaki pants and golf shirts, mostly white but sometimes blue or even green. So he was visible and above the radar, a pose that he felt necessary to avoid scrutiny. He had light brown hair that he kept medium short and wore small semi-rectangular, rimless spectacles, but only indoors when he might need them to read. He was thin and ran six miles nearly every morning.

His reason for disappearing so suddenly from Cynthia's life five years ago (and dropping the tag "Trek") was somewhat bureaucratic. He had switched his identity when he switched employers. NSA didn't know his connection with the CIA, and he remained on contract with them while pursing "academic research." It was through the CIA that he went around the NSA in his communications with the executive branch's Waterfall, who contacted his codename OSWL through a thick layer of crafty technical means that ensured mutual anonymity. Someone at the White House even asked him to change his code name (suggestion: "VAPOR") but even though he never acknowledged this, the memos were now addressed to VAPOR. He continued to sign his replies OSWL. He didn't know who Waterfall was, but he was pretty sure he or she was annoyed by his loyalty to his old codename. He deliberately didn't speculate on it, so it would not influence his product. They maintained separation and while he knew that he was probably on a medium-short list of potential OSWLs or VAPORS (he was sure Waterfall speculated!)...he didn't worry about it. He was above board in all respects and had even passed on some valuable information to Waterfall. Most of his "product," even though logical and seeming to support the Obama Administration's suspected inklings, was completely unsubstantiated and unverifiable. In other words, they could take it or leave it but it wasn't traceable to him. He thought it likely he would be caught eventually and always had his story clean and his sources deeply buried.

What Tyler (or OSWL) didn't say was that he had worked closely with Ed Snowden and was trying to sneak away from that fact. He knew there was no official "paper" (or electronic) trail between Ed and himself, at least none that any of them could follow. Ed of course knew who he was, but unless he was captured alive by Team 6 and tortured, Tyler didn't worry about exposure from that angle.

Ed was a true believer and he had envied him for that. But he still thought it safer to begin removing himself from that line of fire.

The price of his entry into this world had been the shedding his sketchy friends, which was a pretty high price. He was still infatuated with Cyn, but he had to admit she had been too young when he had seduced her and realized it could have turned out a lot worse than it did, because who knows what a 17-year-old girl is capable of? He never liked her GG moniker, it sounded like a cross between a French whore and a Southampton Trust Fund baby, so he watched her career from afar, sometimes very close, down to the keystroke. She was one of the best at evading electronic detection and their cat and mouse game gave them both more than mental stimulation. But eventually he started "cheating." He hacked Cynthia the easy way, just dipped into her NSA electronic profile. He had to do a lot of modification to counter her maskings, but it involved some advanced filtering of the big national data dump. He didn't need old school stealth for that.

Attack and counterattack methods were being hacked and morphed almost by the hour and to keep up was a full-time job that he didn't want to do anymore. When Cyn got corporate, even though it was *SwiftPad*-style corporate, she got easy to track. She was almost promoting her public identity. So there was little sport in it after a while, but he still checked her out.

Tyler's working moniker was Sebastian now, and he knew the only way to maintain it all was never to be out of character. His relationship to the great intel breaches of the twenty-first century, WikiLeaks and Snowden, was complicated. His day job with the Agency (no one called it the Company anymore) was overseeing the NSA electronic monitoring intercepts in Europe, which mostly meant Germany. His story, his self-defined assignment, was to prove someone in German intel provided deep cover, as well as moral and material support, to Snowden and Assange. There was just enough of the anti-Old-Europe crowd still in the woodwork to support his quest. So he informed his handlers he needed to stay in touch if they were going to figure out who helped steal the horses once the barn door was opened. The Open Secrets Movement was very strong politically in Germany, especially among the Greens (*Die Grünen*).

He landed in Hamburg and then got on the *Hochgeschwindigkeitsbahn* to Berlin (175 miles by train, only 90 minutes) to access the target. He was into some serious double agent shit now, he thought. Next stop crazy town, because Berlin is mucho *verrückt*. As the flat northern German countryside flashed by, he thought it looked so normal, so picturesque and well kept. This was his second trip to Berlin in the last three months and justifying it required all his skills as a fabricator and dissembler to feed his pay masters in Langley. He had never had so much fun on a weekend as he had on his last trip to the *Haupstadt*, when he had first met his German contact.

Now he was going back to meet her again, right under the nose of all the CIA and all the *Bundesnachrichtendienst* agents who they both knew would be watching them. It gave them both a pornographic sense of exhibitionist thrill. She took pride in it even though she was one of the most active Deep Digital Throats in the world. Nobody dared touch her.

He made his way to edge of the Tiergarten, across the big lawn in front of the Reichstag. He stood slightly hidden in the trees watching her walk toward him. She was older than he was by at least ten years, but she looked amazing. He hardened by the second as she approached.

"Let's go deeper into the trees," Renate Haspinger said. She was Ulrike Von Drossel's campaign manager, chief of staff and alleged lover, although that wasn't exactly true. In the final analysis, she liked men better, even if it was inconvenient for her politically. "So in what way am I to help you slander myself to your spy masters, Sebastian?" she asked, as her hand slipped into his loosely belted khakis, dropping a memory stick into his pocket on the way.

Renate had had an interesting career since her time as an East German honey pot for American soldiers during the waning days of the Cold War. She had only been 19 when the Wall fell.

"What's it really about?" she purred in his ear.

"It's an inside business deal," as his hands slipped around her hips, "The equity takeover firm, the Crockett Group, has hired

GIP to destroy a small power company so they could buy them and – our friend is standing in their way. They want to ruin him by saying he was a spy for your people when he was a soldier. Or even a serial killer!"

"GIP! Can't you control them?"

"Oh my God! Oh Jesus, don't stop!"

Renate pulled her head up and looked at him. "It must have been in a file. Your perverts listened in on our innocent lovemaking. Perhaps a certain Captain Graham, now a General in line for a position on your aptly named 'Joint Chiefs of Staff' might be useful to you?"

"I wasn't asking..." Renate got back to the main business. They heard feet tramping nearby on the tangled edge of Berlin's wooded Tiergarten, but ignored it.

"Oh yes you were," she said as she slid her hips up, aligning for interlock. "I know what you want from me. Out myself publicly, document his innocence after he is slandered? Provide a little leverage to keep your generals under control? Are you trying to trap the villains at GIP? Or me? I have nothing to hide. My past is public. I have even discussed some of this on television."

German television. For some reason Tyler thought of the "Blue Man" group. He pushed his hands under the back of her jeans.

"In any event, my friends here will find all of this amusing and irrelevant if you out me. Tell me, *Liebling*, what do you want me to do?" She suddenly stood, pulling him up, and dragged him further into the woods, his pants held up by one hand, far away from the huge lawn in front of the Reichstag, deeper into the Tiergarten.

"We have stumbled into the gingerbread house Gretel," he said as they settled in a grassy little clearing, and quickly stripped for action. "It is an egregious breach of trust by GIP, using their contract with us to steal information. It plays into your stereotype of us, a cowboy-corporate-government operation that ruins human beings for the betterment of profits..."

"Yes, we know things are done most strictly in Amerika! This line of reasoning has a certain humorous aspect to it that perhaps..." Renate rolled him over like an Olympic wrestler, driving him to ecstasy. Their copse boudoir was immaculate, not a stray plastic spoon or condom to be seen anywhere.

"I doubt that it will come to anything. I can handle it…I think." He lifted her with a wrestler's bridge, driving the pressure to their respective nexus points. "But there is a suspicion that Jim Hunt has. been raping and killing women since his return from his stay in your country during the 1980s. Is there anything you might…"

"…There are reports, detailed specific reports, but I have never seen them. So I can't say, do you understand," she arched her back and groaned. "But I can tell you simply – Jim Hunt was not a spy – for anybody. He was and I suspect still is incapable of lying. I was a double, and worked for the West the whole time and did much to…" Her head arched back as Tyler found the spot, "undress the *Abteilung* – oh…" That was her story, the only one he really had to stick to – the rest could be tailored with facts.

It was some time before they discussed business again. Renate told him that her experience working for the East Germans convinced her that for the good of society all state secrets should always be exposed. No exceptions. Tyler (or rather Sebastian) agreed, but said that the German electorate was much more educable and flexible than the Americans, because when there were only two parties there could only be two positions, so distinctions were never properly understood. They just got put into the US electoral blender. Of course, said Renate, but don't be so certain that German elections will always turn out so well.

Tyler gave her the specs for the "backdoors" in the new Jupiter switches that were going into US Internet exchange points on a micro memory stick. He was almost sure the Germans already had this info, but at least it would cement a layer of trust between them.

They heard groups of school children tromping nearby but as soon as they came close, they veered away, often with giggles and ribald comments. No one seemed to begrudge love in the Tiergarten in late afternoon. They had completed their exchange and finished dressing.

"I will protect your General. If you want to punish GIP, I will help you with that too, if it comes to it. If required, I can prove that

Jim Hunt was not a spy for the East. Serial killer? Jim? Oh please…"
He knew she was about to tell him that the real serial killers were
in the Pentagon, or White House, but she spared him. Not that he
wouldn't agree with her, but it was just tiresome and futile in the
end. "He is completely normal. A real normal Amerikan, a state all
of you strive for every waking moment. You are all so normal – It
must be the American moral imperative? Your highest calling, no?
We were both young after all…you however – you could be a serial
killer – that I would believe."

Chapter 26

Mark, Clearly Disturbed, gets his marching orders to proceed with Outsourcing the KEG's IT Team

The weekend following the BUDHI, Mark left his beloved Bimmer in the Marriott hotel garage, took the Red Line MAX to PDX and then flew down to LAX for a long weekend. He grabbed a van going up Lincoln Boulevard back to his apartment in Santa Monica. Saturday and Sunday he stayed in, lay on his couch and aimlessly channel-surfed with sound off while he listened to Zig Ziglar self-improvement audios and read the new Will Powers business/sales self-help book, *Full Automatic*, or *How to Blow Away the Competition*. His normal cycle of Santa Monica life was completely off – he didn't work out on the grass strip along Ocean Avenue or in the Hollywood LA Fitness gym. He didn't go hang at clubs on Sunset. The new twist to the assignment in Portland had him bummed out. After a week of sleeping with Angie, sex was the last thing he wanted to spend time chasing, and anyway, he realized he was nothing without his Bimmer.

He had a conference call coming up. It was Monday morning and he still hadn't booked a return to Oregon. He really didn't want to join the call because he had nothing good to report. The staff at the KEG, especially that traitor Hunt, had been dragging their feet, running out the clock. DeFonzaro had been AWOL. He really wanted it all to go away. Even Angie – damn it – she wasn't what he wanted – she was exactly what he had been avoiding and now… if he dropped the hammer, what would she do? She was a fuck-ing emotional basket case. He would be thrown off the project, or would have to leave and then what? If he stayed…then what?

It was 6 A.M. and cool with his patio door opened. He waited for his Keurig mocha and thought about Angie and what his week in Chicago had actually meant. He came back to LA to get away and think, because she didn't fit. In Chicago every night had gone the same, grope, robot sex, stare at the ceiling, sleep. It continued last week until Thursday, when he finally booked a flight out of Portland. It was so great to finally land at LAX. But now it was Monday. FUCK!

From every angle, it made no sense. What was wrong with him? Angie wasn't a decision maker, but she had kept that fact down low so as not to get Mark in trouble with the GIP sales guys, but they clearly suspected she was not important and they didn't seem happy using the Marketing Development account to fly her to Chicago. Mark was sure they had told Ken Oren their concerns and he worried it would blow back on him.

Angie had told him she was tired of working at Consolidated. She had been there near 20 years and he didn't help things when he told her it was a done deal that her department was going to be eliminated in a few months. He told her he would help her "land on her feet." She said, "Well, I didn't land on my feet in bed with you last night."

Looking out at the Pacific, he realized he should have laughed when she made that comment, that she must have meant it as a joke. Was she saying she didn't have an orgasm? Or maybe she had hoped he would get her a job at GIP? Women were such a pain in the ass to figure out.

Angie had dimples, but almost no visible cheekbones.

He dialed in.

"Who's on?"

"It's me, Mark. Hi, Persi."

"Good morning Mark! Are you in Oreegone?"

"No, came back to LA to take care of some things and going back up tomorrow."

"I hear you were in Chicago last week. You should have called; we could have had lunch."

"I was overwhelmed, so much going on, but you're right, I should have…"

"Well next time."

His boss, whom he had never met, didn't seem too upset, and he had worried she would be. In fact, he thought, she almost sounded relieved.

BIP.

"Hi, it's Ken. I have Mary O'Hara from the Crockett Group on speaker with me."

"Hi, Ken. Welcome, Mary. Let's get started. Suzanne?"

"Let's get a report from software from David Bromfield."

"Hi, everybody, David here. I read Suzanne's report on the Consolidated Energy Project, so we know that the security problem we ran into with the Social Cloud affects you. FYI, we are re-badging GIP-SS back to Social Cloud. Pretty intense discussions about that during Senior Staff! One of the marketing VPs had a Chevy Super Sport as a teenager, and thought they could get market spill-over, but focus group tests showed it didn't play. In any event, the first indication is that the vendor that sold us the product left some back doors, so anybody who knew how to open them could log in as administrator. We are trying to trace it; it is pretty serious. Theoretically anybody could have added more access or maliciously done anything to our customers' data."

"My God! That is horrible!"

"Worse than that, the hack was left on a black hat chat site."

"Wasn't the previous vendor Jammit? Are we suing them?"

"We are not suing anybody!" Ken jumped in hard. "We are trying to shut this down with no publicity. This is all absolutely on the QT. There is to be NO discussion of this with anyone." Ken paused, for effect. "Does everyone understand? All attendees here will be logged. If it gets leaked, we look for leakers here. Does everyone understand?"

Simultaneous mumbles of "Yes," "Yep," "Gotya," "Understood," and "Uh huh."

"What's the ETA for resolution?"

"End of third quarter."

"This year?" asked Mark. This got a big nervous laugh, which he hadn't intended. Either way, nearly five months out, it might as well be next year as far the Consolidated Electric and Gas project was concerned. He half listened as the software guy detailed all of the steps they were taking to fix the problem, returning to the original, unpatched code, more developers, overseas problems, communication issues, etc. It appeared the decision to outsource development for the Social Cloud was hindering progress. Mark kept quiet. Nothing he said could be useful at this point.

"Well, that is unfortunate. But for our project in Portland it actually simplifies things, right, Mark?"

"Yes, Ken, we need to focus on labor, on their Info Tech staffing in operations."

"Exactly! Mary, I believe you have some comments to make about this aspect?"

"Thanks, Ken. I guess ya'all can te-ell I'm from Texas. We pride ourselves in our knowledge of the In-er-gee bidness. And we think that this here company up in Orreegan can be the ree-all dee-all. If we can jes' get costs down, I think it's ours for $10–12 a share. The ratios look great. We know we can run this company from anywhere for half what they are spending. That is all profit! I understand you are herding them in that direction?"

"We have our best guy on it," said Ken. "Mark, could you give us a status report?"

"Hi Mary, it's great that you are joining our team." Mark paused and felt like he was on the precipice of a…of something…But…he had trouble gathering his thoughts…

"Thank you, Mark. I want you to know that our group is gonna git after anything you need. We'll handle 'the dirty work,' if you git what I mean…"

They were waiting for him. Dirty work? He decided to let that go. "I don't see any significant obstacles. We have management from the CEO, Finance, and the CIO on board. Even the Infrastructure manager is a former GIP employee."

"So you are confident they are all on board?"

"Yeess. I think so," said Mark. Shit, what else could he say? Tell them he had been playing hide the weenie with a key player for the customer, and now that was about to go south? "There are some people who are not happy with us, even though we have not proposed anything yet. But rumors are just that. I have not approached Jim Hunt yet. I have talked to him, but not about... the benefits of working with us – personally – not me personally – personally for him I mean."

There was silence for almost ten seconds. "It sounds like you have it under control. Right?"

"Well..." Mark looked out at the Pacific, and saw a flashing light. He looked for a plane, he thought it must be, although... in the perfectly clear Southern California sky he saw nothing to explain the light. "We need to get Hunt on board. That is the linchpin." Mark put his phone on mute and took a deep breath. He was hyperventilating.

"Mark...?" asked Persi in a worried tone.

"I am sure you have many tools which you can apply. Right, Ken?" Mary sounded worried.

"Yes, we do," said Ken Oren. "We have to convince Mr. Hunt it would be to everyone's best interest that he support our initiative. Just so you know Mark, Mary's group has a couple of operatives in Portland now and have been unobtrusively looking into Hunt, just an FYI to keep options open...We...let's say we'll have a backup plan if things get sticky. Mark, I'll be in touch next week, and we can discuss our 'Jim Hunt strategy.'"

"No problem."

"That sounds great, Ken," said Mary. "Crockett has just the resources required for this backup plan. We are red-dy to go! We'll follow up with contractual issues as soon as this is settled. Great meet-in ya'all. This is gonna be just great!"

Chapter 27

Jim Stalls Takeover by GIP - Raleigh leaves SwiftPad

Jim's work was stopped. Via a terse email from Angelica (she stopped signing her emails Angie), citing a copied note from Frank DeFonzaro, his team was forbidden from pursuing any projects at the KEG beyond routine maintenance of existing applications. Since yesterday most of Jim's crew had been away from their desks, doing "extended desktop support," which meant working directly with managers in other departments, doing custom work, hoping that when the boom gets lowered, they could possibly land in another department as technical support. They all thought their jobs would be eliminated in a few days.

Jim sat through endless meetings with Mark, where Angie would often join late and leave early. Mark insisted on stepping through the duties *ad nauseum* of the whole staff, along with their skills and history with the company. At each meeting Mark would come with a list of names from top to bottom. It was of course implied that the bottom dwellers would be shown the door. And Jim would then talk up the merits of the bottom dwellers, explaining why they were indispensable, stalling for time, pulling Mark off topic, encouraging talk about his old company (GIP) and people who they might know in common (a very short and inconsequential list), breaking abruptly for coffee or to pee at those moments that threatened to be a decisive point, only to do it again, another meeting, in a couple of days with a new list, the order slightly jumbled, with new bottom dwellers to defend. Jim felt like Scheherazade, telling a new story each time to put off the inevitable. He hated it, and racked his brain for a breakout strategy, but for the time being he didn't have one. He knew he had enough support on the thirteenth floor to keep up the delay for a while longer, so for the time being he smiled and continued to delay.

Watching Angelica together with Mark, though, his first thought was Bridget Jones, sans accent. Her awkwardness got worse by the day, as if he and Ruskin were civilized rivals getting set to fight over her. Jim laughed to himself, realizing that if Mark was Mark Darcy, then he must be the Hugh Grant asshole. He didn't want to be either, although it could be worse, he thought.

"What is it, Jim?" Angie asked, as he smiled to himself during a particularly long vacuum of silence, as the three of them sat together in the fluorescence-lit, windowless, glass-enclosed meeting closet.

"Oh – just something Lester said. The team knows we are talking about outsourcing their jobs and they are getting pretty macabre about it."

A cold look from both Bridget and Darcy. How dare he!

"Jim, GIP is working to save the company, to actually strengthen it," said the top barrister. "It will mean that their jobs are actually more secure, when this is over…"

This is where Jim thought to scream "bullshit," but he knew he had to play it straight if he was going to keep the "Thousand and One Nights" going that would put off the inevitable. He nodded and fought back the cynical laughter.

After a particularly brutal meeting, which accomplished less than nothing, she would keep the three of them together, and she talked, without regard to what she was saying. Angie read a memo from DeFonzaro verbatim, and then posed questions that had no relationship to what she just read. Mark would then give long detailed answers, talking about the importance of "business continuity," while stressing the importance of economic operational efficiency.

Jim tuned them both out completely, nodding, and pretending to take notes. He had never seen lovers use so much passive voice with each other before, but then he had only been to London once. So many opportunities for Chaucerian ribaldry, all beaten back into his filthy imagination. The last thing he wanted was for Angie to have a meltdown. That would break the spell and Scheherazade would be sent to the chopping block for sure. It was a fucking horror show, and he immediately went for a run afterward just to take a shower.

~~~

"Come on, hurry up and get dressed. Are we going out to eat tonight after the Board meeting?"

"I don't think I'll be too hungry..." Jim sat on the couch with Charlotte as they put together another mobile, this one of an old lady in a hoop skirt being chased by a mouse, the mouse being chased by a cat, which was being chased by a dog, which was being chased by a Charlie Chaplin cop, who was being chased by the old lady in the hoop skirt.

"We'll just cook up some frozen jiaozi later..." Jim looked at Macy, who seemed in another world. "We better use the leftovers," she said.

"Why is the lady chasing the policeman?" Charlotte asked.

"It's probably his wife," said Jim, wondering why we had to suddenly use the leftovers.

"But why would his wife chase him?"

"Maybe he forgot to put the toilet seat down," said Jim in a loud voice, trying to get a rise out of Macy. Nothing.

"That's stupid."

"Yes. It is stupid, Charlotte. But your mommy looks nice, doesn't she?" Jim said.

"I guess."

"OK – to bed with you," Macy came in and grabbed her hand without looking at Jim. "Come on, the sitter will be here any minute."

"Another *SwiftPad* Board meeting already. I guess it's been a month since we met," Jim said. Macy stopped for a second, as if she wanted to say something, then continued brushing Charlotte's hair. "OK, Charlotte, where should we hang it up?" asked Jim, unwittingly inviting Charlotte to ignore her mother.

"Right there," she said, pointing at the ceiling.

"Don't you want it in your room?"

"No! It's too ugly."

"We can talk about it tomorrow," said Macy.

"I think your mother wants me to get dressed and comb my hair so we can leave."

"Where are you going? Are you going to the stupid art store too?"

"Yes. I'll be at a meeting there."

"Meeting...blah blah blah!"

"Exactly!"

"Carry me to my room," she asked Jim. Macy made sad eyes that she chose Jim, but Charlotte ignored her.

"You are too big. Come on."

They walked into Charlotte's room and she got into bed.

"Do you like my mommy?"

"Yes, I like your mom very much."

"Do you love my mommy?"

"Yes."

"Are you sure?"

"Yes. I am sure."

"Good."

"Good night, Charlotte." Jim had a vague fear as he turned off the light.

Walt's money, twenty million dollars, was already spent and there were lots of blips and hiccups in the process. They took over three more data centers, one in LA (a recently bankrupted gaming company that reneged on their original agreement to leave the power conditioners and battery backups), one in Taiwan and one in Spain and even now, a month later, they were still working on the image ghosting of the machines and that only seemed to work 80%

of the time. In the meantime they were looking to lease space up the Columbia in The Dalles. Everyone says "easy!" until you get to the details. Google had bought up every site and it no longer made as much economic sense as it once did. The days of cheap hosting were long past.

Heber was able to get another fifteen million in financing but at a murderous rate.

Chubby had been working on it eighteen hours every day and Jim had been helping him at night more and more, especially since he was stuck and frustrated at the KEG. Jim left work early almost every day, worn out from deliriously dreary meetings with Mark, and rode his bike over to the Nikolai *SwiftPad* office. And even when at the KEG, he spent a lot of time reviewing projects for Chubby. Spending twenty (now thirty-five) million bucks in a month, wisely, isn't easy. Jim was being pulled in deeper, and was thinking of taking the *SwiftPad* off-ramp from the corporate knife fighting at the KEG.

Macy and Jim rode their bikes down to the gallery, Macy's skirt hiked up, Jim coasting with his arms folded, letting the wind rush through his hair. They zipped down the hill, getting there just in time for Macy to open her wine and cheese bar and for Jim to join the meeting in the back, which had already started.

"So..." said Hariet, "I don't know much, but I do know that the most important factor in any business is timing. I don't know anything about this Internet thing, but I do know that nothing lasts forever. By my count we, all of us, have invested almost 60 million dollars into this venture. Are we ready to begin whatever it is we are beginning?"

Seb Madison, the Nike guy, looked at Mike Kendrick, the Intel guy, who looked at Mitsuro and then they all looked at GG.

"We are scheduled to go totally, completely and permanently live next week. It will be worth it, because we have really improved the product in the last month. We finally have a solid method that allows us to change, test and promote – one that works."

GG had recently turned 27, and looked older, in spite of her retro fashion accessories. Chubby looked at her, and for a moment thought of the hookers in the restaurant the night he met GG. He had been chasing down loose business threads, day and night, for the last month. All he could do was nod. And then smile. "The system is snappy. The testing has been almost perfect. The staff is exhausted, but excited. We are driving them and they have taken the bit. Everybody's working and talking to each other. We have chased every bug...I think it's ready. It wasn't that bad before and I know it is much, much better now. And, Jim, without your help we couldn't have..."

Jim waved Kip's praise off.

"So, Heber," asked Cook Callahan, who had been plugging *SwiftPad* on his blog and radio show, although to be fair he always gave a "full disclosure, I am on the board of the *SwiftPad* organization," not mentioning that being on the board might be lucrative for him, "what are we worth?"

"Two conservative market analysts, both of whom have been on the money more often than not, say if we go public now, we each will make about nine million on just our pro forma share options. So for you, Cook, for your 'sweat equity' of attending board meetings, that is about what it will be worth to you. Be advised, taxes will kill you."

"Wow!"

"However, if we wait and if it is successful, like everyone seems to think it might be, I don't know, 10–20 times that. Or more..."

"What about just selling it...are we getting outright offers?"

"That is a good question. I think we should discuss that after it goes live...we are getting some interesting nibbles. Amazon is the most likely suitor, if we wait and see some success, a huge return. If we sell it then, we'll get about the same relative bump. But then there is the risk..."

"...Of getting fucked a whole bunch of ways. I think we should put it up for sale now, before we fire it up. That way if it blows, we at least get something." It was Raleigh, who had been sitting in the corner and hadn't said a word. He knew he was resented, because he hadn't come through at all. He delivered none of the seed money he promised. The staff was completely creeped out by him after his "date" with Hadley. And now he looked like he hadn't slept in a week. His clothes were disheveled, his hair was flopped over, revealing a rather large, inflamed bald spot. Almost overnight he went from looking in his late forties to mid-sixties. Even though he sat away from the table, he emitted a strong medicine odor that surrounded him like a force field. His arms were still like dock ropes but his chest had lost its solid definition under his tight powder-blue Banlon short-sleeve pullover.

Heber held up his hand to quickly stop the murmuring and rising anger in the room. "OK, before we proceed with THAT motion, Jim, could you leave the room? We need to decide first who gets to vote on what we do. Jim has been *ad hoc* up until now. We need to formally decide if he is a full board member."

"I need a refill anyway," Jim held up his glass as he walked out.

Once Jim left, Heber asked, "Is Jim Hunt a partner?"

"Yes," said Kip. "You were there, Heb, when my dad put up the money. Whose opinion did he he base it on? Wasn't mine as much as it was Jim's. Besides, since Raleigh checked out, Jim was the only one reviewing the infrastructure requirements and verifying them. I couldn't have done it. For lots of reasons he is a full partner."

"What do you mean, 'checked out'?" Raleigh stood up, but Chubby didn't even acknowledge him. "I'm talking to you, Kippy boy!"

Kip measured him with narrow eyes. "If you weren't so pathetic, I'd beat the shit out of you as you stand. You are a fucking creep. I vote that we give this chump some money and his walking papers."

"Do you want out, Raleigh?" asked Heber.

"I want 10 million dollars now."

"What?"

"I've been with this since the very beginning. I was there when Cynthia and Kip met and planned this. Remember that night? You took my card! GG! Code Queen! Remember?" He shook his head with contempt and laughed. "I helped design the pilot infrastructure, which is basically what we rolled out. I have been onsite for all of the launchings. I want 10 mil or I sue."

There was silence. Hariet hit the table with her fist.

"I'll write you a check right now for five million dollars, if you sign off all other rights and get out," said Hariet. "Right now! Take it or leave it."

"Earliest we can do it is tomorrow morning. I need to get the papers written up," said Heber.

"OK. Tomorrow. I'll write the check right now. Heber, here, see what am doing?"

She waved the check at Raleigh and handed it to Heber.

"Starbucks across the street. Ten A.M." said Heber.

"Make it a cashier's check."

"Sure, Raleigh. We'll make it a cashier's check."

"OK. I'll be there." At that Raleigh got up and left.

Meanwhile, out in the Gallery, Jim was leaning against a pillar watching Macy chat up the art patrons as she poured wine. She seemed sad tonight for some reason. He thought about Charlotte's question, "Do you love her?"

"Yes," he whispered softly to himself. "Yes, I do."

He saw her in a reflection watching him. He turned to look at her and saw she had tears in her eyes.

Raleigh came down the stairs from the office and slowly walked toward the door. He looked like shit, Jim thought. What happened to him? Jim slipped behind a pillar as Raleigh looked around the room and then Jim saw him stop and stare at Macy. She looked up at him in horror as he smiled.

Then he was gone.

Chapter 28

The Easy Girl leaves the Bake Shop early with a Gentlemen Caller

After his date with Hadley, Raleigh had returned to the Easy Girl Bakery three times, the first time unaccompanied, smiling slightly, only making brief eye contact with Elizabeth once and then leaving a good tip. Two days later he showed up about 2 P.M. There were only four or five other people there, and he and Elizabeth, the Easy Girl, made small talk about the weather and flirted a bit.

Raleigh listened as she told him that she had left all of her unhappiness in Indiana, and that she loved Portland because everyone was so nice. She said that Portland attracted "Good Souls." He had noticed the picture on the wall from the 2010 Sturgis Motorcycle Rally in the Black Hills. She sat cross-legged in front of a Harley, while two young men stood behind the bike, wearing colorful bandannas and aviator shades. In spite of their attire they didn't look like motorcycle guys. She said she missed riding, and that she hadn't been on a "Sickle" in two years.

Raleigh was low key, whimsical, a bit melancholic, very humble, but not falsely modest. He described his business success as if it was partially a curse. Mostly he listened, acted wistful and wise, and when it came time to make the next move, he backed off, kindly, sheepishly, gently with an almost unspoken promise to be back. People who knew him would not have recognized him.

He decided it had to be a Harley.

He started scanning Facebook and senior citizen chat sites for Harley owners, looking at pictures, tracing user names. *SwiftPad* was no help, and he didn't understand how it worked anyway. Finally, on the "Old Dudes on Bikes" chat site, he found a retired geezer from Forest Grove had a beauty, just what he was looking for, an 883 SuperLow, next to a picture of his old, slightly fat wife. Their friends in Hawaii said – "See you in two weeks" and he replied "We'll be there!" Today was then plus 15 days.

Raleigh put on a white shirt and dark tie, and grabbed some Mormon literature from the front of a local LDS Church and knocked on the door just as the sun was going down, peeked in the windows, and noticed that they advertised what alarm system they used. He peeked in the garage window; there it was. No one answered the door.

Raleigh took his time, disabled the alarm, cased the house, found the keys and the old guy's leathers. They were a little loose, but otherwise fit. He had his own black, calfskin gloves. He quietly pushed the garage door up, moved the bike out and then slowly, quietly closed the door. He coasted the bike down the driveway and pushed it up the block and around the corner and then started it and rode it back into Portland.

Two days later he showed up at the Easy Girl Bakery a third time, on the first Thursday in June, at 2:50 P.M., about 10 minutes before she was going to close.

"Wow! What's that you got out there?"

He just smiled as he looked at her with a slight grin.

"SuperLow! You don't see many of those in Portland." Elizabeth took off her apron and hairnet and shook out her brunette mane. Her eyes sparkled with excitement.

"I guess not." He looked at her as if he was steeling up his courage. "You got plans?" Raleigh acted shy, carefully keeping himself away from the window with his back to the door, as he held his black helmet on his hip with his hand, "You want to take a ride?"

"I have to close up…" She looked at the bike and then at him. He enigmatically smiled.

"Let me help…"

She had a few things to do in the back, wrap up a pie, give the counters a quick once-over. "I'll get the rest tomorrow…" – she was visibly excited.

"I hope this fits." She tried on the yellow helmet. It was a little big, but an easy adjustment.

They took a ride around Sauvie Island, it was in full bloom, and they stopped and walked and talked and even kissed once. They stopped at a U-pick farm and picked a bag of raspberries together, which she held on her lap as they sped back to Gresham on highway 30 then over to highway 84. They pulled into his neighborhood and he shut it down to about 20 mph. He opened his garage door almost a block away from his house and rode right in, skidding to a stop on the concrete floor, which swallowed them as he closed the garage door from his key-chain.

Elizabeth was floored by his house. The interior was all glass and steel, and he had a sculpture that he bought at the 68 Gallery, a completely white plaster statue of a young girl in a summer dress, with a look of wide-eyed surprise.

She called it "funny and disturbing." He laughed and agreed.

She took off her shoes and danced around on the hardwood floor.

"What's this?" she asked as he handed her a white iced drink.

"It's my own recipe for a White Russian. Coconut Almond blend, Molopolowa vodka and a touch of espresso."

"Mmmm," she sipped as she continued to dance on the floor. She became woozy. "I don't feel good," she said. He grabbed the glass out of her hand just as she was about to drop it on his hardwood floor.

She woke in his panic room, naked and strapped to some kind of adjustable stainless steel apparatus.

"Relax," said Raleigh, who came into focus in front of her. "Make yourself at home."

"You motherfucker!" And then she screamed.

He made an unpleasant face. "I'll be back. I have some business downtown." He closed the steel door, which abruptly silenced her terrified screams, and left for the First Thursday *SwiftPad* board meeting. He knew he was going to need some money.

～～

It was 2 A.M. when Raleigh finished. He was exhausted. And rich, he thought. If he could just get the five million transferred to Aruba tomorrow and catch a plane, anywhere south of Panama. He would be on top of the world. There had never been a night like this. Five million dollars! He had been going through his savings and really hadn't had a steady income for several years and was close to default on his house. He needed to move fast. Dump the body, get the check, get a wire transfer from his bank, get to the airport. He ached all over. He ate three more testosterone pills, five big 400-mg ibuprofen caps and then smoked more meth. Did he have time to get to the bank? Sure he did; it was a cashier's check. They wouldn't have him as a suspect until much later. Just a guy making a deposit in a legitimate transaction. Maybe in a few days, he knew that prick detective from Richland would be all over this, but by then the check would clear. They would start looking eventually, he knew. But he just had to think - Plane to Panama, then…Brazil? Then… Gone, motherfuckers! God, he was tired.

Showering and getting dressed was a chore. He just wanted to sleep, but he knew he couldn't, not yet. He smoked more meth and he felt his energy surge. There it is.

Her body was heavy and he struggled with it. He used a hand truck to carry her to the garage, where he hosed her off and then slowly dressed her with a high-necked white gown that he had been saving for just an occasion. He had to shake himself awake when he finished.

Raleigh struggled as he propped her on the back of the *Super-Low*, put the yellow helmet back on her head and he then got on and tied her hands around his chest. He didn't have to worry about leakage, the enema leak had quit a while ago. Leakage. Leakage.

Leakage. He looked at his crouch and saw a dark stain. SHIT! He had to get her back before the sun came up!

The trails of headlights whizzing by lingered in his vision as he raced west on highway 84. The after-images seemed like solid trains of light that never ended. He thought about the trails that he was making on the bike, a palinopsia that must extend behind him for miles. It was relativity in action – as he sped up, his mass increased and time slowed down. He had to slow down or the universe would collapse on him. He screamed. "Einstein, you fucker!" He twisted the throttle and the bike jerked ahead, hitting almost 100 in a few seconds. Then he remembered not to speed because getting pulled over with a corpse tied around his waist might elicit some questions. He throttled down, and then watched the speedometer as much as the road because he had no other way to tell how fast he was going.

Her keys got him into the Easy Girl Bakery. He set her up on the lunch counter, spread her legs and pushed her bridal gown up to...damn, no garter! It ruined the effect, he thought. He moved her hand to her crouch. She had begun to rigor on the ride over so she sat up easily, displaying an ample décolletage. He put a couple gallon jugs of water behind her to prop her up. He wished her face had set with a smile, but at least her eyes were open.

He left the bakery about 4 A.M. and headed down I-5, cutting west at Tualatin-Sherwood Road, and rode the bike up a dirt path that paralleled the railroad tracks to a bog behind the Wilsonville to Beaverton commuter train. He attached the helmets and the leather jacket and pants to the frame of the bike, and pushed it and watched the almost new Harley 883 SuperLow sink completely into the murky water.

Chapter 29

Jim learns real reason for Outsourcing the Keg's IT Team, and meets Chubby at the Easy Girl Bakery

It was after nine on Friday morning. Jim was standing in the KEG's "data center," a humming tangle of cables and racked computers. It seemed weird to him that he was back in this room, where he had sweated out so many near disasters to the company's computer systems. His mind was racing between those years, 13-14 years ago and everything that had happened since. It was so strange to be back where it seemed time had stopped. He suffered from some kind of temporal vertigo and he couldn't focus his mind on what he needed to do.

Lester had cleaned up his snake orgy wire management, and had made an effort to label many of the cables with descriptions and titles. "4th flr HR Aholes" said one bunch of cables, another was labeled, "13th flr no-brain-X-Zeks,, and then there was the hard-to-decipher "7th flr pipe-farts." It definitely related to natural gas somehow. But Jim would be careful not to pass judgment on Lester's housekeeping this morning.

Sonny had been coming to this windowless, noisy room, filled with rubbery burnt machine odors, for at least the last 16 years.

Today he was scurrying in and out of the room, carrying chairs, greeting Jim's staff as they came in, most of them stone faced. Lester, full of gallows humor, explained to Slater and Rainy that they were being led down to the basement of the Lubyanka building for a People's Liquidation Session. Knute, the old mainframe programmer, thought it was funny.

"What is that? Lubyanka?" asked Slater.

"It's the secret Federal Prison in Arkansas where they keep 'the worst of the worst,'" Lester said.

"Yeah, I've heard of it," said Slater. "So what's that got to do with us?"

"You've 'heard of it,' huh?" Lester snuck a sly glance at Jim. "It is so secret that the prison guards there get retired out of the country, mostly to Malaysia, and each gets round-the-clock protection. The Mob and drug gangs still find them sometimes."

"Really?"

"Steve, he is fucking with you," said Janice, her sparkling brown eyes and gold hoop earrings setting off her shiny 1968 Angela Davis afro. "Lubyanka is in Russia. What he is saying, in his totally asshole way, is that we are on the way to get our asses fired. This is some bizarre Stalinist psychological technique. They are moving us here to the noisy data center so when we shout out in fear and anger no one will hear it."

"That's what I thought too," said Slater.

"It's funny, Jim. You come here from GIP and in three months we are being outsourced to GIP," said Arlen.

This was a very good sign, Jim thought, as he silently acknowledged Arlen's comment. He needed to get them riled up and if silent Arlen was getting pissed off about it, then they all would. His plan was to unleash their pissiness.

Jim and Macy had left 68 Gallery and the SwiftPad *meeting and pedaled up Vista Blvd, which got steeper the farther up you got, both of them straining, in their lowest gears, standing on the pedals. Macy had hiked her long dress well up above her knees and tied it in a knot on the side of her thigh. Jim had been breathing hard, in fact had never before made it up that hill until last night, without having to walk his bike.*

"I take it you don't mean 'ha-ha' funny, do you, Arlen? You mean funny as in 'not-so-funny'?"

"No," interrupted Lester, "I think it is 'ha-ha' funny, you coming over from GIP. It could be some long range, sinister plan, first they come, then they go, pretending that you had forced them out. Then they hire you and come again, using you, Jim, our beloved leader, as the Instrument of their own Evil Redemption!" said Lester. "What did Marx say, first tragedy then farce?"

Jim smiled at Lester's theory. "Sometimes a cigar is just a cigar. We are going to wait until everyone gets here and gets settled. I am only going to do this once," he said ominously, and then smiled again. He knew they were looking for cracks of doubt. The smile was like a cool breeze, because they all trusted Jim and knew he wouldn't smile if all he had was bad news.

They had gotten to Macy's house, which was half hidden up and back behind firs, vines and a big willow tree that obscured the whole narrow three-story house. Macy, who hadn't said a word since they left the 68 Gallery, went right to bed, but Jim lay on the couch in the living room, not wanting to go back to his place, not wanting to leave Charlotte and Macy alone. His stomach was in knots. He didn't mention Raleigh's creepy staring to Macy but he thought it was on her mind too. Something else was bugging him and he didn't know what it was. It wasn't the layoffs at the KEG. He had those worries sectioned off. Business was business. No, this was a bigger worry and he couldn't put his finger on it. Raleigh was out. A relief, he thought. But also somehow a threat.

And there was something else. Something was bugging her too, but she clearly didn't want to talk about it. There was time though – they would get it all straight tomorrow, he had thought.

He knew Raleigh would be picking up his check in an hour at Starbucks, only five minutes away by bike. He thought about leaving the KEG to confront him, to warn him away. Away from everything in his life.

Last night around midnight, after staring off at the wall for a couple of hours he had climbed into bed with Macy. Asleep, she had rolled over next to him and put her arm on top of him. And he had lain there thinking.

He had whispered, "You awake?"

Her eyes had stayed closed and she continued to breathe regularly. He had stared at her in the dark for a minute or two, not sure what he was sensing.

Since he couldn't sleep, he had left a note on the kitchen table, suggesting they have lunch downtown, and at about 4 A.M. Jim had coasted his bike down to his apartment, showered, dressed and walked into his office at the KEG by 6 A.M. Sitting at his desk, reading the Oregonian had been Dick Swensson, the KEG's former CEO, now chairman of the board.

"Jim, my boy!" Swensson had gotten up and shaken his hand. Swensson, as always, looked fit and fresh, the quintessential rugged business leader. "You busy?"

Jim had shrugged with a wry smile.

"Come on, let's get out of here. Let's go down to promenade along McCall Waterfront Park. You remember McCall, don't you?"

"I was too young, but yeah, I have heard a little."

"He made this State. He was always the same, in person or on TV. Do you know in the early sixties, the Willamette was one of the most polluted rivers in the country? It actually stunk! Can you imagine, the river stank like a dirty asshole. Now that is behind us, so to speak, thanks to Tom. He was a great guy, fun to drink with."

They walked down Couch to Naito Parkway and crossed the street against the light.

"Jim you grew up in Oregon, didn't you?"

"Out in the Coast Range, west of Corvallis."

"So you understand things better than all these downtown hip cats from California and New Jersey." They stood almost under the Steel Bridge and watched an Amtrak train clank in from Eugene and points south.

Some joggers had gone by and the first rays of the sun had flashed over the Convention Center needle towers, lighting up the patch of sidewalk they were standing on. They had walked under the Burnside Bridge. The "lawn" in the main section of the park was gray-black dirt with a new crop of grass peeking through. They replanted the grass about five times a summer after the various events trampled it into dirt. "What was this for, Cinco de Mayo or Fourth of July?" Since it was early June, they didn't seem like good guesses.

"The Beer Festival or the Blues Festival? Or the Jazz Festival? The Sustainability Festival? Oh, look at that sign. That's what it is. The Bite of Portland, the food festival," said Jim.

"I thought it was The World Championship for Dong Holding!" Swensson had smiled at his little joke and shaken his head and said dispassionately, *"We got a lot of dong holders in this town."* Jim had smiled automatically, pretending he knew what a dong holder was. *"You understand what is going on, don't you, Jim?"*

"I am absolutely sure that I do not understand what is going on."

Finally everyone was in the KEG's Server Room and settled.

"OH MY GOD!" Christine blurted, as she looked at her phone.

"We need to turn off our phones; we have some important stuff to…"

"NO! You have to hear this." Christine was looking at her phone, but others around her were gasping and saying "Oh shit!" "They found a woman, Oh God!"

"Here it is," said Larry Yang. "'Woman found dead in 23rd Street Bakery. Police have yet to identify the victim, but a source close to the investigation confirms it is the proprietor of the Easy Girl Bakery, Elizabeth Kerns, 38. Police have cordoned off the area and are asking anyone who might have seen or heard anything to come forward.'"

Jim felt a kick in the stomach. Elizabeth Kerns, the Easy Girl, his first new friend when he moved back to Portland. He had commented on and praised her pastry on her blog.

It was just like when Regina disappeared. *Was he following me, punishing me?* Jim knew who it was, and realized he had always suspected him. Everything in his life was suddenly becoming indistinct and cloudy again, as though it wasn't there.

They all sat in silence.

"The Crockett Group is paying GIP to make this move. They have a contract to get us to sign away our IT, so they can buy us."

"What? Why? You mean 'Bum' Crockett, the Poison Pill specialist?"

Swensson laughed. "No. You use a poison pill against a guy like Crockett, to keep him from doing a hostile takeover. A poison pill is…anyway, he wants to do a hostile takeover of Consolidated. Bribe our stockholders to turn the company over to him. Crockett is paying GIP to **weaken us.** *GIP can lose money all day and still come out ahead as long as we give up control of our IT systems, and outsource to GIP. Then Crockett buys us easily. Everyone is afraid of breaking IT. Everyone knows that computers* run everything. You break IT, and it all falls apart for a modern company. No email, websites, Tweety, whatever. So GIP takes over IT – and it falls into their lap."

"How do you know?"

"I got a tip from inside GIP, friend from college. But GIP has some bad stuff on me, from the 1997 contract. Bad stuff, if the papers got ahold of it. I am not a saint, Jimmy. My ass is out there…with everyone else's. I can't oppose this or they ruin me."

They stood halfway between the Morrison and Burnside bridges, looking out at the water.

"So what does the memo say?"

"Identify 'weak' members of the staff, create scenarios where they might cost the company money, be arbitrary and cause dissension, divide and conquer. But GIP has orders only to push until we push back. They juiced up that kid, what's his name…?"

"Mark…Ruskin."

"He's just a sacrificed pawn. Keep your eye on the bigger picture."

"You know about him and Angie…"

At first Swensson had tried to seem surprised, but Jim's impassivity caught him out and he had finally nodded. They had looked at each other and Jim knew that Dick knew too. Their mutual silences were sheepish confessions of their casual dalliances with Angie. Swensson had made a face, his 'I-have-something-else-unpleasant-to-tell-you' face. "One other thing. They have something on you too."

"What?"

"Don't you know?"

"Well, it could be a lot of things, I guess."

Dick had laughed. "I understand. Alright, whatever it is, be ready for it. But I have your back! We have your back. Do you believe me?"

"Somewhat. No, not really."

Dick had laughed again. "You're alright. What do they say they need from us?"

"They want to have our people meet theirs and begin individually planning the 'task handover.'"

"Agree to meet. You still have control, if you can keep it. Make a case that the business is at risk if they take over our systems. They lack familiarity or whatever else you can think of."

"In twenty minutes you are going to face the GIP engineers. We cannot put this off for any reason, not even this horrible murder. We have run out of time; it is out last chance to defend our jobs. They are up on nine, waiting to carve you up. Please listen to me! They are here to take your jobs." Jim was in control of his feelings now.

"Take our jobs!" said Lester with a hick accent, and there was a titter of laughter. Apparently everyone watched *South Park*.

"Each of you in the next 15 minutes will come up with about two or three 'Man Years' of work in your area. It shouldn't be hard. Dredge up projects you have thought about, talked about, bitched about, and doubted you could ever do because of lack of money, time or skill."

"Anything?" said Rodney.

"Anything…scripts, data conversions, migrations, upgrades, integrations, anything, it doesn't matter. All of it, of course follows ITIL. You know, change procedures, make sure it goes through DEV-TEST-PROD. Just make them deal with it. Make them do everything that you all always avoid doing. You have to make them work for you, not the other way around. You say, 'We can't turn over the system until this and that is done. So you guys have to do it, because we don't have time.' Don't ask them for advice, just tell them what to do. Don't let them change the subject. If they lose their cool, so much the better. Yes, Lester."

"So, can we ask the GIP Consultants to drop their pants and kiss their own asses?"

"As long as they test it, have a back-out plan, and put it in DEV for a month first so we can see if it is going to work. Keep them off balance. We are the customer. Got it?"

The team talked together about strategies and coordinating the work. Jim stepped back and let it happen. He didn't need to run things now. He realized Dick Swensson had taught him something earlier in the morning.

Jim's phone rattled. "I need to take this outside," he said. "Chubby, what's going on?"

"Just talked to Heb. Highlooper didn't show this morning. He is not answering his phone. Technically, according to one lawyer I just talked to ten minutes ago, he has walked away from the money."

"Didn't show? After all the drama last night at the board meeting? You hear about Liz Kerns?"

"It was her?"

"Apparently." They were quiet for about fifteen seconds.

"You thinking…?"

"Of course I am…"

"We got to go to the police."

"Let's go up to the bakery now."

"I'll be there in 10 minutes or so."

Jim told Lester he had an emergency and to take over. He hurried down to the street, unlocked his bike and was about to ride up to the Easy Girl Bakery, when he remembered Raleigh looking at Macy just before he left the gallery last night. He called Macy.

She didn't answer.

Chapter 30

Petrovich arrives in Portland and proceeds to the Easy Girl Bakery

etective Petrovich was confused as to the best way to get to the bakery on NW 23rd and Truman. The pattern was broken; this one wasn't found buried in a utility vault. If it was his guy, then he was changing, and the caterpillar was becoming a butterfly. And if it wasn't him, then he, Petrovich, was chasing butterflies.

It was a little after ten, and he had been doing ninety since leaving Richland two and a half hours ago. He crossed over I-5, took the Morrison Bridge, and continued up Washington, to 14th then right, north. Wrong way. Turned left, crossed over 405 on Lovejoy, stop and go, when his phone clanked.

"I'm with Sharon Rodriguez." It was Georgia. "It's going to be another three days until they can dig."

"Come on, Georgia! You need to make this happen faster! It's got to be by tomorrow!"

The phone was dead for five or six seconds. "OK."

"Let me know if I have to talk to anybody."

"Don't sweat it. I got it." Click.

He shook it off. Focus, he thought.

He parked down Truman, near 22nd Street, and walked the rest of the way. All up and down the street, people were standing outside their doorways, in front of the shops, with shocked looks. Many were crying and hugging each other. There was a small crowd of around five people, all men except one, standing in front of the crime scene, and they were chanting:

"End the violence now!"

"Your sister, your daughter!"

"End the Violence Now!"

"Your sister, your daughter..."

Petrovich approached the uniform standing in front of the yellow tape barricade. A gnomish man in a button-down plaid shirt, jeans with wide cuffs, dark-rimmed glasses and a full beard yelled directly at the cop, loud and angry, "Sexist Violence! Treating women with disrespect! This is what happens!"

The cop glanced at the guy, then without moving his head, at Lance. "Can I help you?"

"Yes, officer," Lance showed his badge, "I'm Petrovich, Tri-Cities task force. Henderson back there?"

He pointed his thumb toward the back, and Lance clipped his badge on his front pocket, then walked into the Easy Girl Bakery.

"Petrovich, I thought you quit? Why are you here? Did we call him?" The Portland detective looked at his partner, who shrugged.

"Do you know there was a Henderson, a Secret Service agent, who guarded Lyndon Johnson? You any relation?"

Henderson looked at his partner with wide-eyed surprise, laughed and shook his head. "I don't believe so, Detective. Why, pray-tell, do you ask?"

"Well, once Johnson had Henderson stand close to him, so he could take a piss without being seen. And Henderson said, 'Mr. President! You're pissing on my shoes.' You know what Johnson said? You know what the President of the United States said to Agent Henderson?"

"No, Lance, what did he say?"

"'Henderson, that's my prerogative.' Where is the body?"

"This way." They walked back toward the counter and she was lying flat out on the table. The dress was cut away and the techs were going over it. "She was propped up when we got here. We photographed the shit out of everything. See the bind marks? She was propped up and her skirt pulled up and her legs were spread out. She had one of the bakery's muffins stuffed in her mouth."

"Was she killed here?"

"No. No way. Strangled somewhere else. Look at her neck. Sometime after midnight, what, 8–10 hours ago…we've been here since a little after seven this morning. Other than checking for penetration we haven't touched much. The captain is on my ass to zip this up soon so…"

"Yeah, just give me a few minutes," said Petrovich.

Petrovich looked at the body for about two minutes and then scanned the scene. The counters were clean. He walked into the kitchen; it was closed up and cleaned. He opened the big refrigerator. Tidy. "Anything missing?"

"Money is in the till. Two muffins are missing from a tin, one accounted for." Henderson nodded at the body.

"Sex?"

"Preliminary, but yes and no."

"No semen."

"Correct." Henderson watched Lance as he walked around with a look of controlled patience. Lance came back to the body and looked again. Brown hair, tightly combed with an antique silver barrette holding the bridal veil on her head. She had clearly been strangled by hand, gloved hands undoubtedly.

"What's her background? Have you contacted the family?"

"Elizabeth Kerns. Thirty-eight, single, has a female roommate who works here and discovered the body. The roommate is a mess, one of our people is with her, but I don't think she'll be helpful to be honest. Originally from Indianapolis, came here two years ago. Parents divorced, one sister, younger. Contacted the mother."

"That is always tough."

"Yeah – so I've heard. Anyway, she opened the shop about nine months ago. Victim has a website for her recipes and baking blogging. Comments, etc. We're checking that."

"Detective, there's a couple of guys out here, say they have something to tell you."

"Did they see something?"

"No, I don't think so, but – they say they know somebody…it's not clear, but they are insistent."

"I'm going to be leaving in a bit here, Ted. Let me talk to them on my way out. You know why I am here…"

"Sure, Lance. Tell them to sit tight."

Lance continued walking around the bakery again, looking closely at the counters, then behind the counter. He turned to Henderson and started to say something.

"It was all unlocked. We have one witness who thinks he saw her leave yesterday afternoon on the back of a motorcycle with a guy, black leathers, the full drag deal. She closes at 3 P.M. and that's about when. Nice bike, he said. Low slung."

Lance looked up at the shelf behind the counter and saw the Sturgis picture. "This her?" Lance looked at it and then down at her face. "About three or four years ago I'd say." He turned it around, 'Mike and Doug – July 4, 2010.' Lance's expression didn't change.

Lance pulled a pair of surgical gloves out of his coat pocket, opened the plastic with his teeth and pulled them on.

"The guy have a Harley?"

"We're checking."

Lance picked up her hand and looked at the dark stains on her fingers. He looked at Henderson.

"Ink? Berries? We'll check it in the lab."

"Keys?"

"*No encontrado*. Can't find her wallet either. The witness says she was in jeans when she left, wasn't wearing that dress. Roommate never saw it before. He apparently washed her down pretty thoroughly before bringing her back here."

"From her berry-picking excursion."

"Yeah maybe. Lance, you make anything out of her being dressed as a bride?"

"Doesn't sound like my guy, but, you know they change. They want to be seen, to be understood. It is a process of metamorphosis. At least that is what I've read."

"Like meta what? Meta World Peace? Shit, Lance, I never knew you was so smart."

"OK. Thanks, Ted. I'll meet you at your station later this afternoon. We can circle up then. Unless something breaks before that. I'll talk to these guys outside on my way out. If it is nothing, I'll give them to your guy out there, what's his name?"

"Who?"

"Your guy out there."

"Fuck if I know." He looked at his partner, who shrugged.

"You're a nice guy, Ted. I gotta pick somebody up at the airport, so I'll see you later."

"Oh? You flying in your special friend? Your partner, Sweet Georgia, who found the fuck doll? Try out some of your theories?"

"No. I figured I would stop by your ex-wife's house later. I hear she put out an APB for cop dick. It was Patty, right? Or was that the first one?"

Ted waved bye-bye with his middle finger.

Chapter 31

Outside the Easy Girl Bakery, a girl seemed on the verge of hysterics. Chubby was consoling her. Jim watched his friend, big and burly, wearing Army surplus pants, and a tent-like jute pull-over, and still couldn't believe he could be so gentle and empathetic. Jim rarely saw that side of Kip, but it didn't surprise him.

Since they had been boys, they had had a spiky relationship that never gave an inch of sympathy to each other for matters of the heart and soul. Kip's cross was an emotionally cold father and a mother who had abandoned him. Jim's father had fallen into the bottle when he was young, and had been banished by his mother, a woman whose own emotional roller coaster Jim had spent his life trying to get off. Between them, they had an unspoken agreement, an invisible bond, that required neither of them to acknowledge the other one's pain, even though they always knew the other would be there when it counted.

Jim watched the unkempt, bearlike Chubby comfort the distraught woman haunted by the brutal and macabre rape-murder. And although the police had not made any announcements, the first witnesses to arrive on the scene had told a number of people how Elizabeth's body had been left after being brutally murdered – and the story had spread around, which meant that the crowd in front of the Easy Girl Bakery was rapidly growing as the ambulance arrived.

On one level Kip's empathy was an act, staged by the irrepressible impresario, Orson "Chubby" Welles. But Jim knew that Kip was a deeper spirit than he could ever be and that his "act" hid a real and deep feeling for other people's pain. Jim felt a certain coldness, a desire for revenge, rising stronger than his sorrow for Elizabeth. He was angry, but unable to really feel it yet because...he was almost sure it was Raleigh, and that diverted his anger to guilt. Somehow, he had "known" what Raleigh was since the nineties, and felt responsible for not merely banishing him from the KEG all those years before. He should have really brought him down somehow, not just push him out of the KEG. Even if it had meant killing him. He should have stopped him. He realized he knew, on some deep level, and that had been what had driven him to fire him, not his failure to come to meetings. But it hadn't been enough, and now he was being repaid for his weakness. Jim noticed that a cop was watching Kip closely. Kip was the innocent one – he should be watching me, he thought, it is me who is guilty.

Jim was insanely impatient waiting, and wanted to just say fuck it, and ride his bike up to Macy's house on Vista, but now he had to wait for some detective to give his statement. He had tried her phone twice more, still no answer.

"Kip," Jim said, trying to interrupt him. About fifteen, twenty people were hanging on every gesture and word from Kip. His charisma never seemed to fail, no matter the circumstance. He was talking about some unifying principle that would settle it all in a karmic way soon. He excused himself and looked at Jim..."I have to go to Macy's place. I called Charlotte's school, but of course they wouldn't tell me anything..."

"Hang on, Jim, we got to talk to the cops first..."

Jim was just about to hop back on his bike and leave when a wiry old guy with bushy gray hair and a cheap dark suit came out of the bakery and slowly made his way over to them.

Petrovich recognized Jim from the video of his interview with Henderson. He looked for his badge and remembered he put it on his breast pocket. He awkwardly pointed to it as an introduction. "I'm Detective Lance Petrovich. I understand you want to talk about something regarding this…?" Chubby squeezed between them and began talking. Was Hunt coming to confess and was this guy some kind of hippie lawyer?

"Officer, I am Kip Rehain, this is my associate Jim Hunt. We want to talk to you about a guy we know who…"

"More importantly," interrupted Jim, "my girlfriend and her daughter are missing…"

"Well Jim, she might not be missing yet, but…"

Jim held up his hand at Kip and took a deep breath. Petrovich's eyes went back and forth between them. "Listen, Kip, why don't you talk to the detective, I need to get up to her house and see if I can figure out where she is…"

"Hold on," Lance gave a slight smile to try and calm them down. "Have you reported her missing yet?"

"No, I don't know for sure she is missing, but she is not answering her phone and this guy who we want to talk to you about, he is missing too and I am worried. We both knew Elizabeth. It was her, she is dead, right?" Jim spoke clearly without hurry and breathed slowly trying not to show panic. He squeezed his fists to try and keep from shaking.

Petrovich looked at the two men closely. "Yes, she is dead…" Petrovich noticed that the group that had been listening to Kip had followed him over and was hanging on each word. "Let's go to my car. We'll go first to check on your girlfriend's house. Is it far?"

"No, a mile or so up the hill." Jim pointed up 23rd Street.

Petrovich took a mental inventory of the two. Hunt was well dressed. Medium build, sandy hair, an odd, narrow face, clean blue golf shirt, pressed brown Dockers, shiny rubber soled, plain leather brown shoes, typical cube dweller. He was clearly in distress.

His friend Rehain looked more disturbing for some reason, something like the actor Mads Mikkelsen, he thought, wearing a rough cotton or fine woven jute short-sleeve shirt with Inca hieroglyph patterns, and stained, green, old style Army pants. Handsome wide face, brown, floppy hair, he still gave off an odor, something like old fruit wine that had turned.

Jim looked at his badge again. "You aren't from Portland?" Jim was pretty sure he had seen Lance before, but he couldn't place him.

"No, I am from the Richland-Kennewick area. I am helping with this investigation." Just then the paramedics brought out Elizabeth's body. The crowd went silent. Henderson followed them and waved away the crowd and reporters.

"Come on, gentlemen, let's go check on your girlfriend's house." The three of them walked down Truman toward Lance's Nissan. Kip and Jim locked their bikes to a rack in front of a Persian restaurant and jumped in, Kip silently calling shotgun.

They drove up Vista to Macy's house. Kip told Petrovich about Raleigh and his strange behavior the night before at the *SwiftPad* Board meeting and his bizarre failure to show up to pick up a five million dollar check. Jim jumped in and explained his past with Raleigh, briefly describing how he had fired him 16 years ago. He looked closely at Petrovich again. He remembered being grilled by him, years ago, after Regina disappeared.

"There was a woman who disappeared from our company at about the same time," said Jim. "Regina McKenzie. I remember you now. You were in the room when they questioned me about it."

Petrovich listened without comment.

"I know Raleigh did it," said Kip. "He hit me as a hollowed-out humanoid from the moment I met him. He somehow passes for normal with everyone else."

Jim started to say something, but held back.

Petrovich explained he was investigating a killing in Richland that he thought might be related to the two Portland murders, Regina McKenzie and now Elizabeth Kerns. He needed details. He reiterated to them that he was listening to them closely and for them to hold nothing back, no matter how trivial.

They parked outside Macy's house. "Her SUV is still here," said Jim. They looked in it through the windows and saw Charlotte's rubber boots near the door and what looked like some school library books. It was locked.

They hurried up the steps, Lance leading the way. The yellow house was about 30–40 feet above the street itself. Jim started to put the key in the door's lock.

"Wait," whispered Lance. "So do you live here?"

"Some of my stuff is here. I have my own place just down the street."

"Is there a back door?"

"Yes."

"Do you have that key?"

"No."

"Let me go in first," said Lance, taking the key. "You two go around the back and stand by that door, both of you. Stand back. Can you hide there and still see the door?"

"I think so."

"Do it. Check the windows; if you see someone looking out, and they see you, come immediately back here. Otherwise, stay out of sight, especially if somebody comes out. I'll come through and let you in there."

Five minutes later Petrovich came out and let them in the kitchen door. "Let's look around and see if anything looks like a hasty exit. Did she pack anything?"

Petrovich got a call from his partner.

"Georgia, I am busy, what's up?"

"We start digging in an hour."

"I knew you could do it! Let me know when they find her."

If they find her, he thought as he hung up. Otherwise this is a wild goose chase.

Jim, seemingly sleepwalking, led Petrovich through the house. They opened each of the closets and drawers. All neat and no indication it was forced or in haste. Jim softly conceded that some of her lighter clothes seemed to be missing. Her travel bag was missing from her closet too. Kip remembered it from the trip to the compound.

"So who is the girl's father?" Lance asked.

"Charlotte's dad is Chinese and..." Jim looked up. The mobile of the spinning Asian fisherman, with the gull, and the fish... It was gone. He could still see the mark on the ceiling where the tape had been. But the reproductions - of the Monet, the Song Dynasty finches, and the Pollock - they were still hanging on the walls.

"And what?"

Jim looked down for five seconds. "He is in a Chinese prison."

"...and...?"

"...and what? I don't know. It bothers her. She's worried about him and her daughter. But...I am worried about fucking Raleigh. Do you understand? He hates me. He thinks I fucked him over – before when we worked together at Consolidated E & G and now – now that I have been helping at *SwiftPad*, he...I think he blames me....and...he knows – about Macy and Charlotte. He is a fucking monster – I know it. I should have..."

"Should have what?" Petrovich's eyes widened as he looked at Jim. "What?"

"I knew it was him. I saw them – Regina and him...the day before...I don't know why – I...I didn't put it together..."

"It's alright. Jim – I should have known too – years before that. He was my real prime suspect for Kathy Morton – the woman from Richland – before McKenzie...We'll get him, Jim."

"Maybe she left. Maybe she...Let's go look for their passports."

Macy had all her papers arranged neatly in a file box next to her desk. It was very well ordered and labeled. Jim quickly found the folder labeled "Passports," and it was empty.

"This doesn't make any sense," said Jim. "I was with her last night. She..."

"OK, we need to check her daughter's school. Do you know which one it is?"

"Ainsworth, it is just up the street..."

"I'll have someone from Portland Police check it out, see if she is absent or if the mother said anything. Let's look around a little more. You guys have some time? I have to pick up a colleague at the airport and I think you both should meet him. He can help us."

"Sure," said Kip. Jim didn't respond.

They got back in Lance's Nissan and he got on the phone with Henderson and relayed what Jim and Kip told him. The hunt for Raleigh was on.

Kip directed him down to 405 and then over the Marquam bridge to I-84. "So this is about a serial killer. What else has he done?" asked Kip.

"Did I say serial killer? Not sure that is what it is yet. But I think we might have some of his handiwork buried up there. We are trying to dig up another body in Richland now. We'll find out soon," he continued. "But, you have to keep this to yourselves for now. We have nothing yet."

Kip told him how he had met Raleigh on the same evening that he met GG. But Lance was mostly interested in Jim's experience with him 16 years previously, around the time that the Portland woman, Regina McKenzie, disappeared.

"In answer to your statement earlier," said Lance, "yes I was there and yes you were considered a suspect, Mr. Hunt. Some of my colleagues thought you might have been a psychotic mastermind."

"I am flattered. I have trouble mastering my bike lock. That transient getting beat up – if that was what it was...?" Jim looked at Lance, who nodded.

"I know," Lance said. Fucking Henderson, he thought, I would ask him to show me a warrant, if he asked me for the time. No people skills. Lance knew that the same killer had worked at both the Portland and the Richland Bonneville Power office. Same utility box MO. How did I let him slip, he thought. It was Raleigh.

Jim resisted getting angry or indignant at the detective's acknowledgment that he had been a suspect. "I am worried about Macy. I know she would never go with him without a struggle."

Unless he just put a gun on her daughter, thought Lance.

"The house looked normal," said Kip.

But...why did she leave on her own? I want to believe that is what happened, understand? I would rather she just take off without telling me, than for her to be in danger. I don't want to think about it. Because...why didn't she tell me she was leaving?"

"Don't jump ahead. There is an explanation. What else?" asked Petrovich.

"Highlooper had it in for me," Jim said. "And the last time I – we – saw him, he was leaving the board meeting, last night. I saw him look a long time at Macy, too long. She saw him too, and I could tell it freaked her out."

"Did you talk to her about it?"

"She has been acting – I don't know – she's been giving me sad looks lately. I didn't want to – and at work – they are about to lay off everybody that I work with..."

He probably killed the Kerns woman right after that, thought Lance.

"If your girlfriend and her daughter are traveling, this guy we are going to meet at the airport will be able to tell us quickly if she had flown anywhere. He can get airport information quickly. As far as Highlooper goes, everybody is looking for him. We'll check the flights."

Lance's radio said 84 was jammed up, so Chubby had him take the back way, up I-5 past the Moda Center to Columbia Boulevard, cut across the north end and park in PDX short-term parking. They went down into the main lobby and looked at the Arrival board.

"He's flying in from DC. Good. It's late, he should be landing in five minutes."

Chapter 32

A Meeting is Missed and a Memo is Written - GG Thinks SwiftPad didn't Live up to its Promise

After ditching the Harley in the pond, Raleigh walked back along the tracks that ran between the southern-most Portland suburb of Wilsonville and the Beaverton MAX station. He planned to take the train to get back to his house in Gresham, buy a plane ticket on the web, change and get to his 10 A.M. meeting with Heber to pick up his check. Then head to the airport and leave the country. Mexico then Brazil. The sun was just beginning to break in the east.

He had his passport with him, in fact he had checked it three times since dumping the Harley. He could make it on five million, he thought. He knew he was leaving a lot of money on the table, but he also knew that this last little party with Elizabeth Kerns would draw heat. He felt something inside his head, eating his brain, draining out his fluids and solidifying his insides. He knew he had not made a good impression at the *SwiftPad* board meeting last night and was sure the thing in his head had caused it. Another part of his brain told him he was running out of time.

There was a small shopping center behind the Westside train stop in Tualatin, but nothing was open and Raleigh wanted a coffee very badly, because he was suddenly very thirsty. He walked around, and found himself in front of a Starbucks, where he saw a young man preparing for the day's business. Starbucks! It was in his head. Starbucks! He had to get to Starbucks – for something…It was 5:40 A.M. Raleigh waved and tapped on the window.

"Where's my money, Starbucks!"

The young man at first tried to ignore him, but as Raleigh's banging got more insistent, he held up his open hand and one finger, mouthed "six" and pointed to the clock. Raleigh spat on the window and gave one last hard pound and walked away.

He ignored the sidewalk and crossed the bare rail track and hopped a small barrier and twisted his ankle. It didn't hurt at first, but when he tried to stand he buckled over.

"Fuck! Fuck! Fuck!" he screamed into the empty morning. He pulled himself over to the train stop shelter and flopped on the bench. At that moment, a long, loud whistle broke the early morning silence, announcing the arrival of the day's first commuter train.

Raleigh pulled himself up, and limped past the ticket machine directly into the front of the lead car. It was more crowded than he thought possible, considering the hour, and he had to walk to the front to get a seat. Directly behind him sat a fit and sparkly-eyed blonde in tight jeans, a green jacket and matching bicycle helmet. Her old style Raleigh girl's bike with fenders and a round, silver, thumb bell on the handlebars leaned against the opposite of the car. He looked at his name on the bike and wondered if that was what his mother was thinking when she named him. He knew that it was a popular cigarette and that the packs had coupons on the back. His mother saved all kinds of coupons. She probably named him for the cigarettes. Her monogrammed RALEIGH table lighter had a prominent place in the living room. He remembered her ordering it for about twenty cartons of coupons. He suddenly felt that it was his mother sitting behind him, risen up from her grave, belittling him for what he had done. He turned back and looked at her and the woman in the green jacket looked back with eyes that burned him and he turned back away to face the front. He breathed a sigh of relief, but he still felt her eyes drill into him. He turned quickly back around to look at her once more and right away, from her disgusted and sad reaction, it was clear that he looked hideous, and pitiable.

"Tickets, tickets," the conductor announced, walking down the aisle. Raleigh felt himself coming apart.

Be rational, he told himself.

"Sir, I don't have one," he said to the conductor. "I forgot to buy the ticket. I always buy tickets! I hurt my ankle and I forgot. Please sir, I accept punishment. A ticket. I accept it. There is no excuse. I just forgot…"

The conductor looked at him and then pulled back, "Are you getting on the MAX in Beaverton?"

"Yes."

"Will you buy an all-day ticket when you get there?"

"Yes sir! I have credit cards. Absolutely, I will get a ticket…an all-day ticket!"

"OK. If you promise me you will buy an all-day ticket at the station we're square. Don't forget again." The conductor moved away. Raleigh heard the woman in the green helmet and jacket behind him snort, just like his mother used to when he came home dirty. He didn't look at the woman again.

At Beaverton Transit Center, he changed to the Blue Line MAX, still not bothering to buy a ticket. He found a seat at the back, spread out, taking up two seats, and promptly fell asleep.

Later that afternoon, he woke. He had been riding back and forth through the city and between Hillsboro and Gresham all day. They were at the Gateway Transit station near where I-84 crossed 205. He sat up and remembered last night clearly, but without that thing, that insect in his head. That is what it was, a bug of some kind. It must have crawled out of his ear or something.

It was bright, no clouds. The train was filling up. It was a different view of Portland. Just across the Freeway was Rocky Butte, one of several small, dormant volcanoes around the city, cinder cones, that last bubbled up 300,000 years ago. The PDX airport and the Columbia River were just to the north of Rocky Butte.

From the Gateway Transit station, Raleigh could see opposing armies lining up for battle. The enemy was coming from the north, from across the river, moving toward the crisscrossing highways and train tracks, trying to force their way between the high points. Rocky Butte, just across the 205 freeway bypass, was at a nexus point, a place where great events could happen, and maybe a long time ago did happen. He was at a strategic point. Sleep had cleared his mind. He was beginning to see the big picture again. He was coming back and remembering what he had done. It left him sad, but he was composed now. He was no longer regretful like he had been the first and second times he had done...what he had done. He couldn't say the words, even to himself, and now he had to try to forget about it and move on.

He had to get cleaned up. The money. The money! He had slept through the money! He had slept through his meeting with Heber to pick up the check from Hariet, the queen of the ski jackets. She had been very mean to him, had made him feel like dirt when she wrote the check. Why was she disappointed in him, so quick to be disgusted with him? Don't they know what that does to him?

He knew that by now the body would have been discovered and...and what? What were they saying, what were the police saying? Sleep had been wonderful, complete and cleansing. The train he woke on was westbound into the city, and he didn't change to head back toward his house in Gresham. He couldn't be sure it wasn't being watched.

Raleigh kept an office on 16th and Taylor just down from Providence Park. No one knew he had it; it was registered to one of his money laundering partners, a Colombian named Ernesto Guntermann. Raleigh heard that Guntermann had been beheaded six months ago, in Juarez, mistaken for a DEA guy. Now at least he wouldn't be asking for his money back. Raleigh continued to use his office and ignored the letters demanding rent that were slipped under the door every couple of days.

The Timbers were having a game and as they got closer to town, the MAX train became packed tighter with chattering fans in green Timbers jerseys, some carrying horns and drums. His ankle was the size of a grapefruit. When he stood to leave the train at Providence Park, the pain almost knocked him out. He groaned and made a face with every step, and a young woman asked if she could help, but she was too small to lean on, so she just walked next to him with her hands out, in case he fell. Once he got out, the streets were packed with chanting soccer fans marching into battle. They all moved around him on their way to the game.

Portland's upscale soccer hooligans were loud and raucous, without the knifings, no racist chants or trashing of businesses. They were happy hooligans, a wholesome Liverpool/Manchester–like mob of faux-drunk office managers and sales associates shouting and chanting ribald slogans and demands for total loyalty from everyone on the MAX, scouring like Gestapo agents looking for any sign of Seattle loyalty on the apparel labels of the passengers.

But to Raleigh, it was all streaming from the pent-up rage that an anesthetized, feminized prison bottles up. Raleigh smiled sadly to himself. He was a warrior too, against all that oppressive shit, he thought. But he didn't need an outlet, at least not today. A cigarette would do just fine, he thought. There was a pack in the office he was sure.

The hubbub about *SwiftPad* amused him and the economic potential was very real, as Hariet proved last night. But he never completely cared to understand what it was really about and had confined himself to the basic, vanilla IT infrastructure issues. To him it was just another company website and up to now the App's content didn't interest him at all. His slim, infrastructure design contributions were his sweat equity stake, because in spite of what he had always maintained, he never really had any outside investors.

Some of the fans on the MAX had had the *SwiftPad* App up on tablets, and were hooting and booing the postings on the page titled "MLS." The *SwiftPad* American Major League Soccer group was hated by some fans, popular with others, "click-bait" for the Portland Timbers hooligans, perfect eyeball candy. It addition to the distillation of all of the updates and phony stories manufactured in response to the memes both real and generated, the content consisted of reports contrasting MLS teams with foreign teams and the reasons why Americans were no match for Europeans or South Americans.

The American football mentality, brain-damaged, big, strong and brutal, was the first battle line. First, the *SwiftPad* machine-generated post insisted, was to take over the hearts and souls of those American kids who still play football. Second, take it to the sandlot. American kids need to play soccer on the street, avoiding traffic while desperately trying to score or defend. Some would need to die that way. Play in the fading light of a summer evening, or in the rain of a late fall day without a club or a league. Just kids, no refs, or coaches. Have occasional fist fights while dodging traffic. Then there will be a common understanding of the game, a common dream of the game, dreams of rectifying national humiliations still remembered through a network of communication as old as Roman roads, decades after they happened, holding on to the dream to reverse it, and return honor to the country. Americans had to dream about soccer, not just shout about it.

SwiftPad had a whole interactive story based on just such a boy, raised in rural Pennsylvania, who had never played basketball or baseball or football, in fact didn't even know such sports existed. The App "player" connected with the actor player in the App (assuming the device had sufficient voice recognition, otherwise a keyboard popped up). The young boy, Tad Lopstyk, was not even the star of his youth team, and he worshiped Aldo Donelli. The *SwiftPad* Chooser journey was titled *The Lopstyk Effect*, and it predicted when the US had 18.7 million young boys like Lopstyk, the United States would win the World Cup.

The App player could change history either way, depending on actions. Italy won the World Cup championship in 1934 and beat the US 7–1 in the first game. To make it worse, the Cup was hosted by Italy, or rather by Mussolini.

But the App's Journey changes that fact. An old black and white film print of the game's highlights morphed into a full 90 minutes, importing Lopstyk into the 1934 US team's mid-field. Lopstyk and Donelli strike again and again, matching Italy's goal barrage, with frequent cut-aways to a not-amused Il Duce. In history Italy's win was Mussolini's victory and Lopstyk's time traveling (i.e., The *Swift-Pad* user/Player) changes history. The fascist victory against the US turns into a 7–7 tie and Hitler's enthusiasm for the Berlin Olympic Games two years later was much diminished and with it, Germany's love affair with the Fuehrer. The consequences are only hinted at, because you can only take the Butterfly Effect so far, because…well, it is still happening.

Donelli was the shining example of just who Lopstyk wanted to be. The App, using still shots both real and auto-animated, jumps to the future and Lopstyk stays on the pitch and scores the winning goal in his late twenties, in Qatar in 2022. *SwiftPad* produced a renaissance-like, high holy scene, with angels blowing trumpets and saints gazing with tranquility at an animation of Donelli looking down approvingly at Lopstyk in his interactive uniform that provided a full sensory playing experience for the dedicated fan. (Available in several colors, with free delivery, if you order two. In the future you would catch the highlights in your head, not on ESPN.)

After watching the slightly drunk, green clad fans pass on the street toward Providence Park, Raleigh limped upstairs to his dingy office. A note was posted on the door. Two-week eviction notice. Shit! Two weeks from two weeks ago, almost. He needed to get out of here. He went in and fell into his chair, which broke and dumped him on the floor. He got up on his knees and found a bottle of Percocet in his drawer and swallowed four tablets. He carried his laptop to the floor, plugged it into the wall and fired it up. As he lay on his stomach, he pulled up a browser to the OregonLive site and found the story about his dear, recently departed Elizabeth.

Grisly Murder in NW Portland

A women wearing a bridal dress was found strangled in a NW Portland bakery this morning. Police have identified the victim as Elizabeth Kerns, 38, formerly of Indianapolis, Indiana. Portland Police detective Edward Henderson said they have an on-going investigation and they would be updating the public as new information becomes available.

Kerns was the proprietor of the Easy Girl Bakery. The police have not released any other details.

When asked if there was a connection to the murder of Regina McKenzie, Henderson refused to comment. McKenzie's body was found under a Gresham power vault three months ago.

Raleigh was stunned. How could they not see it! But then, he thought almost simultaneously, how could they ever see it? They weren't at all similar except that they were both women and both dead. He quickly googled the lead and pulled up a webcast of the KOIN newscast. It showed a covered body being brought out behind a young woman news reporter, the annoying KOIN News Girl, holding the microphone like a...in that tight dress, the camera pans, what was that? He stopped the broadcast and slid it back. That couldn't be...his hair is white. Has it been that long? That fucking cop, that couldn't be him? He had almost forgotten about Richland. But then, really he never thought of anything else.

He genuinely needed the money now. He let go of the mouse and laid his head on the floor and realized now he had nowhere to go. Why had he missed that meeting this morning! He knew why, he had undersold himself and now understood why he had not gone to pick up his check. If they multiple it by one hundred, maybe! Maybe wait a week and multiple it by a thousand! He had signed nothing! He was still in the game! It was time to move on *SwiftPad*. To take it all! That was his goal now! He didn't have much time. His leg throbbed. It was time to pull out all the stops, to cash all his chips, to release the hounds! That cu...cun...she was a...he took a deep breath. She had always tried to...he would bring her down. One for the road, he thought, managing to unscrew the childproof prescription bottle.

To an outside observer it would have appeared Raleigh was passed out on the floor. But even though the Percocet kept him from lifting or even moving his head, his mind continued to flash forward, imagining and planning.

Earlier that morning, GG woke up from a bad dream with a start and hit her head as she suddenly sat up in the narrow trundle bed that she had tucked in close to the slanting attic roof struts. She rubbed her head and looked at her big Android phone lying on the bare, unpolished, wooden floor next to her. Ten in the morning, time to get ready to get over to the airport. She was flying back to DC to visit her parents for the weekend, for a happy homecoming, and maybe look up Tyler.

It was hot, in spite of the electric fans she had installed in both the front and back windows. It was an old house, well up the hill in Northwest Portland on 25th and Overlook. Seven or eight of *SwiftPad's* senior coders occupied the second and first floors with various and shifting sleeping arrangements. The house was really the technical command central for *SwiftPad*, and GG was the only one with any smattering of privacy. She had a lockable door at the bottom of the steps that led up to her quarters. She had never had occasion to bolt it however. The close proximity to her crew created the perfect atmosphere for designing an app like *SwiftPad* and the project was exactly what she wanted, personal, intimate, alive, constantly changing, and in general a big group fuck of energy and sharing. She knew it wouldn't last, that it would evolve to the mean, as everything eventually did, and that made it so much better to be here now, when it was still fully alive. She had no idea what the future would hold. She supposed she would be rich, but that didn't really mean anything to her. Maybe she would take up golf, or be a housewife. A mother even, who knows? Fishing with Kip had been a blast and playing with Macy's Charlotte probably set off some biological alarm clock, she thought.

Sleep had been rare and far too short when it occurred, a some-time thing during the last few weeks, but especially in the last few days. The bizarre board meeting last night, with Raleigh finally taking the hint and leaving with way more money than he was worth, had been particularly disturbing. But if she had as much money as Hariet, she would have paid double just to get rid of him.

The App was a hit, there was no doubt about it now. Every hour, the sign-ups were increasing, actually at an exponential rate; in fact, at the current rate, in less than a month, every smartphone and computer user on the planet would be signed up, so they should be reaching "saturation" soon. And the infrastructure was holding. Heber, with Jim's help, had outsourced all the local management of worldwide data centers and had picked the right partners – small-scale teams with imagination and energy. He also farmed out all of the advertising and sales. It was getting out of control, completely unmanageable. They had to do something fast.

Raleigh had been an idiot taking five million! GG thought of Dr. Evil, returning to the present from the 1960s to demand "ONE MILLION DOLLARS!" from the world powers to save the planet. Why would he accept it? He must have been in a very big hurry.

She scrolled through the Big Bored. The Great Firewall of China had, as yet, failed to block *SwiftPad* significantly. Prankster-like praise of the Party and Mao and of the great things that the Cultural Revolution had done for the masses seemed to be taken at face value. One article written in the impatient, schoolmaster style Mandarin of the *People's Daily* (and more or less accurately translated for the slightly apologetic English language *China Daily*), pointed out how the Cultural Revolution (文化大革命) had broken the Mandate of Heaven and the cyclical nature of power in China. Apparently the post had confused enough Party intellectuals to allow general access to the application, at least until now.

There were pictures floating around the *SwiftPad* App of Chinese party officials getting out of expensive German cars with descriptions explaining that corruption must be understood from the inside in order to be combated properly. In a dialog bubble, one official seemed to be wrinkling his nose as he thought, "The inside of this new car stinks!" (新车臭味!) A *chengyu,* or proverb, that the post attributed to Zhuangzi, the 2nd century BC Daoist. He was talking about how a new chariot wheel covered with pig grease could ride as fast as a Tianma, a flying horse, but only first if you killed a boar and coated the axle with the fat. The official in the car suddenly grew a pig's snout. A yin-yang thing apparently. This won't last, she thought.

The limits of discourse within the App were quickly being reached. There were some discussions that did not lead to reason or clarity, issues set in stones that would never move. Israel-Arab discussions led nowhere. Each side saw that the more they supported a peaceful strategy, the harder the other side's line would become and vice versa. It wasn't because the opposing sides didn't understand the other. They understood each other too well, if anything, and it was the same with most international big power issues. It was too deep and too ingrained to be influenced by rhetoric of any kind.

GG had tried to keep the *SwiftPad* App focused on her original design but had failed. Kip had pushed for the easy laughs and the controversy and now it was already starting to wear. Chubby (she laughed to herself as she thought of Jim's name for him) was just too powerful to resist. She thought of that first night that they met. He bowled her over. His influence on the younger developers, even though he knew nothing technically, was taking its toll on her "pure" vision of what the App should be. On the plus side it was at least temporarily pushing up the potential price, if they decided to sell it to somebody.

She had meant the App to be a tool to discover and solve serious issues. Kip told her about Ellsberg's game theory, where the easy-short-term-less-likely-to-succeed actions always seemed to override wiser, long-term actions that didn't pay off immediately. That had been his idea, the idiot! So why did he let those other coders ignore it for cutesy ironies. Kip had told her about Ellsberg! And then...he bamboozled me, she thought with a smile.

Exposing our addictions, to war, oil, eye-candy of all kinds, corporate "quarterly results," and the constant eating of next year's seed crop was what she had hoped would be the result of the App. That people would state an opinion and the App would respond and steer them away from their expectations, so they could confront their fear and anger at whatever it was they were bitching about. Race relationships, education, the environment...put us on the right track. If something is viral enough...anything can be done. You just have to sacrifice either Time or Quality or Money. Choose two. That is what it takes to do anything. That seemed like old-fashioned, Ben Franklin advice. That was her target but she could see already that easy success was dooming that goal and the *Swift-Pad* itself was taking the easy way out.

She didn't have much to pack. She would be back in Portland Monday night. Three days in DC. Catch the streetcar over to the MAX, then over to PDX.

The Percocet began to wear off and Raleigh slowly came around and was able to pull himself up off the floor and sit at his desk. Lonnie Wolfe needed to strike. Ken Oren, the GIP VP, had told him that he wanted to do business. It was time to call in the chips. The way to do this was start at the bottom. Raleigh laughed to himself, because he couldn't get any lower than Mark Ruskin.

> *MEMO: From the Desk of Raleigh Highlooper – AdVenture Capitalist*
> *TO: Mark Ruskin, Executive Expeditor, GIP*
> *FROM: Lonnie Wolfe (aka Raleigh Highlooper)*
> *SUBJECT: SwiftPad Business Vulnerabilities*
>
> *Re: Our previous communication referencing Cynthia Oglethorpe: From my position on the Board of the **SwiftPad**, it is now clear to me that the organization is dysfunctional and disorganized. It is ripe for a hostile takeover.*
>
> *Cynthia, known as GG, is the linchpin of **SwiftPad**, she conceived it and is the application's architect. Now she is rudderless, an easy target for the right approach.*

If properly executed, you, Mark Ruskin, can run the table. Their board is weak and the management is a joke. They have no experience at the top. The principal executive is the spoiled son of a lumber baron. Their finances are poorly accounted for, and in every respect it is amateur hour. But regardless, the application, for the moment, anyway, is very hot. To effect a successful takeover two steps are required.

1. *Lawsuits – for possible patent breaches (GIP has invented everything relating to computers and the legal team at GIP is world renowned), we can bring them to their knees.*
2. *Psychological pressure – Persuade Oglethorpe to turn over the technical direction of the company to GIP. Psychological pressure along with a logical presentation of its merits will work with her. She is under enormous strain, and is out of her depth. There are many advantages that we can suggest such as professional staffing, high redundancy, and top technical and business talent.*

The key is to move fast and move hard. We need to isolate her from Kip Rehain and Jim Hunt, the same Jim Hunt you are dealing with at Consolidated. I would like to discuss tactics with you or with auxiliaries to your legal team.

Lonnie Wolfe

Chapter 33

GG at Airport - The First body found - Jim Makes a Decision

GG got off the Red Line train at PDX with just a backpack. Operating *SwiftPad* was becoming very complex, but she was still up to handling it herself from anywhere with her laptop if things went south over the weekend. Last week, she had hired ten developers to work on automating tasks. It was hard to find good people. The first crop she brought in had been amazingly good, but each new round of recruiting was worse and worse. She was already beginning to lose some control. There were new algorithms in the App that she didn't like, but they were already too deeply embedded to remove without deep testing. And because they never came into the office (there was no space, but now that they were on the Internet all the time, she had enabled total remote access for all developers), she didn't even know some of the people writing the new functions.

Raleigh was gone, but she was still uneasy. She had had a dream that morning that scared her and now she couldn't remember it. It was violent and Tyler was involved somehow. She was sure she dreamed about him because she was thinking of looking him up when she got to DC later in the evening. As far as Raleigh's contribution went, it was generalized BS and no real work, not even coherent planning documents. That, and he was fucking creepy. She hoped she never saw him again.

She had arrived more than two hours before her flight and the security lines were short, so she thought she would waste some time at the Powell's Bookstore Outlet in the main concourse. She had her tablet, filled with SciFi eBooks. Kip had been trying to turn her on to the old stuff, drug-fueled stories that treated insanity as normal, and vice versa. Older, hip people annoyed her, although Kip was OK for some reason, probably because he was beyond hip. But others acted like they had lived through some traumatic revolution, and when you asked for details, most of it came down to drugs.

To GG the final frontier was total normality. She had tried almost everything once. She understood the attraction and was pretty sure if she allowed herself, she would have been high all the time, but she chose to almost never be high, mainly because her metabolism was very fragile. She only allowed herself one cup of tea and two light meals along with a half hour of yoga every day. She knew that when she was doing (for her) really good programming, she was one of only a handful of people in the world, and that gave her all the ecstasy she needed. Even a couple of beers at night could knock her off kilter for a day or two. Some day she would be able to go on a vacation and forget about being "productive." She felt she was almost there.

She read about Easy Girl on the MAX ride to the airport. It scared and saddened her. Kip had talked about how much he liked the atmosphere at the bakery, but she had never made it in to try her pastry. The murder had sparked a lot of comment, particularly on *SwiftPad*, regarding sex and serial killers. Rumors said that Elizabeth Kerns had actually left with a strange guy on the back of a motorcycle the afternoon before, and someone had heard a motorcycle leaving the bakery about 5 A.M. this morning. So she knew her killer and maybe was "dating" him. Figures, thought GG.

SwiftPad semi-generated a story that said that 96% of all hookups with strangers result in no physical or financial harm, but 67% are referred to years later as "dreadful mistakes." We're slipping already, thought GG. *SwiftPad* is starting to suck. Soon we would be highlighting celebrity news.

She knew that her parents would read about the killing and use it as another reason to try and coerce her to leave Portland and come back to DC, to the peppermint and honeysuckle of Northern Virginia.

Her sister was picking her up at Dulles. She had told her parents over a year ago where she was, and before that had let them know through her sister that she was all right. She had dropped her rebellious stance sometime after she quit black-hat hacking and gone to work for JAMMIT, talking to her father once a month, just hi, how are you. They seemed to think she had a boyfriend, and she never denied it and then confirmed it by refusing to give them any details, which she did to throw them off the scent. Her sister had come through Portland once at the height of the *SwiftPad* start-up, so they hadn't really had much time together. This little trip would be good, she told herself.

She looked for a book to buy on the plane, and picked up Fannie Flagg's *All-Girl Filling Station's Last Reunion*. It wasn't technical and it looked sloppy sentimental from the cover. She needed to get in touch with her mother. That would be the trick. Just be Mommy and Daddy's little girl for three days. She wasn't too optimistic it would work out that way but she was determined to try.

As she browsed the shelves in Powell's Airport bookstore, she heard Kip's *basso profundo* voice float past the bookstore's open door out on the concourse. She moved slowly toward the store entrance and kept the book just above her nose and watched as they walked down to the north terminal (United Airlines) entrance.

Kip was walking with a skinny, older guy, with bushy gray hair in a suit a half size too big. She paid for her Fannie Flagg book and slithered along the side of the concourse, moving quickly so she could duck into a store if they turned around.

They didn't stand in a security line, but went to the adjacent waiting area and sat down. Waiting for someone to arrive. She pretended to shop at the Brookstone store just opposite the security line, trying on headphones while watching. She would have to get through the line in another 15–20 minutes or so, so what was the plan?

She chased away a sales clerk with a smile, just browsing, she said. The key was the older guy, who was he? They were standing up!

Something on the old guy's hip.

She grabbed a pair of pink Barska binoculars off the shelf. She focused in on the bushy-haired old guy. Yep, there's the gun, must be a cop. Kip seemed pretty relaxed. They were getting up. The cop was waving. She turned the binocs toward the entrance. It was Tyler. That fucking bastard!

Slow down, she thought, this is Tyler. She smiled. He has to be here to see me, she thought. But I am leaving to see him! Something is off, though. Tyler looked at his phone. He looked up and around quickly, up the concourse, behind him from where he just disembarked. Then in her direction. She was behind the Brookstone window; she tried to hide and that was her mistake. He saw her move. That bastard hacked my phone! She had all location services off, so hacking in was the only way. She looked back at him with her pink binocs. He was smiling.

GG walked out of the Brookstone and tried to look angry. She was working herself up to be pissed off. She got up to him and he was smirking, as was Kip.

"You could have called me, instead of hacking my fucking phone!"

"This is weird. We appear to have walked into an awkward moment, Detective."

The cop smiled weakly at Kip, but seemed preoccupied.

"This is Detective Petrovich," said Kip. "He is investigating the murder at the bakery."

She ignored Kip and the cop. "Why are you here?" she asked Tyler.
"Well…"

"How do you two know each other?" asked Kip.

Both GG and Tyler looked at each other, then both reddened a bit.

"It was a long time ago. I haven't thought about it," said GG.

"I thought about it on the plane."

"Well, good for you then. Why are you in Portland?"

"I am on official business." Tyler looked unconvincingly hard and steely at GG. "It came to our attention that Detective Petrovich is looking into..." he looked at Lance who nodded, "...serious criminal activity, through the misuse of data collected by an unnamed government agency. As well as other crimes. I am here in an unofficial capacity to help the detective."

"Hacking my phone is serious criminal activity too..."

"We think Raleigh is the killer," said Kip.

GG continued to glare at Tyler and took a deep breath. "It had crossed my mind," said GG. "It makes sense, I just hadn't..." GG realized how much time she had spent with Highlooper over the last six months. "Jesus!"

"I am just here to help," said Tyler.

Petrovich smiled. On cue, the detective's phone rang and he walked away to take it.

Jim appeared, coming up from Terminal E. "She's not here. I bought a $50 ticket to Seattle and checked all of the gates."

"What?" asked GG.

"Macy and her kid are missing."

"My God! Why are you looking here?"

"Their passports are missing...I don't know, I am hoping..." Jim struggled not to seem hurt by her question.

GG went up to Jim and hugged him. Jim was struggling to maintain.

"Kip – I am leaving for DC. Right now," she said. "Remember I told you..."

"What!" said Tyler. "No! Wait."

"Why do you think I am here at the airport? Did you think your magic phone summoned me? I am going home to visit the family." She held up her ticket.

"No. Can't you postpone it? On second thought, maybe you should go, considering all that has happened. It might not be safe."

Tyler could see her wheels turning as soon as he said it.

Petrovich came back from his call. "They found the other body! We've got him! Let's go."

As they walked toward the airport exit, Petrovich gave the others a quick overview of the murder and the burial of Kathy Morton in the Richland utility vault and her just-now completed exhumation. His partner had just called to tell him that they hadn't identified her yet, but Lance had enough for Henderson to bring in Raleigh for questioning for the McKenzie murder. They had worked out the judicial mechanics in advance and by the time he arrived at Raleigh's place in Gresham, he expected Portland PD to be there with a warrant, decked out in Kevlar and a battering ram.

"I am just going to be a distraction, Lance," said Tyler. "When you bring him in, I can help, but..." Tyler was staring at Cynthia, looking a bit lost.

"No – we need to find Jim's girlfriend and her daughter. Can you find out if she flew anywhere this morning?"

"Yeah – give me her name – it will probably take a half an hour – clearance issues mostly."

"We can take the MAX back into town," she said.

"I thought..."

"I'll cancel it. I bought a refundable ticket." GG got on her phone with the airline without looking back at Tyler.

"I'll call you, Sebastian," said Petrovich, looking at Tyler. Without another word, the scraggly old cop ran up the stairs like a jackrabbit to the pedestrian bridge over to the parking garage.

GG, Kip and Jim took Tyler on the Red Line MAX back into downtown and went over to the food trucks by the Galleria. Tyler got some Greek eggplant pastry, Kip and GG split a goat cheese pizza and they walked over to O'Bryant Square park to eat. They sat in the shade and watched the skateboarders try and jump off of a two-foot ledge and keep their ride. Jim wasn't eating.

"They aren't very good," said Tyler. One of the boarders flew by, dreadlocks-over-heels, right past them onto the sidewalk.

"So what is this Sebastian shit anyway? What happened to Trek? Are you still Tyler?" GG asked.

He looked at GG and shrugged. "I can't keep track of my *noms de guerre* anymore anyway."

Tyler pulled up an email on his phone.

"OK, here it is. She left on a Singapore Air flight direct to Hong Kong out of SeaTac about ten minutes ago."

"Shit. I knew it."

"Macy Ming Cosino and Charlotte Ming. Does that stack up?"

Jim nodded. "I should have grabbed a flight when I was at the airport!"

"You wouldn't have gotten there in time. Or been able to stop her," said GG.

"She used to be just Macy Cosino, but..." Jim was staring off, "...I think she is divorced. But I'm not even sure. She is using her husband's name in the middle. Can you tell if anybody else is with them?"

"Give me a minute..."

"She must have left after I left, which was about 2 A.M. Jesus! It still doesn't make sense. Either somebody picked her up or she called a taxi and caught a Horizon Air shuttle to SeaTac. I guess they could have just walked down Vista to the MAX. Why?"

"She's OK, Jim. Macy can handle herself," GG reassured him.

"Why didn't she tell me?" He looked down at his phone and didn't say anything else.

GG wrapped her arm around Jim and put her chin on his shoulder. "It's going to be alright." He shook his head, absorbed with his iPhone.

"So I guess this Highlooper has fooled a lot of people, including all of you," said Tyler. "From what I gather, Highlooper might be responsible for more killings than these. Lance says he is a high-functioning, self-controlled, sado-sexual serial killer."

"How could we have missed it?"

"Why didn't he pick up his five million dollars this morning?" asked GG.

"Maybe he is planning something else," said Kip. "Or else he is losing it. He was off the rails last night at the board meeting."

"So how does this relate to you?" asked GG, who had been looking hard at Tyler since they sat down.

"We had a breach. A well-known corporation has abused the trust the government extended to it and accessed some personal data from the NSA database. We are not sure what that has to do with Raleigh, but he has been in communication with an agent of the company that received the stolen data."

"I know what this is about," said Kip.

"I am not sure you do." Tyler looked at Jim. "But Jim might know."

"This is something to do with when I was in the Army?"

Tyler made one of those faces that said, "I didn't say anything, but…"

"It's GIP, isn't? They are trying to rat fuck me so they can take over the KEG."

"Perhaps. But catching this guy Highlooper is the main thing to concentrate on."

"I think you are here for something else," said GG smiling.

"What's that?" said Tyler smiling back.

"Oh. I don't know, Tyler. I know it's not me, is it? I think your overseers in Spytown ordered you to figure out how to, let's say it nice, how to handle *SwiftPad*."

"*SwiftPad!* Let's see, a software company struggling to stay afloat in a world where the Internet is about to change. But the change will be to your advantage as long as you are as successful, as it appears you will be. You will soon be part of the Corporate Club that makes the rules."

"You've got to be shitting me! Are you kidding?"

"Big companies like yours will be able to afford the toll gates on the information superhighway…If you make it to be a big company – which – might not be in everyone's best interest."

"Is that what you mean? No! No! Tyler! Are you the same guy…"

"Alright," Kip's face was red. "Let him say what he means."

"It is true you are perceived by some as a threat and there are people in my sphere of activity that mean to take you down." Tyler paused and let that sink in. "But, what is more important, for now anyway, is I am your friend."

"So you are betraying your colleagues, the people you work with and who depend on you," Kip willed himself to tranquility.

Tyler looked at Kip. "Oh, it's not as dramatic as all that. But, I guess so. It wouldn't be the first time."

"Great! That's great." Kip got up and shook his hand. "Let's get something to drink. Sebastian, Tyler – whoever the fuck you are – do you want to come by and see the original *SwiftPad* data center, the rec room and office? Hey! Note to self, sell tickets to the office. The Origins of *SwiftPad*! GG Slept Here! We could get a Madame Tussaud's to make a 'GG' dummy."

Tyler laughed and looked at GG. "You ready?"

Kip watched another white Rasta boy fall off his board, sprawling out on the sidewalk, and wondered what really was going on between G and Tyler when Jim looked up with a faraway look in his eye.

"Hey, Stan. You're pretty ballsy on that board."

"Hey – Dude! No snow Dude! Long time! 's'up? The plane, right?"

Jim stood up and shook the skateboarder's hand. "You OK?"

"Yeah – a little scratch…"

"Yeah," Jim looked at GG and the others, "we sat next to each other coming into Portland. I knew I'd run into you again…Your girlfriend still in law school?"

"Oh, yeah, well, no, yeah sort of…she moved back to Boston last week. I think we broke up. Anyway she is going to try again next year back east somewhere. But that's cool. It's all good. I got a new squeeze. How about you?"

Stan popped his skateboard up in the air with his foot and it spun around and he caught it as it hung in the air next to him.

"I am heading to the airport now – chasing my squeeze down. I can't let her get away…she moved to Asia without me."

"Really? Wow. We got the bitches bailin', Dude! What's up with that?"

Jim gave him an exasperated chuckle.

"Don't let it bum ya. Oregon, dude! I mean…this is a rocking town. Wow. Who knows…?"

"Take it easy, Stan."

"You too, Dude."

Kip and GG stared at Jim. Tyler looked at the three of them.

"Yeah – that was Stan – an old friend…" Jim laughed to himself. "Anyway, I'm leaving. I am going to catch the MAX back to the airport right now. I just bought a ticket to Hong Kong. I gotta go catch the flight."

"Jim, why don't you wait. Once we get Raleigh, I'll come with you," said Kip.

"No, I've got my passport. Since my Army tour, I always carry it. I am going now, before her trail gets cold."

"I'll have our people keep an eye on you, and her if we can," said Tyler. "All your IDs will be tracked or soon will be. If she pops up on the radar, I'll ping you if I can. I'll know where you are, but once you are inside China, if that is where you are going, then it doesn't matter. China is not fucking around, they are crushing the Falun Gong. I looked up you girl friend's husband. He is in deep shit."

"I know. Thanks. I'll be fine."

"Jim, don't go," said GG. "Macy can swim in any ocean as long as she isn't sandbagged. You might draw attention to her. You could get her…"

Jim looked at her. "It doesn't matter what anyone says. I'm going to Hong Kong to find her. I can take care of myself too. I'll be careful."

"Bye, Jim," said GG as she hugged him. "Just be yourself and trust yourself."

Jim squeezed GG's hand and nodded. "That's the best advice. Chubby – get that fucker. But be careful."

"We got it – get back home quick with her, will you?" They hugged.

"Yeah." He waved and turned quickly away and started walking up to catch the MAX train.

GG turned to Tyler as Jim left. "Come on back to my place, you can get cleaned up and rest a little."

Chubby coughed.

"What?" She looked at Kip with stony eyes.

"Have fun, guys," said Kip. "Give me a call if you want to get together with me and Detective Petrovich. You heard him when he left, he needs me. He needs me to help catch Raleigh."

"We will meet you at the office in a couple hours," said GG. "I suggest you go take a shower and put on some clean clothes."

Kip smelled his own armpit and made a face like a slightly dissatisfied chef. "I'll go over to Cascade Sportswear and buy a new shirt. Repay Hariet for her generosity."

Chapter 34

<u>Government Lowers Hammer – Mark discusses Takeover @SwiftPad</u>

"Mark, thanks for your report. Where are you now? Are you still in Portland?"

"Yes. I intend to stay here through next week."

"Ah, uh…"

There was dead air for about ten seconds.

"Well Mark, this is a lot to digest. There are a number of issues you have brought up that are new to us and I think the team needs a little time to reflect on…"

"Well, as I said, time is the biggest issue." Mark was in shock, worse, he was afraid, angry, and at a complete loss. He couldn't think of anything else to say. Ken Oren was on, and yet, had not spoken at all during his entire ambitious presentation. In fact, nobody did; it went over like a dry turd. Nothing. No enthusiasm. Hostile silence. What happened?

He had laid out a road map for takeovers of both Consolidated E&G and *SwiftPad* with coordinated moves that took advantage of Jim Hunt's dual involvement. He wanted injunctions on *SwiftPad* for patent infringement. He recommended they release the "news" about Hunt being investigated for espionage while in the Army, hint at indictments pending, a call for Cynthia Oglethorpe to be arrested for Cyber-terrorism as the perpetrator of the hacking of the GIP Social Cloud. Destroy *SwiftPad*, then move in and buy it cheap. Push Consolidated E&G to fire Hunt, back off and let the outsourcing of IT operations proceed. Use the one thing that GIP still had – clout.

He tried again. "If it is true, that Hunt is being investigated for espionage…then – what is the hold-up? He's a traitor."

There was more dead air.

"There have been some changes since we last talked, Mark. We cannot go forward with that line of…" It was Suzanne and she was obviously struggling to think of what to say. "OK. What you suggest, this…this…plan is not viable. The information that you think we may or may not have…this information is not to be used…it's not viable…do you understand? Mark, it is imperative that these lines of inquiry be shut down."

"No problem," Mark said. Fucking assholes, he thought. He waited, but no one else said anything. He was a tethered goat.

"You understand? We are done. Mark. Do you understand?"

"Like I said, no problem. I guess I am done."

No one disagreed.

The team heard a beep.

"Is he off?" asked Ken Oren. "Everyone still on say your name."

"Suzanne."

"Mary O'Hara, the Crockett Group."

"David Bromfield, software."

"Persi, Outsourcing."

"John, sales."

"Five? Six beeps minus one right? OK, he is off. Comments?"

"Run away, run away!" said David. There was a titter of laughter.

"I think this is a mistake. This project is still viable, in our opinion," said Mary.

A muffled "Jesus!" was heard in the background.

"You haven't heard the worst," said Suzanne. "I don't know how to begin…but here it is. We, GIP, as in Kathy Snorkiss, the CEO, we have received a letter from…let's just say 'the Government,' but it is very high level and a very big deal, telling us we are being investigated and that serious criminal charges are about to be lodged against us."

"You mean..."

"One of our contractors working for...the Government... accessed and passed to us information regarding an earlier espionage investigation against Jim Hunt. It is not clear how Mark got ahold of the information..." She paused ever so slightly for Ken Oren to speak, but he didn't. "...but we have to stop it and stop Mark before any of it is made public. And as far as the plan to use Crockett resources to 'detain' this woman involved with *SwiftPad*... am I wrong or have we gone off in the deep end of the pool?" Of course Suzanne had known about the plan, and had written up the vague contract for it.

Ken Oren knew he was being pushed out of the igloo, but it was better than turning on one another and having it get worse. He had another job already anyway. Everyone else took Suzanne's lead and began silently rehearsing surprise and indignation about this egregious abuse of power.

"So, GIP is pulling out?" asked Mary without any embarrassment at the obviousness of the question.

"Ken?" asked Persi. Ken, as they all knew, had been the one to pass the purloined intel about Jim Hunt's activities in the Army 25 years ago.

"I'm here." Ken knew his career was over at GIP and he was hoping to get out with as few scars as possible. He already had an offer for a VP job at a Credit Card company. "My advice," said Ken, "is to put Mark down slowly. Don't fire him yet or even hint that anything is wrong. We have to keep this under the lid. I'll call DeFonzaro and tell him we are out. As far as this *SwiftPad* business, we have instigated nothing. Correct?"

What Ken Oren knew and no one else on the call did, was that they would all be laid off within a month. GIP was getting ready to launch "Operation Gold Dust," one of their herd culling exercises, to impress the stockholders looking in on the monkey cages. About 30,000 people would be let go. So it really didn't matter. GIP was trying to jettison its past again, and they were all in the rear view mirror, ghost workers.

"No, well, no. I think we are clear..." said Suzanne, "...we have done research, personal research, which, if it gets to court, could be subpoenaed. We just have to make sure..."

"Mary...?"

"I'll have our people in Portland stand down. But this is a mistake – what did Churchill say, 'When going through hell – keep going.'"

"Excuse me? Stand down? Could you explain?" Suzanne asked, as if she didn't know.

"We had two operatives who have been in contact with your contractor, Lonnie Wolfe. They have been inactive. I will order them out of Portland next week, once we know..."

"...I would do it now," said Ken. "I mean – don't wait. Get with them right now and order them out of that fucking city."

"Anything else?"

Someone coughed.

"Fucking Portland. What did ol' man Bush call it?"

"Little Beirut," said Mary.

After five seconds of silence there were five BIPS.

"Don't answer it," said Raleigh.

"It's my boss." Mark looked at Raleigh, who shook his head ominously. Mark looked at his phone. "Alright, fuck. OK," he cut off the incoming call.

Raleigh shook his head. He was on Mark's GIP laptop and ("Hey, I am not supposed to use that computer for chat rooms!") was watching a seldom-posted-to chat group that discussed Arsenio Hall's possible return to TV. Lonnie Wolfe was a long-time active member of the group, often calling for a return of "real entertainment" to late night TV. He used slightly coded messages on the chat site to tell the two Crockett Group operatives he wanted to plan and execute the operation tonight. The reply was simple and clear. "We are out, done. Over."

"We are free now, Mark. It is all ours."

"What are you talking about?" Mark stood at his closet and looked for a shirt.

"Obviously your people are pulling out. So it is ours to keep."

"What about those guys from the Crockett Group? Aren't they supposed to meet us?'

"They are out. Gone. It is just you and me."

"Then so am I! I am not going to get fired. I am going to call my boss." He only brought four shirts, plus the one he had been wearing. He couldn't decide which one...

"I don't think so," said Raleigh. "First of all, your career is over at GIP. Don't you see that? You are done. They are not ever going to use a guy involved in a dirty project like this. They advertise at the Olympics and the Masters, the holy of holies. You are a toxic floater waiting for the flush. And your girlfriend at Consolidated..." Raleigh laughed. "What is your job anyway? The only thing you know how to do is fuck up a company."

"That's not true! Angie is still...I can manage projects. I am a certified Project Manager. I..." He thought for a minute. "What am I supposed to do then?" Mark wanted to go home, to his condo in Santa Monica, but what if it was true? Three thousand a month rent, plus management fees and even his Bimmer cost almost two hundred a month to park...Fuck it, he thought; he picked out the one with the solid blue collar.

"Look? You want money, right? A lot of it, right?"

"Yaah," he said. He was missing SoCal. He had to get out of here. "Yaah! I need money," he said. He put on the shirt, buttoned it, but then unbuttoned it so he could roll some deodorant on.

"How's that working out for you at GIP? Are you making money there? As soon as they know you are out of Portland, you are done at GIP."

"You are right. I need more money. And GIP...fuck...you are right."

Raleigh got up, but grabbed the edge of the chair and winced in pain. His ankle was killing him. He pulled himself up, and limped a few steps, and stood opposite Mark. Raleigh smiled and straightened the wide dark blue collar on Mark's acrylic shirt, which was also dark blue on the sleeves and on the stripe down along the buttons. The rest of it was light blue, a retro-Vegas look. "You look good. I like the way you dress. Not like these hippie leftovers here in Portland."

Raleigh was wearing a blue sweatsuit with a white stripe down the side, which he had borrowed from Mark while his clothes were being "express cleaned" by the Marriott concierge services.

"So what do we do?" Mark got up and looked in the mirror to see how Raleigh had straightened his collar. Behind him, he saw a reflection from the window – a light – a flash of light! "Did you see that?" He turned and pointed to the sky above the OMSI Museum across the river.

"What? What are you talking about?" Raleigh walked to the ninth floor window and looked out at the Morrison Bridge and the Willamette. Upriver a bit was Tilikum Crossing, the new street car and bicycle bridge. To Raleigh, it looked like a broken Slinky. The Willamette was like the Nile, it flowed straight north. No wonder this town is weird, he thought. "The key is the bitch. Cynthia Oglethorpe or GG, as she calls herself. She is the brains, plus she has about a 30–35% stake in *SwiftPad*. I have at least 10%."

"I thought you sold that for..." Mark went to the window and looked out.

"I haven't signed anything!" Raleigh shouted. "If we can control her, we will have 45–50% of the company. And between us, 99% of the brains! We just have to move..."

"But isn't that kidnapping?"

"We just want to have a discussion. She will just come with us because we are offering her a way to escape from the losers, Rehain and the rest of them. I can handle her. I know how to handle women. That is the difference between you and me."

Mark's face reddened perceptibly. "How do we do it?"

"You still work for GIP, right? Call her up and tell her GIP has a business proposition. She will listen, no reason for her not to, right?"

"Call who up?" Mark stared out over the Willamette.

"Oglethorpe! The cunt GG! Pull your fucking head out!"

"But..." He kept looking up and down the East Bank Esplanade. "Didn't you see..."

Raleigh pulled him around and shook his shoulders. "Once she agrees, we switch, take out GIP and get other money into it. I have access to money. A lot of it."

"Can I call Angie?"

"No! No! We have to move. Where the fuck are my clothes; what's the extension for the concierge?"

There was a knock at the door. Raleigh checked the mirror and straightened his hair and opened the door. A bellhop delivered the cellophane-wrapped package.

"You're late, asshole," said Raleigh. He slammed the door.

Chapter 35

Petrovich announces they found Killer's Lair - Kip steals Tyler's phone

Angie looked over at her door from her computer. "Jim! Come in! Close the door, sit down…"

"I'm not staying. I am leaving. I guess I am quitting…"

"What? No! No! Jim, you won! You were right! GIP is getting the boot! DeFonzaro! You should stay around just to see him! Just seeing him with that hangdog look is worth it all. You won! What is the matter?"

"I am in love, Angie, and she left and I need to go find her."

She looked at him and brushed away something from the corner of her eye and shook it off. "The woman you told me about?"

"Yeah. She is in some kind of trouble, or she is trying to help someone in trouble. I have to go help her. I am flying to Hong Kong now, I need to get to the airport. I have to catch the next train, so I just stopped by to…" he tried to give her a handwritten note.

"Stop! Resignation not accepted! Not accepted! Take care of things. We are in good shape here. I'll cover for you. I'll pay you as much as I can and if it takes longer, I'll figure out how to get you a leave of absence."

"Don't worry about any of that. But OK. We'll see when I get back. But you should start thinking about a Plan B. Can I make one suggestion?"

"Sure."

"Put Lester in charge while I am gone. Make him the boss of the crew. Make him...I think he would be great, to be honest."

Angie looked at Jim as if he were crazy, but shrugged. "OK. I was thinking of Janice – but she never comes to meetings. I'll work with him."

"That's it. I gotta go. Are you alright?"

"Yeah, Jim. I've decided something. I am done! I am through with you know who. Best that we forget all that. I had to see what was on the other side. Fini! All gone. Never happened! Don't need it."

They both stood up and hugged, quickly but without awkwardness. "I'll write you. A real letter – but It might be a while."

"It's OK. Lester is in charge."

They both laughed and he left.

"Hey Dad," Kip said into his phone.

"Kipling! How's the boy! Making money for me?"

"We are doing good."

"Good to hear. So what's up? Are you going to try and make a go of it or sell it off to the highest bidder?"

"I think we need to sell it off."

"Why?"

"Dad...come on...It is getting so big and mistakes are starting to get real expensive."

"Business is hard work and common sense. What about Jim? Isn't he helping?"

"That's what I wanted to talk about. Is Alice there?"

"She is here now..."

"I wanted to tell her...Macy and her daughter seemed to have... gone off to Asia, probably China, without telling Jim. Jim left today.

He's following her...to Singapore or Hong Kong I think...Something to do with her ex-husband, who we think is in jail over there."

"Oh...[It's Kip, Jim went to China. – What?] Hold on..."

"I don't think he knows where she is."

"Hi Kip, it's Alice. Well, I understand. I am proud of him – he is finally following his heart. Relationships are complicated. Jim will figure it out."

"Uh huh." Kip didn't want to get into a long conversation about life and relationships with Jim's mother. He felt he had enough problems of his own.

"That murder in Portland...what is going on with the world?"

"Yeah. I knew his last victim..."

"What? His last victim?"

"It's a serial killer..." Kip stopped himself. Normally he loved shocking people. Saying outrageous things to scare or otherwise pull on people's chain. But not today. "The cops are on it. They are going to catch him pretty soon I am sure."

Kip's dad heard something in his voice. "You be careful," he said gravely. Then his tone switched. "So you are making money right?"

"Not really. But the perceived value is going up like a rocket and that's all that counts. On paper, you are at least ten times richer than you were last month. Well...of course it ain't made until we have it, and taxes will kill us, but I am sure Heber will figure it out."

"I don't trust him as far as I can smell him. You keep an eye on him. I can see him skipping out with some 18-year-old girl for Brazil and leaving his wife and six kids high and dry."

"Yeah, right!"

"Oh yeah! That goes double for you!"

"Love ya, Dad, best to Alice."

"You too, kid."

Kip hung up the phone. For the first time in his life, he was actually worried. It was Friday night and the *SwiftPad* headquarters was nearly deserted. GG and that spook were probably humping like hamsters.

He had so much work to do that if he stayed at it all weekend, he would barely dent it. He was depressed. The company had changed fast. Heber had rented most of a new office building in Hillsboro, where the new hires were being stowed until they could be on-boarded, or else working from home, logging in remotely to work. Heber was staying in Portland almost permanently. He was running scared too, trying to keep it together. He had made it clear that they had to sell or bring in a whole new management team, but that was too big of a decision to make yet.

Kip was depressed because he didn't go to Asia with Jim, which was what he wanted to do, what he should have done. But he was stuck doing what he hoped that he could have talked Jim into doing.

He felt guilty, if for no other reason than he and the Easy Girl had flirted and he never did anything about it and now she was dead. In spite of *SwiftPad*'s seeming success, he felt like everything he had done lately had been a fuckup, just like always. Nothing had changed.

And somebody had drank all his Sangria too.

His Android phone rattled.

"Kip, it's Lance Petrovich. Is Tyler there?"

"No."

"He hasn't been answering his phone," Lance hesitated. "Listen, I want you to be careful. Raleigh is the guy, no doubt now. We found his lair. It is worse than I..." Lance's voice cracked a little, "He video-recorded it all. A couple of the Portland cops could not take it, retching...Anyway we found your name on some kind of death-list in his house. He doesn't like you much. You have to be careful."

"No idea where he is?"

"We are watching everything. We got his car. The techs are going through everything in his place out here. I have to say this again. I want you and Cynthia to be extra careful. He is the worst monster I have ever come across. Where is she?"

"With Tyler. I assume catching up on old times."

"I guess that is why he wasn't answering. OK, you ever eat at the Paradigm?"

"Yeah, it's pretty good."

"Let's have dinner there. It's in the Pearl, right? I'll meet you in an hour, hour and half. I'm not quite done out here yet. If you see or hear from Tyler or Cynthia, try to get them to come too."

"Alright."

About five minutes later he heard someone coming up the stairs. Raleigh still had a key to the place, he was pretty sure. Kip pulled out his serrated pocket knife, opened it and went to the top of the stairs. Take him from the high ground, he thought.

"Wow. You scared me! You're not mad, are you Kip?" It was GG. He had to look twice to recognize her. She had glamourized herself with an elegantly draped red dress, droopy gold earrings and a simple string of white pearls the size of malted milk balls draped around her long bare neck. She had washed out the black dye and her honey blond hair was half up and half down, surrounding her earrings.

"Jesus!" She smiled at him slightly. Behind her, coming up the rough wooden stairs, was Tyler, looking pressed and sharp in black slacks, blue shirt and skinny red tie.

"Too much?"

Kip nodded. "What's going on?"

"Well, we aren't sure," said GG. "We got a strange call from that GIP guy who has been pestering Jim over at the power company... Mark Ruskin? Was that it, Tyler?"

"Yeah."

"He wants to meet me. Just me, he said...downtown at a restaurant, the Chinese place, the Mandarin Harbor."

"What's he want?"

"He says he has an offer to make from GIP for our company."

"Which is bullshit," said Tyler, sitting down across from Kip. "He has been cut off from GIP. They are pulling up stakes completely on both of his Portland projects. The GIP CEO is shitting Legos over losing their NSA contracts. We need to get there early so I can watch him."

"Lance called and said to watch out for Raleigh. They found some horrible shit at his house."

"Uh huh," Tyler said.

"It's definitely him?" asked G.

"Yeah, definitely. By the way, how do you know so much? How did you know GG was in the airport earlier?" Kip turned on his serious radio voice.

"You mean my magic phone?" Tyler took the phone out, smiled goofily at GG and passed it to Kip. "See? I even created an icon with an old picture of her. Don't even need to log in to activate it." He smiled with a smug, satisfied look that annoyed Kip.

"It is fucking creepy," said GG, hiding a smile.

"Well," Kip was going to make a comment about it not being that creepy, based on what he guessed they had been doing since they went to her little alcove attic apartment. Had she always had those clothes? But he held his tongue. He also noticed Tyler's phone was the same color and shape as his.

"OK, let's get this over with," said Tyler. Kip handed him back a phone and they all got up. "Where are you going?"

"I'll be up in the Pearl having dinner with Lance. I guess Raleigh had a torture room in his house."

"Yeah, I am on top of it. OK, we'll catch up with you later tonight," Tyler replied.

"Detective Petrovich told me to ask you to come with me to the Paradigm."

"Naw. We're going to go see what's up with this GIP dick."

Kip shrugged. "What's the...why all dressed up?"

"Sometimes a girl just wants to feel pretty," GG said.

Chapter 36

<u>**GG's meeting with Mark to Discuss SwiftPad's Future is Interrupted**</u>

It had become a little chilly and started raining in the late afternoon, and the dark clouds had sent the sun to bed early. Tyler and GG stood at the bar at the Veritable Quandary, knocking back potato vodka gimlets. "I'll go first," said Tyler, "follow me in five or ten minutes."

Tyler left the Quandary and walked down 2nd Avenue to the Mandarin Harbor, an upscale, older restaurant that stayed within the taste range of its largely non-Asian clientele. Its entrance was close to and visible from both 2nd and from Columbia. The spotless white cloth covered tables were spaced far enough apart for diners to talk candidly. The bar was packed. Tyler squeezed in and ordered a Lychee Martini.

Tyler knew what Mark looked like, and he saw him come in and ask to sit at a table next to the door. This set off an alarm for Tyler, and he was just about to text her not to come when she walked in and was recognized by Mark, who jumped up too eagerly and quickly invited her to sit down with him.

Tyler watched them. He knew she had been with that stinky asshole, Rehain. When she told him that, it had – he just didn't know what to think – tonight, he thought, tonight it would be better.

She seemed so unlike the hard-nosed, grungy computer hacker he had known and trained and shared a chaotic apartment with years ago. Portland had fucked her up, that was clear. He knew he could put this out of his mind – put it in the past. He was going to get past that. He had to focus now – forget all that.

Tyler couldn't hear the small talk, but from their gestures, that was lessening, and the serious discussion had started. The GIP Consultant appeared to order a shrimp cocktail appetizer and Cynthia just pointed to the drink menu, probably another vodka gimlet, her third tonight. Slow down, girl, Tyler thought.

The discussion was clearly entering a serious phase. I should have wired her up with her phone so I could listen, he thought. Then Mark got pulled into a conversation with the guy next to him, whose date had gone to the ladies room. The topic was the previous day's murder on 23rd street. Gypsy Jokers was this guy's guess. Motorcycle gang initiation gone wrong. Tyler nodded while watching Cynthia.

She was smiling and laughing as she shook her head, as if rejecting a ridiculous proposal. But then it got more intense. She contracted her hands and was rubbing her fingers. She nodded yes, then no, shaking her head, finally no. The GIP consultant looked away from her and grabbed his forehead as if he had a headache. Tyler had his eye on the door. Something was bubbling. A couple came in and Tyler was looking closely at them.

He didn't notice the leathery faced man with the starched white shirt and bleached flaxy hair come slowly out of the men's room behind him.

Mark got up, stepped around the table, and pulled Cynthia up by the arm.

Tyler stood up from the bar and pulled out his PPX 9mm, but Raleigh shot him twice from behind, in the back and the neck, and Tyler went down like a rag doll.

Raleigh then limped slowly toward Mark, waving his gun at screaming diners, who were diving under their tables. Mark dragged Cynthia over toward the restaurant entrance. Raleigh looked around the restaurant and then pulled Cynthia away from Mark and put his gun to her head.

Mark obsequiously got the door and held it open, while trying to shield his face from recognition. Raleigh laughed at him and then shot him point blank in the face. He turned around.

"Stay down. Anybody talking on their phone gets it in the head. Heads down!" Then he pulled her out of the restaurant.

Almost diagonally across town, at the Paradigm Bar, Lance, Henderson and Chubby were pouring down bourbon almost as fast as the bartender could serve it.

"This sucks," said Henderson.

"I had a great dinner here once. I think..." said Petrovich. "... we better eat and stop the booze. That monster has no place to go now. I have a feeling he's going to make a move soon. He knows the longer he waits, the weaker he will be."

Henderson looked at Lance. "You were right, goddammit. Now this is going to fuck up your superstar record."

"You mean 22 years ago? Yeah. I fucked up."

"Doctors and cops bury their mistakes. It's the way it goes." Henderson turned to Kip to change the subject. "How come you didn't become a cop? You look like a cop. You sound like a cop."

Kip looked at Henderson out of the corner of his eye and smiled enigmatically. "You guys get up too early."

"That is definitely not true. Let's order something to eat," said Henderson, but as he downed the last of his drink, his phone went off. After listening for twenty seconds, he stood up, and said, "Let's go!"

It took them almost ten minutes to get the mile or so across Portland to the Mandarin Harbor. There was a heavy drizzle coming down. Traffic was wall-to-wall, nothing was moving. Henderson used his siren and flasher to good effect though and got them there faster than safety would have normally allowed. They pretty much knew what had gone down from the radio dispatches when they pulled up.

Tyler was just being put into the ambulance.

Henderson asked one of the drivers, "How is he?" He replied by shrugging his shoulders, but widened his eyes in a gesture that said, "Maybe…"

Mark's body was lying where he fell, covered. Four or five cops were interviewing the customers, most who looked extremely shaken.

"It is him. He grabbed GG and shot his accomplice in the face. No question about it. Descriptions match to a tee. He came in earlier and was hiding in the bathroom. One of the waiters was concerned he was in the shitter for so long."

"Did anybody get a description of the car?"

"The door guy said it was a blue BMW sedan, California plates. It took off, up Columbia, didn't see it turn."

"Kip, sorry you have to stay here. Let's go, Lance. I'll drive."

Kip was in shock. He had GG. That shit-monster had GG. He knew all along, everyone knew, that he was some kind of sick son-of-a-bitch, with a good line of bullshit!

Then he felt in his pocket and pulled out Tyler's phone. He looked at the ambulance that was pulling away. The App! The GG App! Tyler didn't need his phone now anyway. He clicked on the icon with the picture of GG.

He looked around. One of the cops had arrived on a black mountain bike and hadn't locked it. Kip didn't even look around, but just jumped on it and took off.

It was a clear night, and the city lights sparkled. GG was trying to keep her head, not to panic, to think, to believe there was a way out. Raleigh slid Mark's Bimmer to a stop in Washington Park just above the Portland Rose Garden. He's not trying to get away, she thought. That means he is going to kill me. She could only think of one thing to do.

"Raleigh, you can still escape, why don't you just leave me here and get out. It is going take them a while…"

"Shut up." He was wincing in pain as he limped, dragging her over the gearshift through the driver-side door. He could barely stand; each step shot bolts of pain up his leg. They moved like mating crabs through the Rose Garden, both drawing blood on their arms and faces as the wet, thorny bushes slapped against them. GG stumbled. He held the gun to her head, pistol whipping her when she fell, and dragged her up and then down a path until they came the Rose Garden Amphitheater. The grassy hollow was deserted and the moss-covered ancient concrete benches seemed to be populated with the ghosts silently watching another ending play out, waiting for another one to join them. He stopped to catch his breath.

Regina McKenzie, watching, leaned forward with her hands on her chin and behind her, half hidden by the darkness, Kathy Morton looked on intently.

"Get out of here!" he screamed at his victims. "Get out!" Regina looked at Kathy and smiled.

He pulled GG to the bottom of the Greek theater, onto the "stage," pushed her down and stood over her while holding the his semi-automatic pistol down, half pointed at her and half at the ground.

"I want to fuck you so bad, Raleigh," GG said, straightforward, no fear in her voice. "Do you want to fuck me? I always have, ever since that night when…it was…you…you made it happen! You made *SwiftPad* happen – it's your company. We – we thought of *SwiftPad*. But it's your baby! We are going to be billionaires. You know you can get off. We can hire an army of lawyers, come on, let's seal the deal. It's going to be OK. First though…let's fuck now. Come on! Come on! I know you always wanted to. This is perfect. We can imagine everyone is all around us, sitting up, watching while you fuck me, Raleigh."

"Shut up!" Raleigh relaxed his grip and looked up. It started to rain harder. He looked over at the amphitheater. The Easy Girl had joined Regina and Kathy. They all sat together and they were giggling and whispering to each other.

"GET OUT OF HERE!" he yelled.

"You can fuck me anyway you want to! Drive it into me! I am getting wet already, come on!" She unzipped and pulled her slinky red dress off, while he watched, seemingly frozen. The rain moistened her skin and her eye shadow began to run. She got on her knees in her thong and bra, and began undoing Raleigh's pants.

"No!" He pounded her on the side of the head with his fist, knocking her to the ground.

She was dazed and muddy, but knew she had to keep her head. She didn't cry, she didn't scream; she got back up on her knees and forced herself to stay in the moment. "Raleigh, I know you are going to do what you are going to, but I don't care now. I just want one last good fuck before I die. Come on! I want your hard cock in me!"

She forced herself to stay upright, while her head reeled from the blow to her head. She went back to his pants and this time he let her unbuckle and unzip him. His was limp, so she pulled his pants down and put his dick in her mouth. Think, Cynthia, you have him now, one hard bite down and a twist of his balls and you can run! But then she heard him rack the slide on his pistol, pushing a round into the chamber. She felt it press against her head. Wait for it, she thought.

"Oh, Raleigh," she said, pulling back, "I want it all in me. I'll make you so hard you'll fuck me unconscious." She started again, working back and forth playing with her tongue. He was hardening. She looked to the side; it was pretty dark down in the Amphitheater.

She could tell he was not anywhere near climaxing. She worked it harder and he began to slowly to get harder. He killed Tyler, she thought. She began to lose control as she thought of him gunning down Tyler in that restaurant. The anger boiled up in her and she could not go on anymore.

"That's it! I told you cunts to leave!" he pointed the gun at the seats and fired three times.

As she felt him take the gun away, she bit down as hard as she could, grinding and ripping and felt her teeth touch and then pulled hard back with all her weight as she clamped down on his cock. She opened her mouth and pushed his bloody dick out with her tongue and pulled away as fast as she could.

He screamed and fell to his knees. He fired blindly in the general direction she moved, and again and again, and he screamed again…

Then he was down. Kip was on him, pounding his head, again and again and again with his fist. When he stopped moving, Kip pulled his gun away and grabbed it.

He went over to GG. She was bleeding. "It's my leg." He had shot her in the calf so Kip ripped off his shirt and made a tourniquet. "The cops will be here soon, I called them as soon as I saw…"

"Kip, I had to…"

"You're alive! You made it!" Kip went back over, stood over Raleigh and pulled him on his back. He had never seen so much blood.

"Jesus! Your dick is almost gone, man! You are going to be a special treat for your cellmate!"

"Help me!"

"Yeah, OK." Kip kicked him hard in the ribs. "I'll help you." Kip pulled out his serrated pocket knife, and with a flick of his wrist cut through the loose skin and veins that were still holding it, and kicked his dick away. Then he kicked him again.

"There, mother fucker!"

"I am going to die, help me!" Kip shrugged and walked back to GG.

GG was spitting and rubbing her mouth with her wrist. "Get my dress, will you? It's over there." They heard the sirens coming up the hill.

"He was still alive when they put him in the ambulance," said Kip, holding her up. "He might make it, G."

"Oh God! Oh fuck! What are we going to do, Chubby?"

"Hey, nobody calls me Chubby but Jim."

"After this, I think I get to call you Chubby."

"OK, G. But for the record, you bit it off completely. Right?"

"Sure," she said baring her blood-stained teeth. "I bit it right off."

Chapter 37

Where some of Our Characters May live Happily Ever After

Raleigh had almost bled out, but the paramedics got him up to Pill Hill (Oregon Health & Science University Hospital) in about 40 minutes and they were able to save him with transfusions and the like. But he was in a coma for two days, and when he woke he was delirious and never really came out of it. The cops kept an audio recorder running next to his bed in the hopes that he might babble something pertinent about other victims, but it was total gibberish, combined with flat-out screaming at someone or something that he thought was torturing him. The *Willamette Weekly* obtained a copy of the audio and their feature guy wrote a long column with extended commentary, suggesting a pattern of lucidity that went way beyond guilt and paranoia, but that it was a secret code similar to Dutch Schultz's equally incomprehensible death-bed rantings, words and phrases that seemed to refer to another invisible world, that only Raleigh could see.

His penis was not found until the next morning, so it was too late to reattach. The next day they asked Cynthia, again, if she really had bit it off, but she stuck to the story. Henderson inexplicably never had Kip searched that night, and Kip never did get rid of his serrated folding knife, although he did clean it thoroughly later.

A month later, Raleigh mercifully came down with some kind of bizarre staphylococcus. He continued to scream in constant horrible pain, even though they shot him full of morphine and antibiotics. Finally they just put in him a morphine coma. He never talked about his other crimes, or victims. They never got the infection under control and he died two weeks later, taking his secrets with him.

The GIP CEO resigned a couple weeks after Mark Ruskin was killed at the Mandarin Harbor, and they hired a new, squeaky clean CEO who promised that transparency would be the watchword for GIP. She immediately laid off 25,000 employees, including all of the Outsourcing team that worked with Mark. Ken Oren went to work as a VP for MasterCard.

The KEG continued to be a locally owned company. There was no takeover or outsourcing and DeFonzaro left for a Houston energy company to be the assistant CFO. The KEG's stock rose five points in the next three months. DeFonzaro made a few nasty comments to a Houston newspaper about Portland and Oregon in general and got a personal welcome to Texas from the Governor.

Swensson had the KEG's CEO rent out Columbia Edgewater Golf Club for a company tournament and barbecue for all employees past and present. Angie got drunk and fucked Lester in a sand trap next to the 17th green.

Heber sold *SwiftPad* for about $8.7 billion to Amazon after flirting with Google and Yahoo and even GIP, for form's sake. Jeff Bezos made the money contingent on "staff continuity" at least for the first six months. Bezos brought in some of his Stanford MBA boys and girls to run things while pretending that Chubby and GG were still in charge.

Amazon wanted the *SwiftPad* "engine" to back-end a new section of the *Washington Post,* which, as you all know, Jeff Bezos also owned. He thought that it would herald in a new form of journalism, and perhaps might lead to a new understanding of the world for his readers. It was fine with GG. She went on TV with Katie Couric and told her how she had pulled and tore at it like a dog and spit it out as she rolled away.

But she lost interest in *SwiftPad*. Chubby took to smoking dope with the key application developers and eventually one of Bezos's MBAs told him he didn't have to come to work anymore, if he didn't want to. GG got the same message for different reasons. She went back to coding full time and kept changing the algorithms to satirize Amazon. But their exploits were part of the lore of the company and the new team seldom ended a staff meeting without someone referring to it and getting a big laugh out of everybody. Creative people are such a hoot. Eventually though, it was clear that *SwiftPad* as an independent App would be abandoned and eventually forgotten.

Bezos ended up keeping an office in Portland, but moved the development team to Seattle. But the *Post's* "Meta-News" creative team ended up moving to Portland. It was a big deal and had a huge influence on the News business. CNN ended up doing a morning show from the top of the Wells Fargo Center and even Al Jazeera America did an entertainment show from Portland. Portland was gradually becoming one of the major media centers of the US. Reality continued to be a major component of what was reported in major media outlets, although it was difficult to empirically demonstrate.

More and more money flowed into the town. It became less weird, although officially was still weird. But sometimes they had to work at the weirdness to keep up the image. Bezos and Paulson, and even Paul Allen chipped in for a series of weird grants, money to deserving weirdos who did their part to keep the City weird. But even with all of that, it was still a good town, if you could roll your eyes at the silliness. The TV show *Grimm*, which took place in Portland, even had an episode about some German Werewolf at a Portland Tech company that seemed like it was "ripped from the headlines."

Tyler survived Raleigh's bullets, but was partially paralyzed for a while. His hands and arms were fine and he could feel his toes right away, but he couldn't walk, which puzzled doctors. The doctors were optimistic of an eventual recovery. He retired from the government on a full pension, and he never heard from Waterfall again. Vapor and OSWL disappeared from the Espiosphere. He moved to Portland to begin his rehab and new life.

But that new life would not include Cynthia. That was his decision, not hers. He was friendly about it, but firm. He never really said why, although she suspected he couldn't get past her carnivorous blow job. He said he didn't love her anymore, and he was sorry he seduced her when she was so young, but that was then and this is now. No drama, at least from him. Cynthia was a bit confused by it, but accepted it. Tyler took up with his rehab nurse. She was an older lusty blonde (who bore a slight resemblance to Renate) and she apparently gave him incentive to get back on his feet. His nurse hated GG and showed it by being really, really nice to her.

Kip's dad had a heart attack about a month after they sold *Swift-Pad*. He survived, but was much diminished in his vigor, mostly sitting in a porch chair wrapped in a blanket, even on warm days. He was now was a billionaire a couple times over, but he was pretty rich before so it meant nothing to him. Alice, Jim's mom, stayed with him, in fact seemed to shine even brighter than before. She took charge of everything. Enrique and Rosa, now completely vested, were still in charge of operations, but mostly they traveled the world, so Alice set up committees to do things. And her friends had lots of ideas. The Compound would no longer be a tree farm but a high-end retreat and village with a Hobbit theme (Alice was chairperson of the credentials committee). It was a combination of barrows and tree houses (with some brilliant architectural innovations that used the forest without disturbing it – too much.) The bottom land became the public areas, but because of certain drainage problems, most of the public structures, such as the theater, the Everything Free Store, the conference center/gym, post office (letters were strongly preferred over email), and the doctor's office (they had no trouble recruiting medical people, even just to work for free) were built on pilings that were disguised and camouflaged so that they looked like moss-covered gingerbread houses floating on the meadow. They were especially impressive when the fog would hang low in the mornings. Gardens were everywhere as were goats, chickens, some sheep and a few horses. They talked about how to keep it a going concern, which would mean schools and more jobs for parents. That would be phase 2 and the younger people could take over then.

Heber figured the venture would cost 40-50 million in the first two years and about a million a year after that. Walt said that they could always re-start the tree farms. Alice laughed at Walt and said that was for the next generation. She invited many of her old hippie friends (and they brought their friends) to live there and they made the best beer and grew the best weed on the West Coast.

As for Stan, the BU White Rasta boy Jim had met on the plane, he and his new squeeze started a Beer Pub Co-op near their townhouse in the Pearl. They had some problems with infidelity, too complicated to detail here, but they worked it out, at least for the meantime.

Chubby eventually moved down to be with his old man and help out with the building of the new community. He began writing the screenplay for what would be his masterpiece, the film that would explain it all, a film that would bring together the various loose strings of history. From the pyramids to the library at Persepolis, to Jesus in India as a boy, the visions of William Blake and Don Juan perhaps told through the eyes of Phillip Marlowe, who walked through a Time Warp wormhole after Eddie Mars spiked a bottle of Old Forester with peyote extract. It would have a budget, a big budget. Clearly now the sky was the limit. It would be shot in black and white with ultra-high speed 50-mm lens. It would be a trilogy.

He got into it and had a lot of ideas and wrote hundreds of pages, and figured he had years to develop it, so in the meantime he helped Alice with her Community project. It was his idea to convert the miniature railroad that ran into Albany to deliver Christmas trees into a semi-high-speed private commuter train that hooked up with the Albany Amtrak station.

Christened "Brook Farm West," Alice's commune (which they never called a commune, although the press did) would eventually become one of the most prestigious communities on the West Coast, with a think-tank spinoff and a yearly retreat that took place in winter so that activity would transpire around big fireplaces in cozy lodges, under crystal-clear roofs that reverberated the patter of the rain. The yearly retreat would eventually attract A-list writers, academics and politicians, with many of the sessions shown on C-SPAN.

GG, after hemming and hawing and stalling and whining, finally decided to leave Oregon, although she promised she would eventually come back. She said she wanted it to be home, but she had to see the rest of the world before she settled down. She never again dressed like a successful urban woman. She returned to pigtails, jeans, sneakers and tee shirts or raggedy sweaters. But she did stop wearing dark eye makeup and dyeing her hair black.

Before she left she came down to the Rehain Compound and stayed with Kip for a month. She and Alice got along and the old man loved her and told her to "knock off the birth control!" She and Kip were very happy for a while. But much to Kip's surprise, she finally did leave. She said she was going to go and find Jim and Macy.

They would get a postcard every month from Jim, saying he was alright and very little else. He noted that he was following Kip's admonition to never use email but to trust the post office. He never touched any of his *SwiftPad* money, which was piling up. The cards were always postmarked from somewhere in Southeast Asia – Malaysia, Vietnam, Nepal, Thailand, sometimes Myanmar. He sent one picture, probably from Vietnam, of himself sitting in a boat, fishing while wearing a conical Asian peasant's hat. He looked calm, but sad. They always came from around China but never in it. He never mentioned Macy or Charlotte.

Chubby was mad at GG for going off to find Jim and Macy and not inviting him, in fact dis-inviting him. The condition of her promise to come back to him was that he not follow or try and find her. It was the only way, she said, they would ever have a chance to be together. He wondered if anyone could ever make any promises about the future. He wondered if people who did were actually the worst kind of liars. He was out in the field helping to clean out a clogged ditch when it started raining. He looked up and let it hit him in the face. Chubby loved the rain.

THE END